HIS FUTUR...
NOT ONLY...
BUT...

As the strange impression hit Daniel with frightening clarity, he wrenched back with a hot chill. He didn't believe in destiny—just cold, hard facts. And he wanted nothing to do with this woman—ever!

Linsey folded her hands in a demure pose that contradicted the wicked streak he knew she possessed. "I apologize for pushing you in the water, Daniel; that was never my intent. I only meant to save you from certain disaster."

He looked her up and down with unconcealed derision. "The only disaster around here is you." Still shaken by his disturbing physical reaction to her, Daniel turned on his heel and stalked down the boardwalk.

"I was only trying to help!" she hollered after him.

Daniel's jaw tightened. He needed Linsey's help like he needed an outbreak of cholera.

"A sassy, humorous, heart-melting tale of love."
Dewanna Pace, author of *A Taste of Honey*

RACHELLE MORGAN

Loving Linsey

AVON BOOKS ◆ NEW YORK

This is a work of fiction. Names, characters, places, and incidents either are products of the author's imagination or are used fictitiously. Any resemblance to actual events, locales, organizations, or persons, living or dead, is entirely coincidental and beyond the intent of either the author or the publisher.

AVON BOOKS, INC.
1350 Avenue of the Americas
New York, New York 10019

Copyright © 1999 by Rachelle Nelson
Inside cover author photo by Dobbs Photography
Published by arrangement with the author
Library of Congress Catalog Card Number: 98-94818
ISBN: 0-380-80040-3
www.avonbooks.com/romance

First Avon Books Printing: June 1999

AVON TRADEMARK REG. U.S. PAT. OFF. AND IN OTHER COUNTRIES, MARCA REGISTRADA, HECHO EN U.S.A.

Printed in the U.S.A.

WCD   10   9   8   7   6   5   4   3   2   1

*In memory of my grandmother,
Kathleen Yarber Badenhoop,
who provided the inspiration*

To Karen N.,

Who would have thought that the day you first put a romance novel in my hands, you would soon after be reading my first manuscript?

I often think that the day we met was one of the luckiest of my life. You've been my co-worker, my roommate, my in-law, the god-mother of my children, and my dearest friend, and for over fifteen years, we've shared our deepest sorrows and greatest joys. You've laughed with me, cried with me, and come to my rescue more times than I can count. You may not have been the sister of my blood, but you'll always be the sister of my heart.

This book is for you.

Love,
S.

Chapter 1

The ill-omened number thirteen has been regarded as a symbol of death, destruction, and misfortune since ancient Roman times.

Horseshoe, Texas
1882

Whoever had come up with the lackwit idea to hold a wake today of all days should have had their brain examined. Surely everyone knew that the Friday after a rainstorm brought bad luck—but when that Friday also fell on the thirteenth of the month, well, bad luck turned pure rotten.

Even so, it took only one look around the crowded parlor for Linsey Gordon to see that prophecy had done little to dissuade most everyone in Horseshoe, Texas, from turning out for Bleet Haggar's wake.

Flames from dozens of floral-scented candles placed about the room managed to dispel a bit of the gloom and cast a yellow glow on the group of somberly dressed gentlemen shuffling between the kitchen and parlor like

1

lost hounds. A score of women in gathered black dresses and wide-brimmed, veiled hats sniffled into hankies. The cry of the Neelys' new baby grew distant as his young mother carried him out of the room for his afternoon feeding.

No, not one of the familiar faces seemed particularly bothered by the fact that the sitting-in was being held on such an unlucky day.

Habit had Linsey reaching for the smooth crystal disk that always hung around her neck, before it hit that she'd not find it in its usual resting spot. With a troubled frown, she let her hand drop to her lap. She couldn't recall where she'd misplaced her Token of Good Fortune, but more than ever she needed its comforting presence. The amulet had guarded her for fifteen of her twenty years, and she could surely use its protective qualities now.

Well, she supposed with a sigh, she'd just have to make do with the sprig of ivy tucked in her right pocket, the piece of coal in her left, and the Lady Liberty coin in her black kid slipper.

Folks could think her peculiar all they wanted, but she'd seen too many of her Aunt Louisa's portents and omens come true to take them lightly; terrible prices had been paid by those who did. Why, just last summer, Ollie James had spilled a saltcellar while dining in the town's restaurant; that night lightning struck his house, burning it to the ground. Then there was the time Elmer Puckett over at the general store lost a whole shipment of merchandise after he walked under a ladder.

And if the Haggars had paid any heed to the cock that had crowed three times in their yard, a black wreath would not now be hanging on the outside of their door.

Linsey's gaze wandered about the parlor, purposely skipping over the pine casket resting on a pair of sawhorses at the front of the room. At least the clock on the sideboard had been stopped, breaking the time cycle so another death would not occur. And several frames on the walls wore shrouds, while other hangings had been turned backside out or taken down all together. There were no bare mirrors where one might glimpse one's reflection, no pictures that might slip from their nails. . . .

The measures taken to prevent another death had the mark of Aunt Louisa all over them, bless her heart, for if anyone understood Linsey's caution, her great-aunt did. Wakes were notorious for being prophetic disasters, and Gordon women just didn't attend them without seeing to certain necessary preparations.

Still, as the respectful hum of conversation continued around her, Linsey couldn't stop wishing that this whole affair would just be over with. It wasn't that she hadn't been as fond of Bleet as the next person; the wheelwright had been a jolly fellow, well-liked by all his neighbors. But she could think of a dozen more sensible ways to pass an autumn afternoon than sitting in a parlor courting disaster.

Her foot began a rapid tap on the floor, as if it could spur the minutes into passing faster. It didn't. If anything, each moment crawled by at a turtle's pace.

Finally the sight of a bow-backed woman making her way down the row provided a welcome distraction. Like the other ladies in attendance, Aunt Louisa wore traditional mourning—a wide-brimmed hat with a half veil over her eyes and a gathered black dress. The camel's hair and Chantilly lace gown that hung on her spare figure was several years old, for one never wore anything new to a funeral.

Linsey immediately stopped the motion of her foot, smiled, and discreetly waved her aunt over.

Aunt Louisa settled into the empty chair beside Linsey and remarked, "I'm surprised Addie isn't here keeping you company."

The old woman's voice, reedy yet beloved, had a marginally calming effect. "She'll be along shortly," Linsey replied. "She had a few papers to grade before the weekend."

"Making excuses as usual."

Linsey bit back a grin. In spite of Aunt Louisa's fragile appearance and failing eyesight, she remained amazingly sharp-witted for an eighty-nine year old woman. Addie hated funerals and would avoid this one altogether if she had a legitimate reason. Linsey couldn't say she blamed her, either.

"Poor, poor Mr. Haggar." Aunt Louisa plucked a black hanky from within her cuff and dabbed at her eyes. "It's just a cryin' shame, isn't it?" she said to the flock of women seated nearby.

A half dozen hat-bedecked heads nodded agreement.

"I can't say I'm surprised, though," Aunt Louisa went on. "I knew something like this would happen as soon as I heard that cock crow yesterday morning." She shook her head, causing one of her silvery braids to slip from its moorings. "As my dear mother used to say, 'Monday for health, Tuesday for wealth, Wednesday best of all . . . '"

Thursday for losses, Friday for Crosses, Saturday no luck at all, Linsey silently joined in the familiar verse. It actually had nothing to do with dying, but in choosing the day of the week a couple should wed; however, Aunt Louisa insisted that it applied it to every occasion.

"What's that you're muttering, Louisa?" Persistence Yearling asked from the next row up, propping her brass hearing horn against her ear.

Aunt Louisa raised her voice for the centenarian's benefit. "A rhyme, Granny Yearling."

"A what?"

People across the room turned to stare.

"A rhyme," Aunt Louisa shouted, her hand cupped at the side of her mouth. "I was muttering a rhyme."

"What in blue blazes did you bring a rind to a wake for?" Persistence shot back. "Normal folks bring flowers."

Linsey suppressed her laughter as Granny Yearling's remark instigated a round of bickering with Linsey's equally feisty aunt. She could always count on these two to liven things up.

Or perhaps "liven" wasn't an appropriate word, she thought with an immediate frown. Oh, Lordy, she really needed to get out of here. . . .

The notion gripped harder a second later when, out of the corner of her eye, she caught sight of Judith Harvey, the mayor's wife, threading her way toward her. *Oh, no!* The determined look in the buxom matron's face sent dread careening through Linsey.

"Aunt Louisa, I need to . . . use the privy," she completed in a rush.

Without waiting for a reply, Linsey gathered a fistful of her black organdy skirts and scrambled out of her chair. The last thing she needed on an already doomed day was to get pinned in a corner by the meddling matchmaker!

She ducked into the kitchen only to find it occupied by two of her male neighbors, both looking quite uncomfortable in their dark suits and stiff paper collars. Oren Potter, the blacksmith, looked up in surprise while Robert Jarvis, the lamplighter, standing at the stove, lowered the metal flask from his mouth and narrowed his eyes at her.

"Yoo-hoo, Linsey . . . "

The familiar trill kicked Linsey's heart into a panicked beat, the clack of her heels on the wooden floor grew louder. Without a second glance at the men, Linsey dashed out a side doorway. Another group of neighbors had congregated in the foyer leading to the front door, but to Linsey's left, a short hallway remained mercifully clear.

Linsey hastened down the hallway and turned the knob of the first door she came to. She didn't care where the door led, only that it offered escape from a woman whose persistence would try the patience of the good Lord Himself.

Slipping inside the room, Linsey shut the door and pressed her forehead against the wood. *Whew, Lordy! That was close!* If she'd had to suffer another afternoon of listening to Mrs. Harvey invent nonexistent virtues about her lazy oaf of a son . . . for the love of Gus, everyone knew Bishop Harvey was little more than a wastrel in training.

Everyone but his mother, that is.

Well, she was safe for the time being. Mrs. Harvey wouldn't think to come looking for her in—Linsey turned around to identify her haven—a bedroom. A pretty little bedroom, too, decorated in shades of peach and blue. A wide tester bed with embroidered pillows at the headboard commandeered the center of the floor, a glossy walnut-stained bureau hugged one wall, and a . . .

Linsey gasped. Her eyes shot wide open.

Avoiding Judith Harvey lost its importance.

Forgotten were the mourners in the next room.

Thoughts of Bleet's unfortunate death scattered like ashes on a windy day.

Linsey's gaze remained transfixed on the sectional mirror making up the back of a curio cabinet set in the corner. Elegant figurines, a

pair of lace gloves, and an onyx ring served as
the backdrop for a horrified image.

Her own.

The mouth-watering aromas of fresh meat
pies and baked bread had Daniel's stomach
growling like a summer thunderstorm before
he even reached the Haggar's porch. He hadn't
eaten since—he paused with one foot on the
bottom step—early this morning? Last night?
Hell, he couldn't remember.

He shook his head and continued up the
weather-warped stairs. God, it had been a long
day. And it would prove even longer before it
was through. He still had today's shipment to
record in the books, instruments to clean, vaccinations to prepare for tomorrow's visit to
Jenny Kimmell's, Reginal Fitz's article on
typhlitis to study . . .

Yet Bleet had been his patient, and in all
good conscience Daniel couldn't let the day
end without stopping by to pay his last
respects.

He nodded a greeting to the trio of men loi-
tering at the corner of the L-shaped porch,
enjoying their cigars and pipes, then stepped
inside an entryway where people were
clumped together as tight as wet batting. Not
surprising, considering Horseshoe sat smack
in the middle of cattle country—a whistle-stop
between the rolling hills of central Texas and
the piney woods of the eastern stretch—and
any occasion, even the dismal ones, beckoned
to folks like sharp whiskey after a trying day.

Still, the thought of including himself in the

mass seemed about as appealing as operating with a cross saw.

With a weary sigh, Daniel squared his shoulders and worked his way through bodies trussed, tied, and stuffed into varying shades of dark calico, gingham, and broadcloth. Humid heat rose from the press of people, making it as hard to breathe as it was to move. But he figured the faster he offered his condolences to Widow Haggar, the faster he could leave.

Daniel fielded a dozen or more greetings, as well as enduring the usual, "Hey, Doc Jr., think you could look at my . . . ?" He'd long since gotten used to the annoying nickname his neighbors had dubbed him with, but getting used to it and liking it were two different bottles of tonic.

Just as he started past the kitchen doorway, a raspy, "If it ain't the devil himself," drew his attention inside, where he spied two friends sitting at a polished pine table, staking claim to what Daniel suspected was the only uncrowded spot in the house.

"Me and Oren were just wonderin' if you'd show up today." Robert Jarvis waved him over. "Join us for a spell."

Daniel allowed himself a momentary reprieve from the crowd and detoured in their direction. The faint odors of lamp oil and horse hide mixed with lye soap and spiced meat, and grew stronger as he moved into the dingy room. "I didn't think this house could hold so many people."

"It can't—that's why we're in here." Grin-

ning with typical good nature, Oren Potter
stretched out his hand in greeting. "How do,
Daniel?"

The blacksmith's meaty grip nearly crushed
Daniel's hand, yet he grit his teeth and bore
the man's strength. "Fair to middlin', Oren.
How's that boy of yours?"

"That tonic you gave him has been workin'
wonders. No more coughing."

The unmistakable pride and relief in Oren's
eyes and voice sent an unexpected pang
through Daniel. God knew he'd never hear
anything like that from his own dad. Daniel,
Sr., was a crotchety old coot who rarely spared
a kind word for anyone, much less his own
son. Daniel knew it was just his dad's way.
Nothing to do but accept it. But sometimes,
when he watched Oren and Bryce Potter
together, or heard Oren talk about the boy, he
couldn't help but envy them their relationship.

"Glad to hear he's doing better," Daniel said
with a tight smile, though the sentiment came
from the heart. Oren had all but destroyed the
Rusty Bucket Saloon a few years back when
his wife died. Daniel didn't want to think
about how his friend would react if anything
happened to his only child.

Steering the topic to lighter matters, Daniel
curled his fingers around the back of a vacant
chair and told Robert, "I saw you at the depot
earlier. Did your mysterious package finally
arrive?"

The thin wiry man slumped back and
snorted. "He-ell, no. It weren't on the train
again."

"Don't know why you're keeping it a such a confounded secret," Oren grumbled. "Just tell us what the dad-blamed thing is."

"Wouldn't be much of a surprise then, would it now?"

"Surprise, my Aunt Wilhelmina! How long ago did you send for it? Six months ago? I'll bet your three hundred greenbacks are supplying some slicked-down swindler with all the fine liquor and fancy women he can handle."

"You'll eat those words when it shows up on next week's train."

Oren harrumphed. "That's what you said last week."

"Ladies . . . " Daniel held up a palm and interrupted, "as much as I enjoy listening to the two of you whisper sweet nothings to each other, I'll have to take my pleasure another time." Jarvis's package had his curiosity roused, too, but his work wouldn't get done by itself. Daniel scowled. Hell, he was starting to think like his father. "Any idea where I can find Emmaleen in this mob?"

"Last I saw, she was in the parlor," Oren said.

Daniel nodded his thanks, then turned just as five feet, two inches of head-bent haste burst through the doorway and slammed into his front. He grunted at the impact; the black-clad figure bounced backward. Daniel reached out reflexively, closing his hands around slim shoulders that could only belong to a female.

Recognizing the fragile construction of flesh and bone under his hands, Daniel instinctively drew her to him. The sweet scent of lavender filled his senses; a lush cushion of breasts pressed against his chest.

Ah, woman.

It had been so long since he'd held a woman this close that he'd almost forgotten what it felt like. That was the trouble with being one of only two physicians in the entire county: his responsibilities didn't allow time for much more than a passing greeting with the local ladies. But if one of life's finest pleasures insisted on throwing herself against him, he'd hardly object.

Especially if she happened to be a redhead, he decided, an appreciative smile inching across his face. He'd always had a weakness for women with red hair, and hers was the color of shimmering copper. A double row of thick ringlets tumbled down her back from the complicated knot at her crown.

All right, maybe he could squeeze a moonlit stroll into his schedule. It wasn't as if he'd be marrying the girl, or even courting her, God forbid. Just spending an evening with someone who wasn't bleeding, broken, or in need of a remedy.

Oh, yes, the idea was sounding better and better.

Until she tipped her head up.

Daniel's smile shrank.

Words he'd been told could charm water from a dry well died on his lips the instant he looked into the face of his own tribulation.

Linsey Gordon.

She stared up at him, her expression dazed,

green eyes glazed and blank, her complexion pale as bone china. . . .

Daniel released her as if she were made of carbolic acid. He'd never touched her before, not once in the ten years he'd known her, and the shock of it made his pulses jump like cold water on a hot skillet.

Despite his best effort, Daniel felt the old resentment surfacing inside him. Swift. Bitter. Uncontrollable. His hands—his prized hands, usually so sure and steady—began to shake. A film of fire crept across his vision. Even his head started reeling.

The strength of his anger toward her, even after all this time, rattled Daniel. He took a step backward, then another. The edge of the door frame finally jabbed him in the back, stopping his retreat. Nothing cowardly about it, he told himself, feeling a muscle in his eye twitch. Not when it took all the control he could muster not to throttle her.

The temptation must have shown in his eyes, for her gaze fell to the floor. A mumbled excuse he couldn't make out—didn't want to make out—cut through the silence in the room just before she dashed past him and the other men, out the back door.

Oren glanced at Robert and jerked his thumb toward Linsey's fleeing form. "What's got her so spooked?"

"Ole Bleet's ghost?" Jarvis snickered as if he'd actually said something funny. Neither Oren nor Daniel laughed.

Instead Daniel glared out the back door, his soul simmering at the sight of the woman running across the yard, petticoats flapping, bustle bobbing. He couldn't begin to either guess or care about whatever force had sent her fleeing from the house. The woman could be running from death itself and he'd be damned if he'd lift a finger to stop it.

As far as he was concerned, Linsey Gordon had earned his malice the day she'd dumped his dreams into Horseshoe Creek.

Blindly, Linsey raced to the top of Briar Hill Road, not stopping until she reached the two-story Victorian-style house built by Great-Grandaddy Gordon nearly fifty years ago. Once she let herself inside, she pressed herself against the heavy oak door as if to barricade herself from the repugnance in Daniel's eyes. Of all the people to run into on the most tragic day of her life, why did it have to be him?

Oh, Lordy, she could hardly believe that for a moment there, she'd almost given into impulse, thrown herself into his arms, and begged him to set her broken world to rights.

How could she have been so desperate?

Worse, how could she have been so tempted?

With a distressed moan, she shut her eyes, then wished she hadn't. Her mind instantly filled with a picture of her laid out in a casket like Bleet Haggar's, wearing her daisy-chain necklace and best blue watered silk gown—the one she hoped to marry in someday. Her hands were crossed over her chest, her face pasty white. She saw Aunt Louisa and Addie clinging to each other, tears tracking down their faces, the sound of weeping rolling down the grassy slopes of the Horseshoe cemetery. . . .

Her eyes snapped open. Oh, Lord, what had she done?

Somehow her legs brought her into the front room, past the massive blond fireplace of native stone to a damask settee surrounded by rose-printed armchairs. She sank down on the cushion, her black skirts billowing about her. Catching a glimpse of a white ribbon peeking out from beneath the sofa, Linsey bent low. A humorless laugh escaped her as she pulled the amulet from its hiding place. Tears sprang to her eyes, and through misty vision, Linsey traced the lucky shamrock trapped between two thin sheets of crystal rimmed in gold. Her Token of Good Fortune. The day she'd found it, Aunt Louisa had told her it would bring her luck. That day it had brought her Addie, the sister she'd always wanted but never thought she'd have. And over the next fifteen years, the good fortune had kept coming.

Where had the four-leaf clover been when she needed it most?

So much for her pocketfuls of charms. All of them had been utterly useless today, for despite them, she had done the unthinkable. She'd looked in a mirror in the house where a corpse had been laid out. She'd seen her reflection.

And now, before the end of the year, she . . . was going . . . to die.

Chapter 2

Should you look in a mirror
in the house where a corpse does lie,
you'll see the reflection of the next to die.

"You did *what*?"

The exclamation resounded through the lace and light oak decor of Linsey's room late Sunday night.

It had taken two days to build up the courage to tell Addie the news. Two full days of anguish, misery, woe, and desperation.

Now as Linsey looked at the fair-haired woman sitting beside her on the canopy bed, she wished with all her heart that she could spare her sister this knowledge. But they had never kept a secret from each other before; this wasn't the time to start. If anyone had a right to know the truth, Addie did. Just because they'd become siblings by marriage rather than blood didn't make the bond between them any less strong. In fact, Linsey often wondered if they weren't closer than true sisters, because Adelaide Witt had been a wish granted rather than

16

a relative forced—proof positive that portents could be wonderful as well as dreadful.

Linsey reached over to clasp Addie's cool hand with her own. She looked deeply into the innocent hazel gaze fixed on her and calmly repeated, "I looked into a mirror at Bleet Haggar's wake."

A taut stretch of silence followed, broken only by the steady tick-tock of the brass clock on her vanity table. Linsey didn't bother expanding on the statement. She didn't need to. The growing look of horror on her sister's face told her that Addie understood the ramifications of what she'd done.

"How could this possibly have happened?" she asked, her tone half disbelieving, half distressed.

Linsey spilled the sordid details, leaving out nothing. Well, except for her encounter with Daniel. Not only did it have no real bearing on the issue at hand, but neither did Linsey wish to relive what a fool she'd made of herself when she'd run into him. Thank God he'd pushed her away before she'd given into the temptation to throw herself into his arms and beg him not to let go. She'd done some embarrassing things in her short twenty years but that would have topped the list—because for all his healing ways, Daniel Sharpe was the last person she could ever, or would ever, go to for comfort.

When she finished relating the events, she folded her hands in her lap and waited, braced for Addie's response. One advantage to knowing someone for so long was being able to anticipate how they would react in certain situations.

She wasn't disappointed.

"I can't believe this!" Addie cried. "How could you do such a reckless thing? You're usually so careful!"

"How was I supposed to know there was an uncovered mirror in the bedroom? All the others had sheets draped over them."

"You shouldn't have been in the bedroom in the first place."

Linsey crossed her arms in a pose of defense. "You'd rather I let Mrs. Harvey trap me into a corner and wax poetic about her darling Bishop?"

"Considering the consequences, yes!" Addie sprang off the bed and began to pace the room in agitation. "There must be something we can do to stop this. Some way to counteract—"

"Don't you think I've tried?" Linsey interrupted. She didn't blame Addie for asking; hadn't she asked the same question herself a dozen times or more? She'd even spent the better part of the weekend searching through Aunt Louisa's book of divinations for possible solutions. Still, it all came down to the same answer. "This isn't something that can be stopped, Addie. It's not like a magic spell that can be reversed, or a contract that can be negotiated: it's an omen. A foreshadowing of a future event. The most I can do is make the best of what time I have left."

"So you're just going to accept it as your lot," Addie accused.

Linsey hitched up one shoulder and sighed.

"I don't see that I have much choice. We all turn up our toes sooner or later. It's inevitable. I figure that maybe I'm luckier than most—at least I've been given warning. You know, time to prepare, to make a few arrangements, to do some things I've always wanted to do but never got around to. . . . "

Addie stared at her as if she had rats crawling in her hair.

"I've been giving this a lot of thought." Linsey rose from the bed and strode to her rosewood vanity. From the middle drawer she withdrew a folded sheet of paper, secured with a wax seal in the shape of a clover. "And I've decided that three months isn't very long to make a difference, but I want to try."

She returned to the bed, pulled an unresisting Addie down beside her, and held out the paper. "With your help."

Reluctantly Addie took the note Linsey handed her. "What's this?"

"Well, it occurred to me that I have not done one memorable thing in my life—or at least, nothing I especially want to be remembered for." The realization had hit home during Bleet's graveside service yesterday morning. An hour of listening to Reverend Simon praise the wheelwright's many virtues had been torture. A stark reminder that one day between now and the end of the year, her neighbors would be gathering around her grave and reciting psalms . . . but little more. Bleet had been remembered for his kindness, his generosity, his honesty . . . what would she be remembered for?

Considering some of the colorful scrapes she'd gotten herself into over the years, the idea didn't bear imagining.

But one thing had become clear: she couldn't just sit around waiting for the hatchet to fall.

Gesturing toward the paper, Linsey said, "I've made a list of things I want to do in the time I've got left."

Addie broke the seal with her fingernail, unfolded the paper, and read, "Make amends to someone I have wronged. Bring a life into the world to replace the one I'm leaving behind. Never tell another lie?"

"I want to be remembered for my honesty."

She continued silently reading the items Linsey had painstakingly scribed in the deep hours of the night: *Go on an adventure. Do something I have never done before. Make a difference in someone's life. Contribute something lasting to the community* . . .

Finished, Addie carefully refolded the paper. "This is quite a list."

"I know." Linsey couldn't remember everything she'd written, but by the time she'd been through, she'd filled all of one page and half of another. "Will you help me?"

Addie jerked to her feet and strode to the window. For a long time she said nothing. She simply stood there with her arms around her middle, looking vulnerable and lost, so much like the little girl who had come to live at Briar House so many years ago.

Oh, Lordy, she'd known Addie would take the news hard. She'd always been the more sensitive of the two, which, Linsey supposed, accounted for why she herself sought so desperately to remain calm, composed, and collected now. To be strong for Addie. The two of them had been like bread and butter since they were five years old, when Linsey's father and Addie's mother sent Addie here to live. She'd been such a shy and withdrawn little creature then, with hair like sunshine and somber olive-brown eyes too big for her face—so opposite from Linsey, who had inherited her father's vibrant coloring and zest for adventure.

Where had all the time gone?

It seemed like just yesterday that she and Addie had gotten caught stealing a rabbit from the local butcher so it wouldn't end up in the stewpot. Then there had been the summer they decided to "cure" Addie of her fear of heights by jumping off the rocks at Turtle Point—it had taken Addie's broken leg six weeks to mend.

Images continued to roll through Linsey in a bittersweet wave. Tea parties at two in the morning. Skinny dipping in the minister's pond. Linsey's first kiss from that awful Harvey boy. They'd practically scrubbed her lips off her face, trying to get rid of the taste. And the day Addie got her teaching certificate—how they'd celebrated by eating so much ice cream that they'd emptied their stomachs on Daisy and Maisy Bender's front porch.

When Addie's sorrow-filled gaze lifted to hers, Linsey knew she'd been remembering, too.

"What am I supposed to do when you're gone?" she whispered. "Who will I turn to at the end of a trying day? Who will help me plan my schedules, sit with me in church, and spin dreams under the clouds?"

Unshed tears scalded the back of Linsey's eyes. "Oh, Addie . . . "

She pushed herself off the coverlet and met her sister at the window. Together they stared out over the yard, where a line of shedding cedars marked the back property line, and the broadleaf sweet gums displayed a riot of burnt orange and gold. Vibrantly feathered blue jays and cardinals dived from the branches, then soared up again in a spectacular aerial performance. In spite of the burst of color outside the window, the waning afternoon remained as drab and dreary as gray wool, matching their mood.

"I never thought anything could ever come between us," Addie said.

Linsey swallowed. A lump the size of Texas slid down her throat. "Me either." Forcing a bright note to her voice, she chimed, "Look at it this way; I'm not dead yet. I have until the year is out—that gives us three good months together."

"At best."

The softly spoken words made Linsey's heart constrict. "Yes. At best."

Silently their heads tilted into each other. Temple pressed against temple. Hands clasped in a plea for strength and courage.

Linsey wished she could find words of wisdom. Of comfort. But there was nothing left to say.

"I love you, Linsey-woolsey."

The childhood nickname nearly shattered her flagging composure. "I love you, too, Addie."

A chilly draft roused Linsey from sleep the next morning. Keeping her eyes closed, she lay still, relishing the breath of October air against her skin. For as long as she lived—be it days or months—she'd not take the sensation for granted again.

The hard part was over, though: telling Addie. They'd stayed up half the night, whispering, reminiscing, planning . . .

Lordy, she had to stop these melancholy thoughts—she had a list to carry out! Kicking her feet from beneath the thick quilt, Linsey tugged her nightrail so the satin folds fell about her ankles. She still wasn't sure how she'd accomplish each task she'd set for herself, but lying abed simply wasted time, and that was not a commodity she had in excess. Surely opportunities would present themselves, if only she looked. They certainly wouldn't come flying through the window into her lap!

That image made her giggle as she crossed the polished oak floor to stoke the embers in the fireplace. No sounds of stirring came from the next room. Addie undoubtedly slept on. Linsey hated to wake her, but school couldn't start without the teacher.

She rapped against the wall that separated their bedrooms. "Addie, time to get up."

"I'm awake."

Assured by the drowsy, muffled reply, Linsey chose a high-necked, black-and-burgundy striped day dress from her wardrobe, then stripped out of her nightgown, tossing it over a chair on her way to the bureau. Lucky trinkets littered the surface: seashells, a Liberty Lady coin, a piece of coal from the first mine of the area.

Her gaze lit on the daguerreotype of her parents. She brushed her fingers along the silver frame. Her father looked as dashing as a knight of old in his calvary uniform. He was a burly man with dark blue eyes, a shock of flame-colored hair, and muttonchop whiskers. Standing beside him with a dainty hand resting on his broad shoulder, her mother represented the epitome of a refined Southern belle. No doubt men of all ages had been swept away by Genevieve's wild black curls and striking green eyes. But she'd chosen Lyle Gordon, the son of a neighboring cotton farmer. They'd married before the War Between the States broke out and Linsey had been born soon after.

When the war ended, Major Lyle Gordon had transferred his commission out West. Mother thought a formal education and stable environment would be better for Linsey than the harshness of military life, so they'd left her in Aunt Louisa's care. Six months later, Genevieve had been stricken down with fever.

Linsey thought her father would come for

her after her mother died. Instead he married again, a young widow named Evelyn Witt who not only supported his military career, she gloried in it—so much so that her only child, a little girl Linsey's age, had arrived on Aunt Louisa's doorstep the very next spring. To this day, Lyle and Evelyn remained in Indian territory.

Would they miss her? Maybe a little, Linsey decided. She knew her father and stepmother loved her, for they came to visit as often as her father's duties allowed. They simply loved each other more.

As the downstairs chime sounded the half hour, Linsey pulled away from the picture before her thoughts turned maudlin. "Addie, you best hurry or you'll be late for school," she called.

Seconds later, Addie's voice sounded from the doorway. "What are you doing?"

"Looking for my lucky earbobs."

"Too little, too late if you ask me," she grumbled.

"It's never too late for good luck." Even in her case. And now she needed all the good luck she could garner. "Aha, here they are!" Finding the pair of rubies buried at the bottom of her jewelry chest, she attached them to her ears, only to stop at the sight of her sister. Her eyes were swollen and red, her complexion paler than normal.

"For the love of Gus, Addie, you can't go to school looking like that! What will your students think if they see you looking like you've tussled with a beehive? Come over here and let me put some cold cloths on your face."

Compliantly Addie allowed Linsey to guide her to the stool in front of the vanity. After Linsey pressed cold, wet cloths into Addie's hands, she picked up a silver-plated brush and started working the tangles out of Addie's straight blond hair.

"Where are you running off to so early?" her sister asked.

"The orphanage. But I want to stop by the smithy first and see if Oren has any nails made. I'm giving Noah and Jenny one of my lucky horseshoes to hang in their new home after the wedding." She didn't dare bring up the possibility that she might not be around next month for the ceremony; Addie looked as if she'd had enough distress heaped upon her.

But the mention of their childhood friend brought a sharp pang of regret. The ache remained with Linsey as she brushed Addie's long pale hair, then twisted it into a chignon at her nape. Linsey had lost count of the dreams she and Addie had shared over the last few years. Of meeting a handsome fellow, marrying in a double ceremony, and building homes side by side so they'd never be apart. . . .

Linsey sighed. Now she would never know the bliss of married life. Even if she did find her true love before she departed this world, she couldn't in all good conscience marry a man who would barely be a 'groom before she made him a widower.

With Addie's hair tended to, Linsey took her place in front of the mirror so Addie could style her unruly red tresses. Yes, unfortunately, it was too late for her to find wedded bliss.

Linsey stilled. *But it wasn't too late for Addie.*

Her gaze shot to her sister's haggard reflection. As long as she could remember, she'd taken care of Addie. But what about when she no longer could? Who would take care of Addie when she was gone?

No one. Other than Aunt Louisa, Addie had not a soul to depend on.

Unless . . .

Of course! Why hadn't she thought of it sooner? If she could find Addie someone to share her life with, then Addie might not grieve so deeply at her passing.

The more Linsey thought about finding Addie a mate, the more perfect it sounded. It would be her parting gift to her sister, to honor the friendship and companionship they'd shared over the years.

After Addie left to collect her lessons for the day, Linsey danced around the bedroom, her mood lighter now that she had a plan. She gathered her basket and gloves, mentally listing the requirements for her sister's future husband. He must be strong and capable, yet gentle and compassionate. Oh, and he must be suitably employed so that he could properly provide for Addie. Addie would have a dowry, of course, but Linsey refused to hand her sister over to some fortune-seeking scoundrel.

And children. He must get on well with children, for Addie loved them so. She always said she could have a dozen and still want more.

And books. Addie loved her books, so he must support her fondness for them.

He could never forbid Addie from teaching, either, for that was a special calling for a special woman—who deserved an equally special man.

But who?

The question echoed in her mind as she descended the staircase. The pungent aroma of fresh coffee and the sweet temptation of apple pastries lured Linsey to the sideboard in the dining room.

There was no sign of Aunt Louisa, which didn't surprise Linsey. The woman often left to visit Granny Yearling before anyone else awakened. When Addie walked into the room a few minutes later, Linsey decided that it was probably for the best that they hadn't run into her. As wan and weary as Addie looked, Aunt Louisa would surely notice something amiss, and Linsey couldn't bring herself to tell the old woman what had happened.

Telling Addie had been difficult enough.

Linsey wrapped a few pastries in a napkin while Addie grabbed her lunch basket from the kitchen. By the time they left the house, Linsey found herself in surprisingly fine spirits for a walking dead woman. The musty odor of wet earth and the sharp fragrance of wild onion rose up to mingle with the sweet perfume of her lavender toilet water. The sun had finally come out after a weekend of wicked thunderstorms, and with it, the promise of an Indian summer before the chill of winter set in. Whipped-butter clouds drifted with lazy grace across the pale blue sky, and miniature rainbows shimmered on the surface of puddles dotting the road.

Five minutes later they entered the business section of town. The buildings were, appropriately, arranged to form the shape of a U. The two-story Horseshoe Hotel and the livery across the way were located at the foremost ends. Wishing Well Lane, in the center of the U, had shops that catered to nearly every need, from a telegraph and newspaper office to a dry-goods store to the understandably profitable Rusty Bucket Saloon, which also provided for a man's, er . . . baser appetites.

Strolling down the lane on the way to the tiny schoolhouse where Addie had been schoolmarm for the last four years, Linsey and Addie passed the public well set in the heart of town. As they had done since they were little girls, they paused by the stone foundation, turned their backs, and closed their eyes.

A reverent silence wrapped around them. For a fleeting moment, Linsey was tempted to wish for prolonged life. But Aunt Louisa always told her that wishes for oneself were selfish and rarely came true. So instead Linsey concentrated on the hope that she would find Addie a life mate, and soon, so she could attend the wedding before she died. Then Linsey tossed a half-cent piece over her left shoulder. Addie followed suit. Two successive plunks sounded from the depths as their offerings hit the water.

"What did you wish for?" Linsey asked.

"You know I can't tell you; it won't come true." Addie gave her a sly, sideways glance. "What did you wish for?"

Linsey grinned. "Wouldn't you like to know?" Of course, if all went well, Addie would find out soon enough. "I'll tell you this much—it'll make you less lonely once I'm gone."

Even the reminder of her impending doom couldn't dampen Linsey's mood. If anything, she felt strengthened by it.

They resumed walking, the snap of their heels against the wooden planks laid in front of the bank matched step for step. As they drew closer to the schoolhouse, Linsey couldn't help glancing about her in bittersweet appreciation. Lordy, how she loved this town! The way the rooftop of the livery stepped up to the Rusty Bucket, then dropped down to the telegraph office, then up again to the dry-good and feed store, the pattern repeating itself along the semicircular road. And the people—from Madame Cecilee, owner of the Coiffure and Millinery, to Frank Mackey, editor of the Horseshoe *Herald,* to cranky old Elmer Puckett at Puckett's Market and Mercantile. All felt like extended family. All had helped watch over her as a child. And when Addie came along, they had opened their arms and their hearts and treated her with the same sense of welcome.

Yes, Horseshoe had been very good to her over the years. She only hoped she could be as good to them in return.

"I can't believe how easily you're taking this

whole thing," Addie said, breaking into Linsey's musings.

"What else am I supposed to do?" Linsey shrugged. "Railing at God won't change anything, and sitting around feeling sorry for myself is just a waste of time."

"How do you think . . . you know . . . it will happen?"

"I hope it's exciting. I want to go out with a splash!"

"Oh, Linsey, you are incorrigible."

Maybe so, Linsey thought, but at least she'd made Addie smile again. "It's better than going in my sleep. Remember when old Chester Sawbuck died? Nobody found him for two days."

"That would never happen to you."

"It could."

"But it won't. I won't let it."

Their conversation was curtailed by the appearance of the Bender twins, leaving the millinery sporting identical new bonnets. Maisy adjusted the left brim of her hat while Daisy adjusted the right brim of hers in comical synchronicity. Linsey and Addie divided, exchanged greetings with the ladies in passing, then united again and quickly chanted, "Bread and butter."

Linsey laughed at the custom.

Addie fell forlornly silent.

"I wish . . . I wish we could find you a Prince Charming," Addie finally sighed. "That way when . . . it happens, he could kiss you and rouse you from your immortal sleep."

"If you made that wish at the well, then you

wasted a perfectly good halfpenny. The closest thing to a prince I've seen is that warty toad John Brewster stuck in your desk last month."

But Linsey might as well have been talking to a lamppost, for all the attention Addie paid her. Her steps slowed to a stop, and she seemed unaware of the traffic around her.

Linsey followed the line of Addie's gaze until it landed on the man emerging from the combined apothecary-doctor's office. *Oh, no,* Linsey mentally groaned. Daniel Sharpe was the last person she needed to see this morning. She'd been able to forget her disgraceful reaction to him the other day, but the sight of him now stirred up a fresh wave of humiliation. She still couldn't believe she'd mistaken the look in his eyes for concern, the warmth of his touch for compassion. Worse, that she'd nearly allowed the illusion to make him seem like a beacon in the midst of a nightmare.

Seeing her reflection had muddled her vision and clouded her thoughts, that's all. Daniel might feel a lot of things for her—hatred, loathing, bitterness . . .

Concern and compassion were not among them.

Disgusted that she could ever have thought differently, Linsey resolutely turned toward the schoolhouse. "Come on, Addie, you'll be late for school."

Absently, Addie waved her hand. "In a minute." Her eyes never left Daniel Sharpe, who gave no sign of noticing her silent worship as he loaded a wooden crate into the back of the buggy.

With an impatient sigh, Linsey crossed her arms over her front, tapped her foot, and began to hum an aimless tune. It was no secret that Addie had been moonstruck over the man since he and Doc Sr. had moved to Horseshoe and opened the apothecary back in '72.

Not that Daniel wasn't worthy of a woman's interest—quite the opposite, in fact. With his dark brooding eyes, clean-cut black hair and broad-shouldered build, even Linsey had to admit that Horseshoe's young doctor was handsome enough to give any woman an attack of the vapors.

Taken apart and examined piece by piece, his features weren't that extraordinary. A high brow. Hawkish nose. Firm, sensual lips and strong chin. Yet put together on the tanned canvass of his skin, there was just something . . . breathtakingly striking about the man. Even the boyish cowlick on the right side of his scalp, which might have made another man look callow, simply added to his rakish appeal.

As if to support that thought, a long, mopey sigh from Addie floated on the morning air. "Isn't he divine?" she asked.

"Oh, for the love of Gus." Linsey let her arms fall to her sides and started to walk away. She had more important tasks to tend to than watching Addie gawk at Daniel.

Linsey stopped abruptly. She spun around. Her gaze flicked from Addie to the young doctor, then back to her sister again.

No.

Oh, no.

Not Daniel!

But then, why wouldn't Addie fancy him? He was, after all, a respected member of the community. Hardworking. Honest. Dedicated. Or so everyone said. His finances couldn't compare to Aunt Louisa's, but neither did the Sharpes appear to suffer the hardships of many folks Linsey knew. Father and son lived in modest rooms above the apothecary, and Doc Sr. had recently bought himself that shiny new stanhope.

Yes, Daniel fit the criteria for the ideal husband, except for one minor flaw. He was about as approachable as a Texas thistle—toward her, anyway.

But one look at her smitten sister made Linsey sigh in defeat. All right. If Daniel was the mate Addie wanted, then Daniel was the mate Addie would get.

No matter how unpleasant the task might be.

"Come on, Addie." Linsey grasped her sister's elbow and started across the lane.

"Where are we going?"

"To talk to your future husband."

Addie came to a screeching halt and wrenched her arm from Linsey's hold. "My *what*?"

Linsey stopped with a huffy breath. "Look, I might have lost my chance for a Prince Charming, there's no reason why you should lose yours, too."

"What in heaven's name are you going on about?"

"You are going to marry Daniel Sharpe."

Addie gasped. "Are you out of your mind? I can't marry Daniel!"

"Why not? You're smart, you're funny, you've got a gentle heart . . . those are the perfect qualifications for a doctor's wife. And I need to know that someone is taking care of you after I'm gone. Who better than the man you've been moonstruck over practically since you were in pinafores?"

"Linsey, he hardly knows I'm alive."

"He will—once you talk to him."

"But I can't talk to Daniel, I'll trip over my own tongue!"

"Don't be a goose. Just walk up to him and ask him where he's taking those crates."

"You ask him!"

"Why would I do that?" Linsey lifted her hands away from her sides in exasperation. "Daniel hasn't spoken to me in two years; I doubt he'll welcome a chat with me now."

"Surely he doesn't still blame you for the stagecoach accident."

Linsey grabbed Addie's arm again and half pulled, half pushed her across the road. That was one incident she'd rather not relive. "Whether he does or doesn't isn't the point. You've been besotted with him almost half your life and this is your chance to let him know it."

"Linsey, no—" Addie's protest died a sudden death as they reached the front of the pharmacy.

Daniel didn't notice them at first—or if he did, he pretended not to. Linsey watched the play of muscle under the white linen stretched across his back as he lifted a crate into the back of the stanhope. He really was a fine figure of

a man, she had to admit. Wide shoulders. Flat
stomach. Straight waist tapering to lean hips,
and long muscular legs wrapped in brown
wool.

And eyes like chips of smoldering coal, she
discovered when he turned to face them.

Sudden trepidation attacked her. She
reached for her amulet and grasped it in a tight
fist. Maybe this wasn't such a good idea.
Daniel would just as soon bed down with a
cottonmouth as have anything to do with her.
Not that she could blame him after what she'd
done. . . .

No, for Addie's sake, she had to put the past
behind her and start fresh.

Squaring her shoulders, taking a fortifying
breath, Linsey manufactured a bright smile
and called, "Good morning, Daniel."

He kept silent.

Addie kept silent.

Linsey jabbed her gaping sister in the ribs.
"Greet the good doctor, Addie."

She opened her mouth, but the only thing
that came out was a cracking squeak. Addie's
face turned the color of a cardinal's wing. Muttering something about being tardy, she hurried past Daniel without another word,
leaving Linsey to contend with close to six feet,
180 pounds of prickly demeanor by herself.

The silence became thick and heavy as curdled milk. Neither made any move to step out
of the other's way. In fact, if Linsey didn't
know better, she'd think he was trying to
intimidate her. And she hated to admit it, but
it was working. Not much intimidated Linsey,

but as those sharp brown eyes continued to drill into her, she found herself fighting the urge to bolt.

Only the reminder that running from Daniel would accomplish nothing kept Linsey from turning coward.

She wracked her mind for something to say, some spark of conversation that might crack Daniel's brittle veneer. "Nice day, isn't it?"

He didn't answer. Then again, why should today be any different than any other?

Still, it was getting rather unnerving, standing out in public, enduring that hot/cold stare. Linsey licked her lips, waved toward the stanhope, and tried again. "Planning a trip?"

Again, not a word came from those tightly clamped lips. Instead he started passed her.

Linsey's patience, never strong to begin with, began to fray. She stepped into his path and reached out, wanting only to stop him from escaping yet again. But the instant she touched his arm, a startling current streaked up her fingertips and didn't stop until it caught her heart.

The surprise on Daniel's face told her that he must have felt a similar shock. For a moment they could do nothing more than look at each other, Linsey's hand on his arm, his head cocked at a baffled angle. He smelled of bay rum and morning sun and a hint of forbidden pleasure. She was seized by a disconcerting impulse to trace the contour of his smooth jaw, to brush the crescent-shaped shank of hair off his brow, to curl herself against the solid warmth radiating from his body.

He recovered much faster than she did, his

eyes going hard and flat as weathered stone, his expression settling once again in that merciless scowl Linsey was coming to loathe.

She removed her hand and curled her fingers into her palm. "You are never going to forgive me, are you?" she asked softly.

No answer. Just that implacable stare at some spot over her shoulder.

Linsey propped loose fists on her hips. "Look, Daniel, you have every right to be angry with me, but for the love of Gus, it's been two years. How much longer do you plan on holding this grudge against me?"

Steam practically rose from under his collar as he stared into the apothecary window, his jaw clenched so tight she wondered that he didn't break any teeth.

"Don't you think you're being a little unfair? You won't accept my apology; you won't accept my offer to pay your tuition. What more can I possibly do?"

That stony-eyed stare snapped around to Linsey. "Go. Away."

Well, glory be, he'd finally spoken to her. Not exactly words to warm her heart, but she wouldn't quibble. "There now, that wasn't so hard, was it? Maybe now we can begin putting the past behind us."

He looked as if the suggestion had cut off his air supply. His face went ruddy; his spiky-lashed brown eyes nearly bugged out of his head. "Because of you, I lost a fellowship to the most prestigious university in the country, not to mention my fiancée, and you expect me to—"

Daniel broke off in midsentence. His shoulders straightened, and he sucked in a deep breath in an effort to control a rapidly spiking temper. "No apology can *ever* make up for what you did, and I wouldn't take a plug nickel from you. Just stay away from me and I'll do the same."

He stormed into the apothecary, leaving her to swelter in the echo of his anger. He headed straight for his office at the back of the shop, knowing he had to get his emotions under control before he broke something.

Like Linsey Gordon's pretty little neck.

How did she do it? he wondered, throwing himself into the well-worn leather chair behind his desk. How did she manage to take a two-year-old event and make it feel as if it had happened just yesterday? All it took was one look, one touch, and his normally staunch composure turned to ash.

It was hard to believe, even harder to admit, that there'd been a time—a long time ago—when he'd been interested in her. Sure, she was lovely. Hell, as much as he hated to say it, she had the kind of beauty that could stop a war—or cause one. Curves filled out the seams in dresses that used to sag on her gangly frame. Eyes bright as polished amber. Lips ripe enough to tempt fate. Even the pumpkin red hair she'd had as a kid had become more golden over the years, the curls looser, somehow softening her features, yet doing nothing to dim her personality.

Then again, there had always been an aliveness about Linsey that attracted him, a carefree spirit that beckoned to him like breath to a dying man. . . .

Daniel wiped his hand down his face, cursing.

He'd been seventeen when he'd entered Tulane, nineteen when he'd gotten his degree. At twenty he'd begun working in the local hospital where he met Charlotte. They courted for a year, but it wasn't until her father arrived from Vienna to accept a teaching position in Maryland that Daniel had grown serious about her. He'd known even then that Ian McIntyre's immense influence and prestige in the medical field had prompted him to propose to Charlotte more than any affection he felt for her.

Then his mother's illness had driven him home. Coming back to Horseshoe, to his mother's debility and his father's iron fist, felt like a death sentence. And Linsey . . . she'd been his glimpse of sunrise from the gallows. Young, refreshing, reckless. Always from a distance, always with discretion, he would watch for her, wonder about her, want her. Charlotte had been the means to a promising future; Linsey had been a forbidden fantasy.

He'd gotten over his insane infatuation the day Linsey had cost him the opportunity of a lifetime.

Of its own will, his hand reached for the varnished box that sat on his desk. It had been a gift from his mother the day she died: a keepsake box, she'd told him, to hold his most treasured mementoes. From beneath

the hinged lid he retrieved a rumpled, water-
stained envelope, the postmark smeared, the
address nearly illegible.

He didn't need to open the letter to know
what it said. Charlotte's blurry script had been
burned into his memory that long-ago summer day:

> *Trustees approved your surgical fellowship. If
> you are not here by the first day of August,
> Daddy and I will assume you have no interest in
> working under his direction.*

It had been the chance he'd been waiting for
his entire adult life.

And it had come and gone without his even
knowing it . . . until a month later, when several townsmen had finally located and fished
the mailbag—and Charlotte's letter—out of
Horseshoe creek.

The rush trip to Baltimore had been a
wasted effort. His apprenticeship, and his
fiancée, had already gone to another. And no
wonder: a chance to study under Ian McIntyre
was a coveted position, especially since a year
later the man had taken his skills back to
Vienna.

It might as well have been the moon, as far
as Daniel was concerned.

He slumped back in the horsehair chair and
stared unseeingly at the ceiling. God. He'd
never wanted anything so badly as that
apprenticeship. He'd worked his fingers to the
bone, socialized with all the right people,

devoted all his spare time to charity work to broaden his skills. There was nothing he wouldn't have done to get it—even committing himself to the life sentence of marriage to McIntyre's daughter.

But in one fell swoop, Linsey had ruined everything.

Forgive her? The letter crumpled in his fist. When hell froze over.

Chapter 3

*If your shadow is touched by a passing hearse
you will be the next to ride in it.*

"**W**ell, that certainly went well," Linsey
muttered.

She glared into the apothecary for several
long minutes, a tenuous grasp on her own
temper, before realizing she stood alone on the
boardwalk, looking through the window like a
vagrant child.

With a frustrated sigh, she turned a half circle and headed toward the smithy shop. How
was she supposed to give her sister the gift of
a life mate if the gift wouldn't cooperate with
her?

Cooperate. Ha! Daniel barely tolerated the
sight of her. She could understand his anger in
the beginning. She'd probably have felt the
same way if the situation were reversed, and
he'd been responsible for the loss of an important letter of hers. But for the love of Gus . . .
two years?

And why was the incident entirely her fault?

43

Had she been the one driving the coach? Had she caused the horses to bolt straight toward the creek's banks and dump its passengers and its cargo into the water?

Linsey stopped at the corner of Wishing Well Lane and the road to Houston, and closed her eyes. No, she wouldn't do this, she chided herself. Aunt Louisa always told her to accept the consequences of her actions, and Linsey *had* been the one to suggest—okay, insist—that the driver turn around after the rabbit had darted out in front of them. Everyone knew that a rabbit dashing across your path meant bad luck would follow, unless one turned around and began the journey anew. And though she'd only been trying to protect a coach full of people, every deed had its price.

That particular one just happened to be someone else's dream.

The weight of regret lay as heavy on Linsey's soul as the heat coming from Oren Potter's furnace. She thanked her lucky stars that he wasn't around. The smithy had a knack for sensing things about people that they didn't always want known, and Linsey didn't feel much like pretending all was well with her world. She strode to the huge workbench to the left of the entrance and sorted through the bins.

Keeping her thoughts from straying to Daniel was like trying to stop a full-speed locomotive with a haystack. Yes, she'd admit he had every right to hold her to blame for his getting rejected by that college back East and, according to the gossip mill, being jilted by the woman he'd intended to marry. Frankly, Linsey couldn't bring herself to shed any tears over that. A woman who would jilt a man just because he wasn't attending her daddy's school wouldn't have made much of a wife— but her opinion hardly mattered here. What did matter was persuading Daniel to put the past behind him and look to the future: a future with Addie.

Since Addie could hardly talk to the man without swooning, the responsibility of getting Daniel to notice her rested on Linsey's shoulders. But unless she settled this storm between them, she'd not be able to convince him to talk to Addie, much less court her. If only there was some way to make it up to him—

Her hand froze upon a pile of two penny irons. Her head snapped up.

Make amends to someone I have wronged.

That was it! That's how she could make things right with Daniel—by replacing the bride he'd lost with an even better one! And by matching him with Addie, she'd fulfill two wishes with one stroke!

Her spirits lifting with the brilliance of her plan, Linsey shoved a handful of nails into her pocket, dropped a few coins on the workbench, and left the smithy.

Fate seemed to be in complete agreement with her intentions, for she spotted Daniel coming out of his father's store, carrying yet another crate to the buggy parked in front. *Well, no time like the present*, she thought, starting in his direction.

A bulbous black coach drawn by a pair of

mules pulled into the business sector just then, forcing Linsey to wait on the curb while the vehicle lumbered by. Once the way had cleared, she stepped over a puddle onto the road. She didn't get two paces across it before it struck her that the coach rolling down the road was none other than the community hearse.

And it was heading straight for Daniel's shadow.

For the first time since she had taken the job as schoolmistress, Addie wished she were anywhere but inside the stuffy confines of the one-room schoolhouse.

She sat at her desk, Peter Piper's Practical Principles of Plain and Perfect Pronunciation open in front of her, yet in her present state of mind, she couldn't solve a single one of Peter's playful puzzles to save her soul.

She knew she should be furious with Linsey for forcing her into such a humiliating encounter with Daniel Sharpe this morning. Marry Daniel indeed! It was true that she'd dreamed of the day she might share his name and bear his children, but how could she consider marriage to Daniel—or anyone else for that matter—when Linsey . . . when her sister . . . oh, heavens, Addie could barely think the word without a sharp pain gripping her.

Addie wanted so badly to discount the omen. Logic told her that looking into a mirror couldn't kill a person. And yet an unshakeable doubt had inserted itself under her skin, into her mind, causing goose bumps to break out

along her arms. Over the years, she'd witnessed too many coincidental instances to easily brush aside prophecy. Aunt Louisa and
Linsey claimed they'd all been signs. Addie
didn't know what to believe, but she couldn't
forget that her own father had been snakebit
right after his picture had fallen off the wall.

She could have sworn she'd cried herself
tearless, but now she felt them well up again.
She'd already lost her father. And even though
her mother was alive and well, she might as
well say the same about her for all Addie saw
of the woman.

God . . . what if it was true?

What if, before the end of the year, she lost
her sister, too? What if Linsey's glance into that
mirror truly had been a warning?

"Miss Witt, is somethin' wrong?"

The sound of her name startled Addie from
the frightening thought. She blinked back the
sting of tears. A roomful of expectant faces
came into focus, one in particular. "Did you
say something, Bryce?"

"We finished our tests," the eight-year-old
said. He pointed at the book in front of her.
"Do you want us to bring out our primers?"

After a moment's indecision, Addie set the
book atop her meticulously planned schedule.
She couldn't concentrate on schoolwork today,
anyway. "How about taking an early recess
instead?"

A cheer rose up from her pupils. Twenty
freshly scrubbed youngsters ranging from five
to thirteen made a mad dash for the coatroom
at the front of the building. The older children

eagerly helped the younger children don their wrappers, then practically mowed them over in their haste to get outside.

Following along, Addie couldn't blame them for wanting fresh air since the recent rains had undoubtedly kept them inside all weekend, too.

She paused at the back of the room beside Bryce's desk, her attention caught by the drawing on his slate board.

Addie brought the slate closer to study the caricature of herself staring out the window. He'd captured the anxiety on her face with amazing accuracy. Had she been that transparent?

"Bryce?" she called to the boy on his way out.

"Ma'am?" Once he saw the slate board in her hand, the color in his cheeks paled, making his freckles stand out. Defensively, he drew his shoulders back. "I finished my test. I put it on your desk."

"I know you did." He always finished his work well ahead of the other children. "This is very good." She tapped the frame.

The tension in his lanky body eased, though his dark blue eyes remained wary.

"You caught my mood quite precisely. Are my emotions always so apparent?"

He shrugged a bony shoulder. "Not really. You just seemed sorta bothered today."

"Yes, I guess I am. You may join the other children."

As soon as he slipped out the door, Addie returned to the chalk drawing, studying it with a thoughtful frown. It was better than good; it was amazing. In the years since Bryce Potter had joined her classroom, she'd noticed more and more signs of exceptional talent, the least being his swift comprehension of academic studies. This semester alone saw him doing the work of an eighth-grade student. The only thing left was taking his graduate exams.

But then what?

She'd never come across a child with so quick an intellect as Bryce Potter, and he was only eight! Too young for a university, too advanced for her classroom.

Addie swallowed and set the slate on his desk, feeling inadequate.

In the cloakroom, she found little Amy Simmons struggling with the buttons on her threadbare cloak. Addie pushed thoughts of Bryce to the side, and knelt to assist the girl.

Just as she finished and started to rise, a shadow blocked the sun. A sideways glimpse brought into view long, muscle-bound thighs clad in brown woolen trousers. Her gaze rising, Addie took in a blue-and-green flannel shirt stretched tightly over a powerful chest and arms that could squeeze the sap out of a tree. Addie straightened slowly, her pulse beginning to jump at a perplexing and highly irregular rate. "Why, hello, Mr. Potter."

"Miss Witt." He nodded his head without disturbing one strand of the thick black hair slicked back from his brow.

Though not a classically handsome man, with his crooked nose and lazy eye, Oren Potter was what many would term the strong, silent type, with a brawny figure and bulky muscles formed by years of wielding hammer and iron in his blacksmith shop.

"Bryce forgot his lunch this morning, so I took a break from work to bring it by."

She reached to take the pail from him. "That wasn't necessary." His fingers brushed hers and a spark leaped between them. Addie yanked her hand back, shocked by the sensation.

Hoping he hadn't noticed her reaction, her gaze shot to his craggy face. The hooded cast of the smithy's gilded lashes didn't hide the direction of his regard. Teal blue eyes had focused on her . . . on her . . . *oh, my.*

A blush burned its way up her neck and into her cheeks. Addie placed a flustered hand over her bosom and licked her lips. She gave him as wide a berth as the cramped cloakroom allowed, though she couldn't escape the scent of straw and cinder and brazed iron that filled the space. It gave her little comfort to noticed his face had turned an even deeper red than the schoolhouse door. "I-I'd never let one of my students go hungry," she said to break the strained silence.

"I didn't think you would, Miss Witt," he said, worrying the brim of his hat between work-worn fingers.

"I-I always bring a spare lunch. But on the occasion I forget, there is always another child with more than enough food to share. . . . " She couldn't seem to stop babbling. What was wrong with her? Perhaps she hadn't been born with Linsey's open and outgoing nature, but rarely did being in the presence of a man— save for Daniel Sharpe—reduce her to a stuttering idiot. Even then, Addie couldn't recall a single time when Daniel caused sparks to shoot from her fingertips as they done brushing against Oren Potter's knuckles. His *knuckles*, for heaven's sake! And he the parent of one of her students, no less.

The unsettling thought spurred her toward the door. "I understand the inconvenience this errand must have caused you, Mr. Potter, but I do need to supervise the children."

"I'm sure you do." He popped his hat onto his head and opened the door for her, being very careful to step back a goodly distance.

She proceeded him out the door and paused on the stoop beneath the brass bell Aunt Louisa had donated upon the school's construction. Shading her eyes from the sun, Addie scanned the yard, mentally counting the children—though she would have counted grass blades to keep her mind off the man behind her. A group of boys shot marbles beneath the pine tree beside the schoolhouse. Several of the girls played jump rope near the white picket fence. Beyond them, ladies in bonnets or shading themselves beneath parasols strolled past the shops, gentlemen congregated outside the mercantile, and midday traffic preceded down the lane at a crawling pace.

A movement in the street brought her attention swinging back to a red-haired figure in flapping burgundy skirts dashing

across the path of a fast-moving black carriage. Addie's breath dammed up in her
throat. Her heart stopped cold. "Oh my
heavens . . . Linseeey!"

Chapter 4

Eyes, which reveal their owner's thoughts and feelings more clearly than any other part of the body, have always been considered vehicles of strong spiritual power.

She pushed him into a goddamn horse trough.

Daniel cursed himself for not expecting something like this, for not bracing himself the instant he'd seen her racing toward him as though wildfire licked her heels.

But it happened so fast, the shove to his midsection had come so unexpectedly, that he found himself flying ass over appetite over the hitching rail before he could blink.

He sat upright, sputtered grimy water from his mouth, and wiped his eyes. In the street, the horses reared against the traces of the black carriage Ira Graves used to cart folks to their final resting places. The crate of vaccine vials Daniel had been lifting into his father's buggy lay shattered across the boardwalk.

And in the center of it all stood Linsey Gordon. His gaze zeroed in on her immediately, pinning her in place.

Hands clapped against her mouth, eyes wide, she stared back at him with an expression any onlooker might mistake for astonishment. Daniel knew better. He'd been the target of her machinations far too long to believe her apparent surprise was anything other than a cover for spiteful glee.

To his further humiliation, well over a dozen people had seen his ungainly spill and loitered around snickering at their very own Doc Jr., drenched from head to toe and sitting in a damned horse trough of all places.

Hot fury infested his bloodstream as Daniel braced his hands on either side of the trough and struggled to haul himself out of the water—no minor feat, considering the small confines his large body had landed in.

Once he managed to stand, he fixed Linsey with a glare hot enough to make a grown man quake in his boots. "What in the Sam Hill did you do that for?"

She shrank at his bellow. Unfortunately Daniel couldn't savor the satisfaction of making her cringe for long before pride got the best of her.

She straightened her shoulders, tilted her chin at a defiant angle, then damned if she didn't stride right up to him and plant her hands on her hips. "It just so happens that I saved your life."

He tilted his head to the side and squinted at her with quizzical disbelief. *"What?"*

She reached into her sleeve for a scrap of

linen tucked inside the lace cuff. "Everyone knows if your shadow falls on a passing hearse, you'll be the next to ride in it."

He pushed away the hand reaching for his face. "That's the biggest crock of bull . . . nonsense I've ever heard." But not surprising, considering the source. He'd heard so many outrageous things spill from her lips over the last ten years that he could scarcely count them all.

"Nonsense?" Her brows rose. She bit the inside of her cheek. "Mr. Haggar was the first person to die after a rooster crowed three times in his yard. That leaves two more to go, because death always comes in threes."

Daniel moved his face so close to hers that barely an inch of space remained between them. To her credit she held her ground, though a flash of wariness skittered across the bright green of her eyes. Enunciating each word so there would be no misunderstanding, he said, "Bleet Haggar *died* because he was *sick*, not because some stupid cock crowed in his yard." The man had been wasting away for years from a liver disorder—one Daniel had done his best to treat—but beyond doses of roots and ash, and prescribing a morphine and quinine tonic to ease his discomfort, there'd been nothing more he could do. In the end, the wheelwright's death had not only been inevitable but probably a blessing.

Either Linsey Gordon had forgotten that little fact, or she had conveniently used the poor man's demise to feed her crazy delusions.

He suspected the latter.

The two of them stood nose to nose and will to will for several long seconds, so close he could see the starburst design in eyes made greener by the sweep of thick dark lashes against fragile lids. A kernel of respect for her planted itself inside Daniel. This was no shrinking violet. Linsey held her own in a way that Daniel had always admired in a woman but rarely saw.

As their gazes continued to hold, respect gave way to something deeper. A strange and uneasy sensation slithered through Daniel—as if invisible strings were weaving around the two of them, binding them together. In her ever-widening eyes, a vision began to unfold, of himself and Linsey lying together on a grassy carpet, he wearing nothing more than a loose pair of trousers, she wearing little more than a smile. Moonlight washed her skin in the palest of pearls, her eyes shone like emeralds, her hair glistened with amber fire. And as he watched himself bring her hand to his mouth, press his lips against her knuckles, and tuck her head against his heartbeat, an impression hit Daniel with frightening clarity that his future and hers were not only connected . . . but destined.

He wrenched back with a hot chill. He didn't believe in destiny. Or chance. Or fate. Cold, hard facts—that's what he believed in. And the cold, hard fact was that he had never, nor would ever, lie in the grass with Linsey Gordon, or kiss her knuckles, or any other part of her, for that matter. He wanted nothing to do with this woman.

Ever.

As if needing as much distance from him as he did from her, Linsey stepped back a pace and folded her hands in front of her, striking a demure pose that contradicted the wild, wicked streak he knew she possessed. Her voice wavered as she told him, "I apologize for pushing you in the water, Daniel; that was never my intent. I only meant to save you from certain disaster."

He looked her up and down with unconcealed derision. "The only disaster around here is you." Still shaken by his disturbing reaction to her, Daniel turned on his heel and stormed across the boardwalk into the apothecary.

"I was only trying to help!" she hollered after him.

Daniel's jaw tightened. He needed Linsey Gordon's help like he needed an outbreak of cholera. Her and her stupid superstitions. They—and she—had been an albatross around his neck for more years than he cared to count. Thanks to her, half his patients were convinced that charms would protect them from illness better than vaccinations, and the other half swore that paying a doctor's bill in full was considered unlucky.

Causing the stagecoach to flip when a damned rabbit jumped out in its path had only been the proverbial straw that broke the camel's back.

And now all this blather about saving his life from a hearse?

Hell.

Halfway across the shop, a harsh bellow stopped him in his tracks.

"Junior!"

Daniel's eyes slammed shut. A muscle ticked in his jaw. Bad enough everyone in the county had dubbed him Doc Jr.; hearing his dad call him Junior felt as pleasant as a splinter under his fingernail. It was just one more reminder to Daniel that he'd never meet up to the old man's expectations. He schooled his features and turned toward the curtain that divided the examination rooms from the main shop.

The old man appeared a second later, pewter gray hair sticking up from his shiny pate, his sagging cheeks freckled with age spots. "Did you get that buggy—what the Sam Hill happened to you?"

Daniel glanced down at the clothes sticking to his chest and thighs. He thought about putting the blame for his appearance at Linsey's feet where it belonged, yet a strange compulsion made him say, "Hell, Dad, it was so nice outside I decided to go for a swim."

Daniel Sr. narrowed his eyes. "I'm going to assume that you've got time to stand there giving me lip because those crates sprouted legs and loaded themselves into the buggy."

Outwardly Daniel held firm under his dad's disapproving scrutiny, yet inside he found himself battling that old feeling of failure. "I'll finished getting them packed as soon as I've changed into some dry clothes."

"You best put some fire under those feet, then. I'm pulling out at ten o'clock and not one

minute later." Daniel Sr. poked his index finger
into the air. "Efficiency! That's a physician's
creed! If you ever want to make something of
yourself, Junior, you'd do well to remember
that."

As if he could ever forget. The words had
been drummed into his head since he was old
enough to slobber on his father's stethoscope.

"I've got half a dozen kids waiting on those
vaccines and I don't have time for—"

The monotonous tirade broke off as suddenly as it started. Both Daniel and his father
became aware of a third presence at the same
time, and both turned their head toward the
apothecary entrance.

The first genuine smile Daniel had felt all
day inched across his face at the sight of the
stoop-shouldered woman watching them with
amusement.

"If it isn't my favorite doctors sharing a tender moment of affection," Louisa Gordon
greeted them with a twinkle in her rheumy
blue eyes. "Good morning, Daniel."

God, how he loved the way she could make
an insult sound like a compliment. "Miss
Louisa." His mood improving considerably,
Daniel met her halfway across the room,
picked up a veined hand, and kissed her
knuckles. No matter what he thought of Linsey, her aunt had secured a fond spot in
Daniel's heart. Not only was Louisa Gordon
the only one in Horseshoe who didn't call him
by that annoying nickname, but she'd been
nothing but kind to him his whole life. And at
no time had he appreciated her unfailing

warmth more than at the death of his mother six years earlier.

"Took a little bath, did we?"

"Something like that. How are you faring, ma'am?"

Louisa frowned, making the wrinkles in her forehead multiply like pleats in a linen sheet. "Better than Granny Yearling, I fear. I found her lying abed this morning."

"She feeling poorly?"

"She says her bowels are giving her a bit of grief. I was hoping either you or your father would have time to pay her a visit."

Daniel nodded. "If you'll give me a minute to change my clothes—"

"I'll fetch my bag," his dad said at the same time.

Daniel sent a startled glance toward his father. "I thought you were heading out to Jenny Kimmel's place."

"No reason why you can't give those kids their vaccinations." Daniel Sr. reached beneath the counter for a black leather bag as old as he was and retrieved his bowler from a hook on the wall. "Take the stanhope. I'll stop in on Mrs. Yearling, then borrow one of Oren's nags and meet you later."

Daniel bit his tongue to keep from reminding his dad that the whole reason the old miser had forked over money for the plush-seated buggy was because riding horseback aggravated his sacroiliac. But a man didn't argue with his father in the presence of a lady. Not that arguing with Daniel, Sr., ever did any good anyway.

"What are you waiting for, Junior? A brass band?"

Hell, Daniel thought, heading for his room to change his clothes, *what else is going to go wrong today?*

"When you said you wanted to go out with a splash, I didn't think you meant it literally." Addie planted her fists on her narrow hips. "For Heaven's sake, Linsey, what were you thinking, dashing in front of those horses?"

"I couldn't just stand by and do nothing when Daniel was standing directly on death's doorstep."

"So you tried to drown him?"

"Will you stop shouting at me?"

"I'm not shouting; I never shout!"

"Then stop yelling. People are staring."

Made aware of their audience, the bluster went out of Addie. As her body began to sink, Linsey hastened to guide her sister to the bench beneath the apothecary's overhang before she landed in the mud. Then she joined Addie on the seat. All color had left her sister's face, and Linsey worried that she was on the verge of swooning. "Breathe," she ordered, rubbing her hand against Addie's back.

Gradually the trembling abated, and her back rose and fell in an normal pattern.

"Better now?"

Addie released a deep breath and straightened. "Yes. Though I think I've had ten years scared off my life."

"I'm sorry I frightened you, Addie. And honestly, I didn't mean to push Daniel in the water, either. I'm trying to catch him for you, not kill him," she added with a wry grin.

"I know that, but from the look on Daniel's face a moment ago, you won't convince him so easily."

No greater truth had ever been spoken. The man seemed convinced that every misfortune that befell him did so because Linsey commanded it. Even if she had such power, she couldn't imagine using it against anyone. Even Daniel.

Still, why was it that every time she tried to do something good, it went so terribly bad?

"I must get back to the children," Addie said, leaving the bench.

"Do you want me to walk with you?"

"No, no. I'll be fine now, truly. Just try and stay out of trouble, please?"

Once Addie turned away, Linsey did the same, heading toward the livery to rent a buggy. Mr. Graves had led his horses away some time ago, much to Linsey's relief, and though most of the townspeople had also dispersed, returning to their shops and daily business, several lingered behind. She hated looking foolish, which probably accounted for why she had such a difficult time dealing with Daniel. No matter how hard she tried to be civil to him, he seemed to bring out the defiance in her.

Well, it really didn't matter, since Addie would be the one dealing with him—not her, thank God.

Which brought her back to the original problem. How did one go about matchmaking? That was one thing Aunt Louisa had never forced on them: finding a husband, settling down. Linsey suspected it was because Aunt Louisa had been blissfully happy as a spinster for many years before she met Wayne Gordon, and according to Aunt Louisa, he had been well worth the wait. She always said that when they found their destiny, they would know it. He'd make their toes curl, their breath quicken, and their heart sigh just by walking into a room.

Addie experienced all those symptoms around Dr. Daniel Sharpe, Jr., no question.

The problem was, how to get him to feel the same way toward Addie.

The drive out to Jenny's place gave Linsey plenty of time to ponder her plan. She spent the next hour inventing and discarding ideas until her head ached. The only experience she had with matchmaking was the misery she'd suffered at Mrs. Harvey's hands. Linsey shuddered. She refused to put either Daniel or Addie through that.

She'd definitely have to be more subtle. Addie, she was sure, would cooperate; but if she forced Daniel, he might run screaming in the opposite direction. It had to seem natural.

Unfortunately by the time she reached the drive leading to the orphanage, Linsey found herself no closer to an answer than when she'd left town.

The sight of the split-log house never failed to evoke fond memories. Mud fights . . . baseball games . . . sack races . . . but mostly of lavender-scented dresses and warm hugs on cold nights.

As a child, Linsey had often been a visitor to the rambling house. Most times Aunt Louisa brought her, bearing fresh vegetables from the garden—something which a household full of children never seemed to get enough of. Later, when Addie came to live with them, they often stole away to the house to play with the other children.

Yet it had been Jenny whom Linsey had gravitated toward. She'd been seventeen, an old and wise age to a girl of five, and so lively that Linsey used to sit in awe of her. So strong, so independent. She remembered wanting to be like Jenny when she grew up, not understanding then that the girl-turned-woman hid a deep longing to have someone to depend on herself.

She'd found him, finally, many years later. Noah Tabor was a huge man with gentle hands, warm brown eyes, with a pair of motherless girls no one could resist, and who had seen past the wheelchair Jenny sat in to the heart no other man had cared to find.

Wrapping the reins around the brake handle, Linsey gathered her skirts in one hand, the basket of horseshoes in the other, and hopped to the ground. Her heels clacked on the wooden ramp bordered by late-blooming asters making one last lacy showing before the first frost.

As Linsey approached the front door, she could almost hear the walls echoing with laughter and secrets and childish squabbles.

Closer, though, she realized that at least two—
the laughter and the squabbles—were actually
taking place.

She hesitated briefly, unwilling to interrupt
Jenny if she had her hands full.

Then again, she amended with a twitch of
her lips, perhaps an interruption was exactly
what Jenny needed.

Amanda Reed, Noah's young sister-in-law,
opened the door. Amanda and her sister Amy
had often been mistaken for Noah's daughters
rather than the sisters of his late wife, Susan.

An unmistakable sheen in the little girl's
eyes made Linsey's heart melt in sympathy.
She crouched low and brushed the bangs off
the six-year-old's brow. "Amanda, honey, why
are you crying?"

"Doc shot me."

"He did?"

Amanda nodded, dislodging a pair of tears.
"With a pricker this long." She spread her
hands an exaggerated distance.

Linsey tugged a tatted hanky out of her
sleeve and wiped the chubby cheeks. "Oh, I
bet that hurt."

"But he said I was a brave girl, so I got a
peppermint stick. Joseph won't get one 'cause
he cried like a baby."

"Joseph won't have to feel alone because I'd
cry like a baby, too." She gave one last swipe to
the wispy bangs, then straightened. "Is Jenny
here?"

Amanda nodded. "She's in the front room
with the doc."

She stepped back, allowing Linsey to enter

the front hallway into the normal muss and fuss of a household more concerned with love than tidiness. Mud-caked shoes littered the floor; caps and coats hung at cockeyed angles on a row of hooks. It was the complete opposite of the painfully formal appearance of her own home.

Linsey shook off the comparison and followed Amanda to a double-wide doorway gauged with the various heights of Jenny's youngsters. The sight of the man on Jenny's sofa made Linsey stumble to a stop. Why she had expected Doc Sr. instead of Daniel, Linsey didn't know. But there he sat, a knot of children surrounding him, groping at his chest for heaven only knew what.

He reached into the breast pocket of his coat and withdrew a handful of green-striped sticks. The children scrambled all over him likes ants on an apple core, driving him against the back of the sofa. A deep rumble of something sounding suspiciously like laughter struck Linsey dumb. No—she must be mistaken. Daniel didn't laugh. He barked. He glowered. He even bared his teeth on occasion.

But he never laughed.

He managed to peel off the tangle of arms and legs, plucking children off his chest, then his back, flipping one little boy over his head and tickling him until he cried out that he'd pee his pants if Doc Jr. didn't stop.

Jenny rolled into the room just then, an eighteen-month old baby on her lap that Linsey couldn't remember seeing before. He—or she, since it was hard to tell—must have come from the county orphanage.

What compelled Linsey to conceal herself in the corner, she couldn't say, except that catching the staid and dour Daniel acting almost human was a treat she didn't want to miss. And she feared if he spotted her, the hint of softness would disappear.

"I know you only came by to give the children inoculations," Jenny told him, "but I was hoping you'd take a look at little Michael here. He's got a fretful rash, and the cornstarch isn't working."

"I'll be glad to."

"I feel just awful asking you to do more when I can't even pay you proper for all you've done already. But I'll have John load a tub of butter in the buggy along with that crate of layers."

If Linsey hadn't been watching Daniel closely, she might have missed the strained slash of his mouth, since the parody of a smile disappeared almost as quickly as it formed.

"Let's take a look at the little fellow."

As he took the baby, bringing him close to his chest, Linsey forgot all about the conversation.

Her heart turned to mush. Daniel had always struck her as the type of man who kicked puppies and pushed old ladies out of his path. She'd never expected he would be so good with children. Oh, so he was a little gruff, his hands a little awkward as he examined Michael, as if he didn't quite know what to do with the wriggling bundle of drool in his lap. Somehow it made him more endearing. What a confusing man he was: so hard-skinned on the outside, so soft-hearted on the inside.

She could almost forgive him for being such a cad earlier—

Until he caught sight of her.

The twinkle in his eyes dulled, and the compassionate aura turned hard. He set the child away as if she'd caught him doing something sinful. "What are *you* doing here?" he grumbled.

Linsey moved into the room, the tender feeling inside her giving way to annoyance. "Bringing good cheer. You look like you could use a double dose."

"Linsey! This is a nice surprise."

Jenny's welcoming smile lifted Linsey's flagging spirits. At least someone was glad to see her. "I brought you a gift. Horseshoes to put above the doors and nails to hang them with—not those old store-bought kind, but real ones made of Mr. Potter's own forge and fire."

"How thoughtful."

"Make sure when Noah hangs them that he keeps the ends turned up, or the luck will run out."

Abruptly Daniel shut his bag and stood. "Miss Kimmel, I'm finished up here—unless you need anything else?"

"No, but thank you for coming all the way out here."

"Just rub this salve on Michael's bottom at

each changing and that rash will clear up in no time."

As he strode out the door in that no-nonsense walk of his, Linsey fought a battle with annoyance and lost. She glared at his back, then gave in to the childish urge and stuck out her tongue at him.

A giggle came from nearby, and as she turned she caught sight of Amanda standing beside a broadly grinning Jenny.

"Honestly, I don't know what Addie sees in him," Linsey said in way of defense.

"Is your eyesight failing you, sugar?"

"Of course not. Obviously the man has a few attractive . . . assets . . . " Linsey frowned. "Okay, a lot of attractive assets. But looks aren't everything; he's got the disposition of a porcupine. You saw him: he all but threw quills the minute he set eyes on me."

Jenny handed the toddler over to Amanda, who aided his wobbly steps toward the children playing tea party in a far corner of the room."Did you ever consider that maybe he doesn't know any other way?"

"Oh, please. How hard is it to be polite once in a while? Or to smile? Do you realize that I've never seen that man crack a grin in all the years I've known him?"

"It can be impossible for one who never learned how."

"Surely you don't mean Daniel!"

"You know how stern and exacting Doc Sr. can be. Imagine living with that day in and day out for twenty-some-odd years. Remember that not everyone is as lucky as you, Linsey. Not everyone was raised in a family who loves them for who they are."

Linsey almost laughed at the irony. Her "family" consisted of a castaway stepchild and a doddering old aunt. She wouldn't trade Addie or Aunt Louisa for anything in the world, for Jenny was right, they did love her. More, they needed her.

But deep down inside dwelled a yearning for something bigger. To belong to someone who needed her on a deeper level. Someone who needed her as woman, the way Noah Tabor needed Jenny Kimmel.

The squeak of wheels rolling on the hard wooden surface pulled Linsey's attention to Jenny.

"Do you remember when Noah brought Amy and Amanda to me? He didn't know the first thing about raising two little girls and the thought of it scared him to death."

"Nobody would have thought any less of him had he not raised them. It's hard work being a parent."

"But he wanted to. He just didn't know how. All he needed was a little faith in himself."

"You gave him that."

She smiled softly. "Well, I like to think I helped. It was always inside him, though."

The only thing inside Daniel was a heart of ice. Linsey sighed. "This is different, Jen. We're talking about Daniel, not Noah."

"They aren't so different. Maybe all Daniel needs is for someone to show him how to smile."

A yearning to be the one to put a sparkle in his eyes, to be the one who taught him how to smile, gripped Linsey with a swift and sudden fierceness. She abruptly shook the notion away. That was Addie's job, not hers. Addie was the teacher, after all, and Daniel's future wife. "Where is Noah, anyway?" she asked in an effort to divert her thoughts.

Just the mention of the man's name put a light in Jenny's eyes and a rosy glow in her cheeks. It was getting positively disgusting, the way men had the power to change a woman's entire bearing.

"He's over at Widow Hutchin's place, mending the fence her mule busted. Work has been picking up, thank heavens. For every step we take to get ahead, something winds up pushing us back. I don't know what I would have done if Doc Jr. hadn't been willing to take his services in trade."

Linsey's skeptical expression must have given her away because Jenny remarked, "That surprises you?"

"Daniel just doesn't strike me as a man willing to do anything that doesn't gain him in the long run."

"He's a doctor. It's in his soul to heal."

Linsey decided not to voice her doubts about Daniel even having a soul. Instead she told her friend, "If things are that hard, I wish you'd let me help."

"Oh, no. You know that Noah is too proud to take charity."

"It wouldn't be charity. It would be a donation for the children."

"Thanks just the same, Linsey, but we'll be fine. Are you in a hurry today? Do you have time for a visit?"

Knowing that this might be the last time she'd see her friend, Linsey spent the morning visiting with Jenny, helping her with the few chores she couldn't manage on her own, and entertaining the children, whose energy seemed endless. She soaked in all the little nuances of life and living that had seemed so trivial before: the creative comfort of baking pies, inane chatter over the latest fashions, the soft innocence of a child's hand clasped in her own. . . .

If Jenny noticed that Linsey got a little weepy-eyed now and then, or that she lingered at her side more than usual, she didn't say anything.

Neither did she bring up Daniel's name again, much to Linsey's relief, though he continued to hover at the back of her mind. She kept seeing him lolling on the sofa with a passel of children, kept hearing that rumbling from his lungs—that almost-but-not-quite laugh . . .

Linsey finally took her leave after she and Jenny put the children down for their naps, her heart aching at the thought that she might not see her friend again, yet knowing she could tarry no longer with all the things yet left to do. Back in Horseshoe, after she returned the carriage, she decided to stop by Granny Yearling's to see if Aunt Louisa might like company on her walk home.

Granny Yearling lived in a little cottage on

an offshoot road behind the schoolhouse. To get there, Linsey had to pass by the apothecary.

Voices coming through an open window at the back of the building clashed through the air like swords. Linsey's steps slowed. She knew she shouldn't eavesdrop, but something about the tone tugged at her, compelled her to pick up her skirts and wander closer.

Reaching the sill, she stood on tiptoe and peeked inside an examination room. An open doorway in the far wall gave her an unobstructed view into the office across the hall. Daniel stood stiff and square-shouldered in the doorway while his father paced the floor in front of him.

" . . . the right, telling her she didn't have to pay?"

"She didn't have any money, Dad. I accepted the chickens as trade."

"We aren't running a charity, Junior. We have a service to perform, and by God, if folks want that service they've got to be willing to pay cold, hard coin for it!"

"You know as well as I do that every penny she and Noah make goes into those kids and that house. If we demand money, we might as well be stealing food from the children's mouths. Even you can't be that heartless."

"Heartless has nothing to do with it. Just you try paying the university admissions office with a bunch of damned farm animals, and see where that gets you. They want money, Junior." He slammed one fisted hand into the palm of the other. "And every penny you give away adds one more day to getting into the university."

"Don't you think I know that?"

The reply came out in a harsh, anguished whisper that cut Linsey to the core.

Doc Sr. stared up at his son for several long, tense seconds before he finally said, "Yes, Junior, I suspect you do know that. And I'm beginning to wonder if you want that surgical degree as badly as you claim you do."

He then burst out the door, out of sight. Daniel remained behind, alone in the room, his head bowed, his shoulders slumped.

As Linsey watched, her mouth agape, little things she'd given no significance to before started clicking into place. His pinched expression when Jenny told him she couldn't pay. His constant burning of the midnight oil, visible from her bedroom window on the hill. The fixed weariness in his features.

She'd had no idea he was still pursuing an education. It had been her impression that when he had lost his scholarship, he'd decided to remain in Horseshoe and help his father with his practice.

Obviously she'd been mistaken.

But if the reason Daniel couldn't attend the university was because of finances, why did he continue to refuse the money she offered in reparation? And why in the world would he tend the sick and infirmed, knowing he wouldn't get paid?

It's in his soul to heal.

The scene of him with the children replayed in her mind over and over like a melody on the phonograph. He never actually cracked a smile, but his hands were gentle and his voice soothing. That much had not changed since he'd tended Addie ten years ago.

It's in his soul to heal.

A germ of an idea began to form. A broad grin broke out on her face. She'd have to put that nature to the test, then, wouldn't she?

With a deep sigh, Daniel pushed away from the doorjamb and left his father's office to find someone to take the half-dozen layers Jenny had given him. He'd known even when he took them that he wouldn't keep them. He had no more use for the chickens than he did the sows, the quilts, or the buckets of coal that the majority of his patients paid him with.

He couldn't fault any of them; times were hard. But, damn, if this kept up, he'd never get into Johns Hopkins. Never regain his dad's respect.

Not that he really cared what his dad thought, he told himself. He just hated being reminded of his failures.

As he stepped outside, he caught a glimpse of a familiar redhead strolling down the road beside the school yard. She stopped, stooped, picked something up off the ground and tucked it into her pocket, then continued on her way with a cheerful spring to her step. Seeing Linsey stirred a long forgotten hunger for impulsive touches, sparkling conversation and laughing—just for the sake of laughing. It was as if she had no care in the world, and that cupid's-bow mouth of hers was forever smiling.

What brought out such a carefree spirit in a person? Why did it seem as if burdens were not a portion of her plate?

Daniel started, then cursed. What was wrong with him? Why this renewed fascination with her?

If not for her he'd be in Maryland right now, working to prove himself in the medical field under the tuteledge of the most renowned surgeons in the country, a member of an elite team of surgical pioneers discovering new and innovative treatments for some of the most perplexing disorders known to man.

He sure as hell wouldn't be stuck in this one-horse town, taking orders from a sour-hearted old codger determined to mold him into his own image.

Daniel's eyes squeezed shut. No, he wouldn't think about this. It was done, it was over.

The only thing he could do was make the best of the hand dealt to him. But as he reached for the crate of hens in the buggy, he vowed that one day he'd leave Horseshoe and become an accomplished surgeon, even if it took him ten years to save the money. And nothing or no one—especially not Linsey Gordon—was going to divert him from that plan.

"You keep scowlin' like that, Dan'l, your face is liable to freeze," a scratchy voice teased.

Daniel glanced up and spotted Jarvis and Potter ambling toward him.

"Wish it would," Oren piped in. "If he went ugly, the ladies hereabouts might give the rest of us saps a shot."

"Speak for yourself, Potter; I've got wimmen chasing me from dawn to dusk."

"Yeah, with a rolling pin."

His friends continued to hurl insults at each other, but Daniel paid them little notice. Normally he would have found the exchange between his pals amusing, but today . . . well, Daniel just didn't find himself in an easily amused mood.

He lifted the crate out of the stanhope and set it on the back stoop.

"Heckfire, Dan'l what's got you so down in the mouth?" Jarvis prodded.

Daniel raised up and brushed his hands together. "Linsey Gordon."

The lanky lamplighter grinned. "What did she do, try drowning you again?"

"You heard about that?"

"It's all over Horseshoe."

Wonderful. "Don't these people have anything better to talk about?"

"You oughtta know better than that, Daniel," Oren said. "A body can't go to the outhouse without everyone knowing about it."

Daniel didn't argue that. He raised his forearm against the wall and leaned into it. "Tell me something, fellas. You ever get the feeling someone is plotting your downfall?"

"Someone like . . . " Oren made a rolling motion with his hand.

"A woman," Daniel finished.

"You're askin' us?" Jarvis exclaimed.

"Well, yes." Who else would he ask? His father? Any time he brought up the subject of women to his dad, he wound up listening to an hour's worth of "They're a trap, boy, and you don't got time for traps. . . . " Maybe Jarvis and Potter weren't experts on the gentler sex, but he had to get this off his chest, and they were better than no one.

"See, it's like this. I've run into her more times today than I have all year." Daniel recounted each incident, ending with, " . . . then she shows up at Jenny Kimmel's when I'm examining that new batch of kids she got."

Jarvis shuddered. "Jesus, Dan'l. Linsey Gordon, kids . . . you've just planted the seeds for a year's worth of nightmares."

Daniel knew the feeling. Hearing the two in the same sentence was enough to give any sane man a case of hives. "The question is, why?"

"Maybe she's taken a shine to you." Jarvis grinned and winked.

"Don't even joke about that." The thought of Linsey setting her sights on him made a tremor of apprehension surge through his veins. "But I am beginning to wonder if this is just coincidence and I'm overreacting, or if she's got something up her sleeve and I've got a right to worry."

"If ya ask me, you got a right to worry. The safest thing you can do is stay as far away from that gal as you can."

"Isn't that the truth," Daniel muttered.

"Here pal, I've got just the cure for what ails ya." Jarvis slyly afforded Daniel a peek at the flask tucked into his inside coat pocket. "Cooter Hobart's special blend."

The cure? More like the kill. "No, thanks. That stuff'll peel the hide off a steer."

"Didn't hear no complaints the last time."

Hell, that's because it had about blistered Daniel's gullet. He'd hardly been able to swallow, much less complain, the day Jarvis had decided to help him drown his sorrows over losing his fellowship. "Some other time, Robert. I've got a shipment to unpack before my dad has an apoplectic fit."

"Suit yourself." The lean man shrugged. "We still on for Saturday night? You can help me take Potter for everything he's got."

"Shee-oot, Jarvis here is the one with pockets deeper than his pants."

"Why not?" Daniel said without much enthusiasm. "If you fellas are so eager to throw away your money, you might as well throw it in my direction."

"Throw it away, hell. I'm the poker king."

Oren snorted. "You're the poker something, but it ain't king."

As his friends continued down the road, Daniel shook his head. It was pitiful that his weekly poker game was the highlight of his existence. What had his life come to?

That wasn't a question he really wanted to explore. He had a feeling if he did, he'd discover a vital element he'd lived without for a long time, and start missing it again.

No, the only question he wanted an answer to was . . . *What the Sam Hill was Linsey Gordon up to this time?*

Chapter 5

Sneezing: One for a kiss, two for a wish.
three for a letter, four for a better,
five for silver, six for gold,
seven for a secret never to be told.

When Linsey got that look in her eye, trouble wasn't far behind. Addie had been led down mischief's path too many times not to recognize the eager gleam and know that it didn't bode well.

She rose from her chair and stacked the books littering her desk. "Whatever idea you're cooking up, just leave me out of it."

"But this is the perfect plan!" Linsey exclaimed.

"The last time I let you talk me into one of your 'perfect plans,' I nearly wound up in jail." She gathered the books, her gloves, reticule, and lunch pail in both arms and rounded the desk.

"I told you to knock on wood when you said that the mayor might catch us." Linsey grinned, falling into step beside her as she

marched down the aisle. With a conspiratorial
wink, she added, "But you must admit, that
wine would have been worth spending the
night in the calaboose."

"There are those who still don't believe we
were hiding from a tornado," Addie grumbled. Thank goodness her students remained
ignorant of the real reason they'd snuck into
Mayor Harvey's cellar two years ago. She'd
never live down the disgrace. And if their parents had any inkling of half the antics she'd
engaged in thanks to Linsey, she'd be booted
out of teaching altogether.

"C'mon, Addie, this will be different; I
promise."

"Says the spider to the fly."

Linsey brought her to a halt outside the
school-yard gate, a mere ten paces from the
apothecary. "Haven't you always been sweet
on Daniel?"

"Yes, but—"

"And haven't you said time and again, 'If I
were Daniel's wife . . . '?"

"You know I have, but—"

"Then go into his office and pretend to need
medical attention."

"For what? I'm in perfect health."

"Tell him . . . " As if looking for answers,
Linsey studied the empty school yard. "Tell
him your arm hurts."

"But it doesn't."

"*Act* like it does."

Addie's brow lifted. "I thought you wanted
to be known for your honesty."

"This isn't dishonest, it's . . . creative." A

proud grin brightened her face. Then, in the cajoling tone Addie had come to dread, Linsey pressed her point. "If only you'd have seen him with those children, if you'd seen the care and attention he paid them, you'd feel as certain as I do that Daniel can't resist a person in need. Why can't that person be you?"

Oh, Addie hated how easy Linsey made it sound! How plausible. And she hated how tempted she was to go along with such a ridiculous ruse.

But hadn't that always been the way of things? She balked, Linsey coaxed. . . .

And Addie usually lost the battle because it was easier to go along with Linsey's harebrained schemes than risk losing the only sense of belonging Addie had ever truly known.

Still, a thread of reason prevailed over her weakening will. "That's all fine and dandy, but you're forgetting one important detail. I'm no good at playacting—no, I'm worse than no good; I'm downright horrible. Don't you remember that summer I had to play Maid Marian's lady-in-waiting? I practically got booed off the stage because I couldn't even— Ow! What did you pinch me for?" Addie rubbed the stinging spot above her right elbow.

"Your arm hurts now, doesn't it?" Without waiting for a reply, she all but dragged Addie down the boardwalk, pulled open the apothecary door, and pushed her over the threshold. "Now, go in there and make that man notice you."

The string of cowbells attached to an overhead hook jangled at her entrance. Daniel, sitting behind the counter, glanced up from the stack of papers spread out in neat piles in front of him.

Addie remained rooted to the spot, frozen and clutching her books to her bodice like armor, unsure how to proceed. How could Linsey have put her in this predicament? What should she do? What should she say?

This sudden plunge into the role of coquette left her feeling unbalanced and completely out of her element. She'd never imagined she'd find herself any closer to Daniel than the width of Wishing Well Lane. She'd been perfectly content with adoring him from afar, much as she would a priceless painting or an invaluable statue. At least then she didn't make an utter fool of herself. At least then, he couldn't reject her.

But, oh, he was so handsome. If there was ever a time when Daniel Sharpe, Jr., hadn't made her knees weak and her head spin and turn her insides to mush, she couldn't remember it. She'd been ten years old the day they'd met. And of course Addie could lay the blame at Linsey's feet for that, since it had been her idea to jump off the rocks at Turtle Point.

With her leg broken in two places, the pain had been unbearable. But the instant Doc Sr. walked into her room with Daniel in tow, she'd forgotten her agony. Even at seventeen, Daniel had been mesmerizing. Straight, silky black hair, a stubborn jawline, mysterious eyes. And as he helped his father set her leg, his soft voice and gentle touch had soothed her faster than any laudanum drops.

From that point forward, not a day passed when she didn't think of him, didn't equate him with the peace he'd brought her, and yearn for that feeling again.

The idea that she could be this man's wife . . .

A sudden attack of nerves nearly had Addie swooning.

"Can I help you, Miss Witt?"

Addie tried. Heavens, how she tried to think of some witty or—at the very least—polite reply. But her tongue seemed swollen to twice its normal size, preventing any sound from issuing out of her mouth. Her brain went to ash. Even the blood decided to clot in her veins.

She simply stood there, staring like a complete halfwit at the most handsome man God put on this earth and wishing she were anywhere but here.

"Miss Witt, is there something I can do for you?"

She swallowed several times, finally managing to croak out, "It's my arm."

"I see. Follow me, please?"

Anywhere! she thought. Still, several seconds passed before she could make her feet move. Daniel led her behind the old ice-cream counter, around the register, through a curtained partition, and down a paneled hallway to a room bordered with black-walnut beams and a linoleum floor that squeaked beneath his soles. Addie halted in the doorway, her heart beating thrice its normal rate.

"Have a seat on the table, please. I'll be with you in just a few minutes."

Addie stared at the table he indicated with a wave of his hand, scolding herself for her complete lack of courage. For heaven's sake, he was only going to examine her arm, not ravish her. Yet she couldn't banish the feeling that this "perfect plan" was not going to turn out as well as her sister predicted. If only she had half of Linsey's confidence. . . .

But left with the choice of walking out like a coward, standing in the doorway like a dunce, or taking a seat on the table and seeing this plan through, Addie chose the last.

Hesitant steps brought her to a waist-high table covered with a bleached sheet. While Daniel washed his hands in a blue-speckled basin, Addie hoisted herself onto the table and tried to distract herself with her surroundings. She looked around at the certificates on the whitewashed walls. The glass-fronted steel cabinet was filled with wicked looking instruments, whose purpose she didn't even want to guess.

"You said your arm is giving you trouble?"

Addie nodded, but kept her gaze fixed on a crack in the linoleum as he moved closer. She just couldn't bring herself to look at him. *But heavens, he smelled nice. Clean and manly with a faint hint of—*

"Achoo!"

Oh, bay rum. Addie fished for her handkerchief and wiped her nose. She'd always had a embarrassing reaction to the scent. Even now, she felt her eyes water and her lungs swell.

She sneezed again. A flush slid up her cheeks.

"Have you been feverish?"

Only by the grace of God did she manage to shake her head and keep her seat at the same time.

"Are you sure? You're looking a bit flushed."

She kept her gaze trained on the button of his vest as the blush intensified. If Linsey weren't already dying, Addie would strangle her.

"Which arm?"

"My right," she whispered.

"How did you hurt it?"

Addie stilled. The deception chafed her nature like raw wool, yet she didn't see any dignified way out of this situation other than to be as truthful as possible. "I just felt a . . . pinch."

"Well, let's take a look at it. Would you mind rolling up your sleeve?"

Though his voice was brisk and impersonal, he might as well have asked her to strip naked and dance on the tabletop.

With clumsy fingers, she managed to unbutton the cuff and pull the ruffled sleeve past her elbow. Her hands shook. Her nerves quivered. Tears of guilt and humiliation burned at the back of her lids. Still, she thought she was doing well holding on to her rattled composure.

Until Daniel placed his cool, smooth hand beneath her elbow.

His touch made the room close up like a clamshell. A numbing fog swept through Addie's brain. And as her muscles lost all control, Addie made a vow to kill Linsey, just before she slithered off the table onto the floor in a dead faint.

Nibbling on a thumbnail, Linsey paced the length of the boardwalk, doing her best to curb her impatience and failing miserably. What was taking them so long? For the love of Gus, it wasn't as if she'd *broken* Addie's arm!

Another glance through the sheet-glass window displaying a collection of tonic and bitter bottles, a shiny silver manicure set, and a grouping of engraved pictures frames, gave Linsey no further clues than the last time she'd looked inside. A curtain of burgundy-and-green damask behind the ice-cream counter remained drawn shut, blocking off any view inside.

"Well, now, if it isn't Miss Linsey Gordon, peeping in windows."

She jumped a foot in the air and slapped one hand to her pounding heart. "Bishop Harvey, you scoundrel, you scared the wits out of me."

Noticing that his gaze had followed the route of her hand, she dropped her fist to her side. Her nose curled. He smelled of spirits and his eyes were blurry. And God only knew when he'd last changed his clothes. They were wrinkled beyond repair, and the collar of his shirt bore smudges of what Linsey felt certain was cosmetic paint. Wouldn't the mayor be proud if he saw "our country's future congressman" now? "You're drunk, Bishop Harvey."

"Not so much that I can't recognize a beautiful woman when I see one." He moved closer.

She stepped back, more out of annoyance than alarm. For all his faults, Bishop wasn't a violent man. Just a pathetic one.

"If you've got a hankering to peep into windows, be at my place at midnight and I'll give you something really worth looking at."

"You are disgusting."

"And you, Linsey-woolsey, are even more beautiful when you're riled."

That did it. She poked her finger into his chest. "Why you horrid, impertinent *cad* . . . don't you *ever* call me that!" Only her family called her by the pet name, and she'd be hanged before she'd allow this pitiful excuse for a human being to sully something she treasured. "I've not given you permission to call me Linsey, much less something more personal."

"Don't like it? Fine. I'll call you pet. Or sweet muffin. And you can call me—"

"An undertaker if you don't find another corner to haunt. I've told you time and again that I am not interested in your attentions, and I swear on my mother's soul, if you don't leave me alone, Bishop Harvey, I'll . . . I'll put a curse on you!"

She spun on her heel and wrenched the apothecary door open, smirking in satisfaction at the pained howl that followed as it smacked into him. She hope she'd broken his dad-gum nose.

Linsey crossed the shop and plopped down on one of the stools bolted to the floor in front of the ice-cream counter. It had been put in long ago, when Mrs. Sharpe was still alive, and Linsey remembered sitting here countless times as a child, watching the woman churn her homemade blends, waiting for that first sweet taste of heaven.

It had been years since she'd eaten ice cream, years since she'd sat at this counter, but she recalled the pleasure clearly. Thanks to Bishop, even that was being denied her. God, but she loathed that man! No, she'd not insult the gender by calling Bishop Harvey a man. He was a toad. No, a worm. No, the slime a worm left behind—

The sudden appearance of Doc Sr. interrupted her thoughts, and brought back to mind the scene she'd witnessed through the open window earlier.

Linsey hoped the smile she gave him didn't look as strained as it felt. What she'd seen had been personal and private, and frankly, she wished she hadn't seen it at all. Until today, she'd never had reason to question the relationship between Daniel and his father. Perhaps they didn't show outward affection, but she hadn't imagined that they didn't have at least an amicable relationship.

Linsey pretended interest in the swirling pattern of the counter's tiles and tried to decide if she should strike up polite conversation or just keep silent.

Luckily Addie emerged from behind the curtain just then, coming to her rescue.

Or so Linsey thought, until she caught a rare flash of anger in her sister's eyes.

Snatching up her reticule, Linsey fell into step beside Addie, who kept walking right out the door into the street.

"What happened?" Linsey asked.

"What happened? I made a complete fool of myself, that's what happened! I knew this was a stupid idea. Marry Daniel Sharpe indeed—I can't even be in the same room with the man!"

"You didn't make him notice you?"

"Oh, I got him to notice me, all right—after he had to pick me up off the floor and pass an amonia vial beneath my nose to rouse me. Now, if you are finished making me the brunt of another perfect plan, I have a meeting with a parent."

If Addie could have found a hole deep enough, she would have crawled in and never come out. How could she ever, *ever* have let Linsey talk her into such a ludicrous scheme? She'd known from the beginning that it wouldn't work. If only she had listened to her instincts. But she hadn't. And now—

Oh, how could she ever face him again?

Well, she was done. Through. No more letting herself be swayed by Linsey's outlandish schemes.

From now on, she would focus soley on what she was good at, what she felt confident enough to handle.

Her children.

Arriving at the double doors of the blacksmith shop, Addie retied her bonnet, brushed the wrinkles out of her skirts, and patted her cheeks. Once she made herself as presentable as she could, she took a deep, restoring breath, then entered the structure to meet with Bryce Potter's father.

After days of deliberation, she'd finally come up with a way to promote the boy's talents. The only thing left now was to discuss it with his father and get the man's permission.

Despite the cool wind and crispness of autumn outside, inside the smithy it felt like the middle of August. Fired coal, hot iron, and horse sweat mingled with the steaming heat radiating from the huge cast-iron box in the center of the barn-like structure. One side of the smithy had been reserved for hay stacks and tack, while a half dozen stalls took up the other side. Horses nickered from within.

Mr. Potter emerged from behind a pyramid of barrels, and Addie's mouth dropped open. Bare from the waist up, save for a pair of elbow-length leather gloves and a soiled apron, his tanned skin shined with perspiration.

A treacherous warmth curled inside her belly. Her fingers itched to smooth the wild mane of black hair swept back off his brow.

"Miss Witt?"

The sound of her name wrenched her out of the fantasy. Forcing herself to look into his eyes—and only into his eyes—Addie managed to say without stuttering, "I hope I'm not disturbing you."

"Not at all."

Heavens, he actually sounded pleased to see her.

He stabbed a poker into an ovenlike structure, and orange sparks sprayed the air. He tugged off his heavy gloves and motioned toward an upended crate by a room crowded with saddles and other equipment. "So. What brings you here this afternoon?"

She sat straight-spined and press-kneed on the crate, doing her utmost to ignore the splinters poking through her petticoats—and the man leaning his bare shoulder against a thick support beam.

"I wished to speak with you about Bryce."

He straightened and alarm streaked across his craggy features. "Nothin's happened to him?"

"Oh, no, no." Once he relaxed again, Addie toyed with the cuff of her gloves. She had to be very careful how she presented her observations. The little boy's future depended on how she approached the man who ruled his life. It wouldn't do to seem too eager, but neither must she give an impression of indifference. So she settled for plain and simple professionalism. "Mr. Potter, I'm sure you are aware that your son is an exceedingly bright boy. He is merely eight years old and can easily do the schoolwork of an eighth-grade pupil."

A shy smile of obvious pride stretched across the blacksmith's face. Addie's breath caught in her throat at the beauty of the sight, like a mountain kissed by the dawn.

"I'm a simple man, Miss Witt. If he got smarts, he got them from his mama."

Addie swallowed. Clenching her purse strings, she sought to keep her mind on his words and her mission. "I'm not sure that's true, Mr. Potter, but his intellect exceeds that of my top five students combined. What I am sure of—and I'm certain you will agree—is that every opportunity should be made available to a boy of Bryce's obvious gifts."

"What are you saying?"

Forcing any hesitation out of her tone, she stated, "I feel that Bryce would benefit from a far more advanced education than I can give him. There are schools on the East Coast—"

"Hold up a minute—the East Coast?"

"They are very fine schools, Mr. Potter, much better equipped to cultivate the educational potential of children like Bryce."

"I'm sure they are. But Horseshoe is our home. I've got a business here. It's not the grandest business, but it's honest. And me and Bryce get by. Neither one of us has any plans of giving up what we have here."

"No one is suggesting that you give up your business, Mr. Potter. Many of the schools will room and board their students, right on the grounds. Bryce could come home during weekends and holidays—"

"Thank you for coming by, Miss Witt, but I'm not interested."

"Surely you can see that his mind is not—"

His steady, obdurate gaze fell on her. "What I see, Miss Witt, is that you are a teacher. It's your job to teach my boy."

"My resources are limited. Books are hard to come by, and the funds for new material simply aren't there . . . "

Addie let the sentence trail off. The stubborn set of Mr. Potter's jaw and the flatness of his deep blue eyes made it clear that her reasons were of no consequence. And in all honesty, the dearth of proper teaching material was a minor obstacle. They'd held fundraisers before. But books were only as good as the person who read them: her graduate certificate and basic teaching degree were no match for Bryce Potter's level of intelligence.

"Potter!"

Both Addie and the blacksmith swung toward the doors just as Robert Jarvis burst into the smithy, his face wreathed in excitement.

Mr. Potter got up from his seat. "Scram, Jarvis."

"It's here! It came on the train, just like I told you it would!"

"Can't you see I'm busy?"

Jarvis tipped his hat to Addie. "Beg pardon for the interruption, Miss Addie. Come on, Potter—I need you to bring a wagon around and help me load it."

Mr. Potter turned to Addie and sighed. "I'd best go with him before he busts a gut. Believe me, that wouldn't be a sight fit for a lady's eyes."

As he walked out of the smithy with Robert Jarvis, Addie found herself fighting disappointment. She lowered her gaze to her tightly clasped hands and pressed her lips together. How was she ever going to foster Bryce's prospects if his father refused to even discuss the matter?

Perhaps Linsey might have an idea.

Addie shook her head. This was her project, her mission. All her life, she'd relied on her sister to fix her problems.

Well, not this time.

With sudden determination charging through her bloodstream, Addie shot to her feet and left the smithy. Somehow she would make Oren Potter understand that sending Bryce away was the boy's only hope for a proper education.

And somehow, she would do it on her own.

Chapter 6

To comment openly on another person's beauty or health or any other advantage that he or she enjoys may bring misfortune down upon that person.

"**D**aniel's coming to dinner? Tonight?" Half the people in Puckett's Mercantile swung their attention toward the front of the store. Linsey calmly continued rifling through the rack of dresses, unaffected by Addie's outburst.

Aware that she'd caught the interest of several gossipmongers, Addie lowered her voice to a whisper. "How could you do this to me?"

"If you want someone to blame, blame Aunt Louisa. She's the one who invited him and his father, not me. I only learned about it a few hours ago when she got back from Granny Yearling's." Linsey looked through the assortment of muslin, linsey-woolsey, and calico gowns with a displeased frown. There really wasn't much to choose from.

"And I suppose you had nothing to do with

it?" Addie asked, brow raised, arms folded across her bodice.

"I would have if I'd thought of it. But apparently Doc Sr. had to pay Granny a visit yesterday and he got her feeling sprite and perky, so Aunt Louisa wants to thank him." Hmm, the yellow muslin was pretty. High neck, poofed shoulders, leg-o'-mutton sleeves. She glanced at Addie, then shook her head. No, something bolder. More enticing.

She slid one hanger after another across the bar, searching for the perfect frock. If she had more time, she'd have Hazel Mittermier sew up one of her special gowns. But even Hazel couldn't be expected to create a masterpiece in only a few hours, so she'd have to make do with the limited selection Puckett's offered. "Frankly, I couldn't have planned it better myself. Daniel would never accept an invitation from me, but no one with any sense would turn down Aunt Louisa."

"I *cannot* sit across a table from Daniel," Addie contended through clamped teeth.

"Oh, Addie, you can't let one little setback stop you from going after the thing you've wanted most of your whole life!"

"A little setback? I fainted at the man's feet, for pity's sake!"

"All right, so maybe a doctor's office wasn't exactly the best place to strike up a romance—but this will be different. A little candlelight, violins on the phonograph. And with your hair fixed soft and wispylike, and a flattering new dress—" The divine red gown Linsey raised against Addie's front covered the dreary paisley frock she wore. "Daniel simply won't be able to resist you."

Addie pushed the dress out of the way. "Changing the wrapping around a plain old box doesn't change the fact that it's still a plain old box."

"But bright paper attracts notice so one will *open* the box and see the gift inside." Linsey wished Addie wasn't so hard on her looks. If anyone had cause to complain, *she* did. She'd been cursed with short legs and a short body. While many might consider her petite, Linsey thought herself . . . well, stumpy.

Addie, on the other hand, had a beautiful, willowy shape and long legs. All right, so maybe her features—pug nose, wide eyes and long chin—didn't make her the most elegant of women. She certainly wasn't an eyesore, either. Now, to convince *her* of that. . . .

"Here, what about the aqua one?"

"Too many ruffles."

"This copper one, then. It'll pick up the gold in your hair, and it doesn't have any ruffles."

"But it shows half my bosom!"

Heaving an impatient breath, Linsey let her arm fall. "Look, do you want Daniel to notice you or not?"

"Linsey," Addie sighed, "even if I managed to stay conscious long enough to survive the evening, I could run naked through the streets of Horseshoe and he still wouldn't pay me any mind. My visit to his office proved that. Face it, sister, I am not the kind of woman a man notices."

"Don't be silly—"

"No." She shook her head. "It's the truth. I've looked in a mirror."

"So have I."

Linsey didn't mean to be so blunt, but the words, once spoken, had a sobering effect on both of them. She turned back to the gowns, unable to bear the instant sorrow on Addie's face. "Now, should we go with the blue or the copper?"

"Land sakes, I'd take them all," came a familiar cheerful trill. Linsey lowered the dresses and peered over her shoulder. "Caroline!" Laying the gowns over the rack, Linsey rounded the shield of shelves to greet their friend. "Did you see a blue flame spark in a candlewick? I was planning on paying you a visit tomorrow."

"Then I've saved you a trip." Caroline's grin made the lines at the corners of her eyes crinkle like opened fans.

"You really shouldn't be wandering about town on your own."

"Don't worry, I'm not. Axel dropped me off for a few minutes while he took the wagon up to your place. Louisa told him he could come by and fetch the compost bin."

"Your garden will certainly benefit from it next spring. Aunt Louisa has been tossing so much roughage in it that it's full to bursting. And so are you, it seems." Linsey cupped her hands around Caroline's swollen belly and smiled at the powerful kick she felt against her palms. "It won't be long now, will it?"

"Another month. Land sakes, Linsey, it can't be soon enough. He's beating me black and blue from the inside out! And what I wouldn't do to fit into one of these again." She eyed the rack of gowns with longing. "Oh, I sound like I'm complaining, don't I? I just feel so clumsy, and . . . big!"

"You'll be back to your natural shape in no time."

"From your mouth to God's ears. Oh, would you look at this!" She picked up a music box from the shelf and twisted the key on the back. The tinkling strains of a Brahm's lullaby wafted through the store. "Wouldn't a baby dream sweet dreams falling asleep to this?"

"Perhaps you should get it before someone else does," Addie softly suggested.

"No, I'd better wait." She managed a feeble grin and placed a protective hand atop her belly. "No sense in spending money on something I might not ever use."

"Stop that kind of talk this instant, Caroline," Linsey scolded. "Everything will be fine this time, I'm sure of it. You've been wearing your eagle stone since the beginning, so you've been completely protected. Isn't that right, Addie?"

"That's right. Before you know it, you and Axel will have yourselves a healthy baby to coddle and spoil. Keep positive thoughts."

"Yes, you're both right; I'm just being emotional."

With good reason, Linsey thought. Having lost her first three babies before birth, Caroline had every right to expect the worst. But the rare and powerful lapis stone Caroline wore in a bag around her neck would surely secure an easy childbirth.

"What brings the two of you to town, anyway?" the pretty brunette asked.

"Addie's looking for a fetching new gown," Linsey replied with a conspiratorial wink.

Lifting her brow in amusement, Caroline inquired, "Any particular reason?"

Addie blushed furiously. "Oh, look at the time." She glanced at the watch pinned to her bodice. "If I don't get tomorrow's lessons prepared, the children will be completely unmanageable."

Linsey watched her go and sighed.

"Who is he?" Caroline whispered.

"Daniel Sharpe."

"Junior or Senior?"

Linsey gave an unladylike guffaw. "Oh, Caroline. Daniel, Jr., of course!"

"Hmm, he'd have been my choice, too. If I'd found him before Axel. . . . " She let out a long, drawn-out sigh.

Linsey rolled her eyes. "Caro, not you, too!"

"Me too, what? The man is handsome as sin—don't tell me you haven't noticed!"

Linsey grimaced. She couldn't help but notice. But at least she didn't make an utter fool of herself over him. "What is it about him, Caroline, that has women practically swooning at his feet?" Literally, in Addie's case.

"The fact that he's got the face and body of a Greek god isn't enough?"

Linsey tilted her head and gave her friend a pointed look.

"No? All right, then look what else he's got."

On her fingers, she ticked off. "The conviction of a preacher, the toughness of a cowboy, and the perception of saloon keeper." She flipped her hands in the air with a flourish. "What woman can resist a combination like that?"

"Oh, silly me—and here I thought it was his charming disposition women couldn't resist."

"I'll admit he can be brusque sometimes, but if you ask me, it only lends to his touch-me-not mystery. Oh, there's Axel now. Come by next week for tea?"

"I'll look forward to it."

As Caroline breezed out the door with as much grace as her bulky body would allow, Linsey shook her head in exasperation. She just didn't understand Daniel's power over women. First Addie, then Jenny, now Caroline. And all of them seemingly sensible women.

Thank goodness *she* was immune to his charms.

Linsey shook her head again. After a final study of her choices, Linsey draped both dresses over her arm. Just as she started for the register to pay for her purchases, the music box Caroline had been coveting made Linsey pause. She studied the pastel-painted box for a minute, then, pressing her lips together in a stubborn line, plucked it off the shelf. Caroline would bear a healthy baby this time; Linsey refused to think otherwise. Especially not now. She did have a romantic evening to arrange, after all.

Daniel stood on the veranda and stared at the brass knocker of one of the finest houses in the county. Damn his father for doing this to him. After tending to one severed foot, a case of atrophy, and an ear infection, the last thing he felt up to was supper in the house of perpetual catastrophe.

Yet here he was, stuck here alone, performing his "social duty."

Well, he'd stay an hour, and by God, not a minute past it.

Squaring his shoulders, he gave the knocker a curt rapping. Louisa Gordon opened the door a moment later, looking resplendent in a cream-colored dress with a cameo broach pinned to the lacy jabot at her throat.

"Daniel, how good to see you. Let me take your overcoat."

He shrugged out of the calf-length cape and passed it over. After hanging it on the coat rack beside an entrance table, Louisa peered around him and asked, "Isn't your father with you?"

"He asked me to send his regrets, but he was unexpectedly detained."

"A patient?"

Daniel nodded. "Pete Morris down by the Triple J got kicked by a horse."

"Oh my, what a shame. I hope it isn't anything serious."

"So do I."

"Well, perhaps he'll make it next time."

Daniel doubted it, but didn't see any gain in telling Louisa that his dad could rarely attend any function without being called away to tend a patient. Daniel hadn't understood that as a boy, but as a physician himself, he'd quickly learned the way of the life. Even if the old man had the time, social forays weren't high on Daniel Sharpe, Sr.'s, list of priorities.

His sole purposes in life were equally split between driving himself into the ground and making Daniel as miserable as possible.

And speaking of misery . . .

A glimpse of the woman strolling along the upper balcony almost made Daniel say to hell with social responsibility and walk out the door.

Until she stepped onto the landing at the top of the stairs.

"Jesus," he whispered, his mouth going dry.

Daniel felt as if he'd taken a blow to his midsection. Linsey looked . . . incredible. Her hair was pulled back from her temples, held in check by a circular band with dangling charms, and a mass of fat curls spilled down her back. A black velvet choker circled her slim neck. An off-the-shoulder gown hugged her cinched waist and rounded hips like skin, and the drape of her gown pulled tight across the front of her thighs . . .

Daniel tried his damnedest not to appreciate her beauty, but he'd have to have been made of stone not to notice how the copper threads of her gown brought out the highlights in her hair, or the creamy swells of breasts pushed up from her bodice.

The familiar surge in his groin made him painfully aware that he was far from being made of stone. But this was Linsey: the albatross around his neck, the thorn in his side, the blot in his otherwise clean slate.

That didn't stop his mouth from going dry as charcoal as she gracefully descended the stairs. Each fluid movement seemed designed to fuel a man's imagination. It for damn sure fueled his. If his heart beat any harder, it would burst through his chest.

He hadn't even noticed the woman standing behind Linsey until she reached the bottom of the staircase and tugged her sister forward.

"Doesn't Addie look lovely this evening?" Linsey asked him with a pleased sparkle in her eyes.

Actually Daniel thought she looked quite sickly, but kept his opinion to himself. The shiny green-blue of her gown only augmented the pallor of her complexion. He hoped she wasn't on the verge of fainting again. "Yes, lovely. Your arm is better, I hope?"

She shared an inscrutable glance with Linsey, as if asking permission to reply, then looked down at her hands. "Much better, thank you."

Daniel bit back a scowl. He'd always had a hard time dealing with timid females. He much preferred women with a bit more spunk. That had been the one thing he'd appreciated about Charlotte, at least. She might not have had much loyalty, but he'd never have caught her bowing to anyone or cowering behind someone else's back.

Neither did Linsey, come to think of it.

Except for that one time in the Haggar's house, he couldn't recall an instance when she'd shied away from anything.

"Let's retire to the dining room, shall we?"

Louisa suggested, pulling Daniel from his reverie.

He stepped forward to take Louisa's arm, but Linsey beat him to the punch, leaving him to escort Addie. Even through the thick cotton of his shirt, he could feel the cold and clammy imprint of her fingers against his forearm.

Though he'd paid several visits to Briar House over the years, he'd never ventured into any of the downstairs rooms. The dining room, with its cream wallpaper and brass fixtures, was smaller than he'd expected it would be and had a simple elegance reminiscent of Louisa. A table big enough to seat eight people had been formally set for five with blue-leafed china and enough silverware to finance a dozen medical students through school. A soup tureen surrounded by dried rose petals acted as a centerpiece. Braces of flickering candles on the sideboard and on stands in each corner lent the room an intimate atmosphere. It was all a little too feminine for Daniel's taste, but he couldn't help but be impressed that they'd gone through so much trouble for a supper guest.

Daniel assisted Louisa to the seat at the head of the table, then politely pulled out the scroll-backed chair to the right of her. Linsey and Addie began whispering and shuffling, elbowing each other in the arms, acting more like children than grown women. When Linsey caught him watching their antics, she stopped abruptly, straightened, then with all the dignity of a queen, marched around to the other side of the table. Daniel bit the inside of his cheek. She really was a contradiction: half imp, half lady . . . *all woman*—

He gave himself a sharp shake.

Then, aware that the only place settings vacant were the one next to Addie or the one next to Linsey, he hesitated, feeling as if he'd been given the choice of sitting beside a shrinking violet or a Venus fly trap: one fragile, safe, and unassuming; the other a sight to behold with a sweet scent that lures in the bait and snaps it up.

With a spear charge of rebelliousness, he moved to the seat next to Linsey. She might have turned his head years ago, but not any more. He was stronger than he'd been back then, more in control of her ability to affect him. If he had to endure an evening sitting beside her to prove it, then so be it.

Louisa started ladling the soup, which was the cue for engaging in light conversation about work, weather, and the townspeople. The topic steered toward Emmaleen Haggar, and how she was coping with Bleet's passing, and Daniel's thoughts once again strayed back to the stunned look on Linsey's face the afternoon of the wake.

It wasn't exactly a suitable topic for supper, but Daniel knew that curiosity would hound him until he learned what had driven her from the house in such a state. He leaned back in the chair and rubbed his chin with his forefinger. "Linsey, why were you running out of the Haggar house, anyway?"

Silence.

Daniel studied the women from beneath

narrowed brows. Addie looked nervous as a
cat in room full of rocking chairs, and though
Daniel wouldn't have thought it possible, her
complexion seemed even more ashen. Even
Linsey's cheeks seemed to have lost color.

His instincts went on full alert. These two
were hiding something, on that he'd bet his
degree. But what?

"She was avoiding Mrs. Harvey," Addie
finally stated—a little too forcefully, in
Daniel's opinion.

"Again?" Louisa exclaimed. "My lands, I
wish that woman would get her boy married
off and leave my Linsey be."

Louisa might have missed the gratitude in
Linsey's eyes, but Daniel didn't. Whatever
secret these two shared, they were keeping
from their aunt. Not for long, though; he felt
sure of that. Not much escaped Louisa Gordon's eagle eye. The thought almost made him
smile. It ought to be interesting to see how
long they had to dig their graves before one of
them fell in.

"I've always told these girls that hasty decisions make for needless divisions," Louisa
said. "They'll settle down when they've a
mind to settle down."

Daniel smothered a cough. If Linsey got a
mind, he wanted a warning so he could run for
cover. She was dangerous enough when she
didn't think.

"But if you ask me," the old woman went
on, "it's just a cryin' shame when a girl isn't
even safe at a wake."

He didn't dare offer his opinion on that remark. If they asked him, Linsey wasn't safe anywhere—she was a born catastrophe.

"I didn't marry until I was twenty-four, and not for an instant do I regret waiting for my Wayne, rest his sweet soul. He gave me forty wonderful years before his heart gave out." Louisa sniffed the cork on a bottle of chilled wine. Seemingly satisfied, she passed the bottle to Daniel.

While he poured for each of his hostesses, Linsey joined the discussion. "I understand your parents were married quite a number of years, Daniel."

"Twenty-five." Theirs hadn't been as blissful as Louisa's, though.

Linsey accepted her glass, took a sip, then remarked, "There is nothing finer in life than knowing you are loved, and loving in return, don't you agree?"

"For some, maybe. Others might have more important aspirations."

"What could be more important than love?"

Did she want a list?

Supper arrived then, carried in on silver-domed plates by a boy hardly old enough to boast peach fuzz. When the lad spotted Daniel, his brows shot up in surprise. "Hey, Doc Jr."

"Hey yourself, John. I didn't realize you were working for the Gordons."

"Just for tonight. Miss Linsey said she wanted everything to be spec—*Ow!*"

While John hopped back into the kitchen,

Daniel looked at Linsey. Her smile held all the innocence of a cat with a canary in its mouth.

The woman was up to something. He knew it as surely as he knew his own name, but damned if he could figure out what it was.

John returned, juggling two large bowls and a gravy boat. Daniel saw disaster in the making, and apparently so did Linsey; simultaneously they dropped their spoons and reached to help John.

Once the dishes were placed safely on the table, Linsey issued a soft but delighted gasp, directing Daniel's sights to the place settings. He saw nothing unusual, even when Linsey pointed to the small plate between them, where their spoons had landed side by side.

"It's a sign!" she whispered.

"I beg your pardon?"

"Two spoons on the same saucer means a wedding will take place. See, Addie, I knew—" The table jarred, rattling the china, and Linsey shot a glare at her sister, who returned it full measure.

Daniel watched with growing suspicion. What the Sam Hill was going on? The dinner, all this talk about marriage . . .

Maybe she's taken a shine to you.

Jarvis's suggestion made Daniel choke on his wine. Jesus, they weren't looking at him as husband material, were they? Daniel caught his breath and waved away Linsey, who had instantly started pounding on his back. "You can stop beating me. I'm fine. It just went down wrong."

After Linsey had settled back in her chair, the meal and conversation progressed. Daniel participated halfheartedly, still trying to come to terms with the staggering possibility of her developing a matrimonial interest in him. The mere suggestion worried him as much as it astonished him. He figured it was common knowledge that he had no plans to marry; his last foray down that road still left a bitter taste in his mouth.

But no matter how he analyzed it, he couldn't come up with any other reasonable explanation for her behavior of late. He knew one thing, though: it didn't bode well.

Before he realized it, the main course of glazed duck had been served and eaten, and Louisa had gotten herself more than half tipsy on two glasses of burgundy. She was just reaching for the bottle to fill herself a third glass when her hand wavered. Daniel lunged across the table to assist her, and his elbow knocked over several items.

All conversation ceased. All eyes turned on him.

Daniel glanced down. There was nothing much to see: no spilled glasses, no stains on the pristine linen—just a toppled salt shaker.

He sat down, righted the object, and then reached for his own wine.

Still they stared at him.

"What?" he finally barked, chilled by the continued hush.

"You spilled the salt," Addie informed him.

He glanced at the tiny pile of white grains near the tureen, then at Addie, Louisa, and finally Linsey, all of whom wore identical expressions of horror. "I beg your pardon."

Linsey gestured toward the mess. "Aren't you going to throw three pinches over your shoulder?"

"For what?" he asked, genuinely puzzled.

"To avert the bad luck."

The bad . . . Daniel felt his face mottle. If he had to listen to one more superstition—

"Adelaide, will you ask John to serve desert?" Louisa quickly said.

"Yes, Aunt Louisa."

Addie started to rise, but Linsey stayed her with a hand to her shoulder. "I'll get it, Addie. You stay here and entertain our guest."

As she carried the dishes down a hallway that separated the kitchen from the main living quarters, Daniel's gaze strayed to the sway of hips clad in copper satin, and the saucy bow centered high on her bustle. He used to wonder how much of her shape was artificial and how much was natural; used to imagine peeling away the feminine trappings to discover for himself if she was as soft as he imagined, as sweet as he dreamed, as willing as he hoped.

Used to, hell. The old fantasy had been creeping into his thoughts more and more lately since his brief encounter with her in the Hagger kitchen. No matter how much he wanted to forget, Linsey had the disturbing ability to make him remember the scent of lavender, the suppleness of her figure, the thud of her heartbeat against his ribs.

Under his breath, Daniel cursed both his head and his rapidly hardening groin. So much for being in control of her effect on him. No woman should have the power to arouse a man just by a memory. Why could he recall all those tantalizing details about a smart-mouthed, wild-scheming, trouble-stirring vixen? What kind of fool did that make him?

The biggest one in Horseshoe, no doubt.

Daniel lurched to his feet in sudden panic. "Miss Louisa, my thanks for supper and the fine company, but it's getting late."

She glanced at him, surprised. "You're leaving before dessert?"

Damned right; he had to get out of here before his condition became too noticeable. "I have a long day ahead of me."

She started to rise from her chair. Fearing that she'd topple over if she stood, Daniel quickly said, "I can see myself out, ma'am."

"Give my regards to your father, then, won't you?"

"Of course."

"Oh, and Daniel, be careful going home."

He paused at the cryptic remark, then, with a nod to both ladies, excused himself before Linsey returned. He all but tore his overcoat off the rack in his haste to make it out the door.

Once on the veranda, he dragged in a breath of air so deep it stung his lungs. He released it, then sucked in another one, and yet another still . . .

Gradually his tight muscles began to loosen and his blood started flowing a little more freely.

Jesus, he thought—or prayed—he wasn't sure which. How could he desire a woman who'd ruined everything he'd spent years working for?

He crossed the veranda, determination in his stride. All right, so she stirred up his lust. So he hadn't gotten over his weakness for her—there was no use denying it. But just because she aroused him physically didn't mean he'd soften toward her; it only meant that he couldn't trust his body not to betray him. There was one way to fix that—stay the hell away from her.

As he reached the bottom step, the faint, lilting sound of his name drifting out of a window stopped him cold.

Ignore it, Daniel told himself. *It doesn't matter if she's talking about you.* The evening had been mercifully uneventful for the most part; no need to test its generosity. But as his feet began moving toward the sound in complete defiance of his will, Daniel realized he could no more resist the lure of Linsey's voice than he could walk out in the middle of a tricky operation.

Besides, he reminded himself, Linsey had mischief up her sleeve—mischief that in some way involved him. He'd be damned if he'd sit on his hands, waiting for her to plunge the knife into his back. The more he learned about what she was up to, the better prepared he'd be.

Keeping to the shadows, Daniel stole around the corner of the veranda. A door slammed open. He threw himself back against the wooden skirting just as two figures emerged from the back door. Moonlight outlined their shapes as they moved past a shed to a box on stilts, located a good distance from the house. He couldn't hear their words, but from the gestures he'd become witness to some disagreement. He saw Linsey turn her attention to the bucket in her hand, picking through the contents.

Daniel crept closer to the flat-roofed shed near the cage, his footsteps muffled by the thick grass.

"I just don't understand it," he heard Linsey say. "The evening was progressing so nicely! Why would he leave?"

"All I know is that he said he had an early day tomorrow," Addie replied.

"There must be more to it than that. Did you say anything to him?"

"Of course not!"

"Well, that explains it," Linsey cried in exasperation. "What did you do, faint again?"

"There's no need to be cruel—I'm not the one who came up with this ludicrous idea!"

"It wasn't ludicrous; it was a perfectly good idea that just didn't turn out as I'd hoped. That doesn't mean we should give up."

"Oh, Linsey, you are impossible!"

Daniel almost gave away his presence by laughing. Impossible? A mild description compared to those he'd come up with in the past, yet not entirely inappropriate.

Impossible she was. And reckless. And too damn tempting for her own good.

Or his.

That was it: it was time to haul himself out of here before his wayward lust got the best of him again—or worse, before he was discovered. He spun away from the wall and a twig snapped beneath his sole.

"What was that?" Addie asked.

Daniel froze and cursed beneath his breath.

"What was what?"

"I heard something."

Daniel didn't dare move.

The sounds around him seemed to amplify to an almost painful level—the harsh breaths of Linsey and Addie, the scratching of whatever they kept in the cage, and the thud of his own heartbeat.

He had no way of judging how long he stayed hidden behind the shed before Linsey finally said, "Well, I don't hear anything."

"I'm telling you, something is out there."

"It was probably a squirrel."

He sensed more than heard them move away from the cage, and released the breath trapped his lungs. For chrissake, what was he doing, skulking around the Gordon property like a two-bit thief? How had he sunk to such depths? And for all the effort, he had no more clue as to what Linsey was up to now than he'd had before.

At least he could be thankful for one thing, he decided, pushing away from the wall. he'd come out of an evening spent with Calamity Linsey unscathed—

Then he stepped out from behind the shed.

Chapter 7

Never set your hat on a bed.

The slops hit him full in the face. And in the neck, and on the front, dripping down his smart-looking tie, bleached white shirt, and brocade vest.

Addie gasped.

Linsey gaped. The metal bucket she'd flung at their "intruder" fell to the ground with a clatter. "Daniel?" She didn't really need him to answer; she knew who stood there. Only one man in Horseshoe owned such a broad set of shoulders.

"Oh, heavens, Linsey. What have you done?" Addie whispered in horror.

Linsey couldn't answer. She could only stare at the man before her, potato peelings in his hair, curdled milk dribbling down his stern jaw.

She should be mortified. She should apologize immediately, and make some effort to soothe the almost tangible temper simmering behind the rigid features and stiff posture.

She really, really shouldn't . . . A choked

117

chuckle broke through, quickly growing into full-fledged peals of laughter. Linsey tried to pull herself together, clamping her lips tightly, and covering her mouth with her hand. But he looked so adorably pitiful, that it was all she could do not to hug him.

All the while, Daniel simply stood there, moving not a muscle, uttering not a sound.

Then, his long fingers swiped across his eyes, clearing away the mess.

Linsey's laughter dwindled.

If looks were lightning bolts, she'd have been nothing more than a singed spot on the lawn. It was amazing that eyes could be so cold and so hot at once. Even more amazing was that she wasn't used to it by now. Daniel had been looking at her in the same blisteringly frigid way ever since the day the bag of mail had been fished out of Horseshoe Creek.

Even so, Linsey had to admire his aplomb when he did nothing more than nod stiffly and say, "Good evening, ladies." Then he spun on his heel and marched down the hill with all the pride of a military captain.

For a moment, he'd reminded Linsey of her father—a man who barked orders and strode through life as if it were to be conquered and not enjoyed. Where did men learn such emotional control?

"You ought to be ashamed of yourself, Linsey Gordon!"

Linsey turned to her sister and met a look so stern that she almost swore Addie had turned into Evelyn Witt. "Me? What for?"

"I can't believe you threw slops in Daniel's face!"

"How was I supposed to know *he* was your intruder? What was he doing sneaking around out here, anyway?"

"Daniel wouldn't sneak around—he was probably returning from the—oh, no!" Addie's gaze shot to the outhouse, a short distance beyond the shed. "We accosted the poor man for using the necessary!"

Frankly, Linsey thought he'd brought it on himself—he should have averted the bad luck.

"How am I ever to face him again?" Addie wailed into her hands.

Linsey instantly folded her arms around her distressed sister. "Oh, Addie, don't cry. Maybe the evening could have ended on a better note, but all isn't lost. We just have to come up with a new plan."

Over the next few days, that resolve remained with Linsey as she attempted without success to bring Addie and Daniel together. Each day she and Addie returned to the old habit of sitting at the ice-cream counter after school, and though Linsey basked in this precious time with her sister, the most either of them saw of Daniel were his coattails flapping in the breeze. The man seemed to be going out of his way to avoid them.

By the third day, Linsey realized that they were wasting time they didn't have. Sitting around waiting for Daniel to notice Addie was clearly not working. She had to do something, and if she didn't do it fast, Addie would wind up alone and lonely for the rest of her life.

But what could she do?

With a knapsack filled with horseshoes slung over her shoulder, a pocketful of nails weighing down her skirt pocket, and a hammer banging against her hip, Linsey pondered her options on her way to town.

It would be so much easier if she could simply tell Daniel how Addie felt about him, and hope it would open his eyes to the possibilities of happily-ever-after. However, she had a feeling that one whisper of marriage would send him fleeing faster than a spooked horse.

The only other option was nothing short of manipulation: to get Addie and Daniel together in a compromising situation where he would have to marry her for the sake of honor. But that plan didn't sit well, for what if he resented being forced to wed and took his misery out on her sister?

No, it was best to stick to the original strategy—putting them together where he couldn't help but notice her. The trouble was, whenever she did manage to get them together, Addie swooned, Daniel left, or someone interrupted them.

What she needed was to get them together in the same place, at the same time, where neither could escape.

But how?

The question preyed on Linsey's mind as she moved from building to building, adjusting crooked horseshoes already tacked above door frames and fastening the iron charms where none existed to bring good fortune to her neighbors. It gave her a good feeling to know she'd done something to brighten their lives.

When she reached the apothecary, it didn't surprise her to find nothing but a bare shingle above the door frame. Obviously Daniel believed in good fortune as much as he believed in forgiveness.

And therein lay her biggest obstacle. His lack of faith—in laughter, in life, in love. She began to wonder if he closed off his emotions so easily because he had no reason to believe in happily-ever-afters. If so, was that a result of his strict upbringing, as Jenny presumed? Or had the woman he'd planned to marry hurt him so badly?

The possibility preoccupied her as she tapped a nail into the horseshoe above the Sharpes' door and gathered her belongings. Just as she started around the bend fronting the church and school, a stray cat strolled out of a line of bushes. Linsey paused and held her breath. She loved cats, but she was also aware of the power of fortune they held. Especially black ones. She crouched low, and keeping her gaze locked with the brilliant green eyes staring at her, softly coaxed the animal over. "Here, kitty, kitty, kitty. . . . "

It blinked a slow, lazy blink. Then it dipped its head and strolled toward her with a graceful, rolling gait.

Linsey grinned jubilantly and scratched the cat between its ears. If it had dashed away from her, it would have taken its luck with it;

but by approaching her, it gave Linsey the first ray of hope that the day would be filled with good fortune.

Her spirits felt light as air as she rose and continued toward Puckett's Merchandise. Only then did it register that she was the only person in town. She glanced around in puzzlement. Where had everyone gone? Only a second ago, Madame Cecilee had been visiting with Hazel Mittermier in front of her shop, and Mr. Puckett had been sweeping the front walk of his store.

A burst of distant laughter brought Linsey's attention swerving to her left, where a splash of brilliant color peered over the hedge tops. What in the name of Gus was it?

Linsey joined the crowd of townspeople that had already gathered in the empty lot beside the school, where people were pointing and chattering at the peculiar sight.

"Well, glory be. Would you look at that!" Linsey breathed, approaching closer than anyone else dared to venture. It looked like a bubble lying on its side, and was at least fifteen feet wide and God only knew how long. Scads of ropes were stretched out on the ground, and Robert Jarvis appeared to be attaching some sort of basket to the mouth of the slowly swelling bubble.

"What is this thing?" she asked him.

He twisted around and his thick brown eyebrows pulled into a frown. "It's a hah-dro-gin balloon I ordered months ago. Now go away, Linsey. I don't need you jinxing it before I even get a chance to use it."

She ignored him. "What do you do with it?"

"You ride in it, of course!"

"In that?" She gestured toward the panels of purple, green, and gold silk.

"Not in that, in the basket."

She wandered toward the tublike carrier and ran her hands along the woven rim. "But aren't you afraid of falling out?"

" 'Course not. This thing is so sturdy—wait a minute, don't touch those valves, Linsey. I don't got this thing secured down yet."

She pulled her hand away from the odd-looking tanks strapped to the basket. A germ of an idea took seed—not quite visible, yet there nonetheless, struggling for root. "What happens if you twist them?"

"Gases'll blast into the envelope and make it rise. This craft'll go thousands of feet in the air, and come sunrise tomorrow I'll be soaring with the birds."

Oh, lucky Jarvis! How she'd love to soar with the birds, feel the clouds brush her cheeks. Touch the sweet blue sky . . . "But how do you get it back down?" she asked suddenly.

Clearly impatient with all her questions, Jarvis tossed his hands in the air. "Who says I want it down?"

"Surely you don't plan on staying up there forever."

"No," he grudgingly admitted. "When I want to touch ground again, I just pull a lever that opens a flap, but I don't plan on doing that until I've seen the whole country. Now go on and find someone else to pester—I've got work to do."

She sighed and reluctantly backed away from the craft that seemed to beckon to her adventurous spirit. Though she'd love to stay with all the other spectators and at the very least watch Jarvis finishing filling his balloon, her time was better spent finagling a wedding than dreaming of adventure. How *could* she keep Addie and Daniel together without any interruptions?

Suddenly she stopped and glanced over her shoulder. Her gaze traveled up the brightly colored silk panels, slowly but steadily unfurling toward the wide blue sky.

A broad, gleeful smile broke out across her face.

Yep, thousands of feet in the air should solve the problem quite nicely.

Chapter 8

Any journey begun with the right foot is likely to be fortunate, while a journey begun with the left foot will bring misfortune.

"**Y**ou can't be serious!" Addie gasped, staring in horror over the bushes into the empty lot beside the school.

"Why do you keep saying that? Of course I'm serious—it's the perfect plan!"

"You expect me to get into *that*?" She jabbed a finger at the multicolored monstrosity floating a few feet off the ground. Cords connected the circumference of a woven basket to the bulbous sack swaying in the breeze.

"Not for long," Linsey replied. "Only until Daniel gets here."

She looked so smug, so pleased with herself for coming up with another "perfect plan," that Addie wanted to choke her. Mutinously, she set her jaw and folded her arms over her bosom. Linsey may have forgotten how the last two attempts had turned out, but she hadn't. "I am not getting into that—that . . . floating death trap."

"Do you have a better idea?"

"Yes. Forget the whole thing."

"Addie, be reasonable." With a suggestive lift of her brows and a wickedly mischievous gleam in her eyes, Linsey cajoled, "The two of you, alone, together, with only the wide blue yonder and the wind to embrace you? No interruptions, no escapes. And if you faint, Daniel will revive you and you'll still have plenty of time to get to know each other. What could go wrong?"

Setting her finger to her cheek, directing her gaze skyward, her toe tapping a rapid beat, Addie pretended to consider the possibilities. "Hmm, flying miles off the ground in a wicker box over spiky trees and rocky creeks and cliffs? I can't think of a single thing!"

"Nothing is going to happen. You won't be in the air that long, and Daniel will know how to handle the balloon." She fished into her pockets. "And besides, I brought you my lucky seashell and a fresh sprig of ivy and a piece of coal I found just the other day. It hasn't even been used yet."

Addie plugged her fingers into her ears and began humming to drown out the coaxing tone of Linsey's voice.

It was as childish as it was futile, and she knew it even before Linsey caught her hands and pulled them away from her ears. "Look, do you want to marry Daniel or not?"

Addie met the stern green eyes drilling into her with a glare of her own. What a cruel question. What a doubly cruel manipulation. "You know I do."

"Then get into the basket."

"Forget it."

"Dad blame it, Adelaide! It's my last wish to stand up at your wedding, but we are running out of time. I've done everything in my power to see that you and Daniel are given some privacy so he can realize what a wonderful person you are, what a wonderful wife you will make him. Now it's up to you."

The not-so-subtle reminder of her sister's fate and her own promise to help fulfill her last wishes whittled away at Addie's resolve.

Still, she thought she might have been able to stick to her guns if Linsey hadn't given her The Look. The one that said, "I'm counting on you." The one that always made Addie dig deep for her courage and buck up her bravado. She'd never been able to resist it. To do so meant she risked disappointing her sister. Or worse, being left behind. She'd experienced that before, when her mother married Linsey's father, and she didn't care for the emptiness it bred.

"Oh, all right. I'll get into the blasted balloon."

Linsey beamed. "I knew you would. Now hurry, before Jarvis returns. It wouldn't surprise me if he had a crowd behind him, since everyone knows he's pulling up stakes this morning. Unless we want to lose this chance, we have to work quickly."

Oh, this is getting better and better! Addie thought. All she needed was to wind up accused of stealing someone's property. And what was this "we" stuff? she wondered, working herself up into a mild snit as they crossed the few yards between the hedge line and balloon. Who was the one getting into the basket? Who was the one risking life and limb to help fulfill a dying wish? Ha! Not Linsey, that was certain.

Once she reached the ladder, Addie paused and swallowed the heavy knot of panic that stuck in her throat like a lump of clay. The basket didn't hover high off the ground, just two or three feet, but it was high enough to make her stomach queasy.

She forced her foot onto the first rung, then the second, climbing until got her reluctant limbs up the rope ladder. She reached the top and peered into the square basket. It was roomier than Addie had expected, even with the stack of gear along one wall, but that did little to calm her rattled nerves. Already she felt a familiar, chilling anxiety creeping into her blood, rising to her head.

She stepped gingerly over the side and lowered herself into the cube. The balloon wobbled and swayed. Addie clenched her eyes shut and willed down a bout of nausea.

"This is perfect!" Linsey exclaimed from behind her. "Ooh, wrap yourself in those furs, Addie. If Daniel doesn't see you right away, he'll climb inside."

While Linsey oozed exuberance, it was all Addie could do not to scramble out and race for home. Her hands shook so badly she almost dropped the furs twice before finally getting them draped around her shoulders. "What if

he refuses to come with you?" she asked,
unable to control the quiver in her voice.

"Don't you worry; just leave Daniel to me.
Are you comfortable?"

Huddled in the furs, Addie nodded hesi-
tantly.

"Good. Oh, Addie!" Linsey clapped once.
"This is going to be perfect!" she repeated for
the umpteenth time. "Now, stay here. Don't
come out until you hear Daniel, hear?"

Again Addie managed a tremulous nod.

Linsey climbed out of the balloon, pausing
at the top of the ladder to look over the rim at
her. "Remember, Addie, wait for Daniel."

With those words she was gone.

An instant sense of rising made Addie go as
still as a bookend. *Oh, my heavens.* Was the balloon pulling loose? Would she be stuck going
aloft all by herself?

Moving nothing but her eyes, Addie peeked
over the rim at the wavering space between
herself and the ground. A wash of dizziness
suffused her, and she felt herself swept back in
time to a bank of rocks lining Horseshoe
Creek. Addie remembered the place clearly,
just as she remembered an eleven-year-old
Linsey standing beside her, bubbling over
with enthusiasm Addie couldn't imagine feeling as they peered down into the wrinkled ribbon of water below.

"The only way to cure your fears is to face
them head on. C'mon, Addie, it'll be fun!"

Linsey's idea of fun had wound up being six
weeks of excruciating pain and confinement
for Addie while her leg mended. The only

good that had come out of the ordeal was that
Daniel had accompanied Doc Sr. to Briar
House during her convalescence.

The balloon lurched again, straining against
its tethers. Tears sprang to Addie's eyes, and
she gripped the side of the basket in a death-
like clutch. Even as she loathed the fear stealing in, neither could she find the strength to
fight it off.

She couldn't say how long she waited for
Linsey to return with Daniel, but it felt like
hours when, finally, cowardice won the war.

Enough was enough, she thought, pressing
her lips together and lifting her leg over the
side. Not for anything would she go up in this
balloon.

Not even for a chance to become Mrs. Dr.
Daniel Sharpe.

He wasn't at the apothecary. He wasn't in
any of the shops Linsey passed along Wishing
Well Lane. What if he'd been called away?

That thought increased Linsey's sense of
urgency as she hastened down the center of
Horseshoe. She knew better than anyone how
Addie liked having both feet firmly on the
ground, yet she'd all but bullied her sister into
getting into the balloon.

Linsey told herself it was for a good cause.
Still, she refused to leave her sister alone in
that basket for long, even if it meant abandon-
ing such an ideal plan to bring her and Daniel
together.

A sigh of relief burst from her lungs when
she spotted him leaving the saloon.

"Daniel!"

The minute he spotted her, he frowned and turned away. Obviously he still hadn't forgiven her for the other night. But then, that was nothing new, was it?

She hurried forward and gripped his rumpled linen shirt sleeve. Muscles tensed beneath her fingers, but at least he stopped. "I've been looking all over for you."

"Thanks for the warning."

"No, Daniel, you must come with me."

"Not if I were stricken down with malaria and you were the last bottle of quinine."

He shrugged free of her hold but Linsey wouldn't be deterred. "Please, Daniel. It's Addie—she's in Jarvis's balloon."

The note of panic she'd injected in her voice had no effect on him.

"Then tell her to get out."

"She won't come out for anyone but you!" It wasn't a lie; Addie always did as she was told—though admittedly it sometimes took some convincing—and until she heard Daniel's voice, she would stay put.

He blew out an impatient sigh. "Is she ill?"

Uh . . . did lovesick count? "Why else do you think I'd fetch you?"

"If it's a doctor you need, fetch my father. I've been up half the night with one of Rusty's girls, and I'm in no condition to be treating anyone."

Linsey felt her cheeks pale as her glance moved to the saloon, then back to Daniel. For the first time she noticed the shadowed stubble of whiskers, the lines fanning out from bleary eyes, the scent of soap and . . . woman.

Appalled that she could have missed such glaring signs of a night spent in debauchery, Linsey's spine stiffened. "You're right. If my sister needs a doctor, I *should* fetch your father."

"What's that supposed to mean?"

"Simply that I expected better of you." Linsey gave his rumpled appearance a disapproving once-over. "I'm certain that he wouldn't have spent half the night in a brothel, then refused to tend a lady in need. And you call yourself a *doctor*."

Linsey whirled away, sharp needles pricking at her heart. She didn't examine why hearing that he'd been with another woman stung so badly. What right did she have dictating where Daniel spent his free time? None. But still . . . it had never occurred to her that he might visit the upstairs rooms at the Rusty Bucket. How could she have been so wrong?

Heavy bootsteps sounded behind her, but she couldn't bring herself to look at him. "Go away, Daniel. Go back to your doxies. We don't need your help."

"Then you shouldn't have asked for it." He continued to keep pace with her.

The thought of her sister waiting for Daniel added guilt to the emotions already churning inside Linsey. How was she to break the news to Addie? Once she learned that the man she all but worshiped was nothing more than a skirt-chasing rogue, it would break her heart.

Then again, Linsey thought with a furrowed brow, Noah had been quite the ladies' man before he'd met Jenny.

If Daniel had a good woman waiting at home, he'd have no reason to stray, right? All right. She'd let him live a while longer; but if he ever betrayed Addie, she would haunt his sorry hide for the rest of his born days.

They reached the balloon, the silk panels filled to bursting and stretching at least twenty feet in diameter.

She and Daniel paused to study it for a moment.

"Are you sure she's in there?" he asked.

"Positive."

With a deep, resigned sigh, Daniel approached the basket.

Linsey hadn't intended on watching, since Jarvis would be back any minute; but as Daniel ascended the ladder, she couldn't help but marvel at him. Not only did he have the agility of a pole climber, but he had the nicest rear she'd ever seen on a man. The flaps of his coat parted with each upward step, baring long muscular legs and firm buttocks in snug brown wool.

Warmth blossomed in her belly. Her mouth went dry. Her hands tingled. She imagined wrapping her arms around him, running her palms along the smooth curves—

Linsey gave herself a mental shake to jar loose the alarming image. For the love of Gus, she was no better than Daniel's woman of the evening! No, she was worse, for she'd been brought up not to covet anything that belonged to thy neighbor—or thy sister. And here she stood, ogling thy sister's intended's rear.

Mortified, she hurried from stake to stake and hauled on the ropes anchoring the balloon to earth. Just as she started to loosen the fourth and final tether, she heard Daniel holler, "There's nobody in here."

Linsey's spine went taut. "What do you mean, nobody's in there?"

"Just what I said. There's nobody in here." He enunciated each word as if she had a hearing problem.

Or a mental deficiency.

"But she's got to be in there!" Forgetting the last rope, Linsey hastened toward the ladder dangling against the basket's side. "Addie? Come on out." Linsey flipped aside the panel of her fur-lined pelisse, thrust her left foot onto the first rung and heaved herself upward. With only one mooring intact, the craft swayed and bobbed. "Addie, Daniel's here."

The only answer was a sudden rending sound. Then, the craft gave an ominous tug. Linsey went stock-still. Holding fast to the ladder, she called in soft panic, "Daniel?"

Then the last rope snapped.

Addie had just reached for the doorknob when an uneasy sensation made the hair on the back of her neck raise. She couldn't say what compelled her to look over her shoulder, but when she did, the sight of the multicolored ball rising above the church-house steeple sent alarm spiraling through her. Her hand shot to her mouth, catching a gasp. "Oh, no! Oh my heavens, no!"

She shook her head as if to dislodge the

dread coiling through her. Not for one minute did she doubt who at least one occupant of the balloon was. And if Linsey had managed to coerce Daniel into the basket . . . oh, the possibility didn't bear thinking!

The crunch of wheels over gravel and the jingle of harnesses swung her attention to the horse-drawn flatbed rattling toward town. A familiar brawny figure in a flannel shirt and floppy-brimmed frontier hat spurred her into hitching her skirts past her ankles.

Addie flew off the veranda, down Briar Hill. "Mr. Potter!" She waved one arm in a frantic hail. The release of a handful of starched bombazine caused her hem to snag under her swiftly churning feet. She stumbled, then righted herself and cried again, "Mr. Potter, wait!"

He hauled in the reins amidst a duo of raucous neighs. The wagon came to a jerky stop just as Addie reached it.

Her breathing harsh and irregular, she gripped the homespun material of his trouser leg. "Please Mr. Potter, I need you . . . to follow that balloon!"

"Balloon? Jarvis's balloon?"

"My sister is in there!"

"What's Linsey doing in—"

"Please! There is no time to explain, just . . . make haste!"

Before he could object, and before she had time to think about what she was doing, Addie hauled herself unceremoniously up the mounting step, over Mr. Potter's lap, and fell into the empty spot beside him.

Ignoring his look of astonishment, she pointed west. "After that craft!"

With a bellowing "Haw" and a snap of the reins, the smithy set the horses to lurching forward.

"Hurry, Mr. Potter!" she yelled above the clang of harness, the quick clomp of hooves, and the creak of wood. "We must try and catch them."

"The horses are goin' as fast as they can!"

His sharp tone silenced Addie, though her mind urged the mounts to greater speed. Mr. Potter took them through the center of town, scattering people and animals out of his path. The horses galloped across the sideless bridge that arched over Horseshoe Creek, onto the gently rolling grasslands where the road was little more than twin ruts. Untamed weeds as high as the underbelly of the wagon grew between the parallel tracks, making it hard to judge where the road twisted.

Addie clamped one hand around Mr. Potter's muscle-bound arm while her other hand clutched the seat. Wind tore at her chignon and scored her eyes. If her sister wasn't already dying, she'd kill her! How dare Linsey do such a reckless, dangerous thing when her life was already being cut short?

Addie closed her eyes and sent a silent prayer that the winds would ease, that the balloon would drift back to the ground, that Linsey would see the error of her heedless ways and learn to stay at home where she belonged—

A violent bump interrupted the plea.

The wagon tilted, then tipped, rolling onto its side. Addie heard the horses scream just before she was thrown to the ground. A crushing weight fell on top of her. For a moment, she feared the wagon was smashing her—except wagons didn't smell of hot irons and damp leather.

Then she became aware of a button imprinting itself on her nose, and the expanding breath of a human body. "Mr. Potter, please remove yourself from my person before I suffocate."

In the next instant the weight lifted from her, leaving her skin oddly cold.

"Miss Witt, are you all right?"

"What happened?"

"Must've hit a stone."

"The horses! I heard them scream . . . "

A moment's silence wrought with anxiety stretched tightly between them as he glanced around. "Don't see hide nor hair of 'em. Broke free, I reckon. They'll head for home," he said, turning back to her.

Despite the reassuring smile that tugged at his full mouth, worry clouded the blue of his eyes. She hadn't realized until now what a pretty blue they were—a mix of light and dark, like the swirling waters of Horseshoe Creek, with long lashes any lady would envy. Then those lashes dropped over his eyes, his gaze lowered, and then climbed back up her.

Addie's throat went oddly dry. She undoubtedly looked like she'd been roped and dragged. Her clothes were soiled and torn, her chignon had completely come loose from its pins, and she didn't need to look to know how dirty she was, for she felt the grit clinging to her skin.

And still, he looked at her, his gaze growing darker, hooded.

Disturbed by the steady regard, Addie looked away and passed a trembling hand through her tangled hair. What did he think when he looked at her? She knew how plain she was, how dull—and yet, for a moment there, just before his large body rocked to a stand, she could have sworn she'd seen hunger in his eyes.

"Dad gummit," he cussed, standing beside the wagon with his hands on his hips. "I just had this wheel fixed before Bleet kicked the bucket—beggin' your pardon, miss."

"Now what will we do?"

"Ain't no help for it—we start walkin' "

"Walking? Where to?"

"Town, I reckon. It's only a few miles."

"But my sister—"

"Will have to fend for herself," he interrupted. "There's no way we can catch her without horses. And by the time we get to town, that balloon will be long gone. Could be days before she brings it down."

"Days?"

"Yep. Jarvis said some fellas had their airship cloud-borne for a week. Course, they knew what they were doin' up there." Oren shook his head. "Sure hope your sister does."

Linsey clutched the rope ladder with all her strength as the wind lifted the balloon at a rapid rate.

Her eyes watered, her muscles felt like jelly, and her arms were stretched to the point of being yanked out of the sockets.

She chanced a glance down. Her eyes popped wide at the ever-growing distance between herself and the ground. Oh, Lordy! She hadn't expected the craft to soar so high, and not so fast.

To make matters worse, Jarvis chose that moment to enter the empty lot, his arms loaded with items Linsey couldn't identify from her lofty position. Behind him trailed a contingent of spectators, their gestures signaling the excitement of attending such a grand and unique ascension.

Jarvis spotted her a second later. The gear spilled to the ground. He raced forward. Dimly she heard him shouting at her. Waving his arms, stomping his feet, he demanded she bring his balloon back.

If only she could!

Right now, it was all she could do to keep from falling. With a strength she didn't know she had, she pulled herself upward, only to have a gust of wind swoop down and catch the underbelly of the basket. Her foot slipped off the rung; Linsey dangled in midair, a scream lodged in her throat. Was this it then? The end? She'd known her days were numbered, but of all the ways she'd imagined going, plummeting from hundreds of feet in the air hadn't been among them.

The old-timers claimed a person saw their whole life pass before their eyes in the moments before death; Linsey could now support that claim—for in a split second, she saw a five-year-old redhead picking four-leaf clovers on Briar Hill; making faces at Addie while she struggled through one of her piano lessons; the time she dragged Addie upstairs in the Rusty Bucket saloon, just for curiosity's sake, and got an eyeful of Daniel she never dreamed of. . . .

"Daaa-nieeel!"

Oh, please, help me, she prayed, clutching the ropes for all she was worth as the balloon continued rising. Don't let me die like this, in a broken, bleeding heap. Not now, not yet, not when I've got so many things left to do. . . .

Just when her strength reached the verge of failure, she heard Daniel's voice. "Jesus, Linsey!" Then a pair of steely fingers wrapped around Linsey's wrists.

"Grab hold of me; I'll pull you up."

"If I let go, I'll fall."

"No, you won't. I won't let you."

She hesitated only a second before releasing first one side of the ladder to grasp desperately at Daniel's wrist, then the other.

"Now push yourself up."

She didn't think she had any strength left, and yet, as if Daniel were lending her some of his, she managed to fight both the wind and fear, and she climbed. One rung. Two.

Then Daniel's arms were under hers, and around her back, and the next thing she knew, she had cleared the rim. Linsey's knees buckled beneath her and she collapsed against Daniel's chest.

Blessed life pumped beneath the cheek she

pressed against his heart. Linsey savored the strength against her, around her, as she inhaled the glorious musky scent of man, the tang of soap, the crispness of starched linen. Never had smells smelled so wonderful.

"Are you all right?"

Willing her shattered nerves to regroup and her racing pulses to calm, she nodded. "A little shaken is all."

"Do you realize that if I hadn't heard all that shouting, I wouldn't have had any idea you were hanging from that ladder?"

"I know." She lifted her head and stared at him. She didn't care if the worship she felt in her soul showed in her eyes. Daniel had risked his own safety for her, and she could never forget that. "You saved my life, Daniel." And even though she didn't have much of it left, every second was precious.

"If I had any sense, I would have let you fall," he countered in a gruff, almost affectionate tone she'd never heard from him before.

He set her away from him and passed a hand through his windblown hair. It surprised her to see his fingers shaking.

"What the hell were you doing on that ladder anyway?" he demanded.

"Hanging on for dear life."

"That's not what I meant and you know it."

"It wasn't supposed to happen this way, I swear! You were supposed to—" Linsey clamped her lips shut.

His eyes narrowed to slits. "I was supposed to what?"

Appalled at how easily she'd almost let her plan slip, Linsey changed the subject. "Nothing. Let's just figure out how to get this thing down."

Chapter 9

Blacksmiths are credited with magical powers because of their association with fire, iron, and horses.

Nibbling on her thumbnail, Linsey studied the gear secured in the center of a metal hoop above her head and tried to ignore Daniel's taut silence. But she knew she'd have better luck putting out a wildfire with a paper fan.

In a menacing voice, he asked, "What do you mean, figure out how to get this thing down? Don't you know how to work this contraption?"

"How am I supposed to work it? I've never been in a balloon before!"

"And I have?"

"Jarvis is your friend, not mine."

"That doesn't mean he told me how to operate this thing. Until two days ago, I didn't even know he'd bought it. He kept it a guarded secret."

She felt her face blanch. "Oh, no."

"Oh, yes."

So much for her theory that Daniel would know how to handle the craft. "Well, there must be some way to lower the balloon." Linsey searched the interior of the basket. All around the perimeter, burlap bags tied with twine lay in beds of coiled rope. She bent to investigate one of the sacks and discovered it was heavy with sand. "Aha, maybe these will do the trick."

After tying each sandbag at intervals around the rim, Linsey tossed them out of the basket one by one, then leaned over the side to assess her handiwork. The sandbags simply dangled in the air, knocking against each other but doing nothing to weigh down the craft. In fact, the balloon might even have risen a few feet.

"That worked real well," Daniel drawled.

"Got any better ideas?"

"We could toss you out."

She shot him a blazing look. "At least I'm trying. All you're doing is standing there."

"You're the one who got us up here. It's only fair that you get us down."

Though it remained unsaid, she got the impression that he didn't think she could do it. "Okay, let me think, let me think. . . . " Ignoring his snigger, Linsey walked in a circle, tapping her temples. "Jarvis said something about opening a flap." She eyed the swollen panels, then the apparatus at the mouth. "I know one of these valves releases the hydrogen, so maybe the other one opens something to release the air."

But which valve?

She reached up for the one on the right, then the one on the left, then the one on the right again in indecision.

At Daniel's exasperated breath, she settled on the right valve. A sudden whoosh of hydrogen shot the craft up and threw Linsey to the bottom of the car. She landed hard on her shoulder, though the pile of furs cushioned her fall. The balloon stuttered in flight. The basket wobbled but remained upright.

Daniel must have managed to shut off the flow, for when Linsey climbed to her knees and pushed her hair out of her eyes, he was gripping one of the overhead supports with one hand, wiping his brow with the other. "Calamity Linsey strikes again."

"I must have turned the wrong valve."

"Obviously."

"At least we know which one it isn't." She pushed herself to her feet and staggered toward the equipment. "So I'll just try the other one."

"And what, shoot us to the moon?" His hand covered hers over the second valve. Once more, the feel of his warm palm over her knuckles sent a jolt of lightning down her arm. "You've caused enough damage for one day."

Linsey tried tugging away from the disturbing sensation his touch created. "Like you said, I got us up here; I'll get us down."

Daniel's hold tightened. "I'd like to touch ground in one piece, if you don't mind."

Glaring at him, Linsey kept a firm grip on the valve, refusing to let him win this little battle he'd started. For the love of Gus, he could be so stubborn! It would serve him right if he was the one to fall out and not she.

Just then, a cord suspended from the deepest recesses of the balloon caught her notice.

Daniel followed the direction of her attention and also spotted the cord. Linsey reached to grab the line. Daniel blocked her move.

With a frustrated "grrr!" she tried sidestepping around him. He responded in kind.

She couldn't say when annoyance gave way to mischief. Maybe it was when she saw his lips twitch. Oh, he didn't dare crack a smile, but miracle of miracles, there was a luster in his brown eyes hinting that he wasn't completely devoid of humor.

Exhilarated by that competitive gleam, Linsey sidestepped, only to have Daniel thwart the way. Back and forth, around and around. Daniel had height and strength on his side, but Linsey had speed and cunning on hers. And the game was slowly advancing from good-natured fun to a fierce battle to win. But sometimes, Linsey recalled hearing her father say, the best strategy was surrender.

Or at least the impression of it.

She relaxed her body and yawned. Daniel dipped his head and watched her with suspicion. One thing was certain, she thought with grudging respect, he was not a fool. Nor would life with him ever be dull.

Addie was luckier than either of them expected.

After several minutes, Linsey's patience paid off, for Daniel's coal black brows lifted in a cocky expression of victory. Then he made the mistake of letting down his guard.

Linsey sprang.

Daniel lunged.

Both yanked the cord at the same time.

And it broke.

Both stood gaping up at the coils falling out of the mouth of the balloon, around her arm, across his shoulder . . .

When the last slithering echo died away, Linsey rounded on him. "Now look what you did!"

Daniel's jaw dropped. "Me! You're the one who insisted on yanking on the damn thing!"

"There's no reason to curse at me."

That didn't stop him from letting loose a string of profanities under his breath. He braced himself against the rim, elbows locked, one leg cocked. "This is just peachy." He pushed his hair back with his fingers. "I'm stuck in a bucket with the Queen of Catastrophe."

Linsey frowned at him. "I'm no happier with the situation than you are." After all, this should have been the perfect opportunity for Daniel and Addie to become acquainted with each other, not for Linsey to spend some of her precious last hours trapped aloft with the ogre of Henderson County.

It seemed they'd both become the victims of a plan gone absurdly awry.

"Look," she said with a sigh, "We aren't going to force this thing to the ground, so there's only one thing left to do."

"And that is?"

"Enjoy the ride."

"Enjoy! Have you lost every last ounce of sense you were born with?"

"Think about it. What goes up must come down—eventually. So until this thing runs out of hydrogen, we might as well relax and ride the wind wherever it wants to take us—unless you're afraid of having a little fun."

"I have fun!"

"Oh, cow patties. You wouldn't know fun if you sat on it. You're too busy tending to the county's bumps and bruises."

"I'm a doctor. It's my job."

"I'm perfectly aware of that, but haven't you ever heard that all work and no play makes Jack a dull boy?"

Daniel stared at her, his mouth agape.

"There are no patients to tend up here, Doc. Just you, the wind, and the wide blue yonder—so why don't you try closing your mouth, opening your eyes, and enjoying the view." She paused, turned, then whispered, "You might never get this chance again."

He didn't mean to obey her. He sure as hell didn't mean to enjoy the view at her command. Neither one of them knew the first thing about landing a hydrogen balloon much less how to navigate one, and yet he seemed to be the only one who recognized the severity of their situation.

But as his sullen gaze swung away from Linsey and landed on the view below, Daniel couldn't stop the tide of wonder washing through him.

They were coasting above the treetops, some so close that if he wanted, he could reach out and grab a fistful of pine needles off the uppermost branches. A northwestern wind lifted them into the gentle palms of clouds scuttling by, and carried them farther into the open countryside.

The land looked like a patchwork quilt sewn in perfect squares. The rich brown of turned fields, the dun yellows of mowed hay, the gemlike green of grassland, with seams of bluish black water adding to the design. Cattle grazed near ponds, and now and then a lone horseman would look up at them, his eyes shielded with his hand.

They spotted several familiar homesteads. The Chisms'. The Hannickers'. Did old man Arbuckle know he had a hole the size of wagon wheel in his barn roof? Daniel made a mental note to mention it to the cotton farmer when he next came into the apothecary for his monthly supply of camphor.

The scenery continued to roll by as the balloon kept a steady course, carrying them high above a world mired down in duty and survival—and for some, like him, an insatiable need for success. Linsey was right: if she hadn't lured him into this lofty trap, he'd never have experienced the freedom of it.

Though it didn't sit well to admit it, she was right about another thing, too—fun hadn't been a part of his life in a very long time, if ever. He couldn't recall exactly when studying and doctoring had become his sole existence. Once he'd passed all his classes at Tulane, he'd worked at Charity Hospital for a year and half, and it had been fulfilling. Then his mother had gotten sick.

It had been hard losing her, harder than Daniel ever expected it would be. She hadn't been an overly affectionate woman, prone more to bouts of melancholy than cheerfulness, but she'd always been there, as much a part of his days as the sunrise.

Maybe it had been her smile. Small, sad, urging him not to take himself too seriously, to enjoy his youth while he had it. Or maybe it had been the way she'd often taken up for him against his dad. *"Leave the boy be, Daniel. He's got a mind of his own; let him use it."* Almost as if she could sense her son's need to carve his own mark in the world.

When she'd died, so had Daniel's ally. He guessed that was when work had become his solace, his ambition, his weapon and his enemy. Never again his pleasure, never again his calling.

Where had the pleasure of healing gone? Of giving someone a chance at life, and at living?

"Oh, look—there's Jenny's place." Linsey pointed as they passed over the orphanage. Children raced out from under the shade of live oak trees, leaping, laughing, some screaming as they ran toward the pitch-roofed house. Dogs nipped at their heels, bounding, catching the excitement.

Linsey waved energetically, jiggling the basket. Her laughter, husky and abandoned, seemed to reach deep inside him and grab his heart.

When he glanced at her, the expression on her face made his chest tighten and his breath dam up in his throat. She looked so breezy, so fresh, and so damn radiant it almost hurt to look at her. She made him all too aware of the things he'd shunned in his life so that he wouldn't lose focus on what mattered most.

And he could have lost *her*.

When he'd seen her hanging from that flimsy ladder, his heart had plunged to his stomach, then shot into his windpipe. If he hadn't heard the shouting from below, if he hadn't been able to pull her into the basket . . .

The realization buckled his knees.

Daniel sank to basket floor and closed his eyes, willing his pulse to slow and the knot to loosen in his stomach. Damn her for reminding him what it was like to want the forbidden. "Stop dancing before you dump us out of here," he snapped.

"I wonder if they know it's us?"

"I doubt it. We've got to be a thousand feet up, maybe more. Too far to see."

"You're probably right, but I bet they've never seen anything like this." She spread her hands, indicating the balloon. "They'll be talking about it for years to come."

Of that, Daniel had no doubt.

She crossed her arms over the rim. The back of her head tucked into her shoulders in a pose of relaxed bliss. "Isn't this wonderful?" Linsey sighed. "Oh, I just knew this would turn out to be a grand day."

"Let me guess—you found a rabbit's foot under a full moon."

"No, a cat walked toward me."

Don't ask, he warned himself. He was dying of curiosity but he didn't dare admit it. Besides, didn't curiosity kill the cat? Oh, Lord, now he was starting to think like Linsey!

"That's good luck, you know, when a cat walks toward you." She nodded once. "If he walks away, he takes luck with him."

Daniel rolled his eyes and shook his head.

"It's the truth!"

"Who tells you these preposterous tales?"

"Oh, they're common knowledge. But Aunt Louisa is especially wise when it comes to divining the signs. Most of what I know I learned from her."

And Daniel had always thought Louisa such a sensible woman.

"You're scowling again, Daniel. If you don't stop it right this minute, I'm tossing you over the side."

"Anyone ever tell you that you're a brassy bit of fluff?"

She gave him a swift and startled glance. "Bit of fluff?" A smile broke out on her face. The brilliance of it sent warmth spreading through his midsection like a dose of fine Irish whiskey, melting the lingering dregs of tension.

"I've been called lots of things before, but never a 'bit of' anything." A wry grin formed as she gestured to herself.

Daniel inspected her figure. High, full breasts, curvy hips, rounded face—maybe she wasn't the most dainty person, but next to him, she seemed almost fragile. Childlike, even. Except there was nothing childlike about those lush curves.

Gruffly, he said, "There's nothing wrong with you."

"Why, Daniel, was that a compliment?" she asked in disbelief.

"Just an observation. Don't let it go to your head."

"Goodness, more pretty words! I declare, Dr. Sharpe, if you sweet-talk all the girls this way, it's no wonder they're all besotted with you."

Daniel didn't know how to respond to that. He knew women were interested in him, but he had learned to ignore the coy glances and flirtatious overtures rather than encourage them. The only time he let himself get close to the opposite sex anymore was when it related to his profession, as he had done last night at the Rusty Bucket.

The appalled look on Linsey's face when she'd caught him leaving the saloon told him exactly what she thought he'd been doing there. Why it should bother him that she'd jumped to the wrong conclusion, he didn't explore, but with a trace of belligerence, found himself telling her, "I wasn't doing what you think I was doing earlier."

"What, having fun?" Her eyes danced.

"No, when you met me leaving the Rusty Bucket."

The pleasure in her eyes dimmed. She turned away and said, "Daniel, please, I really don't want to hear the details."

"A customer got a little rough with one of Rusty's girls. She was in pretty bad shape."

Linsey shot him a startled look. He was squinting at the sun, his features stoic. A crescent-shaped shock of glossy black hair had fallen over his winged eyebrow, drawing her notice to his sleepy eyes, as dark and inviting as hot cocoa, and framed by thick, spiky lashes. Black whiskers cast a shadow around his mouth and along his jaw. He did look weary. The news that he'd spent the night tending to the woman's needs and not his own gave her heart wings—only because she didn't want her sister hitched up with a rounder, she told herself. "I shouldn't have assumed otherwise."

"No, you shouldn't."

"Will she be all right?" Linsey asked, feeling sorry for the woman.

With a nod, Daniel brought one knee up to his chest and slung an arm over his knees, obviously ending the discussion.

A girl would have to be dead not to notice how the casual pose he struck enhanced the muscles of his thighs and the curve of his rear. The butternut fabric of his trousers pulled so tight along his trunk that it was a wonder he didn't split a seam. She knew all too well that the rest of him was just as firm, and she wondered if the same dark hair that covered his forearm covered other parts of his body.

Once more, her attention roamed upward, passing the breadth of his chest to his profile and centering on his lips, pressed in a relaxed line.

What would he taste like? She'd only been kissed once in her whole life, and the experi-

ence still made her queasy. She had a feeling
kissing Daniel would be nothing like that inva-
sive slobbering she'd endured from Bishop
when she was fifteen. No, Daniel would be
assertive but not forceful. His mouth would be
soft, yet firm. Perhaps even tasting of the peppermint sticks he kept in his shirt pocket for
his young patients. . . .

The treacherous thought flew from her mind
when Daniel reached for the pile of furs
nearby. Her shoulders tensed. He uncovered
the basket she had put together for him and
Addie and flipped up the lid. As he pulled out
a chunk of bread and a bottle of wine, he asked
with a puzzled frown, "Where'd this come
from?"

Evasively, she answered, "Someone must
have left it here."

"Never knew Jarvis to be much of a wine-
and-cheese man."

"You've known him a long time, haven't
you?" Linsey told herself that her curiosity
came from a need to know more about him for
Addie's sake.

"We met in Louisiana while I was attending
medical school. I stumbled upon him on the
wharf one night after he'd gotten roughed
up."

"And you treated him?"

"No, I got him drunk. We've been friends
ever since."

He smiled a lazy smile that made a pair of
dimples dig deep creases in his cheeks, and
Linsey's heart flipped dangerously in her
chest. It was the first time she'd seen him

smile, and the sight stole her breath away. She realized that she'd just gotten a glimpse of the irresistible rogue who had hearts sighing all over the county.

If she wasn't careful, she'd be sighing along with them.

Disturbed by the thought, she folded her cape closer about her shoulders. "My, but I didn't expect it would be so cold up here. Think it will snow?"

"Not this early in the season. Maybe by Christmas."

"I hope so. It would be nice to see snow before I—Oh, Lordy! Daniel, the trees!"

He dropped the wine and scrambled to his feet, then cursed at the sight looming before them: a gradually rising slope wearing a thick and towering coat of pine trees.

"How do we steer this thing?" Daniel hollered.

"I don't know. I'm not sure we can."

"We've got to get it up higher!"

"The valves!"

They reached for the tanks at the same time. Daniel opened the valve, releasing a mighty blast of the gases. After one swift, upward lunge, the balloon began to climb at a steady rate.

Just when they thought they'd cleared danger, a sudden downdraft yanked on the balloon, tilting the basket at a perilous angle.

Pine branches seemed to reach out and seize the silk panels in their clutches like talons upon unsuspecting prey. A horrid rending sound sheared the air. Amidst a vicious tangle of branches, the balloon caught, swung, then knocked against the tree trunk.

The impact threw Daniel and Linsey to the bottom of the basket. Daniel was smashed against the side with Linsey facing him, crushed against his front, her hand twisted in the folds of his shirt, her forehead against his neck. She buried herself against him as pine needles, cones, and branches showered down on them.

Was she to survive the flight from hell, only to meet her end now?

When the particles settled, neither of them moved, though their hearts pounded in unison.

"Am I dead?" Linsey asked once she could speak.

"Not yet, but after we get out of this mess, I'm going to strangle you."

"No, you won't." She lifted her head and grinned. "Admit it, Doc: despite everything, this is the best day you've had in your life."

"If this is the best, I don't think I'll survive the worst. Why did I ever get into this balloon with you? I knew it wasn't safe—hell, I'm not safe with you anywhere!"

She tilted her head back and gave him a quizzical study. "Of course you are, Daniel."

He snorted. "As a lit match in a tub of kerosene."

Of its own will, her hand reached up to cup his whisker-stubbled cheek. "When will you realize that I'd never purposely do anything to hurt you?"

Her touch brought his gaze clashing with

hers. She stared into the dark brown depths, wanting him to believe her, willing him to accept her apology for this transgression as well as those that had come before.

But as they looked at each other, she saw his surprise give way to something darker, more primal. It set off a spark low in her belly and caused warmth to steal up her spine.

Forgotten were their cramped surroundings and their perilous situation. Linsey slowly became aware of the rigid muscle of his chest beneath her breasts, the washboard hardness of his abdomen under her ribs, the power of his thigh aligned with the seam of her legs.

The intimacy of their position uncoiled a heavy knot of longing inside her, flowing into her blood, saturating every nerve ending.

She knew she had to get off of him, knew lying atop him courted danger and threatened every principle she had been raised with. And yet she couldn't make herself move to save her life. He felt so warm, so strong, so powerful. And he smelled of sultry summer evenings and damp sheets, with just a hint of bay rum thrown in to add to his mysterious allure.

Her fingers slipped from his jaw to the corner of his wide, perfectly defined mouth. The pulse at his throat gave a sudden leap. She felt his body tighten, his heart rate quicken, saw his eyes turn darker.

She wanted that mouth, wanted to feel the moist softness of his lips against hers, wanted to taste the peppermint flavor of his breath. As if sensing her hunger, his hand blazed a possessive trail up her back, pressing her toward him. She closed her eyes as he brought her closer, an inch at a time, wishing he'd come to his senses and push her away from him, hoping to God that he wouldn't.

And then the decision was torn from either of them as the bottom of the basket gave way.

Shading his eyes from the glare of the mid-morning sun, Oren scanned the land ahead. Still no sign of Horseshoe, but as long as they kept followin' the train tracks, he knew they'd end up in town eventually. For the sake of the lady who trudged along behind him, he called encouragingly, "Ain't much farther Miss Witt."

"I cannot proceed another step."

Oren glanced over his shoulder. He bit the inside of his cheek to stop from grinning. He never thought he'd catch Adelaide Witt looking anything less than perfectly groomed— but, boy howdy, she was a sight. Her high-necked dress was stained and torn. Her bonnet dangled by its blue polka-dotted ribbons and trailed halfway down her back. Her yellow hair hung in limp strands around a narrow face smudged with half of Henderson County.

Lord, she was a pitiful sight.

He found her cute as a toddler's dimple. Tired, rumpled, but cute nonetheless. "I s'pose it wouldn't hurt none to rest for a spell."

"My deepest gratitude," she breathed, then plopped down on a nearby rock without a care that her skirts flew up past her knees. Oren spied a glimpse of barn-red underdrawers, and red-and-white striped stockings that reminded him of a peppermint stick.

His lips twitched. He'd have never have guessed that the demure Miss Addie possessed such fiery tastes. But figuring Miss Prim and Proper wouldn't appreciate being the object of his amusement, he bit back his grin, sat beside her, and handed her the canteen he carried looped across his chest. "Here, this oughtta wet your whistle."

He expected her to sip daintily from the canteen.

She guzzled like a trail-worn cowpoke.

Oren watched her throat work the liquid down. As far as throats went, hers was a pretty one, he had to say that. Long and smooth and creamy. A drop of water trickled down her oval chin, into the unbuttoned collar, heading to the place only his imagination had ever taken him.

She lowered the canteen and wiped her mouth. "Is something wrong?"

His gaze shot to her eyes.

"You're staring at me. Is something wrong?"

"No . . . no," he said, feeling guilty color steal into his cheeks. This was his boy's teacher, and though Oren considered her one of the prettiest little fillies this side of the Red River, he didn't figure an old skewbald like him had any business fancying a thoroughbred like her.

"Do you think she'll be all right up there?"

It took him a minute to realize who she was talking about. He squinted in the direction they'd last seen the balloon, he nodded, then glanced back at the schoolmarm. "What notion ever got a-holt of her to ride in that thing anyway?"

She gave a tiny shrug. "Linsey doesn't always think situations through. Once an idea takes hold, she . . . well, she runs with it." Hazel eyes shadowed with secret sorrow turned on Oren. "I apologize for involving you in this, Mr. Potter."

"Oren."

She hesitated. "Oren, then."

When she said his name, he half expected harps to start playing.

"I simply didn't know how else to reach her, and when I saw you . . . Oh, heavens!" she gasped, bringing her hand to her mouth. "What about Bryce? He isn't at home waiting for you, is he?"

"No need to fret. He's spending the weekend with his mamaw in Houston. That's where I was coming from when you hailed me down."

"Oh, thank goodness," Addie sighed with heartfelt relief.

Then again, she couldn't imagine Oren Potter gallivanting across the countryside if he'd left his young child at home. Granted, she knew very little about him, although he'd lived in Horseshoe for nearly five years. She knew he'd been married and had lost his wife a couple of years ago. And she knew that his child was a teacher's treasure. Other than that, Oren Potter was as much a stranger to her as that Hobart creature who made spirits in his barn. But he didn't strike her as the type of man who abandoned his responsibilities.

And she realized that she very much admired him for that quality.

She watched him for several minutes in silence before broaching the subject near and dear to her. "Have you given any further thought to our discussion?"

"If you mean about sending my boy away, nope."

"You won't even consider—"

"Nope."

"Mr. Potter . . . "

"Oren."

"Oren, perhaps I didn't make myself clear. Your son has a gift of learning. He absorbs concepts with amazing accuracy, he can solve mathematical equations faster than—"

"And maybe I didn't make myself clear," he cut in with a voice of steel. All trace of amiability vanished from his eyes, leaving them a flinty blue. "I ain't leavin' Horseshoe and I ain't sending my boy away—especially not half across the country to some fancy Eastern school where the only thing they'll teach him is how to become some uppity, righteous Yankee too good for his own kin."

Addie stared at him, feeling his pain as if it belonged to her. Who had hurt this gentle man so badly? "Bryce would never be like that. He loves you."

"And I love him. That's why I can't let him go. Addie, he's all I got."

He didn't seem aware of the slip of her Christian name, but Addie noticed. The sound of it, rumbling through his chest and off his tongue like a caress, made tingles ripple through her nerve endings.

Then he turned solemn eyes on her, and in the clear blue depths, she saw pain and fear that seemed too large for even a man of his size to carry. "I'd be obliged if you didn't bring this up again."

She turned away, unsettled by the urge to cradle his head against her breast and comfort him as she would his son, or any of the other children in her class. Oren was far from being a child. She'd become all too aware of that over the last few days.

"If there's somethin' he needs to know, you can teach him."

"I'm afraid Bryce needs more attention than I'm able to give him within my classroom."

"Then teach him in private."

"Tutor him?"

"If that's what you call it."

"I don't know if I can. His capacity for knowledge is so much greater than mine."

"You don't set enough store by yourself. How are you gonna know what you can teach him if you don't try? And if you need a place, there ain't no reason why you can't give him lessons at the smithy after school."

Against wisdom, Addie found herself pondering the idea. What a challenge! To be able to help shape such a young and brilliant mind. To help a child explore all the opportunities she'd never had the courage to explore herself. . . .

"I'll do it," she said with a decisive nod. "I'll

give him private lessons, and whatever I don't know, we'll learn together."

He smiled at her as if she'd just announced she'd hang the moon for him. "That's the spirit."

Making a decision for herself felt so . . . liberating! For as long as she could remember, she'd lived in Linsey's shadow—

Oh, no! Addie thought, pinching off the uncharitable thought before it fully formed. How could she have forgotten Linsey? How could she have been so selfish, sitting here, enjoying a man's company and making plans for her future, while her sister was in danger?

New urgency made her leap to her feet. "We've rested long enough, Mr. Potter." She gathered the canteen and her bonnet. "I must find some way to help Linsey."

Chapter 10

The four leaves in a four-leaf clover represent good luck in fame, wealth, love, and health.

Daniel lay still, his lungs feeling as if they'd collapsed and turned to lead. He should feel rocks biting into his shoulder blades, or at the very least, the sting of abrasions on his skin, but the fall seemed to have stunned every nerve in his body numb.

"Daniel?"

His name reached him through a fog and roused him from the stupor.

"Daniel, say something!"

Linsey. The alarm in her voice compelled him to ease her panic. "Something."

Dimly he heard the disturbance of pebbles, an urgent rasp against the earth. Then she was there, above him, shading him from the sun with her own body. As she bowed over him, he had to blink a couple of times to clear his blurry vision. If he didn't know better, he'd swear he'd seen a sheen of moisture in her eyes.

"You wouldn't answer at first, and I was afraid . . . are you hurt anywhere?"

Without giving him a chance to answer, she brushed her unpracticed hands along his body, more in an effort to soothe herself, he suspected, than out of any skill in detecting injuries.

"I'm fine. Just a little stunned." As if to prove his fitness to her, he lifted himself to a sitting position. Against all odds, it seemed he'd escaped the fall with nothing more than a few aches and bruises.

He couldn't be so sure about Linsey, though. She appeared unharmed, but he knew from experience that looks could be deceiving. "What about you? Are you hurt?"

"I don't think so. What happened?"

"The bottom fell out of the basket." He rose unsteadily, then reached a hand out to Linsey and helped her to her feet.

At her sudden wince, he frowned, his concern mounting. "I thought you said you weren't hurt."

"I said I didn't *think* I was hurt."

"That's your problem half the time, Linsey—you don't think." Daniel guided her to a flat rock, knelt at her feet, and lifted her hems. He tried to keep the examination brisk and impersonal, tried only to ascertain if she'd broken any bones. But the instant he touched her leg, a spark shot up his fingertips. He gritted his teeth and ran his palms down her calf. Relief at not finding any broken bones almost turned his own to liquid. Daniel told himself he'd feel the same about any patient, but deep down inside, he knew it was a lie. Linsey wasn't just any patient. She was the woman who tormented his days, taunted his nights, and teased his senses until he couldn't think straight.

And he'd almost kissed her. Would have if the basket bottom hadn't given away, and the dozen-foot fall hadn't knocked the notion right out of him.

What the hell had gotten into him? He never acted impulsively. He prided himself in the ability to think a situation through, to consider the consequences before he acted. A doctor could afford to do no less since he often held a person's life in his hands.

But with Linsey, he hadn't thought. He'd just felt.

Even now, as he continued his exploration, his heart banged against his ribs and a fever simmered in his blood.

A hiss when he pressed against her ankle confirmed his suspicion. "You're ankle is sprained."

"Good. It's nothing serious, then."

"It's nothing to take lightly, either. You need a cold compress on that leg to prevent swelling."

"I'll put something on it when I get home." She pushed herself off the rock and tugged at her skirts until the panels fell in straight folds.

"What are you doing?"

"Going home."

"You can't walk on that ankle; you'll just make it worse."

"Well, I can't stay here. Aunt Louisa and Addie will be frantic with worry."

"All the better reason to stay put. I have a feeling Jarvis will have half the town out searching for his balloon, and if we keep to one spot, it'll make it easier for someone to find us."

"But if no one knows where to look, we could be stuck out here till morning, or longer. What conclusion do you think people will jump to if you and I have spent all night together unchaperoned?" She shook her head. "Stay here if you wish, but I have a reputation to think of."

At that, she slowly started limping away.

Daniel watched her hobble along for a moment, then scanned the area with a growing sense of dread. Not so much as a stray cow from an outlying farm broke the monotony of the scrubby remoteness. Instinct told him they should stay with the balloon, but there was merit to what Linsey said. A man and a woman caught together left too much room for speculation, regardless of the circumstances. For all he knew, the damage might already be done.

Folks might be a bit more lenient if they were found making an effort to get back to town, at least. And even if her reputation wasn't at risk, it didn't seem wise being alone with Linsey for another minute, much less a full night—not after the way he'd been tempted.

That thought sealed the decision. Daniel crouched in front of her. "Get on my back."

"You plan on carrying me?"

"I don't see any gilded coaches."

"But we've got to be ten miles from town!"

"Do you have any other suggestions?"

She hesitated for so long that Daniel thought she planned on walking despite his advice against it.

Then with a sigh of surrender, Linsey wrapped her arms around his neck and mounted his back. Daniel curled his arms around her knees and settled her against him.

Blanking his mind, he set one foot in front of the other and began the long trek back to town. As they passed beneath the tree, a shimmer of color made him glance up at the remains of Jarvis's prized balloon, dripping from the branches like silk streamers at a holiday party. Another man's dream shredded to ribbons because of a woman. He jerked his chin in the air at the damage. "*You* can explain that to Jarvis."

"I'll buy him another balloon."

The offhanded remark pricked his pride and his temper. "That's your answer to everything, isn't it? You break it, you buy it?"

"If I can, yes. I never asked for the money, Daniel. My mother was the sole heir to her family's plantation, and when she married my father, she sold it and put the money in a trust for me. I can't give it back, so if I can use it making other people happy, then what's the harm? I've got nothing better to do with it."

"Maybe you should try finding a worthy charity."

"I tried. He wouldn't take it."

Daniel stumbled. Was she calling him worthy or a charity?

Part of him argued that since she had so

much money to throw around, maybe he should let her pay for his enrollment. It was the least she owed him. But he had pride. Accepting an apprenticeship based on his own hard work, sharp skill, and bartering ability was an entirely different matter than taking pity money.

He'd rather earn the fees, even if it took him ten years, than accept one token of Linsey Gordon's wealth.

They traveled quite a while, Daniel focusing on nothing but the solid ground beneath his soles, the chatter of magpies nesting in the trees, and the rustle of small mammals scurrying through the grass, before he realized that the silence Linsey kept had become too quiet, and the weight on his back had grown gradually heavier.

He glanced at her out of the corner of his eye. Her head rested on his shoulder. A tumble of copper curls coiled around her face, against his neck. Dark brown lashes rested against delicate cheekbones.

The shell around his heart fractured.

She looked so innocent. Sweet. Soft.

Daniel clamped his lips together to keep from moaning aloud as desire returned in ever strengthening waves. Sheer force of will kept him forging ahead. Damn her for making him aware of her as a woman! It was much easier thinking of her as a walking catastrophe—at least then he had good reason to steer clear of her.

Then again, nothing had been easy since the day his father had moved them from Houston to Horseshoe. From that point on, it felt as if he'd fought tooth and nail for every gain in his life, while Linsey breezed through each day as if she owned it.

Hell, she practically did.

Daniel latched onto the seed of resentment, hoping—wishing—that it would distract him from the pressure of her breasts against his back, the rocking of her womanhood against his spine, the sensual slide of her thighs along his hips.

But even the old anger wouldn't rescue him from fantasizing about the woman he carried. With each torturous step, the grassy carpet looked more and more inviting. He wanted to lay her in the sweet greenery, fan those glorious curls around her face, watch her eyes darken with hunger as he peeled her gown off her shoulders and bared her—

"Daniel?"

The sleepy voice in his ear sent a tremor ripping across his skin. He swallowed once, twice. "What?"

"Isn't that Mr. Potter's wagon?"

His vision snapped into focus and relief coursed through his veins. He let her slide off his back. Though the urge to get away from her, to let his blood cool, had him ready to race down the hill, Daniel forced himself to check his pace as he went to investigate.

Sure enough, it was Oren's flatbed. Daniel recognized the smithy's emblem of a hammer and horseshoes on its side. "The wheel's broken. Traces are torn clean, off, too."

"I wonder if he was looking for us."

"Probably. But from the looks of this break-age, he's on his way back to town on foot, which puts him in the same straits as you and me."

"What should we do?"

"Keep walking, I suppose."

"Why don't I just stay here and make a bed in the wagon while you go on for help?"

"I'm not leaving you here alone. We don't even have a weapon for protection."

"You can't continue carrying me, either. I'm just slowing you down."

As much as he hated to admit it, she was right on that account. They were both hot, both tired, and 110 pounds or so didn't seem like much until you carried it on your back for over a mile.

Still, he couldn't leave her.

The only other choice was to stay with her and wait for someone to find them.

Some choice.

"Things could be worse, you know," she said.

He made a sound, half humor, half agony. "How could things possibly be worse?"

"We could be dead. And you can thank my lucky amulet—oh, no!"

"What now?"

"It's gone! Daniel, I've lost my Token of Good Fortune!"

"So buy another one."

"You don't understand. This one is special—irreplaceable! I need it to protect me. Any time I've been without it, something awful has hap-pened!"

Oh, hell, not this gibberish again.

At the distant pounding of hooves, Daniel's head snapped up and Linsey spun around. Both spotted the man approaching on horseback at the same time.

Daniel frowned. He'd never known Bishop Harvey to stray any farther than the closest saloon, so what was he doing all the way out here?

"See!" Linsey cried. "The bad luck is starting already."

"Doc Jr., Linsey . . . "

Daniel gave a single nod to the man reining in.

"I am so relieved to have finally found the two of you," he wheezed, mopping his brow.

"What are you doing here, Bishop?" Linsey asked flatly.

"Why, searching for you, of course!" He dismounted his horse and swaggered toward Linsey. "When I heard you were trapped in that balloon, I jumped on the first horse I could find and came after you." He took one of her hands and patted the knuckles. "What an ordeal you must have been through, my dear."

She wrenched away from his touch. "Stop fussing over me, Bishop, I'm perfectly fine."

Daniel glanced from one to the other, sensing a cat-and-mouse undercurrent. So the dandy had designs on the queen of calamity, huh? A rare spark of mischief made Daniel cross his arms over his chest. "Don't let her brave front fool you, Harvey. She's been trying to cope with the pain, but she hurt her ankle badly and needs to get back to town so my father can look at it. Unfortunately, we are a bit stranded."

Harvey tipped the dusty bowler set on his stringy blond hair and bowed with a ridiculous flourish. "I would be honored to assist our fiery damsel."

Still the same pompous ass. But at least Harvey was willing to take Linsey off his hands. "You heard him, Linsey, he'd be honored to help you."

"That's not necessary."

He unfolded his arms. "Get on the horse."

"I'd rather walk."

He should have known she'd be difficult. Nothing with Linsey was *ever* easy. "Either get yourself in that saddle, or I'll do it for you."

"Why can't you take me?"

"Because Harvey's the one with the horse."

"You'd really send me off alone with him?"

"With a smile on my face and joy in my heart." Without further ado, he picked her up and dumped her in the saddle. "Get this girl out of here, Harvey. She's caused enough trouble for one day."

While Harvey hoisted himself in the saddle behind her, it was all Daniel could do not to burst out laughing at the fury blazing in Linsey's eyes. Damn, she was pretty when she was riled.

"You'll be sorry for this, Daniel."

She was right about that. As he watched her ride off, he did feel a pang of regret.

For not kissing her when he'd had the chance.

* * *

Linsey held herself as stiff in the saddle as possible, cursing Daniel with every jarring breath. How could he have just packed her off with Bishop without a qualm? How could he not know what a shady scoundrel Bishop Harvey was?

As his hand inched its way across her leg yet again, Linsey clenched her teeth together and said, "If you touch me one more time, you'll be the one seeing Doc Sr.—to surgically reattach your fingers."

"Dear Linsey, you know you've been dreaming of the day we would be alone together. I know I have."

His mouth came disgustingly close to the bare skin of her neck.

"Let me down," she demanded.

"I've only just now gotten you where I've been wanting you. In my arms, soft, helpless—"

He made the mistake of reaching for her face. "I'll show you helpless!" Linsey grabbed his wrist and sank her teeth into the heel of his hand.

He howled in pain, and she used the distraction to slide off the horse.

She hit the ground hard on her bad ankle. Her knees buckled. A shard of agony speared through her heel, up her leg, crippling her.

Hearing the thud of boots upon the ground, Linsey reined in her agony and, knowing she'd never be able to outrun him in her condition, searched the ground for a weapon. She gripped a fist-sized rock and waited with bated breath until the sour odor of whiskey closed in on her. A quick twist to the right put her out of Bishop's reach and he fell to the ground.

Linsey reared up onto her knees and raised the paltry rock over her head. "Stay away from me, Bishop."

"Now, Linsey, is this any way to act toward your intended?"

Linsey almost choked. She'd eat poisonous berries before she ever married a snake like him. "I'm warning you for the last time, stay away from me."

"Why are you being so difficult? We are perfect for each other—your beauty and money, my social position . . ."

So that was it. She'd always suspected that Bishop lusted after her trust fund, but he'd never admitted to it until now.

"Now put down the rock, and let's get down to some real sparking."

At the gleam in his eye, Linsey scrambled back, just before he lunged. His hand wrapped around her sore ankle, his fingers biting into the injured muscles. An agonized scream of pain and fury erupted from her throat.

Linsey didn't think, couldn't think past a desperation to make him leave her alone. She simply brought the rock down on his skull at the same time a loud *pop* rent the air.

He dropped like a sack of grain.

Linsey stared at him, stunned, paying little mind to the echo of a report swirling around her. "Oh, sweet Jesus, what have I done?" Her breath came in heaving gulps. God, what if she'd killed him?

Holding panic at bay, she leaned forward

and reached for his neck. A pulse beat strong and regular against her fingertips. She slumped back on her heels, relief rolling through her. He'd always been an irritating rodent, but she'd never have wished him dead. Especially by her own hand.

"Miss Linsey?"

Startled, Linsey twisted around. Through a cloud of dust, she discovered Jarvis sitting on a big bay, holding the reins to an extra roan, and Oren Potter dismounting a cream-colored gelding, a shotgun ready in his hand. She was amazed that she hadn't heard them approach.

"Did he hurt you?" Oren asked.

She got up off the ground and brushed the dirt from her skirts. "Not as bad as I hurt him. He'll have a knot the size of a lemon and a whopping good headache when he wakes up."

Both men looked first at Bishop, who lay face down in the dirt, still as a stump, then at her, then at Bishop again.

Oren moved to his side, rolled him over with his foot, and studied him closely as if making sure he was still breathing.

Linsey tamped down a swell of guilt. It was his own fault, she thought defiantly. He'd only gotten what he deserved. If he hadn't been pawing at her, she wouldn't have bashed him over the head.

"Mine or yours?" Jarvis asked of the blacksmith.

"Hers. Other than a bump on the head, there ain't a scratch on him."

Linsey listened to the exchange with puzzled curiosity. Only when Jarvis holstered his pistol did it click in her mind that the pops she'd heard hadn't been Bishop's skull cracking, but gunshots fired by one or both of these men. "It seems I owe the two of you my thanks."

"And it seems you didn't need our help," Mr. Potter replied. "You handled him just fine on your own."

"Nonetheless, thank you for coming to my aid."

"You can thank *me* by telling me where you left my balloon."

"A mile or two back that way." She pointed east, deciding that this wasn't the time to tell him what had happened to it. "I expect you'll find Daniel between here and there, too."

"You didn't clobber him, too, did ya?"

"Of course not," Linsey snapped. Though she probably should have, for sending her off with Bishop. "Last I saw, he was in perfect health and waiting by Mr. Potter's wagon. He figured you might have been looking for us," she told the smithy.

"Your sister hailed me down. She's mighty worried about you."

His voice was so gentle it almost brought tears to her eyes. "I figured she would be. I'd be deeply grateful if one of you could take me home."

"Can you ride?"

"No. I've always meant to learn, but—"

"That's fine; I'll take you up with me." Oren turned to the lamplighter and said, "Jarvis, why don't you go on and fetch Daniel while I see Miss Linsey home?"

After Jarvis set his heels to the roan's flanks, Linsey gestured toward Bishop. "What should we do about him?"

"He'll have to walk. There ain't enough horses."

"He has his own horse," Linsey felt compelled to point out.

With a delightfully wicked glint in his eye, Oren gave the animal a deliberate smack across the rump and sent it galloping off across the prairie. "As I said, there ain't enough horses."

Something wasn't right. Daniel felt it in his bones. He couldn't put his finger on it, but as he strode back to where the balloon had crashed, there was a knot in his gut that wouldn't go away. He'd had this same feeling just before he'd gotten the letter from his dad telling him to come home because his mother was sick.

Was his Dad ill now?

No, he didn't think that was it. It was something else. Almost as if someone needed him. But who? The only one he'd ever had the slightest connection to was his mother, and she was beyond needing anyone.

Daniel shook off the mysterious uneasiness. He could no more explain the feeling than he could explain why he was returning to the balloon to search for a stupid bauble.

Yet twenty minutes later, that was exactly what he was doing, scouring the crash site for anything that might resemble a good-luck token. A glint of gold in the grass near the spot where they'd fallen caught his attention. Daniel bent down and extracted a delicate chain. *This* was her powerful protection? A four-petalled leaf trapped between two glass disks?

She seemed to think so. He'd never heard anyone sound so convinced about anything as when she claimed that awful things happened whenever she was without the charm.

His brows pulled into a sudden frown. She'd noticed the amulet missing just before Harvey had shown up. Before that, she'd twisted her ankle because the basket had ripped. Daniel recalled each development in backward sequence. The almost-kiss, the crash, the broken equipment, the ripping up of the stakes . . .

If she'd lost her token when they'd first arrived at the empty lot—

Daniel cut off the thought with a disgusted grimace and shoved the amulet into his trouser pocket. No sane, rational, logical person believed in such flights of fancy. And he was nothing if not sane, rational, and logical.

Except there was nothing rational about the way he felt around a woman who was as nutty as a pecan tree.

The pounding of hooves created a welcome diversion, and Daniel raised his head just as Jarvis reined in his horse. He dismounted, walked toward the tree in a daze, and stared up into the branches with an expression of such comical despair that Daniel might have laughed if he didn't feel so bad. Jarvis had been fascinated with ballooning ever since he'd come across an article about Montgolfiers when he was fifteen. And though he'd been saving every spare cent he made, and often talked about seeing the country, Daniel hadn't realized until recently that he meant to do it in one of the hydrogen crafts.

A few steps brought him to his friend's side. Daniel pressed a consoling hand to Jarvis's shoulder. "I'm sorry about your balloon, Robert."

He shook his head. Shaggy brown hair brushed the upturned collar of his box coat. "She ruint it, Dan'l. That consarned female ruint my air ship. Three-hunnerd dollars right down the shitter."

Daniel didn't know what to say. He was glad, though, that Linsey wasn't around right now. Jarvis in a temper was not a pretty sight, and the farther away she got from him, the safer she'd be.

"Maybe we can fix it. Mrs. Mittermier is supposed to be magic with a needle and thread. I'll wager she can mend the tears."

"That's the least of the damage. There's still the busted tanks, the car, all my meters . . . " He ripped his hat off his head and flung it to the ground. "*Damn* that girl! I shoulda let Harvey have her."

Daniel's attention swerved from the tree to Jarvis. "What did you say?"

"I said I shoulda let Harvey have her. Me and Oren saw him gettin' a little too friendly with her, so we fired off a couple shots to scare him off. And this"—he lifted both hands and jabbed them in the air at the tree—"*this* is what I get."

You'll be sorry for this, Daniel. He saw again the contempt in her eyes, heard again the accusation in her voice. He'd thought it humorous to send her off with the pretentious sot, thought it might even the score for all the trials he'd suffered at her hands.

He'd never once considered that he might be putting her in danger. "Where is she now?"

"Home, probably. Leastwise, that's where Oren said he was taking her."

Without pausing to think about his actions, Daniel strode at a clipped pace to Jarvis's horse. He'd just inserted one foot in the stirrup when Jarvis clapped a hand on his shoulder.

"Where are you going?"

"To check on Linsey."

"You got a death wish? That woman has been a curse to you for years, and you're willing to go off half-cocked because some fella was rolling in the dirt with her? What's gotten into you?"

For a moment Daniel just stared at Jarvis. Then the haze in his eyes slowly receded. Good question. Hadn't he already learned that his weakness for that girl always resulted in disaster? Besides, when had he been appointed her protector? She was safe, being escorted home by a man more than capable of protecting her from harm.

He dragged in and released several deep breaths. "You're right." Again he said, "You're right; I'd only be asking for trouble."

"That's the gospel truth. Hellfire, Dan'l, for a minute there you had me worried that you might be going soft for Linsey Gordon."

Soft? For Linsey?

His wits might have been rattled up a bit lately, but he hadn't lost them completely. "No need to worry, my friend. The day I go soft for Linsey Gordon is the day Cooter Hobart gives up moonshining."

Chapter 11

An itchy nose means you will be kissed, cursed, or vexed, run against a gatepost, or shake hands with a fool.

By the time Daniel got back to Horseshoe, the sun had long since fallen behind the horizon, plunging the town into shadows. He made his way wearily up the stairs to his room, tossed his hat on the bed, then stripped out of his filthy shirt. He'd felt it was only fair that since he'd taken the first—and last—voyage in his friend's balloon, he should stick around and help him haul the mangled craft home. Now all he wanted was a bath, a meal, and sleep—all at once, if he could manage it.

Wearing just his trousers and socks, he returned downstairs to fetch the wooden bathing tub. He set the tub in the middle of the kitchen, placed an oil lamp with the wick turned down low in the center of the small table, then stoked the stove to boil water.

He'd just placed a metal pail under the sink pump when a grumpy voice invaded the peace.

"About damned time you decided to come home."

Daniel glanced over his shoulder at his father, standing in the doorway. The tassel of his long flannel nightcap draped over his shoulder and brushed against his protruding stomach, which was covered by a matching red nightshirt that barely hid his knobby knees.

"I had to help Jarvis get his balloon out of a tree," Daniel said.

"I heard you and the Gordon girl crashed the blamed thing."

No, Linsey had crashed the balloon. But Daniel didn't bother correcting his father.

"What in Sam Hill did you think you were doing, Junior?"

He closed his eyes for a moment, then lifted the filled bucket out of the dry sink. "Not now, Dad."

"Not now? Not now? I had to cancel visits with four patients and close up the shop just to come searching for you."

It figured. Daniel Sr. couldn't dredge up any concern for the welfare of his only son, but he had plenty to spare for his practice. With a wry expression, Daniel replied, "You shouldn't have gone to the trouble on my account."

"What were you thinking to take off in that contraption?"

Daniel sighed. It was the same question he'd asked himself a thousand times during the afternoon. It always came back to the same answer. "I don't know."

"Where was your sense of responsibility?"

"I *don't* know."

A critical gaze touched him clear to the bone as he poured water into the huge vat atop the stove. Daniel, Sr., had never been one to hide his disapproval, but tonight Daniel felt it keener than ever.

"You'd think for all the money I spent on sending you to Tulane, they'd have taught you some damned common sense!"

He'd never let him live down the fact that he'd paid for Daniel's schooling, would he? "Not when it concerns Linsey Gordon. I doubt even a genius could figure out what goes on in her mind."

"It don't take a genius to see that she planned this whole thing just to get herself alone with you. A gal sets her sights on a fellow she fancies, then traps him into marriage by claiming he compromised her."

Was that what happened between his mother and his father? Was that why they'd been so miserable together?

Daniel didn't let himself dwell on the question. He wasn't sure he wanted the answers. "That's a fine theory, Dad, but if she's so bent on forcing me into matrimonial bliss, why was she the one who insisted on walking back to town so her reputation wouldn't be tainted?"

"Who knows the way a woman's mind works?" Jabbing his finger in Daniel's direction, his dad said, "But mark my words, boy, that gal's husband-hunting, and she's marked you as her victim."

"Then she can just set her sights in another direction."

"First sensible thing you've said in years. A woman'll drain the life right out of a man— wear him down till he can't think straight. And you've got more important matters to concentrate on than a marriage-minded spinster, if you're ever gonna make something of yourself."

Like you? Daniel was getting sick of being compared to a man whose biggest accomplishment was opening an apothecary in Cowtown, Texas.

No, that wasn't fair, he thought with an inward sigh. For all it's remoteness, Horseshoe did have its own quaint appeal. He was just tired. No sleep, the events of the day, his turmoil over Linsey . . . all were beginning to take their toll. "Go on back to bed, Dad. I'll be up once I've finished in here."

"Don't be too late. I've got a long day ahead of me and I don't want to be kept awake by a bunch of rattling down here."

After Daniel, Sr., left the kitchen, Daniel stayed by the stove, waiting for the water to boil. Snatches of the dinner conversation at Louisa's flickered in his memory. Talk of courtship, of marriage, of love. He'd had a feeling then that Linsey had designs on him, but he'd rejected the idea as being too ludicrous to believe. Now he wondered if his dad might be right.

He didn't know why he was having such a hard time believing that Linsey might be scheming to trap him into marriage. In view of all that had been happening over the last few days, it wasn't exactly inconceivable.

The question was, why? Why him?

Daniel scratched the side of his nose. He hated mysteries. They made him feel powerless, out of control. He'd much rather know what he was dealing with so he could plan his next move.

But Linsey was as unpredictable as the weather. One moment as calm and breathtaking as an autumn sunrise, the next moment wicked and stirring up more havoc than a spring storm.

The worst part of it was, Daniel had always been in awe of nature's power. He loved to watch the lightning flash and hear the thunder roar. It set a fire in his bloodstream, a hunger in his soul.

Yet for all that he admired in a thunder-cracking, rain-pelting, lightning-forking performance, he also knew that only a fool stood out in the middle of one.

With a grim turn to his mouth, Daniel emptied the heated water into the tub, added cold, then shucked his clothing and climbed in. As he settled his neck against the rim, he made a vow to himself. Whatever Linsey had planned, he refused to fall for it. She'd exposed his weakness this morning: the crazy attraction he couldn't control. But he knew better than anyone that under that frivolous, flighty exterior he'd been so drawn to, hid the wicked heart of a woman who cared little who she hurt in her pursuit of what she wanted.

And for reasons he couldn't fathom, she suddenly seemed to want him.

* * *

"Addie . . . " Linsey snapped her fingers in front of her sister's face to break the trance she seemed to have fallen into. "Aaad-deee . . . are you in there?"

It wasn't the first time Linsey had found her like this. Addie had been acting strangely since the day before yesterday, wandering around the house with a faraway look in her eyes. Linsey might have found it amusing if it wasn't so insulting. One would think that with their remaining time together so uncertain, Addie would spend a little more of it paying attention.

At last she raised her head. "Hmmm?"

"Haven't you heard a word I've said?"

Blank hazel eyes slowly focused. Addie straightened on the sofa and pushed a needle hastily into the fabric stretched across her embroidery hoop, but Linsey could see she was still distracted. Probably pining over Daniel again. Linsey frowned. She hadn't seen him in a couple of days, although Doc Sr. had stopped by to examine her ankle and given her the same warning Daniel had: to keep weight off it. But distance from the junior Dr. Sharpe hadn't lessened the indignation she felt toward him for brushing off the loss of her token, and then forcing her to go off with Bishop.

And to think that she'd come a hair's breadth away from kissing the wretch. The thin air must have dulled her wits. Not only would she never wish to betray her sister like that, but no woman in full command of her senses would let herself fall prey to a man of such churlish temperament.

If she never went near Daniel again, Linsey would spend the rest of her days in utter bliss. If it weren't for the fact that Addie would wither up from misery without the arrogant, self-absorbed, unforgiving oaf, Linsey would forget the matchmaking plan altogether and concentrate on the other tasks still left undone.

Unfortunately she had to put her own feelings aside for her sister, and that meant keeping any derogatory thoughts regarding Daniel to herself. "I asked you if Mr. Puckett got that letter off to my father."

"He said he put it on the first stage heading west."

"Good. I only hope he gets it in time to visit before I turn up my toes."

"The way you're courting death, that will be sooner than you think."

Linsey rolled her eyes. "Please, the scolding you and Aunt Louisa gave me is still ringing in my ears."

"It's no less than you deserve for making us worry like that. However, I suppose I can take some comfort in the fact that you won't be pulling any more dangerous stunts for a while." She glanced at the clock on the mantel, then set her embroidery in the basket beside her. "I have to run an errand. Do you need anything from town?"

Linsey shook her head, hoping Addie couldn't see how impatient she was to have the house to herself for a little while. Either she or Aunt Louisa or both had been hovering over her the last couple of days like mother hens.

As soon as Addie left, Linsey set aside the catalog she'd been leafing through and scooted off the sofa. Her ankle was still tender, but at least she could walk on it without horrible pain. And if she didn't get out and get some fresh air, she'd go stark, raving mad.

Besides, she'd promised to visit Caroline for tea this week, and that visit was long overdue. It would be worth suffering through another of Addie's lectures if she could just get out of the house for a while.

Linsey returned to her room to fetch her cloak, gloves, her Lady Liberty coin, and the music box she'd picked up for the baby. She stood for a minute, trying to think if she had everything she might need. She had no desire to chance her luck by returning to the house for a forgotten item. Deciding she had everything, she limped into town to hire a horse and buggy.

Caroline and Axel lived on a farm five miles west of Horseshoe, and the drive gave Linsey too much time to think. Perhaps was being too harsh with Daniel. After all, she had been the one to lure him into the balloon, not the other way around. She supposed she might have wanted to exact some revenge if he'd cut a similar shine on her.

Upon further reflection, she wondered if perhaps some of the anger she directed at him didn't go a little deeper than the issue with Bishop. Daniel, for all his surly ways, was just too darned tempting for his own good.

Or for hers.

Hard as she tried to forget, she couldn't rid herself of the memory of being crushed against him. Of feeling his chest against her breasts, his hand against her back, his breath against her mouth . . .

Thank goodness the basket bottom had given way, or she feared she would have made the mistake of her life.

Well, once she got him married off to Addie, that temptation would disappear. In the meantime she'd simply steer clear of Daniel and accomplish her matchmaking from a distance.

That thought had her feeling much better by the time she pulled onto the driveway leading to Caroline and Axel Goodwin's homestead. Free-roaming chickens pecking at the ground scattered out of her way. A herd of Angus beef, penned in the pasture behind the barn, lifted their flat faces to study the visitor. Only Frisky, the misnamed, lop-eared hound, lay sprawled in the middle of the yard, unperturbed by her arrival.

Linsey parked the buggy under the shade of an ancient oak tree, and after leaving the horse a bucket of oats to feast on, walked up to the one-room house.

When she heard the muffled keening, like that of an animal in distress, she knew something was wrong. Linsey hastily opened the door. Inside she found Caroline lying abed, her face pale, her hands shaking, her clothes and the bed linens drenched in sweat.

"Caro!"

"Oh, Linsey, thank God . . . "

She dumped her packages onto a chair and hastened to her friend's side. "Caro, what's happened?"

"My water broke."

"Where's Axel?"

"He left for Houston yesterday morning. He won't be back till Tuesd—" A keening wail cut off further words and grew to a tortured scream.

Linsey grit her teeth as Caroline squeezed her hand hard enough to snap bones. How could a woman want a child if this was what she had to endure, as if she were dying a slow death a thousand times over?

When the pain ended, Caroline lay panting, sweating, sobbing. "Somethin's wrong, Linsey. Its too soon. I'm gonna lose him, I just know I'm gonna lose this baby, too."

"You are not going to lose this baby." Linsey searched the cabin and found a pile of folded cloths inside a chest. After filling the basin with tepid water from the pitcher, she soaked one of the cloths and bathed Caroline's clammy brow. "How long have you been having the pains?"

"All morning. They're worse than I've ever felt. Oh, sweet Jesus—" She clutched her belly as another pain ripped through her. The walls echoed with the cry of sheer suffering.

Linsey peeled the blanket off her belly and went pale at the sight of the blood staining the sheets. "I have to get the doc," she whispered.

"No, Linsey—" Caroline grabbed Linsey's skirt. "Please don't leave me."

"I have to." God knew she didn't want to

leave her friend, but she didn't know beans about birthing, and the closest midwife lived halfway across the county. "I won't be gone long, Caro—I swear it on my mother's soul."

Daniel arranged the bottles on the shelves, grouping those with the skull and crossbones on a high shelf while others sat at eye level or lower in the glass cabinet. The symbols had been on the bottles for as long as he could remember. A closed eye on the chloroform; a broken bone for laudanum; the letter C divided by a squiggly line on the carbolic acid.

He'd learned the purpose of each drug from the labels before knowing the names. Another of his dad's methods in teaching Daniel the trade before he'd been given a chance to decide for himself. Though Daniel didn't regret his decision, and suspected he would have gone into medicine anyway, sometimes he wondered if things wouldn't have turned out differently if his father hadn't driven him so hard.

Even now the old man wouldn't let up. The last couple of nights, while Daniel had been studying reports documenting the advantages of surgery versus herbal treatment in female problems—a subject that had fascinated him for years—he could hear his dad in the background, finding fault with some procedure or another that Daniel had done.

Though it only made Daniel more determined to pass his entrance exams and get the hell out from under his dad's thumb, several times Daniel had caught himself drifting off in thought, seeking escape from the constant hounding. The closest he came was in remembering the view from Jarvis's balloon—the sense of freedom he'd found with the wind in his hair and laughter in his soul.

Invariably his thoughts would stray to Linsey, the woman who'd torn him from the burdens he bore, and how for a moment she'd looked at him as a woman looked at a man she wanted—not as a doctor to cure all ills, not as son who failed at every turn. Just a man.

And it made him wonder if his dad might be wrong. That maybe a woman didn't always drag a man down to the depths of misery, but sometimes brought him to the heights of contentment.

Daniel abruptly shook his head to dispel the notion. He'd seen with his own eyes what happened when a man let himself become diverted by a pair of sparkling eyes and winsome smile: he became resentful and unsatisfied; she drew into herself so deep that nothing mattered anymore.

The smartest thing he could do was stay as far from Linsey as possible.

Just as he finished stocking the cabinet, the door flew open, hitting the wall, knocking the cowbells clean off their hook.

And who but Linsey skidded inside.

Clutching the door, she cried, "Daniel! Thank God you're here. Come quickly."

"Forget it, Linsey," he said, twisting the key in the lock. "I'm not falling for that trick again."

She rushed toward the counter and slapped her hands on the tiled surface. "It's no trick. Caroline is hurting something fierce. She says the babe is coming."

"The babe isn't due for another month."

"When it's due and when it comes aren't always the same thing. You should know that better than anyone. Daniel, please, there is no time to waste! For the love of Gus, she needs you now!"

The escalating panic in her voice made Daniel waver in indecision. What if she wasn't lying this time? Could he really take that risk? "I'm warning you, if this is another ruse, so help me . . . "

He grabbed his bag from beneath the counter. Linsey pushed out the door and had climbed into the buggy out front before Daniel even got across the boardwalk.

She scarcely gave him a chance to get into the vehicle before she set the horse in motion with a slap of reins and a sharp "Ha!"

The drive to Caroline and Axel's was wrought with an anxious silence. Linsey gripped the reins in pale fists, her features tight with a worry that appeared genuine. Daniel regretted giving her such a rough time. Even Linsey couldn't fake the fear he saw in her eyes.

Before he could stop it, his hand reached across the seat to squeeze her leg. "We'll get to her in time; don't worry."

She gave him a feeble smile before returning her attention to the road.

Finally they pulled off the country road and

drove up to the cabin. The buggy had barely come to a stop when Linsey leaped down. Daniel grabbed his bag and raced after her inside.

Linsey hastened to her friend's side and dropped to her knees next to the huge tick mattress. "I'm back, Caro, just like I promised. I brought Daniel with me. Everything's going to be fine now."

"I'm going to lose him, I know it," she wept.

"No, you won't. Daniel won't let anything happen to this baby."

Daniel wished she wouldn't put so much faith in his abilities. He was only a man, not a miracle worker, and he'd seen healthier women than Caroline deliver stillborns. She'd already lost two babies midterm, and a third in the last trimester. The odds that she'd deliver a healthy child this time were slim to none.

Still, strangely enough, Linsey's confidence also gave Daniel a strength of purpose he hadn't felt in a long time: to not fail the two women who trusted him to do his job.

He set his bag on the foot of the bed. "Linsey, gather up all the lamps you can find. I'll also need hot water, a piece of rubber sheeting if you can find it, and a pile of towels."

While Linsey hastened to do his bidding, Daniel rolled up his sleeves and scrubbed his hands in a tin basin. Several items—a pair of scissors, a whole garlic clove, a cartridge and a comb—littered the surface of the bedside stand. Three horseshoes had been nailed to the inside of the headboard of the cradle waiting between the bed and the fireplace.

No one needed to tell him that Linsey had been responsible for the extra touches. If it would have done any good, Daniel would have ordered the nonsense taken away. But he didn't have the time or energy for an argument. He needed to save both Caroline and her child.

He finished scrubbing his hands and had just begun to press on Caroline's belly to judge the position of the baby when Linsey set five lanterns on the trunk at the far side of the bed, and a stack of towels on the nightstand. Then she knelt beside Caroline and brushed the tangled brown hair from the woman's eyes in a gesture Daniel couldn't help but find touching.

God knew, Caroline would need a friend today.

As he examined her, he knew she was in trouble. Wave after wave of contractions rolled through her, pain twisting her gaunt, perspiring face. Blood trickled from her bottom lip where she'd bit through it against the pain.

"Doc Jr, please do something. Don't let my baby die. I can't lose another one."

"I'm going to do everything I can, Caroline." Not only for the babe but for the woman. He didn't think she'd survive another miscarriage. "I need you to work with me, though."

"Whatever it takes—*ahhh*!"

"Take deep, even breaths. Don't push—even if the sensation becomes unbearable, hear?"

"I hear. Don't push."

Daniel poured carbolic acid into a pan to sterilize his instruments, then over his hands. Many physicians didn't put much importance on cleanliness, but one of Daniel's professors insisted that patients fared better, and over the years, Daniel had come to agree. "Linsey, inside my bag there's a small brown bottle with the symbol of a closed eye on it. Dribble a few drops onto a piece of flannel, then press it against her nose and mouth until she passes out."

Linsey's head snapped up. She looked at Daniel in astonishment. "You're putting her to sleep?"

"It's necessary. I have to cut her open."

Cut her open? She'd never heard of such a thing! Granted, she'd never attended a birthing before, either, but she knew how babies were delivered—and it didn't involve cutting anything open.

The panic must have shown in her eyes, for Daniel told her, "If I don't perform this surgery, Caroline and the babe will both die. She's too small to deliver it through the canal, and the placenta has already begun to tear away."

She heard the anguish in his decision, yet his eyes shone with a steely confidence. He knows what he's doing, she told herself. He had a degree to prove it.

Even so, her hands trembled as she fished under rolls of bandages for the group of bottles, searching for the one he specified. It wasn't that she didn't trust Daniel, it wasn't that she doubted his abilities. It was herself she didn't trust, herself she doubted. He wanted her to help him and she feared that if she failed, it would mean the death of one of her dearest friends.

But if she didn't help him, Caroline or her baby would most certainly die. Did she really have a choice?

"Caro? Daniel says we need to give you this to make you sleep."

Questions swirled in her pain-riddled eyes. "What for?"

"So he can save the baby."

"Tell her to breath deeply when you put the cloth over her nose and mouth."

Linsey repeated Daniel's order, and whispered, "Don't be afraid, Caro."

"Don't leave me, Linsey."

"I won't. I'll be here the whole time until you wake up."

And though she knew it was a necessary procedure, her eyes grew moist as she pressed the drugged cloth over her friend's face. In just a few seconds, Caroline's eyes closed, her tight muscles relaxed, and the hand within Linsey's went limp.

Linsey couldn't bring herself to watch when Daniel set his knife beneath Caroline's navel. She turned her head, hunched her shoulders, and gripped Caroline's work-worn fingers.

The click of steel hitting steel, the thump of a clock, the consistent yap of a dog, all had her nerves on edge.

She focused on Daniel's steady breathing, willing it to calm her. Amazingly, it did. Slowly the tension left her neck and shoulders, and the anxiety seeped from her body.

After a while she even managed to brave a glance at Daniel. His cowlick drooped low over his forehead, creating a frame for his right eye. The mouth she'd once longed to taste was pressed together in a relaxed line.

His composure really was remarkable. While she battled hysteria, he remained unflaggingly calm and self-assured, almost as if he worked on a mechanical object instead of a person. Maybe that was what made him so capable—being able to separate himself from his emotions.

"Wipe my brow, please."

Grateful to be of some use, she snatched a square of flannel and stood to blot the beads of sweat from above his eyes, then sat down again. If he needed anything, she'd be happy to comply, but unless he asked, she figured the best thing she could do was just keep out of his way.

"Talk to me," he said a few minutes later.

"About what?"

"Anything your little heart desires." *Click. Snap.* A curse.

She caught a flash of white; felt the tension in Daniel's shoulders as his movements turned swifter. Only then did she realize that he wasn't as detached as she thought. That he would seek a sense of normalcy, of comfort, from her made her heart do a little flip.

"Jenny asked me to stand up in her wedding," she said.

"She did, huh?"

"Will you be there?"

"I plan on it."

It went unspoken that sometimes his plans didn't always work out the way he wanted them. "She asked her girls to wear blue. It's a lucky color."

"You wearing blue at your wedding?"

"I would if I married, but I'm afraid that won't happen."

"The right man'll come along."

She longed to tell him that even if he did, it was too late. "And you Daniel, have you set your eye on a lady yet?"

"Nope. Haven't looked, either."

"Sometimes you don't have to look. Sometimes she's right under your nose."

His hands paused. She felt his gaze on the top of her head. Her scalp tingled.

"Thread the needle on that tray with the cat gut. And fetch me a warm blanket."

"The baby's out?" she breathed.

"Will be in two seconds."

The next few minutes passed in a rush of activity: Daniel's hands nothing more than a blur above the sheet covering Caroline; Linsey hurrying to and fro bringing him items he requested, sometimes even before he requested them; blood-soaked cloths tossed heedlessly into a metal basin. . . .

And then the announcement she'd been waiting for.

"Caroline's got herself a fine girl child."

The next thing Linsey knew, he'd placed a screaming, squirming bundle in her arms. She took the baby across the room to get her cleaned up while he finished with Caroline.

"What a little cherub you are," Linsey crooned, wiping a damp cotton cloth along the wriggling body. She couldn't weigh more than five pounds, but she looked pink and healthy despite the mottled complexion of her wee face. Even more incredible was that such a painful experience could have brought forth such a beautiful creature.

And as she counted the fragile fingers and knobby toes, an ache grew inside her, so sharp she wondered how she bore it. She'd never hold a child of her own, never nurse it from her breast, never watch it take its first steps.

"Linsey?"

Daniel's concerned tone almost shattered her. She'd always been the strong one, and for him to catch her weak and weeping . . .

"A bit overwhelming, isn't it?" he commented softly from Caroline's bedside.

She swallowed, then nodded, as deeply moved by his insight as the tender compassion in his voice.

"No matter how many times I see a birth, it never fails to humble me."

For the first time since she could remember, he wasn't jeering at her or recoiling from her or cursing her to perdition. He was simply listening. What's more, he seemed to understand that some things couldn't be put into words.

"Oh, Daniel . . . " She lifted her gaze to his across the room, and in a voice hoarse with emotion, said, "Caroline and Axel will be so grateful. You have given them a gift beyond measure."

He shifted and dropped his gaze, clearly discomfitted by the praise. "I don't know about that; I just did what I've been trained to do." As if one compliment deserved another, he said, "I couldn't have done it without your help."

His praise created a warmth in her belly.

"So how does it feel to bring a life into the world?"

Linsey suddenly brightened. "I did, didn't I?" It hadn't occurred to her during the activity, but she had. Her smile widened. She'd actually brought a life into the world! "I guess that's another project off my list."

"List?"

She thought about telling him, but he'd only laugh at her. Or worse, ridicule her, and she didn't think she could bear that after being the recipient of his praise.

They continued working together in companionable silence, and when Daniel finished with Caroline, he examined the baby and pronounced her fit. Caroline awoke shortly after.

She was a bit groggy, but Daniel expected that. Her stomach would be quite sore for a while, too, and she'd need help with the baby. As he watched Linsey place the baby in the new mother's arms, and listened to them gush like only women could do, an unexpected swell of pride rose inside him—pride in Linsey, pride in himself. Damn, but they'd worked well together, almost as if they'd been made to be partners. He'd always wanted that "perfect fit." That sense of being part of a team. He couldn't have asked for a better set of extra hands.

He hadn't expected to find that with Linsey. But, then, she was forever surprising him.

After he had all his instruments cleaned and put away, he returned to the women. Caroline was looking weary.

"Why don't we go outside for a bit?" he whispered in Linsey's ear.

"I promised Caroline I wouldn't leave her," she whispered back.

"You're not. You're just getting some fresh air. We'll leave the door open so she can call out if she needs you."

After a second's hesitation, Linsey rose from the bed where mother and child snuggled and let Daniel escort her outside onto the front porch. A swing hung from the rafters. He gestured toward it. Linsey smoothed her skirts along her rear and thighs, and sat. Daniel lowered himself next to her.

She took in a deep breath of cool, fresh night air and stared at the stars. "Have you ever wished on a falling star, Daniel?"

He hesitated. He didn't feel up to bickering with Linsey tonight. "I wouldn't know what to wish for," he finally said.

"Why, whatever you want. Wishes on falling stars are always granted—that's how I got my sister." She smiled at the sky. "Nights like this are magical. The moon, the stars . . . And even if you don't believe in the power of a falling star, the miracle behind that wall is enough to make a person believe anything is possible."

He said nothing, just watched her for several moments while the peace of the evening surrounded them. "If anything was possible, what would you wish for?"

"If *anything* was possible?"

Daniel nodded.

"A child. Holding that baby in my arms makes me ache for a little girl of my own."

He knew the feeling. Every now and again he'd get that pinch of longing, too. "You'll have one someday."

She swallowed visibly, then whispered, "Some women just aren't fated to be mothers."

There was such sorrow in the words that Daniel found himself wanting to pull her close. He wondered how she could be so certain that she'd not hold a child of her own, but it was too personal a question to ask.

He hoped that when he finally married, his wife would want children as badly as Linsey seemed to. His sons and daughters would need to know they were loved, and important, and accepted for what they were.

God knew, he'd never felt that way.

He suspected she'd make a good mother, though. She had a way about her that attracted youngsters. A zest for life, a mischievous twinkle, a nurturing aura.

A swift and fierce longing gripped him, to watch her grow big with child, to be there at the child's birth, to share in the wonder of creating a miracle.

And who knew? He might get his wish. The child just wouldn't be his.

Linsey braced her hands against the seat and set the swing in motion with her toe. "How did you know what you had to do? I mean, didn't you worry that you'd hurt the baby when you cut Caroline open?"

"No. I've assisted with a cesarean section before, so I've had some experience with the procedure. But there are other risks involved with the operation. A doctor has to weigh those risks versus trying something a little safer, or doing nothing at all. Most of the time, you follow the feeling in your gut and hope it's the right decision."

"Well, I don't claim to know anything about surgeons and their skills, but what you did back there was nothing short of incredible."

Daniel nodded his head. It had been amazing. Ten years ago, he wouldn't have dreamed he'd attempt such a risky operation. But after the progress he'd seen in the field of medicine. . . . "You wouldn't believe some of the life-saving techniques being discovered today. Blood transfusions, tumor removal. The next thing you know, someone will have discovered a cure for cancer."

"And you want to be a part of that?" she asked with a smile.

Yes, he did. He couldn't remember the last time a procedure had given him such satisfaction. As if his knowledge—and his hands—were worth something.

Once upon a time, he'd arrogantly believed those two things could change the world. That arrogance had fed his ambition, had become the driving force to complete his school and dare the impossible.

When had he lost it?

He squinted at the scattered clouds in the distance. "I don't expect you to understand."

"I think I do, though. It's as if you are standing on the edge of the frontier. Your heart is thundering and your palms are damp and you've never felt so glorious in your life because you know that there is something extraordinary out there. Something no one else has seen or experienced before. And if you don't reach for it, don't grasp it in your hands"—she pressed a fist to her middle—"there's an emptiness inside you that never goes away."

Daniel listened in stunned silence. He'd never heard anyone describe his feelings so accurately.

"I really am sorry for losing you that scholarship, Daniel. I wish you would believe that."

He didn't want to talk about this with her, not tonight, not when he'd had his first taste of triumph in such a long, long time. He didn't want to be reminded that underneath the soft, generous, competent woman he'd worked with lay a conniving hellion who had caused his fall. "It's done and over with."

"Is it?"

"Let's just forget it, all right?"

"I wish I could. But a day hasn't passed since that I haven't felt just terrible about your letter winding up in the creek."

He couldn't reply even if he wanted to.

"What I *don't* understand is, what's so special about that eastern university? What's there that isn't here?"

"It's more a matter of what *isn't* there that's here."

"And that is?"

"My father, for one."

"He can't be all that bad."

"You've never had to work in his shadow."

"Maybe instead of clashing with him, you

could find common ground. Perhaps a shared interest."

"We have no shared interests."

"You have your passion of medicine."

Did they? Daniel scoffed at the thought.

"I just know that if my father were nearby, I wouldn't squander the time we had together on earth with useless quarreling," Linsey said.

"You could always go West to visit him."

"If I showed up in Indian Territory, he'd send me back on the next train. He says it's too dangerous for a young woman."

Daniel had to smile at that. "I can't imagine the dangers would stop you from going to him if that's really where you wanted to be."

"Maybe you're right. Horseshoe has been my home since I was child and I am happy here—I'm needed here. But sometimes . . . I can't help but wonder what else is out there."

There it was again. That wistfulness. That hint of sorrow.

Yet it seemed vastly important to Linsey to be needed by people. A human trait, Daniel supposed. And who knew? Maybe that's why he stuck around here. The people of this county needed a physician, and Dad couldn't do it all, though he dared any man to tell him that.

Other than that, though, no one needed him as a man. But he preferred being rootless—as soon as he saved the amount necessary to take his entrance exams, he'd be gone. It was better not to tie himself down. "If being needed is what you crave, maybe you should go into medicine. You never know what you'll encounter, either."

"Ha! I don't have the time or the patience."

They laughed at the pun. And as before, the sound wrapped around Daniel's vitals and gave a gentle tug.

"You really do have a beautiful smile, Daniel. You should try it more often."

Yeah, maybe he should. It felt . . . good. At least, it felt good smiling with her.

"Well, I'd best get back inside," she said with a sigh. "I'd hate for Caroline to awaken with no one near."

Just as she rose, Daniel sprang to his feet and caught her arm above the elbow. "Linsey, wait." He wasn't sure why he'd stopped her. Maybe because she seemed to want something from him he just couldn't give—forgiveness. Too much had been lost as a result of that coach overturning, and too much muddy water had passed under the bridge since then. Daniel still felt mired in it.

No, he thought with an odd sadness, forgiveness wasn't something he could find it within himself to give her.

But he could give her something else.

He cleared his throat, reached into his coin pocket, then pressed her amulet into her palm.

Linsey glanced at their hands. Her eyes widened. "My Token of Good Fortune!"

Speechless, she took the amulet with excruciating care, as if he were handing her one of the stars she'd been watching. "Where did you find this?"

"In Jarvis's balloon. The basket, actually. It

must have gotten caught when the bottom fell out."

Right when they'd almost kissed.

Neither said it, but it was there, in her startled eyes, in his treacherous thoughts. Daniel reeled them in, knowing that if he let himself dwell on that moment, he might fall into the dream and never climb out. Linsey had that ability: to make him want to forget everything but her, to lose himself in her provocative touch and capricious grin.

He cleared his throat again and shoved his hands into his pockets. "I heard Bishop Harvey tried forcing his attentions on you."

"He's been doing it for months."

"I'm sorry, Linsey. It was stupid of me to send you with him. I know we've had our differences, but I wouldn't want anyone to hurt you."

She let out a little laugh and hugged herself. "Except you, right?"

He caught her gaze, held it. "I *never* would have sent you with him if I'd have known."

To his astonishment, tears welled up in her eyes. "Thank you for that." She lifted and lowered the amulet. "And thank you for bringing this back to me." She smiled.

Daniel forgot how to breathe.

He couldn't remember a single time when a look had been so trusting. A fragrance so inviting. A smile so beguiling.

And in that moment, he wanted her with an intensity that made everything else pale in comparison: the fellowship, his father's respect, his own surgical practice.

Nothing had ever surpassed that dream.

Until now.

Until Linsey.

It didn't make a goddamn bit of sense. She was reckless. She was irresponsible. She was high-strung.

She was the most beautiful creature he'd ever seen in his life.

And as his gaze came to rest on that ripe, cupid's-bow mouth that had been taunting him forever, he knew if he didn't kiss her, the not knowing would drive him mad. He had to taste her—just a sample, just once. . . .

Even as his hand reached up to cup her jaw, Daniel knew it was a mistake to touch her. Even as he took a step closer, he knew he was playing with fire. Even as his mouth lowered to hers, he knew he'd regret it. This woman was trouble.

But damn, trouble had never tasted so sweet.

It was a simple kiss, a mere brushing of his lips across hers, but he felt the shock of it clear to the bone. His lungs pumped hot and heavy as, still cupping her jaw in his palm, he pressed his forehead to hers. Her shallow breaths teased the skin at his collar. And he knew then that one taste would never be enough.

A kiss to her forehead led to one to her brows, then to her eyelids, and each eye, the spiky brown lashes still damp with unshed tears. Across to her temple, where copper tendrils of her hair grazed his cheek.

If she'd backed off, if she'd given a token of

a fight, if she'd resisted in any way whatsoever, he might have been able to keep his desire in check.

Instead she started kissing him back. A tentative press of her lips on his shoulder, then his collarbone, then his neck.

A moan rumbled between them, and it awed Daniel that the sound came from him. He tipped her chin up and covered her mouth in hot, hungry need. And still, he wanted more. He swung an arm around her neck, drawing her closer, bringing her flush against his front. His mind rebelled, but his body craved her heat.

Her breasts pressed into his chest, and her fingertips bit into his skin. He deepened the kiss further, sliding his tongue along the seam of her lips. There it was, what he sought—the flavor of high winds and silvery smiles and innocence unearthed.

A sound like the purr of a cat caused the fever in his blood to rise, and scalpel-sharp need sliced through Daniel from heart to heel. The temperature around them spiked. Their kisses became faster, harder, more urgent. Seeking, searching, devouring. With Linsey, there was no coyness, no reserve. Everything about her was open and reckless and uninhibited.

And that made her dangerous as hell.

Even so, his fingers delved through her hair. Silky soft curls wrapped around his wrist like lust itself, teasing his flesh, binding him tighter to her than iron sutures.

He wanted to break free. He wanted to push himself away from her.

He wanted to bury himself so deep inside her that nothing could separate them.

The madness continued to spin around his senses and through his veins, making him aware of nothing but her hands tightening around his back, her fingers clutching his shoulders, and the scent of lavender flirting with his control.

The muscles in his body went taut as a tug-of-war rope. The blood drained from his scalp, rose from his toes, and met smack in his groin, where it went from a slow, swelling simmer to a furious boil.

As if she detected the swift change in his body, in the atmosphere itself, Linsey pushed against his chest. Daniel broke the fusion of their mouths and loosened his hold on her. Then he stepped back and ran a shaking hand through his hair. He couldn't look at her, couldn't trust his own resistance.

"Daniel?" Linsey's confusion reached out, touching him with tentative fingers. "Why?"

Because I was an idiot? Because you were there, and I haven't kissed a woman in months? A dozen jibes sprang to mind. That she was willing, that she was able, that all women looked the same in the dark.

Instead Daniel found himself confessing, "Hell if I know." He only knew that Linsey had this ability to make him do things—feel things—that had no rhyme or reason.

A tiny cry from within the cabin brought both of them back to reality.

Linsey cast a glance through the front window. "I need to get inside."

Daniel nodded. "There isn't much more I can do here. For now, Caroline just needs rest. I'll be by to check on her tomorrow, but send for me if she exhibits any signs of complications."

"I will." She headed for the open door, then paused with one hand on the jamb. "If you could stop by Briar House and let Addie and Aunt Louisa know where I am, I'd be grateful."

He nodded again. Crazy how they could have such an inane exchange after experiencing the most staggering moment of his life.

Once she stepped inside and the door shut behind her, Daniel fell back against the cabin wall. Why *had* he kissed her? Hell, he'd only meant to give her back her stupid amulet. Instead he'd all but ravished her on a neighbor's front porch.

And the most frightening part was, he'd do it again given half a chance.

Inside the cabin, Linsey stood with her back and palms flat against the door, her gaze glued to a soot stain above the stove pipe.

Daniel had kissed her.

And she'd kissed him back.

How could she have betrayed Addie like that?

She pressed her fingertips to her lips, still feeling the imprint of his mouth on hers. So much for keeping her distance. She couldn't have been closer to him than if she'd crawled inside his skin.

And the worst part of it was, for a walking dead woman, she had never felt so alive.

For the first time, Linsey understood what Addie had been going through all these years. When Daniel looked at her, her tongue tied itself into a knot. When he touched her, her heart sighed, and when he kissed her . . . Linsey felt like swooning.

It was more than his extraordinary looks; Linsey couldn't believe herself so shallow as to have her head turned by a pair of sensually brooding eyes and a sullen mouth. It had been more than his touch, too, though that had ignited a wildfire inside her.

Deeper down, Linsey had sensed something more intimate. A loneliness that had spoken to her without words. A neediness that called out to the nurturer in her, beckoned to the woman in her who longed to make him laugh and smile and believe in luck.

Oh, God. She buried her face in her hands. *He* was what—and who—she'd been waiting for. *He* was the reason she'd remained single well past the age when most girls were already married and bearing children. Not only did Daniel make her toes curl and her heart sigh and her skin tingle, but he challenged her wits, tempted her soul, and teased her spirit.

He was a man she could fall head over heels in love with.

And he belonged to her sister.

Chapter 12

There is nothing luckier any day of the week than a chance encounter with a chimney sweep.

For two days, Linsey wrestled with the guilt and shame of her behavior. She thanked her lucky stars that Caroline's recuperation prevented her from returning home, for she didn't think she could bring herself to look Addie in the eye—not after what she had done.

Then Axel Goodwin got back from Houston, and Linsey could put off facing her sister no longer.

When she entered Briar House late Tuesday afternoon, a wave of relief rolled off her shoulders at finding the house empty. She headed upstairs and set down the valise Aunt Louisa had sent over yesterday morning, then lowered herself onto the bed.

If only she could talk to Addie—ask her to help make sense of these confusing feelings Daniel stirred inside her. But what could she say? "Addie, I kissed the man you love, and now I can't stop thinking about him?" It would break her heart.

No, she thought with a despairing sigh, no matter that she and Addie had always told each other everything, this would be one secret Linsey took with her to her grave.

As always when something weighed heavily on her mind, Linsey sought diversion in activity. She spent the day cleaning Briar House from top to bottom—polishing the banister until the beeswax coating made it so shiny and slick one could slide down it with ease; rubbing the silver so bright it could blind a person; ironing linens; carving soap bars into eccentric shapes; rearranging the goods in the pantry . . .

But no amount of work stopped Daniel from plaguing her every moment. Image after image assailed her. The bright look on his face in the balloon, his tender handling of Caroline and her baby, the tentative smile he'd given her when she'd praised him.

Even more shamefully, she recalled with acute clarity the wild sensation of his mouth on hers, and those hands—those gifted hands—along her back, cupping her bottom, pulling her so close she could feel his heart thudding beat-for-beat against her breast. . . .

She slammed the cupboard shut. This had to stop. What happened between her and Daniel should never have happened—could never happen again. He belonged to Addie, and the sooner she got them married, and Daniel out of temptation's reach, the better.

Sooner came sooner than she expected.

As Linsey walked outside to empty a pail of dirty scrub water, she spotted Noah Tabor leaning a ladder against the house. She barely recognized him at first. He was dressed in his work blacks—jet shirt and matching overalls. Brushes, brooms, and rods stuck out at all angles from the pack strapped to his back, and soot stained his hands and face, leaving all but the whites of his eyes and striking green irises visible.

He released his hold on the ladder to tip the bill of his cap. "Afternoon, Linsey."

"Hello, Noah," she greeted, her hand shading her eyes. "What brings you to our neck of the woods?"

"I ran into your aunt in town, and she asked me to stop by. She said you've got a swallow stuck in your chimney."

"We do?"

"That's what she said. Mind if I have a look?"

"Of course not." It gave Linsey some comfort hearing that Aunt Louisa had hired him. Noah might be too proud to accept donations for his ever-growing family, but he never turned down honest work, and often tended to odd jobs unfit for one of the local youngsters. "How's Jenny faring?"

"Skittish as a doe. I'll be glad when we get the knot tied and life gets back to normal."

"Only a couple more weeks left to go. What about you? Are you suffering any jitters?"

"Not a one. I knew she was the woman for me the second time I kissed her."

"Not the first?" Linsey teased.

Noah winked. "A gentleman never tells." He tipped his bill again and, whistling a jaunty tune, scaled the ladder to the roof.

Linsey watched him for a moment, then turned on her heel to resume her own work. In all the years she'd known Noah, she couldn't remember seeing him so happy. He and Jenny would have a wonderful marriage—

She stopped short as an idea struck. That was it! The perfect way to bring Addie and Daniel together. What better way to generate thoughts of one wedding, than by celebrating another? But she didn't dare wait until Noah and Jenny actually exchanged vows; she couldn't guarantee she'd be around that long. What if she threw them a party—an engagement party, with everyone in town invited? There'd be dancing and merriment—lots of opportunities to plant the seed of matrimonial bliss in Daniel's mind. And with a crowd of people around, there was no risk of the episode at Caroline's repeating itself.

Linsey's spirits took an upward swing. She dashed into the house and up the stairs, eager to begin her plans. So maybe having Addie play injured hadn't turned out so well. And maybe Aunt Louisa's dinner party could have ended on a better note. She'd even concede that the balloon incident had been nothing short of a catastrophe. But not *every* effort could turn out so badly. After all, a chance meeting with a chimney sweep was the harbinger of good luck.

This plan couldn't possibly fail.

* * *

It was a total disaster.

Days of planning and preparations went down the pipes within a matter of hours.

A rainstorm blasted through the small community, causing over half of their invited guests to cancel out—including Addie, who had left that afternoon to run one of her mysterious errands and had yet to return. Bishop Harvey got drunk on Aunt Louisa's burgundy wine and passed out directly on top of the dinner table, ruining the banquet it had taken Linsey two days to prepare.

And Daniel . . . he hadn't been there for more than ten minutes when his father stole him away to help with some emergency.

By half past eight o'clock, all the guests who had braved the storm to attend the party had collected their cloaks and headed for home, leaving her sitting on the bottom step of the stairwell alone and frustrated and near tears. Why was it that every time she tried to do something good, it turned out so badly?

At the sound of shuffling heels, Linsey hastened to get her emotions under control. She sniffled and wiped her eyes.

Unfortunately nothing missed Aunt Louisa's keen eye. Crossing the tails of her shawl around her middle, she took a seat next to Linsey. "What is it, child?"

The gentle tone undid her. Tears welled up again, blurring her vision. Linsey blew her nose into a sodden hanky. "Everything is ruined. I thought the evening would be perfect, but nothing went the way it was supposed to. At this rate, I'll never see them get married."

"I doubt this will dissuade Noah and Jenny from marrying."

"Not Noah and Jenny, Addie and Daniel."

"Addie and Daniel?" She shook her head in confusion. "I must be spending too much time at Granny Yearling's. When did he start courting her?"

Even if she hadn't made that vow of truth, Linsey could never lie to Aunt Louisa. "He isn't exactly, but I've been hoping to change that."

"Playing matchmaker, are we?"

At Linsey's nod, the old woman brought her arm around Linsey's shoulders and drew her close. "Child, matters of the heart have to be handled delicately. If one tries to force love where love is not meant to grow, it will only cause misery for everyone involved."

"Addie has always loved Daniel, though. They are perfect for one another."

"Are they?"

"Of course. Daniel is just having a little trouble realizing it."

"Perhaps, then, they are not as perfect for one another as you might think."

"Are you saying that I'm wasting my time? That Daniel will never learn to love her?"

"Not if he isn't her destiny."

"But if Daniel isn't Addie's destiny, who is?"

With a tiny shrug and a whimsical smile, she said, "Only Lady Fate knows the answer to that."

Linsey stared at the paper streamers she'd

strung from the chandelier to each doorway. If Daniel wasn't the man for Addie, then who was? Who was the man who would comfort her sister, be there for her through all of life's joys and sorrows, give her the family she longed for and the love she so desperately needed? "Aunt Louisa, *I* need to know."

A twinkle entered the rheumy blue eyes. "Then ask her."

It felt strange sitting in the Potter's quarters behind the smithy, listening to an eight-year-old boy read eloquently from Charles Dickens's, *A Tale of Two Cities.* Rain poured down on the tin roof with a steady drumming, a fire crackled merrily in the hearth, and several lamps placed about the room gave the knotted pine interior a warm, cozy glow.

It felt even stranger having the boy's father in the same room, cooking up something that had a heavenly aroma.

Addie sat at the kitchen table with Bryce, trying in vain to ignore the man whistling at the stove behind her. She'd been paying visits to the Potter's quarters throughout the week, and each day found herself lingering longer and longer. She told herself it was because Aunt Louisa and Linsey were so busy planning Noah and Jenny's engagement party that neither of them were ever home, and that Bryce's education was too important to let anything stand in her way. If there was a chance that she could give him the advantages he deserved without separating him from the only family he had— how could she ignore that?

In all honesty, though, Addie knew that Bryce wasn't the only reason she went to the Potter's.

Not anymore.

She hadn't expected that Mr. Potter would want to sit in on the private lessons with Bryce. At first he had kept to the shop, working while she and Bryce studied. Then one day he showed up just as she'd been setting her books out, and began cooking dinner. Over the next few nights, he did the same thing.

Now he seemed to always be around. Not interfering, but just there. Strong. Silent. And too intriguing for Addie's good.

She caught her gaze straying in his direction once more, and abruptly turned her attention to the window. Only then did she realize with a start that it was almost pitch dark. She glanced at the watch pinned to her bodice. Six o'clock? Oh, goodness. Linsey was going to kill her! She stood and began to gather her books and papers. "I didn't realize it had gotten so late. I'd better start for home. Linsey is expecting me at Noah and Jenny's party."

"It's still raining, though," Bryce said.

"Don't look like it'll be letting up anytime soon, either," his father added. "Why don't you stay to supper with us, Miss Witt?" The smithy gestured toward the countertop, where a basket of biscuits sat beside a cast-iron kettle and pitcher of milk. "Everything's finished. Nothing fancy, just rabbit and greens, but it's fillin'."

An immediate refusal sprang to Addie's lips. Not that she had anything against rabbit and greens—she simply didn't think it wise to remain in this man's company any longer than necessary. "I really shouldn't. My family will be worried."

"I'm sure they wouldn't expect you to venture out in this weather."

Oren obviously didn't know Linsey very well. She'd been planning this party for days, throwing herself into the preparations like a mad hatter, and all she could talk about was how perfect an opportunity it was for her and Daniel to forge an attraction. Addie should be grateful that her sister was doing everything possible to make Daniel notice her, and should also have thrown herself whole-heartedly into the plans.

Instead she'd spent the last few days buried in books with an eight-year-old and fighting a traitorous attraction to his father.

"Please stay, Miss Witt," Bryce said. "It's been a long while since we've had a lady sit to supper with us."

Her resolve weakened. She never had been able to refuse the entreaty in a child's eyes, Bryce's especially.

"All right, I would be honored."

Somehow the simple acceptance of the invitation made it seem more personal. Intimate, even. In the four years since she'd been teaching, she'd shared countless meals with the parents of her students. This time shouldn't have been any different.

It shouldn't have been, but it was.

From the moment Mr. Potter pulled out a chair for her, Addie felt pampered and special in a way she'd never known before, as if her presence was the most important event in their lives. Bryce scrambled around putting his books away and digging in the cupboards for linen napkins that looked as if they had never been used, while his father yanked on drawers and banged cabinet doors on a mission for dishes. The pair bumped into each other several times in their effort to ready the table for a guest.

Finally the males took their seats, Bryce to her left and his father across from her. As they ate, Addie couldn't resist stealing glances at him from beneath her lashes. With all his physical imperfections, Oren Potter could never be considered a handsome fellow, yet there was something about the way the firelight softened his craggy features that made him compelling to look at. He had a gentle voice, too, and, she'd discovered, a witty humor.

And more patience than she'd ever known a man to have. Even when she'd been on the verge of hysterics the day Linsey had absconded in Robert Jarvis's balloon, he had remained solid and sturdy as the pine tree he'd been named for. She set down her spoon and dabbed at her mouth with the napkin. "I don't think I ever thanked you for bringing Linsey home the other day, Mr. Potter."

"Oren."

She smiled. "Oren."

"It was the least I could do. From what I hear, it's a good thing she weren't anywhere near that contraption when Robert found it."

"She ordered him another balloon from

Philadelphia. Perhaps when it arrives, he'll feel a little more lenient toward her."

"I expect it can't hurt."

But he sounded doubtful. In all honesty, Addie didn't think anything Linsey did from this point forward would make Jarvis forgive her.

"Have you ever been in a balloon, Miss Witt?"

Addie felt color steal into her cheeks at the child's question. "Only for a brief while. I'm afraid I suffer a dreadful fear of heights."

Mr. Potter gasped. "Me too! Can't hardly stand on a ladder without gettin' dizzy."

"Remember when Miz Bender's cat got caught on Mr. Puckett's roof, Pa? And you had to climb up there and get it down for her?"

"I done went and passed out cold. Wound up callin' in the bucket brigade to fetch me down. Took four of 'em to load me in a blanket and lower me to ground."

Unabashed laughter filled the room at the image of the big, burly man being lowered from the roof by a blanket. One story led into another, and soon Addie found herself confessing a few of her own escapades, including the real reason she and Linsey had been caught in the mayor's cellar two years ago.

It surprised her how easy it was to talk to Oren. Here he wasn't the town blacksmith. Here he was a loving father to his child. A man of the house.

A widower.

She became achingly aware of that thought as she studied him over the rim of her water glass. She tried to remember when she'd ever felt this comfortable in Daniel's company, and couldn't. Around him, she felt as if she were standing before a giant. Though Oren topped him in height by at least a head, and his build was much more bulky, he seemed much more approachable.

So much more affable.

Infinitely more appealing.

At the traitorous thought, Addie set down her glass harder than she intended. She loved Daniel. She had loved him for as long as she could remember. How could she be so aware of another man?

Realizing Bryce and Mr. Potter were looking at her curiously, Addie cleared her throat. "Gentlemen, the evening has been a pleasure, but I'm afraid I must be getting home." The rain had stopped some time in the last hour, and the winds had settled down. It was almost a shame that the storm passed.

Oren nodded. "Yes, ma'am, I reckon it has." He scooted back in his chair. "Bryce, you best get on to bed."

"Aw, Paaa."

"Go on now, son, you've got school in the mornin'. I'll be up there in a bit to turn down the lamp."

"Yessir." The towheaded boy's head hung in clear disappointment as he dragged himself out of the chair. "Good night, Miss Witt."

"Good night, Bryce."

After Bryce disappeared into the loft, an acute silence descended on the room.

Mr. Potter slipped her wrap off its hook and

held it out for her. Addie thanked him with a wobbly smile, took her woolen cloak, and draped it over her arm, feeling suddenly too heated to wear the heavy garment.

In companionable silence, they left the private living quarters and strode through the blacksmith shop, where the scent of his work lingered in the air—fire, coals, leather, and iron. Horses whinnied at their passing, and now and then one of the animals would poke its head out to receive an affectionate pat.

Addie had to smile. He always had a kind word or a gentle touch for those in his care. "It's easy to see how much you love this place," she observed aloud.

"Yes, ma'am, I surely do."

"And Bryce, too."

"He's a good boy. I wish I had a dozen more just like him."

"You do? I mean, that's a coincidence, as I always wanted a dozen children, too."

"I lost my first wife in childbirth. My second wife, Bryce's mother, passed on from the cholera. And Maggie, my third wife . . . well, you might as well know, she was leaving me."

They'd reached the doors and Addie paused, feeling a dart of rivalry at the mention of the women he'd had in his life. "I'm not sure you should be telling me your personal business."

He stopped, looked at her, then bowed his head. "You're right. A lady like you wouldn't be interested in hearing about my past."

"It's not that," she hastened to clarify. "I just thought . . . it might be too painful."

"Painful?" He inhaled a deep breath, then searched the smithy as if looking for words. "I wouldn't exactly call it that. I needed a mother for Bryce, so I put an ad in the paper for a bride. Maggie answered it. Texas was nothing like she was used to: too hot, too dirty, too uncivilized. One day, she packed her bags and said she was going back to New York. I wouldn't let her go, so she stole away in the middle of the night." His gazed dropped as well as his voice. "Her train wrecked a few miles this side of Memphis."

Addie's heart went out to him, and it was all she could do not to step closer, to hold him. "Was that the night you made such a shambles of the saloon?"

He nodded.

"I never knew. The only thing I'd ever heard was that she was visiting family back East."

"What man wants the world to know his wife was leaving him?" he remarked softly. "Miss Witt, I'd be lying if I said my marriage to Maggie was a love match. It was just a necessity—but I was fond of her. And I wonder lots of times if I'd just let her go when she asked, then maybe she'd have taken a different train and might still be alive today."

She knew the guilt he must feel. She often wondered if she hadn't been cold the night her pa went out to the woodpile, if he wouldn't still be alive today. "My aunt always says we cannot hold ourselves responsible for other people's choices, but sometimes what we know in our heads isn't always what we feel in our hearts."

"Amen to that." He breathed with a curious force, and giving Addie a crooked grin that made her heart skip a beat, he pushed open the door. As they walked out, they encountered a massive puddle at the threshold. Mr. Potter straddled it the best he could, but even his wide-legged stance didn't extend from one side to the other. One foot wound up buried up to the ankle in muck. Not a word of complaint left his mouth, though. Instead he reached for Addie.

She paused for several long, wary seconds. Intuition told her that if this man touched her, nothing would be the same again.

Then she chided herself for the foolish thought. What could be the danger? Mr. Potter was as sweet and gentle a man as they came.

But there was nothing sweet or gentle about the jolt of awareness she felt the instant his hands fit around her waist, and hers came to rest on his powerful shoulders.

Addie's mind swam as he swung her clear of the puddle and set her on dry ground, her knees as weak as melted butter. She stared up at him, astonished by her reaction. She couldn't see his features clearly in the misty darkness, but the longer they stood there, the hotter she felt his gaze grow.

A knot of longing unraveled deep in her belly.

She knew she should release her hold on him. Knew the sensations Oren Potter awakened in her defied every virtue she believed a woman of her position should hold. Yet as his head inched forward, paused, then inched forward again, Addie wanted nothing more than to be kissed utterly, completely insensible by this man.

Just as she thought her wish would be granted, he drew back and said, "You best run along home, Miss Addie, before I forget I'm a gentleman and that you're a lady."

Addie's gaze snapped to his tight features. He didn't want her. She'd thought . . . she'd hoped . . .

With a tiny cry of mortification, she picked up her skirts and fled.

She couldn't recall the trip home, but when she arrived, all the windows were dark save the one in Linsey's room.

She removed her cloak and hung it on the coatrack. Burning with embarrassment, she hurried up the stairs and down the hall, wanting only to nurse her emotions in private.

But as she passed Linsey's room, the door flew open. "Where have you been?" her sister demanded.

Addie came to a guilt-stricken stop. "I—I've been tutoring Bryce Potter."

"At this hour? You missed the entire engagement party!"

"I know. Time simply got away from us. Then the storm hit. . . . " Addie shook away the memory of her wanton behavior. "How was the party?"

"I'll tell you later. Right now, we've got to get down to business."

Business? Addie wondered as Linsey seized her hand and pulled her into the bedroom.

What kind of business did one conduct at this hour?

Once on the bed, Linsey held out a worn, leather-bound book Addie had seen a hundred times in the parlor. "Do you know what this is?"

"Aunt Louisa's special collection of love charms and divinations."

"Exactly. I was talking to Aunt Louisa earlier, and she said something very interesting. She said that in order to get you and Daniel married, we must first find out if he is your destiny."

Addie's hand shot to her mouth. Daniel! Oh, heavens, she'd forgotten all about him! How could have yearned for the kiss of another, when she'd always believed Daniel was the only man for her? How could she have completely neglected her self-made commitment to marry him? "Yes, yes. What do we do?"

Linsey must have gone through the book already, for several places were marked by bits of ribbon. Linsey opened to one of the sections, then twisted around and reached for a strand of beads on the bedside table, where a lamp shed a mellow pool of light onto the floor.

"It says to toss this over your shoulder. When the beads hit the floor, they should land in the shape of the first letter of your true love's name."

Addie took the set of blue beads from Linsey and clutched them tightly in her hand. She closed her eyes, willed the Fates to be kind, and tossed the beads over her left shoulder.

They landed on the floor with a pinging clatter.

Addie spun around. She stared in shock. "It's an O," she gasped.

"No it's not, it's a D!" Linsey contended. "See the straight edge along the side?"

Addie didn't see any such thing. All she saw was the craggy face of a man standing before her in a leather apron, trousers and gloves, his bare shoulders glistening with sweat, his dark blue eyes watching her with a predator's intent.

She blinked away Oren's sudden appearance in her mind and stared hard at the beads, willing herself to see what Linsey saw. She wanted to believe, but the evidence was right there: save for a slight indentation near the upper left side, the beads had made a near perfect shape of an O.

For Oren?

But he couldn't be the man she would marry! She loved Daniel. She wanted to be *his* wife!

Didn't she?

Feeling weary and slightly faint, Addie rubbed her brow where a knotting headache was beginning to form between her eyes. "Linsey, I'm going to bed."

"You can't go to sleep yet; we've got to burn our hair."

"Burn our hair?"

"Yes, and we don't have much time."

Linsey grabbed her hand and led her to the small fireplace. A candle had been set upon a blanket, along with long matches, two small squares of linen, and several leaves Addie didn't recognize.

"It's pointless for me to do this, but the book calls for two girls and I don't want to take any chances that it won't work for you."

Once they'd seated themselves on the blanket across from each other, Addie asked, "What now?"

"We wait for the clock to strike midnight. As soon as the last chime sounds, we must in complete silence pluck twenty hairs from our head, one for each year of our age, then wrap them in the cloths with the true-love leaves. When the clock strikes one, we burn each hair separately and say, 'I offer this, my sacrifice, to him most precious in my eyes. I charge thee now come forth to me, that this minute I may see.' And you'll see an image of the man you will marry walking about the room."

"That's silly."

Linsey glanced at her in surprise. "What's gotten into you, sister?"

"What do you mean?"

"You've never called the divinations silly before."

How did Addie put into words the questions she'd harbored over the years?

"Burning hairs, reciting verses . . . how can that foretell who a girl will wed?"

"I don't know, it just does."

"But . . . haven't you ever wondered if things happen because we want them to happen and not because they are meant to happen?"

"Why would I wonder that?"

Addie's sigh of defeat made the candle flame dance. "All right, let's see what the Fates have in store for us."

~~Chapter 13~~
Chapter 14

If you find a horseshoe, pick it up
and all day long you'll have good luck.

Linsey sat cross-legged on the blanket spread on the floor, watching Addie with mounting concern as she settled opposite her. Was it her imagination or was her sister acting strange tonight?

No, it wasn't her imagination, she decided. Addie seemed . . . distant somehow. Distracted.

Oh, Lordy—Addie hadn't somehow learned of her indiscretion, had she? Linsey didn't know how she could have—unless Daniel had said something to one of his friends, and they in turn mentioned it to someone else until it finally got around to Addie. But why would he boast of a kiss that he regretted as much as she did?

Maybe she should just confess to Addie, get it out in the open, and rid herself of this guilt. Once, when they were thirteen, she had borrowed Addie's favorite silk reticule and accidently dropped it in a bucket of axle grease. Linsey had kept it secret for weeks before finally confessing, only to find out that Addie had known all along.

She had forgiven Linsey, of course, and seemed satisfied with the new purse Linsey had bought to replace the old one.

But borrowing a purse and stealing a kiss were not the same thing at all, nor could the hurt she'd inflict on Addie be repaired by money.

The clock began to toll the midnight hour, giving Linsey a welcome reprieve. Later, she promised herself. She'd tell Addie later—when she had more courage. For now, the task before them needed all her concentration.

The divination called for complete silence, and she and Addie followed the edict as they plucked twenty hairs from their head, one at a time, then wrapped them in the cloth with Aunt Louisa's precious store of true-love leaves.

When the clock struck one, they fed each hair separately into the candle flame and recited, "I offer this, my sacrifice . . . "

Then, with the rank odor of singed hair filling their nostrils, they waited.

Thunder rumbled in the distance. Rain poured down outside. The heat of the fire grazed Linsey's cheeks like a lover's kiss. She steeled herself against the disturbing sensation, and focused on keeping the mystical passages open so that Addie could see her destiny.

And then, oddly enough, a hazy image began to form in the periphery of Linsey's mind. Her brow crimped in a puzzled frown. Surely she couldn't be seeing the face of her own husband; she wouldn't be around long enough to find the man, much less marry him. So what in the name of Gus could it be?

The shape moved around the room, touching the lucky tokens on her dresser, studying the picture of her parents.

"Do you see him, Addie?"

"Yes," she whispered with a breathless catch in her voice.

Who do you see? Linsey wanted to ask. She couldn't, of course. Proper carrying out of the divination forbade Addie from saying the man's name. But it didn't stop Linsey from wondering.

And it didn't stop her from puzzling over the appearance of a man in her future, either.

Finally the form leaned against the bedpost, arms crossed in a pose that started a curl of uneasiness in Linsey's middle.

Then he started coming into focus. Dark hair. Big shoulders. A chill broke out over Linsey's arms. The features became more distinct. Dark brows. Straight nose. Full lips.

A pair of dimples.

Her eyes snapped open. It couldn't possibly be . . . she couldn't have just seen . . . Daniel?

No, she denied with a sharp shake of her head. There must be some mistake. It just wasn't possible that she and Daniel were meant to be together, that *he* was destined to be her husband. Aside from all the presaged reasons, they barely tolerated each other!

And yet, there he had stood in all his brooding allure, looking real enough to touch.

She glanced at Addie, whose eyes remained shut. Twin patches of pink-colored cheeks. Tangled strands of damp blond hair framed her face. Slowly, her lashes lifted, and in her eyes, Linsey glimpsed bittersweet yearning. Had she seen Daniel, too? How could they both have seen him?

"Let's do one more," she told Addie.

With a discouraged slump of her shoulders and a lackluster sigh, Addie started to rock herself off the blanket. "Linsey, I feel like I've been wrung out to dry. Can't we do it another night?"

Addie did look weary, and she did have school in the morning, yet Linsey knew she'd not rest a wink if she didn't prove to herself that the vision had been a quirk of circumstance. "One more—it will only take a minute." Linsey flipped through the book, searching for another divination. "Here, then let's do this one. 'Point your shoes toward the street, tie your garters around your feet, pin your stockings under your head, and you'll dream of the one you're going to wed.' " Linsey shut the book with a determined snap. Yes, one more. By morning, she would know without a shadow of a doubt that she was matching her sister up with the right man.

Linsey dreamed of Daniel that night.

It started out innocently enough. She was

a child, perhaps eleven or so, sitting beside Addie at the brand-new ice-cream counter in Doc Sr.'s apothecary. Mrs. Sharpe stood behind the counter, her raven hair pulled back in a haphazard bun. The apron covering her ample figure bore the stains of her efforts as she mixed up yet another tub of ice cream.

Linsey was waiting with eager anticipation for the next batch, wondering how chocolate could possibly taste better than vanilla, when Daniel walked in, home on holiday. Even at eighteen he'd been handsome enough to throw a girl's senses off balance, as Addie proved when she swooned face-first into her bowl.

The years rolled forward to the Christmas of '75. Daniel returning from Louisiana for his mother's funeral, looking so lost and empty that it hurt to see him.

Then 1880, the day he'd held his precious letter in his hands. Linsey tossed and turned, trying to escape the contempt in his eyes.

The color blue drifted across the picture—a pure, vivid shade of joy and freedom. She lay still, tranquillity claiming her, echoes of laughter making her feel light as a cloud. And Daniel's smile, with that flashing dimple, made her heartbeat quicken and her breath come in shallow gasps of wonder. Even his eyes no longer held bitter emotion, but something hotter. More elemental.

Need.

Raw, dark, dangerous need. Growing wilder and more powerful as he held her.

The image switched abruptly, replaced

with wind-brushed fields of clover—the symbol of a long and prosperous relationship. Amidst the fragile foliage stood Daniel in a black Sunday-go-to-meeting suit, beside him a lady in a flowing blue gown trimmed in lace and pearls . . .

A wedding.

His wedding.

Linsey's mouth curved in a bittersweet smile. Her wish, coming true. Daniel and Addie, together at last. Happiness claimed her, balmy and poignant—

Until he lifted his bride's veil and the face beneath belonged not to her sister, but to herself.

Linsey jerked awake. She snapped upright, swung her legs over the side of the bed, and pressed a trembling hand to her brow. Beneath her bed she spotted her kid slippers, set in the manner specified the night before.

What in the name of Gus was happening? This made it twice she'd seen Daniel in one form or another, and it was beginning to alarm her. She had no right dreaming of him, no right wanting him. Daniel belonged to Addie—not to a woman with one foot in the grave.

There had to be an explanation.

Linsey tossed her hair out of her eyes. It was all the time she'd spent with him—that had to be why she kept conjuring him. That and the thoughts of weddings—both Noah and Jenny's upcoming one, and the one she was trying to finagle for Daniel and Addie. But they were no closer to getting married than they'd been a month ago, and at the rate it was progressing, she'd be dead and buried before the two exchanged a word.

The time had come for drastic action.

Oren ran a finger along the paper collar that seemed to get tighter around his neck with each passing minute he stood on the schoolhouse stoop.

He felt like a durn-blamed fool. He was thirty-four years old, standin' outside in the pourin' down rain, goin' a courtin' to a woman young enough to be his daughter. Okay, maybe that was stretching it. His sister, then.

But fourteen years. He'd been married and widowed three times in those years. He'd married the first time out of youth, the second time from loneliness, the third time out of necessity. He knew the routine. Court 'em, kiss, wed 'em, bed 'em. He was getting to be an old hand at this.

Except this time he felt green as a new shoot. This time, he'd fallen in love.

He hadn't thought it possible. He'd about given up ever findin' the woman he wanted to grow old with. Who woulda thought she'd be right under his nose?

Now he could only hope she'd taken a shine to him, too.

Oren pulled out the posy from under his coat, where he'd tried to keep it safe and dry. Since it was almost winter all he'd been able to find were a handful of asters, and even they were looking pretty pitiful. But it was the best he could do.

Would his best be enough?

"Miss Addie," he practiced. "I know I ain't much to look at, and we ain't known each other but a couple years or so, and I can't be sure of your feelin's, but I'd be right proud if you'd take me . . . " Ah Jeez, he couldn't say that. She might think he meant *take* him. Not that the idea hadn't crossed his mind every second of every day for the last month, but a fella just didn't blurt something like that out to a lady. Whispered it in the dark maybe, but didn't blurt it out in broad daylight.

He took a deep breath, gathered his thoughts, and tried again. "Miss Addie, I'd be plum tickled if you'd step over the broomstick with me."

The schoolhouse door swung open, and Oren jumped back just in time to miss getting skewered by an umbrella.

"Mr. Potter!"

Oren stiffened in alarm. She hadn't heard him, had she? He hoped to God not. What a knucklehead she'd think him.

"How long have you been out here?" she asked, lowering the umbrella.

Long enough to get cold feet.

"Did I miss a lesson with Bryce today?"

"No." His voice came out in a croak. He cleared his throat and repeated himself. "No, ma'am, no lesson."

"Then what are you doing out in this weather? You'll catch your death."

"I—I . . . " *Hell, Potter, stop bein' such a yellowbelly—just ask her! Say the words, "Miss Addie, would you step out with me tonight?"*

Yet hard as he tried, they stuck in his throat.

So they just stood there, she in the doorway looking as pretty as a summer daffodil and him on the stoop, staring like a drowned half-wit, trying to think up a sound reason for standing out in the pouring rain.

Then the chance went to seed all together as his son came bursting through the school-yard gate, hollering,"Pa! Pa, come quick! Your mare is foaling!"

Oh, hell! "Beggin', your pardon, Miss Adelaide." Oren went to tip his hat, forgetting that he held the durned thing in his hand, and poked himself in the eye. Blushing to the roots of his hair, he turned on his heel and fled down the lane after his boy.

As Addie watched them, she couldn't help the twinge of disappointment. The last person she'd expected to find on her doorstep was Bryce's father—the man who, according to the divinations, would be her husband.

She didn't dare tell Linsey that she'd dreamed of Oren Potter, or that she had seen him walking about the bedroom last night. Linsey was so determined to see her wed Daniel, that she'd likely die right then and there if she thought her plans weren't coming to fruition.

Besides, marrying Daniel was what Addie had always wanted—to become his wife. So why were the divinations pointing to Oren? Why was it *him* stirring up all these feelings inside her instead of Daniel? And why, with each thought of Oren, did it feel as if she were betraying Daniel, even though he'd never indicated he returned her affections? And where did that leave her promise to help Linsey accomplish her list of last wishes? Addie pressed a hand to her brow. Oh, heavens, she'd never been so confused.

A spot of color on the stoop caught her notice. She bent down and plucked up the sodden posie of flowers, tenderly touching the wilted petals and smoothing the crushed stems. It was a miserable offering as far as flowers went, but she'd never seen anything so beautiful in her life.

Her gaze returned to the man and boy dodging people and wagons in their path. What compelled her to follow, she couldn't say; she simply picked up her skirts and went after them. By the time she arrived at the smithy, she was soaked to the skin.

She found Oren in one of the middle stalls, kneeling beside a cream-colored mare lying on its side, its stomach bulging from the life it nurtured within. "Is this the expectant mother?"

The look of surprise and pleasure on his craggy face made her heart leap.

"Yes, ma'am."

That said, Addie didn't know what to do. So she stood there, clutching the folds of her wet skirt in her hand, chiding herself. It wasn't like her to make impetuous decisions, and now that she'd done so, she was at a loss as to how to get out of it with some shred of dignity.

Then Bryce walked into the stall, a pile of coarse blankets draped over his shoulder. "Why, hello, Miss Addie. Have you come to help, too?"

Oh, dear. Help? What did she know about horses? What did she know about anything? "I'm afraid I'd just get in the way."

"You'd never be in the way, Adelaide," Oren told her. "If you want to stay, just pull up a blanket."

They were the sweetest words Addie had ever heard.

And then it didn't matter what she knew or didn't know about horses, or what she did or didn't know about anything. The only thing that mattered was that this big and gentle man and his brilliant, charming son wanted her with them. Her. A plain, prim, faint-hearted, unwanted corn farmer's daughter. She knelt between them on the bed of straw, looked into Oren's fathomless blue eyes, and asked, "What can I do to help?"

"Caroline, you must take every precaution against having more children," Daniel told the woman as he drew the sheet over her scarred stomach. "I can't stress enough how risky this delivery was."

"Louisa Gordon says that children of cesarean birth are supposed to be of unusual body strength and have the power to find hidden treasure."

"She is a strong little girl," he conceded, "but take my advice: if you want to be around to see her grow up, do *not* conceive again."

"Am I to ban Axel from my bed, then?" Caroline asked, tucking the baby close. "Would you like it if your wife denied you your husbandly rights?"

A flashing thought of Linsey crossed his mind. Daniel banished it instantly.

"No, ma'am, but if her health were at risk, I would do whatever was necessary. There are other means of protection that I'll discuss with Axel. The only thing I want you to concern yourself with is rest."

Daniel shut his leather bag, and with the brim of his hat pulled down low, braved the downpour. He'd be glad to see sunshine again. It had been raining for two days—a steady, gray rain that created rivers of red mud through the streets of Horseshoe. The buildings across the way looked like sad old men, an apt reflection of Daniel's mood.

He couldn't place the source of his glumness. Over the last couple of days, business at the pharmacy had been brisk, he'd seen enough patients to choke a horse, and he'd been able to review several clinical dissertations. He'd even managed to douse a few arguments with his father and avert any further disastrous encounters with Linsey. He should be thankful for small favors.

Instead, an unidentifiable restlessness plagued him: an impulse to shuck his duties for the rest of the day and run barefoot through the grass. To watch the clouds drift across the sky. To do something other than drive himself into the ground for a goal that seemed constantly out of his reach.

He couldn't, of course, and he didn't understand this sudden urge to want to. This craving to experience laughter, to experience life, to experience Linsey—

With a curse, Daniel urged the horse faster. He'd told himself he wouldn't think of her anymore. Wouldn't start wishing again for pleasures he'd long ago forbidden himself until he reclaimed the dream that was lost to him long ago.

When he reached town, he handed the reins of his horse to a stableboy and started for the shop. Mud caked his boots and pant legs, making them stick to his skin, and his shirt stuck to his back despite the overcoat and hat he wore. Swift, purposeful steps took him down the boardwalk toward the apothecary, where he anticipated a bath, a hot meal, and twelve hours uninterrupted sleep—in that order.

Just as he passed the Herald the door opened, and the unexpected appearance of Linsey stepping out of the office brought Daniel to a quick stop. This was the first time he'd seen her since the birth of Caroline's baby, and a shaft of desire sped straight to his loins.

The air all but crackled between them. He wondered if she ever thought about the kiss they'd shared. He wouldn't blame her if she hated him. In fact, he was surprised she hadn't slapped him senseless for taking advantage of her during a moment of vulnerability. He'd been little better than Bishop Harvey.

She didn't look angry, though. She looked ravishing. Refreshing. Utterly and too damned desirable, standing there with her face flushed and her breasts rising and falling with each rapid breath she took.

He yanked on the reins of that runaway thought, schooled his features to keep them from showing on his face, and nodded once. "Linsey."

"Daniel."

His name on her lips caressed him like the dawning of a summer day, soft, breezy, breathless.

"What are you doing out in this weather?" she asked.

He shifted his weight from one leg to another. "Seeing patients. And you?"

Her face jerked toward the letters painted on the window, then to the strap of the reticule around her wrist. "Just tending a bit of business," she replied with a wobbly smile. "You take care in this rain, now. It wouldn't do for you to catch a chill."

Without further ado, she hastened past him and down the lane. His gaze followed her, baited by the enticing sway of hips, the bob of a bustle, the rustle of skirts. She really had grown up to become a comely woman.

But more, she had a rare knack of making the dreariness of the day brighten, the cloudiness inside him lift.

He thought of the patients he'd seen over the last few days and how useful it would have been to have her assisting him. He bet she would have been able to calm the Neelys' fretful child and soothe the widow's grief. Hell, she could probably charm the birds from the trees if she put her mind to it.

The idea of keeping her around held a dangerously seductive appeal. He imagined her gracing him with a proud smile when he mastered a difficult operation or pressing a consoling hand to his arm when circumstances looked grim. And at the end of the day, after the sun went down and the night beckoned, they'd come together in wild abandon and soar to heights beyond those of any mortal.

Would that kind of life be such a trial? Would it bring as much misery as his dad claimed?

He frowned with sudden curiosity when she stopped, stepped off the curb, and picked something up off the ground.

She'd done this before, he remembered, and like the last time, he expected her to tuck the object in her pocket.

Instead, she held it up and closed her eyes. Then she . . . *spat* on it? Daniel shook his head and felt a rusty chuckle rise in his throat. Just as he started to turn away, he felt a stinging whack to the side of his forehead.

"What the . . . ?" His hand shot to the spot and came away smeared with blood. He spun around. Linsey had continued her stroll in blissful ignorance. And at Daniel's feet lay a discarded horseshoe.

Hell, leave it to Linsey to knock some sense back into him.

Chapter 15

Never clip your fingernails on a Friday or Sunday.

Daniel set the small pair of scissors on the bureau top, then brushed the crescent-shaped clippings into the wicker trash basket. Amazing what a bath, a clean set of clothes, and a good night's sleep did for a man's mood. Now all he needed was a few of the eggs he smelled his dad frying below. Of course, the old coot had probably eaten them all just to spite Daniel, but a fellow could always hope.

Mindful of the three stitches above his left eyebrow, Daniel ran a comb through his damp hair, grabbed his hat, and strode downstairs.

Even the weather seemed benevolent. The storms of the last couple of days had swept through, leaving the sky a pale, dusky blue, like it had been the day he and Linsey had gotten trapped together in the balloon.

The memory made him grin. That day really had been the most fun he'd ever had, though he couldn't admit it to anyone.

Especially not the man sitting at the kitchen table, wearing black trousers, white shirt sleeves and suspenders, and drinking coffee from a huge black beer stein. Surprisingly, several overeasy eggs had been left on the plate in the middle of the table.

Daniel slid into his chair and grabbed the plate, his mind still on Linsey. "Dad, do you believe in luck?" he asked at length, sliding a forkful of eggs into his mouth.

Daniel, Sr., glanced up from his plate. "What kind of question is that?"

"Do you?"

" 'Course not," he groused. "There's no such thing. A man carves his own way in the world by the sweat of his brow and the blood in his veins. Luck doesn't have anything to do with it." He drained his mug, got to his feet, and slipped his coat off the back of the chair. "You planning on getting those orders written up or are you going to laze around here all day?"

He was tempted to say yes. Tempted even more to tell his dad that it *he* might try doing the same thing. That maybe, if Daniel, Sr., stopped to smell the lavender once in a while, he might actually find something to smile about instead of being in such a goddamn grumpy mood all the time.

Ah, hell, Daniel thought, brooding into his coffee cup after his dad left. If that wasn't hypocritical, he didn't know what was. Over the years he'd become a mirror image of the old man, with all of his faults and none of his merits. He sure hadn't found anything to smile about until a reckless redhead careened back into his life. It didn't make sense that a woman who had brought nothing but grief down upon his head could be the same one who showed him that enjoying himself didn't necessarily mean he had to give up his dreams.

So why was he having such a hard time accepting a simple apology from her? She'd forgiven him without hesitation for sending her off with Bishop Harvey. Was he overreacting? Had the stage accident been just that—an accident?

Maybe it was time he stopped being so hard on Linsey, he thought, picking up the untouched newspaper folded in the middle of the table. If he was overreacting, if it really had been an accident as she claimed, then the least he could do was stop using his anger over that day as a weapon. He knew what that felt like. He'd experienced the sting of someone's disapproval too often in his life, and he hated it.

Strangely, the decision made Daniel feel quite pleased with himself. With a loud, relaxed sigh and a cup of coffee in his hand, he leaned back in his chair and snapped open the paper to the front page. He read with interest the article reporting that the notorious outlaw Frank James had turned himself over to the law, skimmed over an accounting of Judith Harvey's quilting bee last weekend, and was just about to turn the page when his name jumped out of the headline on a sidebar column:

WEDDING BELLS FOR SHARPE, WITT?

Coffee spewed from his mouth, spattering

everywhere. *What the . . . ?* Daniel blotted at his shirt as he scanned the article. "In many parts of Texas there's a nip of winter in the air, but in our own beloved community, romance seems to be blossoming between the younger Dr. Sharpe and our own schoolmarm, Adelaide Witt."

Flabbergasted, he scoured the rest of the article. It read more like a pedigree than report, citing all of Daniel's accomplishments, Addie's talents, and both their contributions to the community, ending with, "Don't be surprised to see these two handfasted by the end of the year."

For chrissake, where did the *Herald* get such a ridiculous story? He and Adelaide Witt? Married? He'd barely looked sideways at her all the years he'd known her—why the hell would anyone think he was planning to marry her?

A sudden flash of three women and a supper conversation sparked in his mind. Was one of the Gordon women behind this? He dismissed Louisa immediately. She'd never struck him as the manipulating type, and she'd said herself that the choice of mates had been left up to her nieces.

Addie? He couldn't imagine that. The woman was afraid of her own shadow.

So that left . . . Linsey.

Daniel slapped the paper onto the table. He should have known better than to let his guard down with that woman.

Oren's mare gave birth just after daybreak. The foal lay in a bed of straw, covered from head to hoof in a disgusting film, and disturbingly still.

"Is it alive?" Bryce asked in a hushed voice.

Oren cleared the mucus from the foal's muzzle, then breathed into its nose and mouth.

Spellbound, hands together in prayer, Addie watched through misty eyes as the huge man blew life into the foal while its mother prodded it with her fuzzy nose. The incongruous sight touched her beyond words. "Come on, little one," she whispered. The mare had labored all night to bring the colt into the world, and it seemed unfair that all her pain and effort could be for naught.

At last, a slight jerk of a hoof made her breath catch in hope. Then, with a visible rise of its chest, the little one raised its head. The mare whinnied to her baby and licked it with her coarse tongue.

Oren backed away, and while the mare tended her young, he plunged his hands into the bucket of water and washed his face. The beaming smile he wore was identical to the one on his son's face.

"You did it, Oren!" Addie exclaimed.

Bryce let out a loud whoop.

Jumping up and down, Addie hugged the child, then turned to Oren, cupped his face, and kissed him full on the mouth. The instant their lips met, it hit her what she'd done.

She froze.

Oren stilled.

Wide eyed, she stared into startled blue eyes. "Oh, my!"

His gaze darkened. "My words exactly."

She should move away. It would be the proper thing to do. The wise thing to do.

But at the moment, Addie wasn't feeling very proper or very wise. Her pulses raced. Her nerves sizzled. Her blood hummed like the strains of a violin, and Oren was the only man who could play the tune. He smelled of horse and birth and rumpled hay, but Addie didn't care. The intoxicating combination had her feeling as if she'd imbibed too much wine.

Oren's face tilted and his mouth came closer. She lifted her chin to receive the kiss. The hands cupping his cheeks moved around the thick cords of his neck to lock behind his nape. He tasted of salt and spice and man, and she opened her mouth, hungry for more. She moaned when his tongue slid between her lips. A delicious ache uncoiled in her belly and spread to her breasts, making them heavy and sensitive and eager for the feel of him.

With a boldness she hadn't thought herself capable of, Addie pushed herself against him until his heart and hers pounded against one another. His powerful arms wrapped around her back. His tongue twined around hers, coaxing, exploring, enticing Addie into wanting to touch every part of this man—and have him touch every part of her.

He must have sensed her yearning, for he pulled back, his incredible blue eyes dark with desire. "Addie . . . " he breathed.

"Oren . . . " she whimpered.

"Pa?"

They released each other so fast that Addie

fell back onto a mound of straw. Oren reached for her instantly and helped her to her feet. She looked so dad-blamed adorable, standing there trying to pluck straw from her mussed hair, her cheeks bright pink, her green-gold eyes alight with need. He'd never wanted a woman as badly as he did this one.

The time had come for a chat with the boy.

And much to his regret, it should be now. "Let's get this mare some oats, son."

They left Addie in the stall, giving her privacy to do whatever it was that women did after they'd just kissed a man dumb.

Bryce was quiet for a while until they reached the end of the shop where Oren kept the feed stored. Then he asked, "Are you sweet on her?"

Oren shoved the bucket into the bin of flakes. "Reckon I am."

"Is she going to be my new mother?"

"I've been thinkin' about it."

"I've been thinking about it, too."

Oren looked down upon his son's bent head. He'd been thinkin' about having a mother? About having the schoolmarm for a mother? "And?"

"She smells nice."

"Yep, she surely does."

"She has a real pretty smile, too."

"She does, at that."

"And she reads like an angel."

"Couldn't agree with you more."

"I think we should keep her."

Oren couldn't stop the silly grin from spreading across his face. "Take these oats to the mare while I finish washin' up. Then we'll see how Miss Addie feels about being kept."

With a toothy grin, Bryce grabbed the bucket and scampered back to the stall.

His spirits soaring higher than Jarvis's balloon, Oren stripped off his shirt and scrubbed himself from neck to waist with lye soap and rainwater, whistling a merry tune. The thought of Addie someday scrubbing him down like Maggie used to had him grinning like a mule eatin' cactus. Except he'd bet bathin' with Addie would be as wild an adventure as breakin' a mustang. Glory be, that gal had a way of making his blood run hot.

A whack against the shop made him glance toward the open doors. Lying in a wedge of morning sunlight was the weekly newspaper.

Oren flipped a clean shirt over his damp torso, picked up the paper, and snapped it open.

His gaze stopped on a pair of names in small but bold print.

His whistling ceased, and it felt as if someone had shoved a hot poker through his heart.

Adelaide? His sweet Adelaide was marrying Doc Jr.?

The rustle of footsteps drew his deadened gaze to the woman who only moments ago had been crushed against him, pulling at his hair, making his heart thump like a stallion's hooves and his body go hard.

"The mare is nursing!" she cried. "I declare, that is the most amazing thing I've ever seen in my—Oren? What is it?"

He shook his head numbly. "I thought . . . there was something between us, Adelaide."

Pink color rose in her cheeks. "Well, yes, I suppose there is."

"Then why are you marryin' Daniel?"

Her face went as pale as day-old milk. "Where did you hear that?"

"It's in the paper." He held the *Herald* open to her view.

"Oren . . . it isn't what it seems."

"Then what is it?"

"I can't tell you," she whispered.

He let his arm fall to his side. "Do you love him?"

"Once . . . maybe . . . " Her expression crumbled. "I don't know . . . "

Oren steeled himself against pulling her into his arms. He wanted answers, even if he had to drag them out of her. "Has he already asked you to be his wife?"

"Not exactly."

"You don't know if you love him, and he hasn't exactly proposed. Are you . . . have you and he . . . " He could hardly think it, much less say it.

"Oh my stars, no! How can you suggest such a thing?"

"What else am I supposed to think?" he cried. "You kiss me like there's no tomorra; then I find out you're fixin' to marry another fella, and the explanation I get is a bunch of hemmin' and hawin'? The least you can do is tell my why!"

"Because I made a promise!"

Oren dragged in a deep breath through his

nostrils and looked at the rafters, shamed to the bone that his eyes were getting damp. Aw, damn. He hadn't expected this. Hadn't expected it at all. He'd gone and fallen for a gal who'd promised herself to another man—worse, a man he'd called friend.

There was only one thing he could do. He turned away from her and, with the words ripping from someplace deep inside, told her, "I made the mistake of not letting go once. I won't make that same mistake again. If Daniel is who you want, I won't stand in your way."

Then he walked out of the shop and headed straight for the Rusty Bucket.

With the paper clenched in a white-knuckled fist, Daniel pounded on the Gordon's door with force enough to make the brass knocker rattle against its plate. God *damn* that girl. All this time he'd thought she was the one who'd set her cap for him. Instead, she'd set her sister's cap for him.

The peep-window slid open a few moments later. "Who on earth is beating down my door?"

"Miss Louisa, it's me, Daniel. I need to speak with your niece."

"Be more specific, Daniel; I've got two of them."

Through gritted teeth, he said, "Linsey."

"She's out back doing the wash."

Long, hard strides brought Daniel around the side of the house to the backyard. Clotheslines had been strung between two posts,

weighed down with frilly things that looked
like kites on parade.

Fighting his way between a wet cotton shift
and a cloying set of pantaloons, Daniel finally
broke free on the other side of the line. His foot
immediately sank into several inches of soggy
ground. The source, he discovered, turned out
to be a ten-gallon washtub overturned on its
side, the sudsy water creating puddles in the
already saturated ground.

Then he heard her.

"Shoo! Shoo! Get out of here, you dirty
scamp!"

Circling the tub, Daniel slogged through the
puddles into the next aisle.

The sight of Linsey stopped him dead in his
tracks. She stood on an upended crate between
a row of whites and one of prints, a wash paddle raised over her head, soaked from head to
heel.

He didn't know which shocked him more:
seeing her hopping in the air, swinging the
wash paddle over her head, or his own reaction
to the temptation before his eyes. Her navy blue
skirt, heavy with water, molded around the
flare of her hips and the enticing curve of her
rear, and her paisley blouse stuck to her like
skin, outlining the upper slopes and under-
swells of her breasts with a detail that made
Daniel's mouth go dry. He'd felt those breasts
crushed against him, knew their fullness. Had
been haunted by dreams of touching the
creamy texture and tasting the heated sweet-
ness that belonged to Linsey and Linsey alone.

"Don't you dare perch on my line, you scallywag," she scolded the unidentifiable intruder. "I don't have enough time left as it is, without you trying to cut it shorter." She took a swing with the paddle.

Jarred from the fantasy, Daniel ducked in time to avoid getting brained, then popped back up. How in blazes could such an innocent temptress be so damned dangerous? "What the Sam Hill are you doing?"

She spun around so fast that she fell off the upturned tub.

Daniel sprang forward, caught her by the waist, and hauled her close—dangerously close—against him.

The feel of her in his arms had an instant impact. The breasts he'd admired were flattened against his chest, searing his skin despite the layers of clothing between them. Her stomach, hips and thighs branded themselves against the length of him, their bodies fitting together as if they had been poured into the same mold.

An image of ripping off her clothes, of feeling nothing between them but skin and sweat, appeared in his mind with stunning clarity. Daniel's heartbeat picked up speed. The hands pressed against her back sizzled. His manhood hardened.

Linsey's hands squeezed his upper arms. She licked her lips, drawing his attention to the moist pink flesh. He could almost feel their softness under his, taste the sweet pad of her tongue, imagine the tiny sigh of surrender.

No—he'd actually heard that.

He dragged his gaze from her mouth to her eyes. He found her staring at him, his own lust reflected in the emerald pools.

"What are you doing to me, Linsey?" he asked in husky voice he hardly recognized as his own.

"Nothing." She shook her head in denial, sending damp tendrils of copper hair brushing against his skin. "I'm not doing anything."

"Yes, you are. You're bewitching me, and I don't like it." Daniel abruptly released his hold on her and stepped back, needing distance between them before he lost all control. She closed her eyes and brought her hands to her flaming cheeks. Any other time, he might have taken arrogant pride in the way he made a woman's knees go weak and her hands tremble and her eyes glaze over with desire.

Now it made him mad as hell.

He unrolled the newspaper clenched in his fist and held it up for her to see. "Explain this."

She gave a shake of her head, as if to clear her thoughts. A glimpse of the *Herald* made her go still. "It's a newspaper."

"I know it's a newspaper. I want to know who printed this hogwash."

"I suppose Frank Mackey did, since he's the edit—"

"No, how did it get in there?"

"Well . . . " She licked her lips. "I don't know all the particulars, but I think he sets blocks with letters in a plate—"

"Don't play games with me, damn it! I know you had something to do with this, so don't deny it. Did you have this announcement printed up in the *Herald*?"

"All right—yes." Linsey's spine straightened and she brought her shoulders back. "I did."

His mouth fell open. Wanting the truth was one thing; hearing it was another. "What the Sam Hill for?"

"It was the only way I could think of to get you to notice Addie."

"Addie? For God's sake, why? What did I ever do to make you hate me so much?"

"Hate you?" she gasped. "I've never hated you!"

The honest-to-God astonishment in her voice made his mind stutter. "Then why are you so hell bent on meddling in my life? Do you get some twisted sort of thrill out of watching me go to ruin?"

"I did this for my sister, Daniel—not out of animosity toward you. In fact, I'm actually doing you a favor—you won't find a more capable wife. I've been hoping you would come to realize that on your own, but when you didn't, I had to do something to make you sit up and take notice."

She'd done that all right. "So you wrote a gossip column for the newspaper?"

"If you had just cooperated and started courting her like you were supposed to, I never would have gone to such public measures."

"Does your sister have any idea what you've done?"

"Not exactly—but once she does, she'll thank me for it."

Daniel let loose a bark of disbelieving laughter.

"She will!" Linsey insisted, planting her hands on her hips. "Addie has loved you since the day you and your father moved to Horseshoe. You've just been too blind to notice."

"She couldn't have been more than a kid," he argued.

"She was ten years old, and in her eyes, you hung the moon and the stars. It almost crushed her when she found out you were marrying another woman."

Part of him felt flattered that he could be the object of someone's affections for that long; another part of him reeled in amazement that he hadn't had a clue.

But it didn't change what she had done. She'd manipulated his life, just as his father had always done, and he'd not stand for it. "Whatever your reasons, I have no feelings for Addie, and no plans to marry—not her; not anyone." He took a menacing step forward. "I'm going to be a surgeon, do you understand that? I'm going to work with the best in the field, and then I'm going to build my own surgical practice. But I won't get any of that accomplished being saddled with a wife and a passel of kids. And if I ever do think about taking a wife, by God's teeth, she will be one of my choosing, not one you've assigned to me. Do you understand me?"

Her eyes flat, her tone flatter, she replied, "Perfectly."

* * *

Addie stumbled for the third time as she raced home, blinded by the tears coursing down her face. She didn't even know why she cried, why she felt this terrible, searing pain in her heart. She kept seeing a craggy face wreathed in agony when he set eyes on the newspaper, kept feeling over and over the sting of him turning his back on her and walking out of her life.

How could it hurt so badly to be rejected by a man she'd scarcely known a month?

It did, though. She'd never felt a pain so fierce, so unbearable as when Oren had walked out of the smithy, wounded and angry.

How could Linsey have done this?

Her soles pounded up the steps of Briar House. Halfway across the veranda, her shoulder knocked against something hard and unyielding. Firm hands gripped her around the arms to keep her steady.

Looking up through blurry eyes, Addie started in surprise at discovering the man she'd once adored. "Daniel!"

"Miss Addie." He let her go and shoved his hands into his pockets.

They stood facing each other, he looking as awkward and uncomfortable as she felt, neither knowing what to say to each other. She wiped at her face with trembling fingers, though he had to have noticed the tears on her cheeks.

"You must have read the paper, too," she finally said, seeing the tight lines around his mouth and the lingering anger in his dark eyes.

"Yes. And I already know that your sister orchestrated the whole thing."

"You do? She did?"

"Yes. As a matter of fact, I was just on my way to find you."

Addie went still. For more years than she could count, she'd heard Daniel say words like those in her dreams. But now that she actually heard him say them . . . where was the funny thrill in her heart? Where was the giddiness?

All of a sudden, pressure built in the back of her nose; she twisted just in time to avoid spraying Daniel with a sneeze.

"Are you all right?"

Addie blushed to her roots. Some things never changed."Fine, fine." Taking a backward step, she plucked a hanky from her sleeve and wiped her nose. "You said you were on your way to find me." It was the most coherent sentence she'd spoken to him in her life. Not one stutter, not one mumble.

"Yes. *Ahem.* Miss Addie, there is no easy way to say this, so I'll just come right out with it—I don't want to marry you."

She stilled. Her mouth fell open in astonishment.

"It isn't you," he hastened to add. "I'm sure you'll make some man a fine wife. That man just won't be me. Even if I had the time . . . well, I just don't feel that way about you."

For a moment, Addie could do little more than stare at him. Amazing. The man she had worshiped for years had just stated that he didn't want her, and she felt . . . nothing. No heartache, no regret, no sorrow. Just . . . nothing.

How could that be, when a short while ago, her world had been shattered by a man she'd known only a fraction of that time?

She walked a few paces away, wrapped her arms around her middle, and tried to make sense of her confusion. "A year ago—a month ago, even—I would have been crushed to hear that."

"And now?"

"Something has changed," she said carefully, as if testing the fit and feel of the syllables. "I've changed." Addie smiled through her tears. A weight had rolled off her shoulders, just by voicing the words that had been lingering in the back of her mind lately, words she hadn't dared voice until now. "I've always been a basket of nerves whenever I get near you. You are too strong, too powerful, too overwhelming. I could never feel like your equal."

As she spoke the words, another realization came. With Oren, she never felt that way. With him, she felt cherished. Desirable. Strong and independent. All the doubts she'd been carrying around about herself didn't exist when she was with him.

But when she'd promised to help Linsey fulfill her last wishes, the last thing she'd expected was to fall in love—with the wrong man.

She had, though. She'd fallen in love with Oren Potter. She'd wasn't sure when it had happened, or how, but she suspected it had been the day he'd stood out on the school-house stoop in the pouring rain with a handful of drowned blossoms.

Her promise to Linsey had never felt like a heavier burden.

"Let me see if I understand this: you don't want to marry me, either?"

She shook her head slowly.

"You didn't have anything to do with article in the *Herald*, or inviting me to supper, or the balloon, or any of the other schemes against me?"

Again she shook her head.

"But if I don't want to be with you, and you don't want to be with me, why is Linsey so hell-bent and determined to see us wed?"

She closed her eyes. Why did he have to ask her the one question she couldn't answer?

"Tell me the truth, Addie—why is Linsey so determined that we marry?"

A door opened, then shut, and suddenly Linsey was there. "Because I'm dying."

Chapter 16

Red hair, whether "ginger," auburn, or copper-hued, is supposed to be a sign of fiery and ungovernable temperament, or of a passionate disposition in love.

The words hit Daniel like a sledgehammer, driving through his middle, stealing his breath. Linsey . . . dying? No, it wasn't possible. Not Linsey. Not this vibrant creature who could brighten a room with just her presence.

His blood turned to ice.

"What the hell do you mean, you're dying?" He searched her face, looking for some clue as to what affliction she might be suffering from. She looked perfectly healthy to him. Still the same glowing ivory complexion, the same glossy red curls, and the same sweet curves and hollows that made a man want nothing more than to tumble her in the grass. "From what?" he managed to ask.

"I don't know exactly. I only know that before year's end, harps will be heralding me to the pearly gates."

272

He looked at Addie, who stood pale and shaken, her head bowed and her hands clasped, offering neither dispute nor explanation.

Jesus.

Daniel's legs folded beneath him. Numbly he sat. The thought of Linsey—reckless, cursed, passionate Linsey—cold in the ground . . . "How long have you known?"

"A month or so. No one knows but me, Addie, and now you."

"You haven't told your aunt?"

"Not yet," she said, settling down beside him, filling his senses with the intoxicating fragrance of lavender and reckless winds. "I'm not sure her heart could take it."

"Did my father make the diagnosis?"

"I never saw your father."

"Then who?" he demanded. "I'll contact your physician and get a full report of your symptoms, take them to my colleagues. Hell, I'll give you an examination myself and compare findings. He could have misdiagnosed you. Even doctors make mistakes."

She hushed him with a hand to his arm. "Daniel, I appreciate your concern, but there is no cure for my condition. I can't even say I've contracted a disease."

"Then how do you know you're dying?" he cried in frustration. And, he admitted, fear.

"I saw my reflection at Bleet Haggar's wake."

For a moment, he simply stared at her. He couldn't have heard right. She was dying because she'd *looked into a mirror*?

He threw back his head and laughed.

He laughed until his ribs hurt and his eyes watered, partly from relief, partly from genuine amusement. Of all her nonsensical claims, this one had to take the prize.

A glance at Linsey caught her staring at him down the slope of her nose, her eyes narrowed. "I fail to see the humor in this, Daniel," she said.

Daniel wiped his eyes; his laughter abated to bone-quivering chuckles. "You had me there for a minute, Linsey, I'll give you that." He shook his head. "Oh, damn. Here I was, thinking you were serious."

Her mutinous expression grew. "Make light of it now, Mr. Skeptical, because you'll be choking on those chuckles when they're shoveling dirt over my coffin by year's end."

The iron-clad ring of certainty in her voice rendered him mute. "You *are* serious!"

"Of course I am. Do you think I'd joke about something like this?"

"For chrissake, Linsey, you don't really believe that looking into a mirror will foretell your death!"

Her refusal to answer spoke for itself.

Events began clicking in his mind: the day she'd run into him at Bleet's wake, the horrified expression on her face; her mysterious and hasty compulsion to marry him off without his consent.

She believed it. She honestly thought she was going to die because of some crazy superstition.

Humor turned to irritation. "Linsey, do you know how absurd that is? People die because they get sick, or because of their own stupidity, or another's carelessness. They don't die just because a hearse crosses their shadow or because birds land on their clothesline or because they look into a mirror."

"My mother did."

The flat sobriety in her voice had a quelling impact. Linsey had never spoken of her mother that he could recall, but with those three little words, he understood how deeply the woman's passing had affected Linsey. He didn't know whether to console her over her loss or shake her for the ludicrous idea that a mirror had somehow caused it.

Before he could do either, Linsey gathered her skirts in her hand and rose with stiff hauteur.

"I understand that you don't put much store in the power of portents," she told him, "but mark my words, Daniel, this will come to pass. By year's end, I will no longer be around to ruin your life. That should make you blissfully happy."

At that, she marched into the house. With commendable loyalty, Addie followed, little more than flash of wrinkled paisley and ruffled hems.

Daniel stared at the closed door long after the echo of its slamming had faded away. The tremor in Linsey's voice, the sheen of tears in her eyes, disturbed him more than he wanted to admit. He'd been trained to ease pain, not cause it. Yet that's exactly what he had done, and to the one person whose laughter and passion and spice of spirit had stirred more life in him in the last month than he'd felt in all his twenty-seven years put together.

He rubbed his brow. Life had been so much simpler before it had been invaded with Linsey's quirky notions and manipulative schemes. He'd never found himself fighting for control. Or resisting the pull of the forbidden. Or treading that thin line between lust and something deeper. . . .

No, his staunch hold on his emotions had only been shaken when one reckless, irrepressible redhead charged into his well-ordered world and waged war.

Happy? Just the thought of anything happening to her made the bottom fall out of his soul.

From the parlor doorway, Addie watched her sister furiously flip through the pages of a *Harper's Weekly*. A hasty swipe of her wrist across her eyes told Addie that her instincts had been right on the mark; Daniel's reaction had injured Linsey deeply. She didn't know who she felt more sorry for: Linsey, Daniel . . . or herself. So many lives were being affected by one woman's misguided determination.

"Linsey?"

She briefly glanced up. "That man makes me so angry sometimes that I want to scream!"

Addie knew the feeling. Linsey made her feel that way sometimes, too.

"Can you believe the nerve of him?" her sister continued. "I trusted him with the most shattering secret of my life, and he laughed—

laughed!—at me." She turned back to the cata-
logue and pitched several more pages over.
"Thank God I'm not the one planning to marry
that insufferable wretch—we wouldn't last
beyond the wedding feast before I had his
head on a platter."

The fiery tone couldn't hide the hurt behind
the heat. It was puzzling. Linsey barely
seemed to tolerate Daniel, yet he was the only
one Addie had ever known who could make
Linsey cry. Could she . . . was it possible that . . . ?
No. Addie dismissed the notion instantly. Linsey couldn't possibly have developed feelings
for Daniel. The two clashed like paisley and
flannel.

Addie perched on the edge of the sofa
beside Linsey, folded her hands in her lap,
and approached her as she would have one of
her students. "I know you meant well when
you had that article put in the paper, but
surely you knew it would upset Daniel when
he saw it."

"Actually, I'd hoped it would give that hard-
headed mule's behind a shove in the right
direction."

"You shouldn't have gone to such extremes."
Such public extremes. Not only one secret had
been revealed today, but two.

"You're right." Linsey agreed without com-
punction. "I should have shoved him in the
horse trough again, instead."

"It wouldn't do any good. He doesn't want
to marry me, Linsey. He doesn't want to marry
anybody—he told me so."

"People often say things they don't mean

when they're angry. Daniel is a bit miffed right now, but he'll come around. Don't give up hope."

Addie felt the tight hold on her composure slip. "I can't give up something I don't have. For heaven's sake, Linsey, love isn't something that can be forced. The heart latches on where it wants to, where it feels safe and secure and loved in return. We have no control over that—sometimes it happens without warning!"

"Exactly! Isn't that what I've been saying all along? Given time, Daniel's heart will latch onto you; then all our wishes will come true."

"Oh, Linsey, why can't you simply accept that I am not meant to be Daniel's wife?"

When Linsey turned her head, Addie found herself pinned with an implacable stare.

"Because I love you, Addie, and because I'll do whatever it takes to make sure you are happy—now and always. And if that means seeing you married to the man of your dreams, then by God, before one grain of Texas soil falls on my casket, I *will* see it done."

Stunned numbness descended on Addie. Hadn't Linsey heard a word she'd said?

No, obviously she hadn't. She wouldn't even listen. She refused to. Her mind was so set on her own goals, her own set of wishes— last wishes—that she couldn't even consider that maybe the man of Addie's dreams and the man Linsey deemed she should marry were not one and the same.

Torn between wanting to clout Linsey over

the head and bursting into tears, Addie sprang
from the sofa and flounced into the foyer. She
stood outside the door, clenching and
unclenching her fists, fighting tears of shame
and frustration. Why couldn't she simply tell
Linsey that her feelings for Daniel had
changed—if, in fact, they had ever existed at
all, except in her own foolish imagination?
What was so hard about being honest about
the fact that it wasn't Daniel she wanted to
spend her life with, but Oren?

She hated her lack of courage, especially
where Linsey was concerned. But how did one
change a trait that was as much a part of her as
her love of teaching or her fear of heights?

She closed her eyes, but a tear escaped anyway to trickle down her cheek. A yearning to
seek comfort in Oren's arms, to feel his quiet
strength surround her, stunned Addie with its
force. After this morning, though, she doubted
Oren wanted anything to do with her—and
she could not bear his rejection atop everything else that had happened.

Feeling as lost and alone as she had the day
her mother had stuck her on a coach bound for
the unknown, Addie wiped her cheek with the
back of her hand and drifted outside, her
shoulders slumped with defeat.

To her surprise, Daniel still sat on the top
step. "Daniel? You're still here?"

He jerked his thumb toward the house.
"She's angry with me, isn't she?"

Addie glanced over her shoulder into the
window, then back at Daniel. His black hair
looked as if it had been combed back with a

pitchfork. His eyes had gone dull. Troubled, even. That was peculiar since, in the past, he hadn't seemed to care a whit how Linsey felt about him. "She loves to laugh," Addie explained. "But she hates to be laughed at."

"I wouldn't have laughed at her if she hadn't concocted that absurd story!"

"Is it absurd?" Addie asked softly.

He turned on Addie. "Don't tell me you believe that drivel!"

She hesitated, once again torn between a lifetime of habit and an onslaught of practicality. Finally she shook her head. "It doesn't matter what I believe."

"Damned if it doesn't! If you believe it, then you're as daft as she is. And if you don't, then why in the hell aren't you doing something to convince her otherwise?"

"Because it isn't that simple, Daniel! You, of all people, must know how opinionated she can be. Once she gets her mind set on something, a wedge and hammer couldn't pry it loose."

Linsey's strength of conviction was a trait Addie had clung to for years. Often she'd envied Linsey the ability to stand firm, no matter what windstorm swept through her life. Only recently had Addie begun to see that Linsey's strongest virtue could also be her deepest flaw.

And Addie's most indomitable foe.

Suddenly weary, she slipped the hat pin out of the back of the net-and-felt concoction perched on her head, removed the hat, then lowered herself to the step above Daniel, far enough away that his aftershave would not send her into a fit of sneezing. "Look, the truth is, I don't know what to believe. Sometimes there will be a sign, and something wonderful or terrible will happen. But other times, good fortune comes my way with no warning. But Linsey . . . there is no doubt in her. She honestly believes she will not survive beyond the end of the year."

"Because her mother died?"

"Because her mother died after seeing her reflection in a mirror at the wake of her husband's commanding officer. Three months later, she was stricken down with the cholera."

The tight set of his jaw an indication his cynicism, Daniel squinted into the glare of morning sun that cast an amber glow across the autumn-kissed landscape.

At length, Addie softly told Daniel, "I think that deep down, Linsey feels that there was something she could have done to change things, some way she could have prevented it—or at least been prepared for it."

"Where'd she get a fool notion like that?"

"A combination of things, I suppose. Coincidence, Aunt Louisa, her own fanciful imagination."

"Cholera wiped out entire settlements— there is no way to prepare for that."

"But Linsey needs to control things, and divining the signs is a way that she can feel as if she has some power."

"And that includes trying to get you and me married."

Addie sighed. It registered that this was the first actual conversation she'd ever had with Daniel, and the fact that it was getting them nowhere only confirmed her belief that he and she would never make a good match. But now that the truth was out, and Linsey's secret in the open, Daniel at least had a right to an explanation.

"My father died when I was very young. Three, maybe four. He'd been bitten by a snake while collecting wood. We'd lived in Kansas then—at the end of the world, my mother used to say. Sometimes months would pass before we saw another living soul. She said she could endure the solitude for my father's sake, but after he was gone . . . well, she didn't have it in her.

"Then one day, the cavalry passed across our land. My mother literally got down on her knees and begged them to take us. That's how she met Linsey's father. Fell head over heels at first sight, she says, but I think she was just lonely, and scared—at first, anyway. As the years went on, they found love with each other. Their existence revolves around each other. It leaves little room for anyone else— even their daughters.

"Linsey and I are all each other has had since we were five years old. She's determined to see that I have someone to take care of me when she's gone, since Aunt Louisa won't be around forever. Linsey's convinced you are the person I need to help me get through my grief."

"But there won't *be* any grief," Daniel argued, "because there won't be any death."

Addie lifted her hands in a gesture of exasperation. "Haven't you heard a word I've said?"

"I've heard, but beliefs can change."

Good heavens, he was as bad as Linsey! "Linsey's beliefs won't change just because you say they should. They're too ingrained in her."

"That's why we have to prove to her that all these crazy signs she puts so much store by are nothing but folklore."

Addie went still, the words igniting the first spark of hope since the day Linsey had told her the news. If Linsey could be persuaded to put aside her notions—or at the very least, doubt them—then maybe there was still a chance for all of them to seize happiness. "How, Daniel? How can we prove it?"

"Hell, I don't know. I'm a doctor, not a magician. I've never dealt with anything like this."

Slowly, a bright smile spread across her face. "But I know who has."

Addie didn't understand how she kept getting involved in these plots. First with Linsey, now with Daniel. All she'd ever really wanted was to be a part of something outside herself, to love somebody, to be loved in return. To know that she meant something. What that something was, she couldn't name, but watching and dreaming of Daniel had been the closest she'd ever come to finding it.

Until Oren.

Even that was doomed, though, negated by a promise she'd made to the one person who'd ever been loyal and true to her.

Unless she took charge of the situation and helped Daniel prove Linsey wrong. And the best person to help them was the one person who understood Linsey better than anyone.

It took them an hour to track down Aunt Louisa. They found her at Granny Yearling's house, a tiny clapboard structure on an off-shoot road behind the church.

"Now remember, let me do the talking," Addie said as they waited for someone to answer their knock.

"What will you say?"

"I don't know yet, but Aunt Louisa's faith in superstition is almost equal to Linsey's, so we must be very careful that we don't cause her any distress."

The door opened a second later.

As she and Daniel stepped inside, the place reminded her of an open hope chest with a hundred year's worth of memories crammed into one little cubicle. Every available surface was cluttered with memorabilia, doilies, lamps, quilts, figurines, miniature tea sets, embroidery hoops, picture frames, and wall sconces of brass, silver, and copper . . .

It made a person dizzy just looking at it all.

They sat on the edge of a thick-cushioned sofa crowded with pillows and dolls. Aunt Louisa and Granny Yearling sat across from them, Granny's hearing horn propped idle on a table beside her, the pipe in her mouth puffing smoke like a steam engine.

Daniel kept to his word and let Addie do all the talking. It amazed her as much as it appeared to amaze him that not only could she actually say so many words in his presence, but that she could spin them into a coherent tale.

"This . . . friend," Aunt Louisa hedged when Addie finished, "you say he looked into a mirror at a wake?"

Addie didn't bother correcting Aunt Louisa's error in the friend's gender—the less chance she might associate with Linsey, the better. "Yes, ma'am."

"Oh, dear, then he is surely doomed."

"Bah, superstitions," Granny scoffed with a dismissive wave of her hand. "Bunch of horse patooey if you ask me."

"You don't believe there is any danger in looking in a mirror, Granny?"

"The only danger is the simple act of looking into one."

"What do you mean?" Daniel asked.

"When a body looks into a mirra, most times they see who they want to be and not who they truly are."

Daniel leaned forward and tapped his fingertips together. "One of the things I've discovered, though, is if someone believes very strongly in something, they can actually will it to happen."

"Well. Then that person needs to find something worth living for," Granny grumbled.

Louisa's face became animated. "You know,

Granny, you may be on to something there. What if . . . " Her shoulders slumped. "No, it would never work. The power of mirrors is simply too strong."

Daniel and Addie both straightened.

"What is it Aunt Louisa?" Addie asked. "Even a slim chance of saving our friend is better than no chance at all."

"Well, if a woman is made to feel beautiful, she becomes beautiful to herself. If a weak man is made to feel strong, he will begin to see his own strength. Perhaps fate can be conquered in the same manner: combat the power of one belief by pitting it against a stronger, more powerful belief."

"How?" Daniel asked.

"That, dear boy, is something you will have to discover for yourself."

For the first time in many years, Daniel had a craving for a healthy dose of Cooter Hobart's special brew, but he wound up settling for the next best thing—whatever Rusty had on the shelf. Louisa and her cryptic goddamn messages: pit the power of one belief against another. What kind of horse shit was that?

He shook his head as he strode into the saloon that evening. The whole thing was just too damned much to take in. Linsey's manipulation, her confession, his own turbulent emotions. . . .

Catching sight of Jarvis at the far end of the bar, Daniel shouldered his way through a fog of cigar smoke, whiskey fumes, and bodies that smelled of stale sweat and painted

women. The Rusty Bucket was full to the brim,
unusual for a Friday night, until he overheard
a few crusty cowpokes regaling others with
tales of their recent trail drive. Not too many of
those going on anymore; this part of the country was heading for the winter lull.

"Howdy, Doc," Jarvis greeted when Daniel
bellied up to the bar next to him. "What the
hell did you do to rile Potter?"

"Didn't know I did anything."

Jarvis jerked his thumb over his shoulder,
then downed a shot. "He's been sittin' over
there all afternoon planning your funeral."

Daniel spotted Oren, alone at a table in the
middle of the room. "Guess I better find out
why." He swiped the glass of whiskey the bar-
keep had poured him, then ambled to where
Oren sat. He looked like hell, slump-shoul-
dered and stinking to high heaven. "This seat
taken?"

He lifted his head. Bleary blue eyes went
sharp as nails. "Go away, Doc Jr. I ain't normally a violent man, but right now I'm itchin'
to shove your ass through a brick wall."

"Any particular reason?"

"You stole the only woman I ever loved!"

Daniel reared back in surprise. He couldn't
mean *Linsey*.

"How'd you do it? Did you smile at her?
Women are always falling all over themselves
for your smile."

"I think there's been a mistake, Potter."

"Your intentions—are they honorable?"

"I don't have any intentions, honorable or
otherwise."

"You son of a—you're toying with her?"

Daniel took a step back. Only a fool wouldn't put some distance between himself and a charging bull. Daniel didn't consider himself a small man by any means, but compared to Oren, he was downright puny. He'd seen what Oren in a temper could do to a room. "Whoa there, pal . . . "

An iron finger jabbed Daniel in the solar plexus. "Don't tell me 'whoa'; I ain't a dad-blamed horse. And don't call me pal, either. A friend wouldn't fool with a friend's lady."

"I didn't know you had your cap set for anyone."

"Well, I did. But she loves you. And a woman's feelings are fragile, so you better treat her with honor and respect or I'll rip you in half."

Before Daniel could defend himself, Oren stalked out of the saloon, slamming the bat-wing doors so hard that one hit the wall and fell off its hinges. What in the Sam Hill was that all about?

Slowly Daniel became aware that every eye in the place had turned onto him. He lifted his hands away from his sides and barked, "What?"

A few eyes blinked. Someone snickered.

"I'm not compromising anyone, hear?"

With a snort of disgust, he seized his glass and tossed the whiskey down his throat. Maybe Linsey was right to think she was going to die.

Right now, Daniel wanted nothing more than to strangle her.

Chapter 17

A horse with a single white stocking is considered lucky, while a horse with four white feet is considered unlucky.

With a frustrated sigh, Linsey stabbed the quill into its stand and raked her fingers through her hair. Her Last Will and Testament lay spread out to dry in front of her. Her inheritance would be split equally between Addie and Aunt Louisa, after a large portion was divided between the church, the school, and Jenny's orphanage. Addie could have whatever personal belongings she wanted, with the rest being donated to whomever she deemed appropriate. Linsey just couldn't find the energy to care anymore.

Beckoned by a chattering outside the library window, she lowered her hands and watched a pair of mockingbirds dive to the ground, then swoop back into the branches of a silverleaf maple with their prize. She listened to them bicker and imagined them standing beak to beak, feathers ruffled, each claiming the branch for their own.

Much the same way she and Daniel did.

She should be furious at him for the way he had ridiculed her yesterday—she *was* furious at him. And she wished now that she hadn't told him her secret. If it hadn't been for her vow of honesty, she wouldn't have told him. But she'd been skirting the edges of that promise over the last month, and when he'd all but cornered Addie with his demands of the truth, she'd been left with no choice but to tell him the dreadful news.

And what had he done? Laughed at her.

She might have reveled in the rare sound of it, might have been overjoyed that she'd found something to crack that frigid facade of his. Not when it was at the expense of the most tragic event of her life, though.

Yes, she should be utterly seething toward the insensitive lout.

Except Daniel had a way about him that made even the unforgivable forgivable. Maybe because she knew that under his brittle exterior beat the heart of a tender, compassionate, lonely man whose smile had the power of a pocketful of charms.

And to her continued shame, he made her feel more alive than she'd ever felt before. She only had to remember the forbidden kiss on Caroline's porch, when his touch had awakened a desire within her that she had never even known existed. Or recall the smoldering way he had looked at her just yesterday in the backyard, as if he were fire and she the tinder he planned to devour.

Linsey shook away the thoughts jostling against each other in her mind and pushed away from the secretary. Lordy, if she didn't find something to keep her occupied, she'd go daft. It seemed that the harder she tried to elude thoughts of Daniel, the more doggedly they pursued her. She couldn't sleep anymore without seeing him in her dreams, couldn't walk down the street without searching for a glimpse of his broad-shouldered form, couldn't even update her will without his sensuous gaze appearing in her mind.

As if coveting her sister's beau wasn't bad enough, Linsey found herself shouldering the ever-growing strain of eluding St. Peter's call. If there wasn't still so much to do, she thought she'd simply collapse on her bed and let eternal sleep claim her.

But she hadn't completed half the items on her list yet, and knew she'd not rest easy until every last task was accomplished.

Drawing the list from her pocket, she ran her finger down each item.

Marry Addie off to Daniel.

Working on it, though she'd plumb run out of ideas.

Make amends to Daniel.

Working on it, despite his fighting her at every turn.

Go on an adventure.

That she'd done, and from heights she hadn't expected.

Bring a life into the world.

Also done.
Contribute something to the community.

There—*that* she could do. And it might even help to distract her traitorous mind from thoughts of Dr. Tall, Dark, and Handsome.

Returning the folded list to her pocket, Linsey paid a visit to the pantry and brought out several sacks of salt. What better thing to contribute to her neighbors than a bit of good fortune?

Twenty minutes later, Linsey had the salt loaded into an old pull-wagon from the garden shed. She opened a painted parasol above her head, gathered her camel's-hair skirt in one hand, and started for town.

The wagon bumped and rolled behind her. She reached the smithy and waved at Mr. Potter, who looked unusually careworn as he sat on a half-barrel, greasing the hub of a wagon wheel. "Good afternoon, Mr. Potter."

He returned her greeting with torpid effort. Wiping his hand on a rag, he met her at the door. "What'cha got there, Miss Linsey?"

"Salt—the emblem of wisdom, friendship, prosperity, and protection." She lifted a sack and presented it to him. "May it keep you safe from ill-will."

"I don't reckon it could make things worse," he said, taking the offering.

"Are you troubled today?"

He managed a smile, but his eyes remained dull. "Nothing to concern yourself with, but thank you kindly for asking."

Knowing there was little she could do to ease whatever burdens the man bore, she continued on her way, stopping at each store to deliver a pillar of good fortune. To her surprise, the smiles she received in return actually began to lift her downtrodden spirits—until she walked out of the Rusty Bucket.

Her heart dropped to her toes at the sight of Daniel and Addie standing side by side at the livery corral. Though they did nothing improper—they weren't even touching—their heads were bent toward each other, and they seemed engaged in private conversation.

Intimate conversation.

Realization struck with the force of a whiplash. It was happening. Daniel and Addie were talking.

Linsey had wanted this. She'd wished for it. Planned it.

She'd just never expected it to hurt. Never counted on the stab of jealousy sliding into her heart at seeing the two of them standing so close to each other.

What was wrong with her? She had no right being jealous of either one of them, no right feeling as if she were dying inside.

But the feeling was there despite her wishes—a bruising of the soul, a battering of the heart. Making her eyes sting and her throat tighten. She wanted to grab Daniel to her, clutch him close and never let him go. At the same time she wanted to keep as far away from him as possible, for he had the power to make her wish for the impossible.

Impossible because he belonged to Addie, and because she had one foot in the grave.

Linsey squared her shoulders, swallowed the lump in her throat, and pasted a smile on her face.

And as she strolled toward the couple, she prayed no one could see that her heart was breaking.

The time had come to put their plan into motion.

Several lengthy conversations about Linsey's superstitions had finally resulted in a strategy.

Armed with Linsey's list of last wishes, Daniel eyed the horse penned in the livery corral, then checked his timepiece. "I thought you said she was on her way," he remarked to Addie.

"She should be, any minute. She's making her way around the horseshoe, delivering salt to all the neighbors." Addie, too, checked her timepiece. "Where is Bryce? I asked him to meet us at half past one . . . oh, there he is now."

The towheaded boy raced up to them, a tight grip on the scraggly black cat clawing its way up his chest in a bid for freedom. "I found Patches, Doc Jr . . . "

"Good job, Bryce."

Addie knelt in front of the boy. "Now remember, hold on to her until I give you the cue, then set the cat loose. She'll run for her babies. Got it?"

"Got it." The boy smiled, his excitement of being included as bright as a sunbeam.

"If you do your job," Addie went on, "I've got

a brand-new volume of *Twenty Thousand Leagues Under the Sea* with your name on it. Deal?"

He grinned, proudly displaying two missing front teeth. "Deal."

Bryce scampered off to hide on the other side of the corral while Daniel and Addie resumed their wait for Linsey.

"I should probably feel guilty for involving a child in this scheme," Addie confessed with a sideways glance.

"If this convinces Linsey that she won't die, then everyone will benefit . . . you, me"— Daniel jabbed a finger in Bryce's direction— "and even that boy there."

They finally spotted Linsey strolling down the boardwalk, pulling the cart behind her. Once again Daniel found his lungs swelling, his heart expanding, his damnable desire for her escalating, the closer she got.

"Linsey."

"Daniel."

As always, her voice reminded him of warm sunshine and balmy winds.

"We have a surprise for you, sister," Addie exclaimed, pulling Linsey close to the corral fence. "See?"

"A horse?"

"Yes! Daniel has decided to help us complete your wish list. You said you've always wanted to learn how to ride, so he agreed to loan us his horse and give you a lesson. Isn't that grand?"

She looked at him, suspicion darkening her eyes. "You are going to help me complete my wish list?"

He gave her a crooked smile. "Consider it a peace offering." Not giving her a chance to question him further, he cupped her elbow and guided her to the black. Addie strolled along behind them, her hands folded demurely at her waist. "First, you have to look into its eyes and introduce yourself," he instructed Linsey.

She gave him a skeptical look. "Introduce myself?"

"You wouldn't want a stranger sitting on you, would you?"

Her brows pulled together. "I see your point." She took in a breath, and cheerily said, "Hello, horse. I'm Linsey." To Daniel, she said, "I feel silly."

He decided not to tell her that she looked silly, too. "You get used to each other this way."

She nodded, then turned back to the black. "You sure are a pretty girl."

"I think he'd take offense to that. He's a gelding, not a mare."

"Oh!" She dropped a curtsey. "I beg your pardon, sir."

The horse gave a soft whinny and tossed his head.

Daniel bit the inside of his cheek to keep from chuckling. "Hold out your hand. Let him get used to your scent."

She followed his instructions, grimacing when the horse snuffled against her palm and left it moist.

"That's great, you're doing great. Rub his neck now."

With her confidence building, she ran her palms down the twitching muscles of the gelding's neck, along his heaving sides, all the while whispering sweet nothings to him.

Lucky beast, Daniel thought. A swift image of having those same sweet hands stroking him, caressing him, sent a spear`of fire shooting straight to his groin.

"That's enough," he said, his voice gruffer than he'd intended—but a man could only take so much. "Time to get in the saddle."

"Are you sure he won't throw me?"

"He won't throw you. He's gentle as a babe." Daniel bent at the waist and laced his fingers together. "Put your left foot in my hands, and on the count of three, I'll give you a boost. Swing your right leg over his back, hear?"

"I hear."

Just as she placed her hand on his shoulder and her foot in his hands, a sudden flash darted across the corral. The horse backstepped; the hooves of his white-stockinged hind legs sank into a patch of mud.

"Oh, Lordy, what was that?" Linsey cried in alarm.

"What was what?" Addie asked with mock innocence.

"That thing that ran in front of me—it looked like a cat."

"I wouldn't worry about it," Daniel brushed aside her concern. "Are you ready? One, two—"

"No, it's a bad sign when a cat dashes across your path." She withdrew her foot and backed up a pace. "Thank you for the offer of a lesson, but another time."

"I thought you wanted to complete your list."

She eyed the horse. "I do, but—"

"Linsey, you may not get another chance," Addie urged her. "Would it make you feel better if Daniel went up with you?"

Daniel shot a startled look at Addie. "Hold on there—"

"You'll take her up on the horse, won't you, Daniel?"

Daniel's gaze flicked from Addie to Linsey, to the horse, then back to Linsey. This wasn't part of the plan. He knew damn well what would happen if he put Linsey in the saddle in front of him. She'd drive him crazy, teasing him with the scent of her hair, the warmth of her skin, the softness of her body.

But he didn't see any way out of it. This had been his idea, after all. And he did have a point to prove.

With a sigh of resignation, Daniel cupped Linsey's foot in his hands and gave her a boost. Once she found her seat in the saddle, he mounted up behind her and wrapped his arms around her.

She squirmed a bit, then held herself stiffly. Her hands gripped the horn so tightly her knuckles turned white.

"You have to relax," Daniel told her.

"If I do, I'll fall off."

"If you don't, he'll sense your fear and toss you off."

"But . . . "

"I won't let anything happen to you, Linsey."

As if his words had the power to calm her, he watched her muscles gradually loosen. "That's it," he encouraged. "Now find your center."

"My center what?"

"In the saddle."

She scooted backward an inch or so. Daniel tensed as her bottom pushed into the cradle of his thighs; the horse sidestepped. With a gentle pat to his withers and a calm tone, he soothed the animal. If only someone could soothe him as easily.

He tried to ignore the heat pulsing in his loins, the dizzying sensation of all this soft female flesh between his thighs and against his chest. "Touch—" Daniel cleared his throat. "Touch your heels to his belly."

The black obeyed her command. The motion tossed Linsey back against his chest, then bounding forward again.

Daniel closed his eyes and moaned. How the hell did he get himself into these situations?

He rode with her around the corral, instructing her, until his control reached the point of snapping. Then he gave a gentle pull on the reins. "That's enough. I think you're ready to go it alone."

"Alone?" she croaked, regarding him with panicked eyes. An instinct to protect her, to keep her safe and sheltered, rose up inside Daniel. But more, he wanted her to feel the same sense of immortality he'd felt when she'd trusted him to deliver her friend's baby. "You can do it, Linsey. You can do anything you put your mind to."

Her smile was slow to unfurl. It blossomed like a summer rose, innocent and fragile, and then, reaching full bloom, so glorious that it stole Daniel's breath. The scent of her, the sight of her lips, ripe and moist, beckoned him closer, tempting, tormenting.

In two seconds flat he'd slid out of the saddle and was striding to the corral fence where Addie sat up top with her heels hooked over a board. He leaned against the fence and crossed his arms. If he'd thought watching Linsey ride would be easier on his system than actually being in the saddle with her, he realized his mistake the instant she put her heels to the horse and set it in motion.

Damn, she was beautiful. Glossy curls bouncing against her back, breasts rising and falling in a tormenting rhythm. . . .

"She's doing it, Daniel!"

Addie's voice tore him from the fantasy beginning to unfold. And as he forced himself to see Linsey the way Addie saw her, he couldn't help but smile; couldn't curb the glow of satisfaction. He'd helped her. He'd suffered for it, but he'd helped her, and it was worth it to watch her hair flow in the wind, her smile shone brighter than a noonday sun. She'd caught on quickly, as she did everything, and from the brilliance of that smile, she loved the sense of power over a beast bigger than herself. The horse. The fear.

Daniel knew that feeling of satisfaction. He felt it every time he mastered an illness or performed a difficult surgery.

Still, he envied both her ease of the taming and the taming itself. The ride, the rock of her body on the beast's back. The thought of her rocking against him, riding him with the same abandon as she rode the horse, had his smile ebbing and his pulses throbbing. He could teach her that as well. Finding her center. Settling into a rhythm. Pelvis slapping against groin, wild hair brushing fevered skin.

He closed his eyes and cursed.

He glanced self-consciously at Addie, hoping she hadn't notice the bulge in his trousers. Thankfully, she appeared more interested in something over her shoulder.

Or maybe he should say someone, Daniel amended, following the direction of her gaze.

So *that* was the way of it. It sure explained a lot: the change in Addie, Oren's accusations in the saloon the other night. "Does he know?" Daniel asked of Addie.

She wrenched around to face him. "Does who know what?"

"Oren. Does he know you're in love with him?"

Guilty color flooded her cheeks. "No. I've never told him."

Well, hell, that made a whole lot of sense. Their whole misunderstanding might be cleared up if Addie was just honest with the fellow. If Daniel thought it would do any good, he would have been tempted to tell Oren himself. But the two of them exchanged no more than stiff nods lately—and besides, he made it a practice not to stick his nose into another man's love affairs.

After a moment, she asked, "Do you remember when I broke my leg?"

"Dimly." It had been a long time ago—before he'd even gone off to Tulane.

"You came with your father and helped set it."

Daniel remembered that part. He'd done everything wrong, according to Doc Sr., from grabbing the wrong splints to forgetting the bandages to nearly giving the patient glycerine instead of laudanum.

"I don't think I've ever been in such pain, but you got me through it."

She'd been a patient. It was his job. Back then, it had been his dream.

"I . . . developed feelings for you, but only recently have I realized that those were the feelings of a young girl, not of a grown woman."

Daniel shifted uncomfortably. "I'm sorry I never returned your feelings."

"I'm glad you didn't. I never would have found Oren if you had. Even though nothing can come of it, I now know what it feels like to love. Having that for a moment is better than never having it at all."

"You should tell him how you feel, Addie."

"What difference would it make? I'd still have to choose between him and my sister, and that isn't a choice I can make. Not yet." She squinted across the corral, where Linsey rode like poetry in motion. "What if this doesn't work, Daniel?"

He squeezed her arm. "Then we keep trying. There's too much to be lost if we quit." He
let his hand fall away from her and stepped
away from the fence. "I'd best get back to the
apothecary. My dad will have my hide if I
don't get those bottles labeled."

"You're leaving?"

"There's really no reason to stay. She rode a
horse after a black cat dashed across her path,
and nothing untoward happened. I think we
proved our point."

No sooner were the words out of his mouth,
than a scream cut through the air.

"Nothing is broken; you just have a bruised
shoulder. Keep your arm in the sling and in a
few days you'll be right as rain."

Linsey glared at Daniel, then at Addie. "I
wouldn't be hurt at all if the two of you hadn't
bullied me into riding that beast." The only
reason she'd gotten on the horse was because
she had trusted Daniel not to let anything happen to her, the same way he'd kept her safe
when the balloon had taken off. "I told you
that cat would bring me bad luck, but neither
of you believed me."

The two shared a look that stung her. Linsey
hated the way it made her feel excluded. It was
the same look her father had shared with her
mother, the same one he now shared with
Addie's mother. And it was silly feeling jealous of that look between her sister and the
man Addie would marry, since she'd wanted
them to develop a relationship—if not out of
love, then out of fondness.

"Addie just wanted to help you complete your list," Daniel said as if that could excuse his part in her injury.

Linsey quirked a brow. "And you?" She dared him to tell her the truth. If he thought she'd buy his claim, then she had a gold mine next to the Red River that she would sell him.

He sighed, sounding defeated. "All right—I want you to see the folly of putting so much faith in folklore."

"Is that so? Then how do you explain my fall?"

"Inexperience."

"On the heels of seeing a black cat race across my path?"

"Coincidence."

"Why can't you just accept that there are powers beyond your realm of control?"

Her stomach fluttered at the dimpled grin breaking out across his face. "Obstinance."

Linsey pursed her lips. She did *not* find him amusing. Too irresistible for his own good, but not amusing. There was nothing humorous about the way he made her heart leap and pulse race. Nothing remotely comical about the longing she felt anytime he came around her, or the envy she felt when she saw him and Addie together.

It made no sense. It was completely unreasonable. Everything was going as she planned: Daniel and Addie were getting on well, and from the possessive hand she'd seen Daniel put on her sister's arm when they were at the corral, they would soon be feeling attracted to each other.

So if everything was going as planned, why did it make her so miserable?

Too many questions, too much confusion began to play havoc with her emotions. Linsey knew if she didn't get away, she'd suffer the ultimate humiliation and burst into tears in front of both of them.

She hopped off the examination table, wincing when the action jarred her arm. But the pain couldn't compare to the one she carried inside.

"Linsey, don't be this way," Addie implored.

"What way? Angry? Of course, I'm angry." Angry at her sister. Angry at Daniel. But most of all, angry at herself. Because despite every reason why she shouldn't, every reason why she couldn't, she'd gone and fallen in love with a man she shouldn't have.

Chapter 18

The rose is a symbol of enduring love.

Linsey settled on the wooden bench beneath the awning of the train depot, her lame arm cradled in her lap. Even with a fox-fur pelisse around her shoulders, the November chill cut to the bone. Linsey numbed herself to it, just as she'd been numbing herself to most everything lately.

Heavy bootsteps sounded slow and lazy against the platform. She shut her eyes. *Please don't be Daniel.* Since the discovery of her feelings for him, she could hardly think his name without weeping, much less see him.

However, the harsh scent of coal and horsehide alerted her to Oren Potter's presence even before he paused by the bench.

"Miss Linsey, are you out here again?"

"Hello, Mr. Potter," she greeted with a feeble smile.

He lowered his powerful bulk beside her and tapped his hands together. "It's awful cold to be sitting outside."

It was awful cold no matter where she went lately. "I'm waiting for my father."

"You've been waiting for three days straight," he remarked softly, as if she needed the reminder.

"He'll be here."

"Did he say when?"

"Not exactly. But my nose has been itching all week, so I'm sure he'll show up any day."

"Then I'm sure he will."

She mentally thanked him for not jeering at her. He was probably the only one left—with the exception of Aunt Louisa—who didn't mock her anymore. Even Addie—sweet, gentle-natured Addie, who had never found fault with Linsey—doubted that she would see her father soon, despite signs to the contrary.

In truth, a distance between her and her sister seemed to grow every day. They rarely spoke anymore. There was this heavy, silent . . . thing between them. Linsey couldn't be sure if it was something she fostered, or Addie did, but it hurt.

"They seem to be stepping out a lot together lately," the smithy said, drawing Linsey's gaze down the road.

Her heart gave a lurch at the sight of Daniel and her sister standing together under the overhang of the apothecary. It was getting harder and harder watching them together. Daniel had never pushed for a retraction in the *Herald*. In fact, for all intents and purposes, he and Addie gave the appearance of a courting couple. And each day that drew them closer seemed to cast

Linsey further away. She had never expected this sense of abandonment. This . . . insignificance. She wanted to hate them for it, for this feeling of being on the outside looking in, and that made her feel small and petty. For despite the canyon developing between them, Addie's happiness meant everything to it. It always had. It always would.

She looked away and swallowed. "It's what betrothed couples should do, I expect."

"I expect so."

The note of forlorn loneliness in his voice compelled Linsey to ask, "Have you ever considered remarrying, Mr. Potter?"

"Are you proposing?"

"We hardly know each other, sir."

Their cheeky attempt to lighten the gloominess around them failed miserably.

After a long lull, he said, "I did consider it once."

"What happened?"

There was a soul-deep sadness in his eyes when he looked at her. "She'd promised herself to someone else."

The train pulled up a few minutes later, wheels clacking against iron rails, the whistle screeching through the crisp air.

Linsey straightened. Mr. Potter rose from the bench and assisted her to her feet. As the steam engine chugged into the depot, hope flourished in Linsey's breast as she sought a glimpse of a burly, mustached man among the passengers disembarking. The letter had gone out weeks ago, and her hand had been itching like mad. Maybe today would be the day.

One passenger alighted, a tall, paunchy man in a pin-striped business suit; then came an elderly lady with florid cheeks and a hat bearing a real bird's nest. Several more visitors made their way out of the cars, yet none wore the dashing uniform of the United States Calvary.

"Are there no others bound for Horseshoe?" she asked the conductor.

At the negative shake of his head, her heart sank to the pit of her stomach.

"Maybe he'll be on next week's train," Mr. Potter said consolingly.

Dejected, Linsey nodded, then turned away from the depot toward home. Against her will, her gaze was drawn to where Addie and Daniel still stood, watching her. She felt their pity reach out with cloying fingers. *What if they were right?* she wondered. *What if I am crazy?* The thought added to her despair, for if believing in the signs all these years had been for nothing, why should she believe in anything?

Her heart heavy, she trudged up the hill, the walk to Briar House longer than she ever remembered it being. She stepped inside and removed her pelisse. Just as she started for the stairwell, a letter waiting on the entryway table caught her eye. It was addressed to her and Addie, postmarked Oklahoma Territory.

From their parents.

Linsey tore open the envelope. An object fell

from the folds. Without scanning the note, Linsey reached for it.

Tears sprang to her eyes at the photographs her father had included in his note, of him and Evelyn.

Linsey smiled. She'd gotten to see him today, after all.

The signs hadn't been false.

Sitting in his office, Daniel leaned forward in his desk chair and rubbed his brow with weary resignation. *Combat one belief with a more powerful belief.* Louisa's words rang in his head like a cavernous echo as he studied Linsey's last-wish list.

Playing the black cat against a horse ride hadn't worked, and putting a salve on her nose to make it itch against a visitor coming to call hadn't turned out as expected, any more than any of the other little tricks he and Addie had tried over the last week. Everything they tried kept backfiring, and frankly, Daniel was beginning to feel like a fool. He was running around town making an ass of himself, to make the very woman who had cost him his future believe she'd have one of her own.

And why? Why go through all this trouble? He had no intention of being a part of that future.

He crumpled her list and fell against the back of his chair. Behind closed lids, he saw her grinning into the wind, dancing on air. Counting a baby's toes, wishing on a star, clutching a four-leaf clover to her heart, curtseying to a horse . . .

He heard her, too—the longing in her voice when she spoke of love and children; whispering to him "this is the best day you've had in your life. . . . "

So many things people took for granted.

So many things he took for granted.

"Daniel?"

His eyes snapped open. Addie stood in the doorway of his office.

"I knocked, but you must not have heard me."

"No, I'm afraid I didn't." He straightened. "But I'm glad you're here. We need to come up with our next plan of action."

She took a seat on the edge of the chair across from his desk. "I think it's time we surrender."

Daniel stared at her in amazement.

"I can't bear to see her so disillusioned," she explained, her voice hitching with emotion. "Let's just go along with her beliefs—what could it hurt?"

"You want to feed this fodder?"

"What else can we do? Nothing is working, Daniel. She believes as strongly as ever."

He pulled himself out of his stupor. "I'm not giving up."

"Why?" Addie cried. "Why not let her have her beliefs? Who is she hurting?"

"Herself. She's wrong. And if we start encouraging these foolish notions of hers, we could wind up losing her. Is that what you want?"

"Of course not. But what if she isn't wrong? What if four-leaf clovers really do bring good luck, and looking into mirrors really are a fore-shadowing of death?"

He refused to believe it. They were the ridiculous concoctions of people like Linsey who wanted to control the uncontrollable.

"Daniel, you might be willing to take that chance, but I'm not."

"What are you saying? That you're giving up? I thought we agreed this is the best thing we can do for her."

"My sister has never asked me for anything in her life, Daniel. She has taken care of me selflessly and without hesitation since I was dumped on her doorstep fifteen years ago, and now is my chance to do something in return. What would it hurt if we pretended to fall in love? What if we did go along with the ruse of getting married?"

Daniel shook his head. "We'd both be miserable, Addie. We can't pretend something we don't feel."

"Hear me out, please. It would just be until the first of the year. If Linsey is wrong and she doesn't die by December thirty-first, then my death-bed promise will be invalid. We will both be free to pursue other . . . interests. Everyone wins, and no one gets hurt."

"And if she isn't wrong? If she actually wills herself to die?"

There was a long, pregnant pause before Addie finally spoke. "Then I would make you a good wife, Daniel; I swear it. And as my husband, you'd have the Gordon money at your disposal. You could go to that university if you wanted—"

"You're willing to buy a husband to accommodate your sister?"

"I'm willing to buy my sister's last wish for her peace of mind. To me, that's worth any price."

"Even Oren?"

Tears sprang to her eyes. "If that's what it takes, yes."

He hated that he was even considering such an extreme. He didn't want a wife. But neither could he bear causing Linsey so much pain, either.

He missed her smiles. He missed her snappy wit. He missed the way she tossed her head in defiance. Hell, he even missed that sparkle of mischief in her eyes.

But was he willing to give up his precious freedom to get it back?

It took him only a second to decide.

"No, Addie; I can't. She's wrong. I feel it in my bones. And whether you help me or not, I'm going to prove it—no matter what it takes."

Jenny Kimmel's wedding day dawned as beautiful as a wedding day could be. Jenny looked pretty as a picture in her white-lace gown. Her brunette hair was pulled atop her head in an intricate knot with fat sausage curls cascading down, and a wreath of silk roses at her crown.

Everywhere Linsey looked, there were roses: in their hair, attached to the pews, in their bouquets . . . The children had even decorated Jenny's wheelchair with satin ribbons and crepe roses.

Organ music drifted through the thin walls of the cloakroom at the front of the church. Biding her time for the cue that would begin Jenny's journey down the aisle, Linsey asked her friend, "Do we have everything?"

"Let's see; something old, something new, something borrowed, something blue, a sprig of ivy in my shoe. Yes, I think we have it all."

A pregnant pause in the music finally signaled the start of the ceremony.

Jenny smiled. "This is it—the day I've been waiting for my whole life!"

Linsey grasped her hands and kissed her cheek. "Be happy, Jen, always."

As Noah's girls raced to take their positions in front of Jenny's chair, to be pushed by John Brewster, Linsey turned to whisper to her sister, "Soon this will be you, Addie."

Addie didn't look at her; instead, she averted her face.

A numbing sense of unease prickled at the surface of Linsey's skin. She had no time to question Addie, though, for the "Wedding March" had begun.

Amy and Amanda, adorable in blue-and-white pinafores and crowns of silk roses, led the procession. Addie went next, with Linsey following behind. The church was full to bursting, two whole rows taken up by all eighteen of Noah and Jenny's children, the rest occupied by the citizens of Horseshoe.

Even though none would miss the wedding of the year, Linsey still wasn't prepared to see Daniel. He sat with his father in the third pew from the front. As Linsey passed by, she met his flat and brooding gaze.

Her heart lurched.

Amazingly, she made it to the front without stumbling. She listened to the service with her eyes closed, clinging to every word Reverend Simon recited.

She imagined herself standing at the altar, wearing the brooch Aunt Louisa's mother had passed down to her, a spanking new veil Hazel Mittermier had sewn of the finest Chantilly lace, Addie's favorite lace gloves, and blue ribbons woven into her hair.

And Daniel would be standing beside her, gazing down, wearing that lazy dimpled smile she so adored. . . .

Oh, why had she ever run from Mrs. Harvey? If she had simply given in and listened to the woman brag about her son, she wouldn't have looked into the mirror. At least then, this weight in her chest wouldn't exist. This sore, churning, heavy aloneness. This irrational fear that she was losing two of the people she loved most—to each other.

The soft clapping of hands pulled Linsey's notice to Noah and Jenny, who looked into one another's eyes, their love plain and powerful.

She inhaled deeply and smiled over the tears beginning to burn behind her lids. Hopefully the guests would think her weepy over her friend's happiness. In truth, she was, though another part of her ached for herself. These were the things she'd miss out on: the loving squeeze of a man's hand around hers, the proud glitter in his eyes, the arrogance in his voice as he vowed to love and honor her till death did they part.

She'd never have that. And unless fate dealt her some mercy, neither would her sister.

Linsey didn't know how she managed to get through the ceremony without bawling like a baby, but before she realized it, Noah was kissing the newly pronounced Jenny Tabor. Applause rose from those in the pews, and many hurried to the front doors, where Noah pushed Jenny through the shower of rice being rained down upon them.

Their spirits light and gay, the guests began to stroll toward the Horseshoe Hotel, where the reception was being held.

Linsey allowed herself to be pulled along with the tide of the crowd. In front of the millinery, someone tugged on her arm. She paused, glanced over her shoulder, and discovered Robert Jarvis behind her.

"I . . . uh . . . just wanted to thank ya for the new balloon. It came in on yesterday's train."

"It did?"

"It surely did, and with enough hah-dro-gin to carry me across the Atlantic Ocean." Gruffly, he added, "You didn't have to do that, Linsey."

"Yes, I did. I never should have stolen the first one."

"I won't argue that, but I'm grateful for the second chance. I'll be leaving at first light, long as the wind holds up."

"Well," she managed a heartfelt smile, "I'm

sure they will cradle you gently." Impulsively, she reached into the reticule dangling from her wrist and withdrew a rusty nail. "Just in case, take this with you for luck."

With a curious look he took the nail, then gave her a smile and dropped it into his vest pocket.

At least she'd made someone happy, she thought, following him into the hotel.

Inside, banquet tables had been set up along the perimeter of the dining room, leaving a large space for dancing. A quartet of county musicians sat upon a raised platform, tuning their instruments.

Then the strains of the violin began to play, and the room went silent.

Linsey listened spellbound as Noah sang a love song to Jenny that brought a tear to every eye in the house. While the violinist continued the ballad, he picked her up out of the chair and into his arms, and danced with her in a way that only lovers danced.

The scene was so touching that it brought an ache to Linsey's heart. She saw Caroline with Axel and their new baby girl; Mayor and Mrs. Harvey.

Everyone in love. Everyone with so much happiness ahead of them. . . .

Overwhelmed by an unbearable sense of loss and self-pity, Linsey headed for the door. The musicians struck up a lively number that had folks dancing like cats on a hot tin roof, but she couldn't dredge up their spirit. She knew if she didn't escape now, she'd shatter.

She didn't get two steps out the door before she bumped into someone coming down the boardwalk.

"Well, now if it isn't sweet Linsey-woolsey Gordon, out for a moonlit stroll."

With music pounding in his skull, Daniel drained the shot of whiskey someone had shoved into his hand. He'd known he shouldn't have attended that damn wedding. Seeing Linsey walking up that aisle, looking like heaven, had put notions in his head that had no right being there.

Well, he'd done his duty, made the social appearance required of him. There was nothing keeping him here. If anyone needed him— and from the amount of spirits flowing, someone would eventually—they could find him at the apothecary.

Adjusting his hat, then buttoning his coattails, Daniel pushed away from the bar and wove his way through the crowd and out the door. Halfway down the boardwalk, an out-of-place sound made the back of his neck prickle.

He went still, glanced around the shadows, and strained to hear.

There it was again: a muffled whimper.

And then he saw her, trapped in the arms of Bishop Harvey. The son-of-a-bitch had her pinned to the hotel wall, his face against her neck, his hand on her breast.

Rage unlike anything Daniel had ever felt pumped through his veins and blurred his vision. He clamped a hand onto Harvey's scrawny shoulder and spun him around. "Get your goddamn hands off her, Harvey!"

Bishop released his hold on Linsey and stumbled backward. Bleary eyes struggled to focus on Daniel. "Jump off a bridge, Doc." He lunged for Linsey again.

Daniel didn't give him the chance to get close. His fist flew, catching Harvey in the jaw. The impact lifted him off the ground and sent him flying backward. He landed with an audible thud.

Two solid steps closed the distance between Daniel and the mayor's spawn. Daniel jabbed a finger into his face. "You ever touch her again, you so much as *look* at her again, and I'll string your innards from here to Houston and back."

Those were the last words Harvey heard before his eyes rolled back in his head.

His chest heaving, Daniel raised his head. Linsey was staring at him, one hand to her bosom, the other over her mouth. Their gazes locked. He saw the shock in her eyes. The relief. And something more powerful.

Pride.

The emotion shook him more deeply than he imagined. He wanted to yank her to him, hold her, keep her safe from all the world's evils. He wanted to shove her from him, curse at her to keep her distance, to let him live in the isolated world he'd created for himself.

He did neither.

He spun on his heel and left.

* * *

For several long moments, Linsey stood alone in the darkened alley, trying to understand what had just taken place. One moment, Bishop had her up against the wall, pawing at her, muttering disgusting things against her neck—the next moment, Daniel was there, coming to her rescue.

He'd punched out Bishop Harvey.

Why? Why had he done such a rash, reckless, wonderful thing?

Her feet began moving of their own will, carrying her in the direction Daniel had taken, and before she knew it, she was racing after him.

"Daniel!"

He kept walking, his feet pounding down the deserted boardwalk.

"Daniel, wait!"

He came to a stop just outside the circle of lamplight, but didn't turn around.

When Linsey finally caught up to him, the emotion she saw in his eyes stunned her: a possessiveness that both thrilled and frightened her. "Why did you do that, Daniel? Why did you hit him?"

"He was touching you."

Simple words, simply said. And they told her nothing.

"Why should that matter to you? You've made it perfectly clear that you'd rather walk barefoot on broken glass than do anything for me. Why would you defend me against the likes of Bishop Harvey?"

He took a step forward. She shrank back, alarmed by the burning fury in his eyes.

"You want to know, Linsey? Do you really want to know?"

She had no chance to respond before he grabbed her by the arms and gave her a shake.

"Because I love you, damn it!"

Chapter 19

A waxing moon is reported to have magical powers and influence blood flow.

The declaration rocked through the air, an explosion of forbidden words and pent-up emotion.

Releasing Linsey as if he'd been stung, Daniel stepped back and shoved a hand through his hair. "Hell, I can't believe I said that."

She stared at him, flabbergasted. "You love me?"

He almost denied it. What stopped him, he didn't know—maybe because he knew deep down that there had been too many deceptions already. "God knows I never wanted to," Daniel said, choking on a mirthless laugh. "I don't even know how it happened—let's just forget I ever said it."

"I wish I could."

The sharpness of her tone took him by surprise. Her cheeks were pale in the lamplight; her eyes glittered with fury.

"You are supposed to be marring my sister,

and you tell me you love me? You are the most selfish, childish . . . cruel man! How dare you do this!"

"What are you talking about?"

"Addie has loved you faithfully for ten years, and you are so consumed with yourself and your desires that you won't even give her a chance."

His mouth fell open. "You call *me* selfish? You're so consumed with controlling the lives of everything and everyone around you that you don't bother listening to see if it's what they want! How do you know I'm the man your sister wants to spend her life with?"

"She told me—she tells me everything."

He gave a snort of disdain. "Obviously not everything."

"What is that supposed to mean?"

He looked down at the hand clutching his sleeve, then into emerald eyes that had been haunting his every waking and sleeping moments for months. This farce had gone on long enough. "Ask your sister."

Addie stood by the window, staring out the pane at the smithy across the way, where a single light burned from within.

Yearning seized her with fierce claws, tightening around her heart and lungs until she could scarcely breathe.

Oren, her soul called.

As if he'd heard it, he appeared in the wide doorway. The glow of street lamps gathered around his powerful frame, caressing him in a way that Addie longed to. Perhaps she should feel shame for wanting him, especially after the way she had rejected him for Daniel, but the only emotion she felt right now was despair.

When his gaze didn't veer from the hotel, she wondered if he knew she stood inside, watching him through the window. Did he ever think about her? Did he ever long for her as she longed for him?

Before she succumbed to second thoughts, Addie moved through the crowd and pushed herself out the door. Oren stilled, then slowly straightened. Heart thumping, breath quickening, she stood on her side of the lane; he stood on his.

For a long time, neither moved. The air between them swirled with longing and pain and wistful desire.

Then, Addie took one step. And another. Off the boardwalk, across the packed road where wind kicked up dust at her feet.

She didn't stop until she stood a heartbeat away from the man she'd come to love more than life itself.

She wanted to say *I'm sorry. I love you. Please, forgive me.*

But the words locked in her throat.

And then, he turned away.

Addie closed her eyes and let her head fall back as grief flooded through every vessel in her body. Through teary eyes she stared at the platinum moon. It looked as desolate as she felt. She'd finally found the man who made her feel strong and cherished. Who made her toes curl and her heart thump. Who made each day something to treasure, and not something to endure.

And he wanted nothing to do with her.

No—she'd not let him walk away from her. All her life, she'd allowed others to fight her battles for her, to shelter her, to rule her every thought and action.

Not this time.

"Oren."

He stopped in the center of the smithy, his body as stiff as the iron nails he made in his forge and fire.

With a sigh, he turned to face her. "What are you doing here, Addie?"

His eyes, those beautiful midnight blue eyes, were bleak and weary. Go slow, Addie cautioned herself. *If you push him, he'll run like a wounded mustang.* "I didn't see you at the festivities," she said, strolling into the shop. "I wondered why."

"Don't feel much like merrymakin', I reckon."

"Oh? What are you in the mood for?"

His gaze traveled down her body with the heat of a full-fired furnace. *Love makin'. Seen' you in that dress, all gussied up, I'm havin' a helluva time not flippin' up your skirts to see if you're wearin' those candy-striped underdrawers.*

His gaze fell. So did his voice. "You shouldn't be here, Addie. Ain't proper for a bride-to-be to be visitin' another man."

She dragged a finger along the edge of a stall door. "I suppose I wasn't in the mood for merrymaking, either." As she looked steadily into his eyes, she hoped he would understand how much she still wanted him.

"What do you want from me, Addie?" he finally whispered. "You want my blessing? I can't give it. You want my heart? I gave it to you. You threw it back in my face. Just what the hell do you want from me?"

She swallowed over the tears clogging her throat. "Another chance."

He gave a harsh laugh.

"Oren, please. I can't bear this," she whispered in agony. "I made a mistake." She hastened toward him, closing the physical distance between them, wishing she could close the emotional distance as easily. "I only promised to marry Daniel because Linsey wants it so badly." She took a deep breath and confessed everything—the mirror, the list, their scheme to trap Daniel into marriage. "All of that happened before I met you— before I fell in love with you. After the night the foal was born, I knew something had to be done. So Daniel and I thought if we proved to her that the superstitions were invalid, she'd realize that she wasn't going to die, and I could tell her about you."

"I know what it's like to lose someone close to you, Addie. But being dishonest ain't fair to anyone—most of all yourself. The only way we've got a chance for a life together is if you tell her the truth about us."

"I know. I planned on telling her—after the first of the year."

"No, Addie. As long as you give her this

power over you, you can never fully be your own self."

"Oren, please try and understand—Linsey is more convinced than ever that she will not live out the year, and I'm beginning to fear she's right. Sometimes I think this is all that's keeping her going. What if she does die, and I haven't lived up to my promise? I'll never be able to live with myself."

His features closed, going as dark and stony as an abandoned cellar. "Then you and Doc have a good life."

As Addie watched him turn away, it felt as if her world had just crumbled to ash. How could he expect her to turn her back on her sister?

Then again, how could she let him believe he would be second to any other commitment she made? How could she let go of the one person she wanted to be with more than anyone on earth?

She couldn't. Before, it had never been important to take a stand against Linsey on an issue—because before, there hadn't been anything at stake. Now there was. If she didn't do this one thing, if she didn't confess her love for him to her sister, if she didn't find the strength to stand up for them, she'd lose him. He'd walk out of her life, and she'd never get him back again.

"All right!"

He stopped, looked over his shoulder, and waited.

"I'll tell her," Addie said in a rush. "I'll tell her tonight—under one condition."

"What's that?"

"You give me twelve more babies like Bryce."

The next thing Addie knew, she was being swept up in Oren's powerful arms.

"You dad-blamed woman—I thought you'd never come to your senses."

"I love you, Oren."

He gave her a slow, wicked smile that had her nerves sizzling and her toes curling. "Show me."

Ask your sister.

The words pounded through Linsey's brain as she searched high and low for Addie. She remembered seeing her in the hotel, but when she went back to look for her, she wasn't there, nor could anyone tell Linsey where she had gone off to. Home, maybe? Why, she couldn't guess, but neither could she think of anyplace else her sister might be.

She crossed Wishing Well Lane, thankful that at least she didn't have to worry about Bishop jumping out of the woodwork anymore. Several of the men at the reception had heard the ruckus and had come out to investigate. Linsey had quickly explained what happened. Her report had aroused the men's protective instincts as well as their outrage, and they vowed to send someone to track down the county sheriff. She'd press charges against Bishop if she thought it would do any good, but the best she could hope for was that the mayor and Mrs. Harvey might at last see their son for what he really was, and take measures to see that he didn't accost another woman.

Linsey frowned, her thoughts once again circling around to Daniel—to his defense of her, to his astounding declaration. She'd never been so angry to hear anything in her life. It just wasn't fair. Even if she didn't have one foot in the grave, she could never betray Addie by stealing the man she adored. Already the guilt of having kissed Daniel, of having fallen in love with him, was almost too much for Linsey to bear.

Ask your sister.

Again the words echoed in her mind. What could he possibly know about Addie that she didn't?

As she passed the smithy, a feminine giggle wafted through the doors, followed by a masculine rumble of laughter. Linsey's steps faltered. There was something very familiar about that giggle.

Linsey pushed on the door with her fingertips. Brows drawn, she peeked inside the shop, the darkness broken only by the mellow glow of a lantern hanging on a hook outside a stall.

She knew better than to barge into a neighbor's property uninvited, and yet the playful noises coming from within compelled her farther into the shop

But when she peered over the stall, she gasped at the sight that met her eyes—a man and a woman, locked in a passionate embrace. She recognized Addie's long, straight blond hair instantly. She couldn't see the man's face, for he had it buried between Addie's breasts, yet Linsey knew only one man would ever be allowed such liberties.

Daniel.

Anguish seared her heart. A tight fist of betrayal plowed into her middle, stole her breath, drove her backward. She choked on a sob and spun around, blindly seeking escape. She stumbled over her skirts, against a barrel, and it toppled over with a crash.

Linsey regained her footing. Behind her, she heard a violent rustling, then a slam of a door being flung open.

"Linsey . . . ! Oh, my heavens . . . Linsey, wait!"

She couldn't. She couldn't bear the sight of them.

"Miss Linsey!"

The deep, drawling voice yanked her to a stop two feet from the smithy doors. Slowly she looked over her shoulder. Addie was hastily buttoning up her gaping bodice. Behind her loomed Oren Potter—his clothes rumpled, straw clinging in hair dark as coal.

"Mr. Potter?" she asked in confusion. "Addie? What's going on here?"

"I didn't want you to find out like this. I meant to tell you . . . "

She sank to the crate. "I don't understand. I thought you wanted to marry Daniel. I thought you loved him."

"No." Addie shook her head sadly. "Oren's the man I love. And he loves me."

"When did this happen?"

"There wasn't any certain day. It just started . . . and grew."

"That long? For the love of Gus, here I've been shoving you and Daniel together, and the whole time you've been rolling in the dirt with the smithy?"

"Now see here, Miss Linsey—"

"No, Oren, please. This is between me and my sister."

It was the first time Linsey had ever heard such backbone from her sister, and amazingly, she'd done it with nothing more than a soft tone and a gentle hand to the strapping man's arm.

Addie stepped forward, smoothing her rumpled skirts and licking her kiss-swollen lips. Her eyes were filled with sorrow, and maybe a little regret, yet Linsey had a difficult time seeing past the haze of betrayal. The whole time she'd borne the burden of guilt for kissing Daniel, the timid, proper sister she'd cared for for fifteen years had been trysting with the local blacksmith—and never said a word about it.

"Linsey, I never meant to keep this a secret from you."

"But you did! How could you not tell me? Your own sister?"

"I wanted to tell you—I *tried* to tell you." She gave a watery laugh. "God, I can't count how many times I've lain awake over these last weeks, trying to find the words."

"Why didn't you just say it?"

"Because you were so busy planning your death and my life that you wouldn't listen."

The statement drove through her like a pickax. Daniel had said almost the exact same thing to her only hours before.

"Linsey, I love you. And I know you had your heart set on me marrying Daniel . . . but he isn't the man of my dreams. Oren is. I want to walk at his side down the center of town. I want to fix his meals and share his home and bear his children. I want to spend the rest of my life looking at him, touching him, being with him. I don't want to look back one day and say, 'I had love, and I threw it away,' and it isn't fair for you to make me feel guilty about that. Because I do love him, Linsey, with all my heart and soul—and if you can't accept that, then you're not the sister I've looked up to all these years."

Slack jawed, Linsey could only sit in amazed silence, partly over the strength of Addie's commitment, partly over her own blindness to what should have been noticeable all along. "I had no idea you felt this way. If I had known . . . " She swallowed and blinked back a film of moisture gathering across her eyes. "Addie, I never would have tried to force you into doing something you didn't want to do. All I ever wanted was to make sure you would be happy."

"I am happy. With Oren."

She was. Linsey could see it in the shy glow in her cheeks, in the sparkle in her eyes. Addie had found her Prince Charming.

It just wasn't Daniel.

He stood on the banks of Horseshoe Creek, skipping rocks in his black coattails, looking

more handsome than a body had a right to.
His Sunday suit fit him to snug perfection,
emphasizing those incredibly broad shoulders, that lean waist, those straight hips and
long muscled legs.

As always, the power of him lured her like a
blossom to sunshine. Linsey picked up a flat-
sided stone and joined him at the banks. She
let the stone fly. It bounced twice across the
smooth surface, making double plops.

"Not bad," he said.

"I used to be better."

The idle chatter didn't cover the underlying
tension between them. There had been so
many words flung at each other, so many emotions brought to the surface. . . .

She was probably making a fool of herself
by coming here and seeking him out. She
imagined what it must have cost this proud
man to say what he'd said earlier: that he . . .
that he loved her. They were the most beautiful words a woman could hear from the man
who had stolen her heart, and what had she
done? Screamed at him like a shrew.

It still infuriated her the way he and Addie
had conspired against her, but he'd warned
her of the consequences of her meddling. By
pushing Daniel and Addie together, she'd
nearly cost Addie the love of her life and saddled Daniel with a wife he never wanted. For
that, she owed him an apology.

Again.

It seemed she was always apologizing to
Daniel.

"I found my sister with Oren Potter tonight,"

she finally said, flinging another stone.

Daniel followed with an impressive triple skip of his own. "She loves him."

"She told me." Linsey looked over at him. He wasn't looking at her but at the shimmer of moonlight bridging across the water. "You've known all along, haven't you?"

"Pretty much."

"And you never said anything."

"It wasn't my place to say."

"I feel like a fool," she said. "Here I was, thinking she needed me to help her find someone who could make her happy. Turns out she didn't need me at all. She did it on her own."

"You might try taking a lesson from the teacher. Be the one in charge of your own fate, instead of letting it be in charge of you."

Linsey stared at the rippled glow across the creek's surface while emotions circled inside her like a tide pool. Fate. What a fickle creature it was. Giving. Taking. Teasing. Forbidding. So profoundly kind . . . Her gaze strayed to Daniel . . . So unbearably cruel.

She committed to memory every detail of the exasperating, arrogant, loveable man who had stolen her heart. The brooding tilt of his eyes. The proud angle of his nose. The stubborn slope of his jaw and the sensuous turn of his mouth.

He turned, and caught her watching him. The moment froze. Emotion swirled between them, captured like stardust on a moonbeam. Past and present merged into one, filling Linsey with a yearning so keen it nearly brought her to her knees.

Maybe he was right. She was so tired of dying. Tonight, she wanted to live. With Addie no longer between them, why squander another moment? She had so little time left.

She took one step forward, then another, and yet another until she stood before Daniel. With a boldness that surprised even her, Linsey reached for the narrow black tie he wore and worked it loose from its knot.

His hands gripped her wrists in a firm but tender hold. His lashes fell, coal fringes against tanned skin. "What are you doing, Linsey?"

"Taking charge of my own fate. I need you, Daniel. I have for months. And I think you've been needing me, too."

He sucked in a swift breath. Desire equal to her own glittered in his eyes. "There's no going back after tonight."

"No, there isn't. There's just now. Sometimes that's all we've got." She slipped the tie from his neck and let it drop to the ground. "Will you share it with me?"

She felt his hesitation, his control. It tightened his body, battered at his control.

Finally his hands, Daniel's beautiful hands, smoothed their way up her arms to her shoulders, leaving goose bumps in their wake. His fingers curled into the ruffle of her sleeve.

And she knew beyond a doubt that the weeks of fighting this unruly attraction had finally reached an end.

With a tug to her sleeves, he slipped the gown off her shoulders. It shimmied down her body to pool at her feet like a satin cloud.

He drew back and his heavy, smoldering gaze raked her body.

One by one, he released the hooks of her stays. Her breathing quickened; her heart began an almost painful thump. Anticipation tightened her breasts as he peeled the corset away, then tossed it aside, leaving her to stand in only her petticoats, chemise, and her Token of Good Fortune. With one fingertip, he drew a line across the swell of her breast. It expanded at his touch, became eager and aching, straining against the flimsy cloth.

The first contact of his mouth at her collarbone made a shiver spiral down Linsey's spine. She closed her eyes, her mouth parted, and her senses filled with the scent of bay rum and cool moon and forbidden wishes. Yes, this was what she craved—for Daniel to awaken every nerve in her body, make her blood hum, and her head spin. Another kiss, moist and tender, to her neck, and another to the pulse beneath her ear, intensified the dizzying sensation.

She unfastened the buttons of his vest, then his shirt, revealing hard male chest inch by tantalizing inch. A tremor rocked through him as she peeled the fabric away. Dusky nipples went pebble hard as the cool night air caressed him. A thick, dark mat of hair on his chest narrowed into a thin line to his waistband, as if pointing the way to pleasure.

Linsey could only stare in awe at the sheer beauty of him.

Rolling his shoulders, Daniel helped her remove his shirt. It fell to the ground and he stood before her, naked to the waist and glorious, kissed by moonlight and loved by the sweet Texas wind.

She flattened her palms against his supple skin, kissed the scorching flesh at his collarbone. Her hands, curious and bold, roamed down the flat, rippled muscles of his abdomen. They clenched, quivered, filling Linsey with a power that made her smile in wicked delight.

"Witch," he whispered.

She tossed her head. "Wretch."

He smiled that dimpled smile that had been melting hearts all over Henderson county for the last decade. Then he covered her mouth in a soul-searing kiss. Linsey's knees went weak. She curled her arms around his neck to drag him closer, even as he swept her against the powerful breadth of his chest.

She felt him guide her to the ground, dimly aware of him spreading his coat beneath her back just before he laid her upon the warm wool and covered her body with his own.

The kiss grew hotter, harder, deeper.

Consumed by the fever of Daniel, Linsey met his open-mouthed assault with a hunger of her own, twining her tongue around his, plunging her fingers through his silky hair, gently scoring his scalp, until nothing mattered but tangled hair—tangled tongues—tangled desires.

Daniel pulled back. Linsey gasped for breath. Their gazes met, and in the dark depths Linsey recognized his hunger, for she felt it, too.

He tugged at the ribbon of her chemise. She shivered, a hot, delicious shiver of eagerness for him to quit this torment and touch her. When he did, she thought she'd died and been launched to paradise. Dragging the folds of her chemise aside, his mouth pressed moist, scalding kisses to the sensitive flesh of first one breast, then the other. His breath teased her nipple; his tongue flicked over the distended bud. Linsey closed her eyes and bit her bottom lip to keep from crying out. Just when she didn't think she could bear the sweet torture any longer, his mouth closed over her, drawing her breast inside.

"Daniel!"

Oh, God! She'd thought his hands gifted, but that was before she knew what pleasures his mouth could bring. Her hands, clutching the tight muscles of his bare back, began to rub up and down the length of smooth skin, anxious, needing something from him she couldn't name, but knew only he could give. Toned muscle surged beneath her palms, a curious bulge hardened against the inside of her thigh.

She whimpered when he drew back and reached for him, feeling suddenly chilled and empty at his desertion. Then she saw him going for his waistband. Licking her bottom lip, Linsey covered his hands with hers. They were clumsy, inexperienced, shaking as she tugged at the stubborn button, yet she wanted to see him, to feel him, touch him.

Daniel finally seemed to take pity on her, for he swiftly worked the fasteners open, then slid his trousers down hard, muscled legs. He sprang free of the confines.

She stared at him in shock and wonder.

She'd never seen a naked man, never imagined that one could be so . . . beautiful. Daniel was. His manhood, rising proud and strong from a mat of thick black hair, should have frightened her. It didn't. It only made her curious, more eager to explore him. Daniel groaned and buried his face in her hair when she closed her fingers around his shaft. She caressed his hardness, gloried in the feel of silk-on-steel leaping at her touch.

His hand slid beneath her petticoat to begin a slow journey up her bare thigh, over her bottom to the sensitive crease of her pelvic bone.

Linsey arched at the wild sensation.

Gentle hands. Gifted hands. Sensual touch. He seemed to know just where to stroke to give her the most pleasure. Her hip, her belly, the mound of curls between her thighs.

Feeling herself grow hot and damp, Linsey clutched Daniel's head to her breast. His finger probed at her entrance, searching, teasing, tempting, until her thighs parted and her hips rose of their own accord. His finger slipped inside her and she caught back a whimper, unable to believe the feelings of wonder, of desire that flooded her.

"Daniel!" His name escaped her on a sigh as he plunged his finger inside her and withdrew it, only to taunt her again. And again. Urgency built inside Linsey. She wanted to beg him to go faster and yet savor the slowness at the same time.

When he covered her, sliding between her thighs, pausing with his strong shaft pressed to the entrance of her body, he took her face in his hands.

"I love you," he said huskily.

She couldn't speak for the emotion clogging her throat.

"I don't want to hurt you."

"I know." She didn't want to hurt him, either. But she would.

She pushed the knowledge to the back of her mind as Daniel, his gaze holding hers, pushed inside her. She felt herself stretch, felt her muscles tense. He withdrew. No sooner did she relax, than with one swift, sure stroke, he plunged himself into her.

Linsey gasped. Her nails bit into his buttocks, and tears sprang to her eyes.

He didn't move. She didn't want him to. The last thing she'd expected was for him to hurt her.

"I'm sorry," he whispered, his voice thick. "I'm sorry."

He kissed her eyes, her nose, her mouth with such tenderness that she almost wept. Gradually his tender homage eased the pain. She hardly noticed it when he began to move again.

He kept the pace slow, sliding in, out. A wondrous pressure began to build. Linsey

tightened her legs around him, let herself fall
into his rhythm, let him take her higher,
higher. A delicious dizziness crept at the edges
of her vision. Stars began to dance in her head.

He thrust harder into her. She arched against
him, panted his name. Oh, God . . .

With a final plunge, Daniel cried out. Linsey
released a keening wail as the world exploded
into blinding color and feeling. Straining
against him, she absorbed every last drop he
spent into her.

At last, limbs trembling, heart thundering,
Linsey fell back, feeling as if she were melting
against the ground. Daniel collapsed atop her,
as limp as she.

They lay entwined for what seemed forever,
body sated and hearts full, when Daniel finally
murmured, "Woman, I think you've drained
the life right out of me. I can't move."

"This has been wonderful, hasn't it? And
you know what?" She gave a giddy giggle. "I
got to do something I've never done before."

"That was obvious—but what you lacked in
experience, you more than made up for with
eagerness."

"You must think me shameless."

"I wouldn't have you any other way."

A slow, satisfied smile spread across Linsey's face. Staring at the endless blanket of
stars, the glowing moon, she combed her fingers through his silky hair and asked, "Have
you ever come to a point in your life when you
think, 'If it never gets better than this, I'll die
happier than I deserve?' That's how I feel
when I'm with you. I wish I could take that

feeling and put it in my pocket and carry it with me wherever I go."

"I'm at that point right now." She felt him grin.

He shifted, starting to relieve her of his weight, but she wouldn't let him. Sighing her contentment, she pulled him close, wishing it could be closer, wishing she could take him with her when she left this earth.

That wasn't possible, of course. Nor would she really want to deny others his incredible skills—as long as they didn't extend beyond doctor-patient relationships. Even she wasn't generous enough to want him to find another woman too soon after she was gone.

"God, I love your hair," he muttered against her neck.

Linsey smiled. "I'm wounded, doc. And here I thought you loved me for my wit and charm."

"I do, I do. And your luscious breasts and your tiny waist and your gorgeous legs . . . "

As his hand trailed up her bare leg, she laughed, just for the sake of laughing, and threw her arms around his neck. "I declare, we've gone completely daft. It's freezing out here . . . "

"Funny, I was thinking how warm it was. If you're cold, though, I know of a very nice way to heat you up."

"And here we are, on the banks of Horseshoe Creek, where anyone can stumble upon us. What were we thinking?"

"Nothing. Everything." He brushed a curl off her brow, then let his fingers trail along her cheek. "The last thing I seem capable of doing around you is thinking. Since the day I've met you, you've turned my world upside down. Blame it on your smile. On the light in your eyes. Hell, blame it on the moon for all I care. I just know I've never felt so damned alive in my life as I feel when I'm with you."

After a long, drugging kiss, he laid his head upon her breast and sighed, seeming in no hurry to dress despite the damp evening chill.

With Daniel's body a warm and comforting weight upon her, Linsey continued watching the stars, unable to believe how incredibly complete she felt. If this was the way her father made his wives feel, it was no wonder they'd chosen to stay with him. She felt the same way about Daniel: anywhere he went, she would gladly go. Of course, she'd never leave her children behind, the way her parents had done.

Not that children would ever be a part of her future—but for however much time she had left, she wanted to spend it here, with Daniel, in his arms. Loving him. Seeing him smile. Hearing him laugh. Even watching him get riled filled her with a peculiar excitement. Who'd have ever thought that one day, she'd feel so thoroughly and completely loved by the man who'd once hated her with equal passion?

The thought dimmed Linsey's peace. "Does this mean you've forgiven me?"

"For what?" The lazy question rumbled against her breast.

"For everything. For Addie, for . . . " her voice dropped to a halting murmur. "For your fellowship."

Daniel grew still. Then he raised his head to look at Linsey. After the passion they'd shared, that was the last question he expected to hear from her, and damned if he knew how to reply. But he knew one thing—he couldn't fool himself into believing that the same woman who went around taking care of people could have deliberately ruined his career.

Scooting up, Daniel tucked her head under his chin and drew her close. Her cheek rested on his chest. Her warm breath caressed his sweat-dampened flesh.

"There was a time when that fellowship meant everything to me. I would have lied, stolen, and cheated to get it, and probably did all three at one time or another," he confessed. "It's not something to be proud of, but there it is. I just wanted so badly to have the power to give others a fighting chance to live their dreams. I wanted to be a part of that 'something bigger' that you talk of, to know that I could make a real and lasting difference."

"And now?"

"I don't know, Linsey. But I feel as if somewhere along the way, I lost sight of the reasons I wanted to become a surgeon in the first place. They seem to have gotten lost in some . . . quest to prove I could do it, despite all the odds."

"Ambition isn't a bad thing, Daniel."

"It is when other people lose at the expense of another's win. You don't go into medicine to prove a point; you go into it because you love to beat the odds. Because you want to make a difference. Because you want to preserve human life. But maybe life isn't worth saving, if it isn't going to be lived." If he'd learned anything from Linsey over the last month or so, it had been that.

He leaned back and tipped her chin up with his knuckles. "So maybe losing that fellowship was the best thing that ever happened to me. I never would have come to appreciate the things I've taken for granted—and I never would have fallen in love with you."

"So you *do* forgive me?"

"Sweetheart, there's nothing to forgive."

In one swift motion she had him pinned to the ground and rained kisses over his face until they were both laughing. Daniel didn't realize what a burden he'd carried until the words were out of his mouth, until he'd let go of the blame.

Then Linsey cupped his face in her hands and placed a kiss on his mouth so tender that he swore his heart melted. One kiss became two, then three, long, deep, intoxicating kisses that stirred his desire all over again. It amazed him how much he wanted this woman. Tonight. Tomorrow night. Every night, for as long as they both lived, he wanted her. With him. Beside him. Atop him. And if that meant giving up all that he'd worked for, and settling for a country practice with his cantankerous father so he could support her and the family they might have, then so be it. There would always be other dreams.

There would never be another Linsey.

"So, do you think you could be happy spending the rest of your life with a fellow who gets paid in chickens?"

Linsey giggled. "Surgeons don't get paid in chickens."

"No, but drug store-owning country doctors do."

She stilled upon his chest. "What do you mean? What of your dream to go to the university and become a famous surgeon?"

"Being with you is more important than studying at Johns Hopkins."

Linsey reared back and swatted at his shoulder. "I can't believe I'm hearing this from you! You would dare throw away something you've wanted and worked for your whole life, for a woman?"

"Not any woman—only you."

If anything, the reply made her madder. "Let me tell you something Dr. Sharpe. No woman worth her salt would ever expect the man she loves to give up something that means so much to him. A woman supports her man's dreams. She becomes his helpmate and he becomes hers. If she doesn't, then he'd best find himself another woman."

"Are you saying you want me to get my degree?"

"If you do not continue your schooling, i

you do not get that surgical degree and start your own practice, you are not the man I thought you were—and I want nothing more to do with you."

Grinning like a lackwit, he tumbled her to the ground and kissed her soundly. "Damn, but I knew you'd make me a splendid wife."

She stared at him in numb disbelief. "What did you say?"

"I said, you'll make me a splendid wife. My dad always told me that a wife would just drag a man down, but I don't suppose my mother was anything like you."

Linsey sat up, pulled her chemise closed, and began tying the ribbons.

A dull sense of dread spread through Daniel when she said nothing. She wouldn't even look at him. "Linsey?"

At long last she lifted her head, and the bleakness in her eyes stole his breath.

"I love you, too, Daniel. I wonder if there was ever a time when I didn't love you," she whispered, "and I can think of no greater honor than becoming your wife. But I can't marry you."

It was hard to speak for the crushing pressure on his heart, but somehow he managed. "Why not?"

"It just wouldn't be fair to make you a widower just after you've become a groom."

A widower? What the Sam Hill

He fell back onto his coat and shoved splayed hands through his hair. "For chrissake, not this foolishness again! I thought you'd come to your senses!"

"Please, don't make this any harder than it is—just stop fighting fate and accept the inevitable."

He pinned her with a steely-eyed glare. "Like you are?"

"What?"

Daniel snatched his trousers from the grass and pulled them on with short, jerky movements. "You'll fight for your sister, you'll fight for your friends, you'll even fight for me, but you won't fight for yourself. Just what the hell are you afraid of, Linsey?"

Her body snapped back if he'd struck her. Goddamn, he was sick of trying—and failing—to convince her that these fears were completely unrealistic.

She recovered an instant later, plucked her blue silk bridesmaids dress from off the ground and held it close to her. "There are some things in life that you just can't fight. Love is one; death is another. I thought you of all people would know that."

"All I know is that I'm tired of watching you put your faith in something that doesn't exist. These damned superstitions of yours have done nothing but ruin people's lives, and until you can see that, we have no future."

"Oh, Daniel, don't you see?" She shook her head slowly. "We never did."

Chapter 20

❦

The hand—man's first tool and weapon—signifies power, both physical and spiritual, and is known to possess healing virtues.

Daniel threw himself into his work, driving himself from dawn to dusk, seeking to keep himself so occupied that by the time he fell into bed, he was too exhausted to think. He'd taken over some of his dad's patients, filled in for Dr. Chelsey in the next county, and even helped out at the hospital in Iron Bluff when the death of their physician left them shorthanded. The nonstop pace left him looking like hell warmed over and feeling twice as bad, but he didn't care. The one time he had let himself care, his heart had been ripped from his chest, stomped on, then shoved back in.

His dad had been right all along: let a woman become a part of you, and she'd drain the life right out of you.

As if thinking about the man had summoned him, Daniel, Sr., appeared in the doorway of Daniel's office just as he unlocked the glass-fronted supply cabinet. When had his dad gotten spectacles? Daniel wondered, noticing the gold-rimmed lenses for the first time. He quickly averted his gaze. The eyewear only served to remind him of the amulet Linsey wore and all that had torn them apart.

"You going out again?" his dad asked.

"Just making the rounds today."

"And avoiding the books. They don't have lice, you know."

Daniel spared a brief glance at the stack of textbooks and journals taking up space on his office shelves. He could hardly bring himself to look at them, much less open one up. Why bother? He'd never make it into Johns Hopkins anyway, and even if he did, what was the point? He'd probably fail at that like he'd failed at everything else. Turning his attention back to his bag, Daniel shoved a roll of bandages into it. "I don't have time to study."

"You had best make time, Junior . . . "

Daniel rounded on his father. He couldn't take it—not now, not with the wounds of Linsey's rejection still so fresh and raw. "Don't call me that! Call me Daniel or Dan—or better yet, call me son if that's anywhere in your vocabulary. But for chrissake, don't call me Junior again."

Daniel, Sr., reared back. "What the Sam Hill has gotten into you, boy?"

Daniel let out a wild laugh. "You can't even say it, can you? Have I been such a disappointment to you that you won't ever acknowledge that I'm your own flesh and blood?"

The old man's eyes narrowed. "What kind of talk is that? Of course you're my flesh and blood."

"Then why don't you say it?" Daniel cried. "Always calling me 'Junior' as if I'm no match for you. Never your equal, always beneath you." Daniel swallowed a raspy knot of emotion. "Just *once* I'd like to hear you say I'm as good as you."

"You won't, because you aren't."

To Daniel's deep shame, he felt his eyes go damp. He swiftly buckled his bag, needing to get out of here, away from the one man whose approval he'd always sought and never gotten, before he unmanned himself.

He'd just reached the door when a biting grip around his arm pulled him to a stop.

"You aren't as good as me; you're better. As a man, as a doctor . . . hell, boy, you're better than I'll ever be."

Daniel's system went into shock.

The grip loosened, then fell away. "You've got a way about you that makes people trust you. That makes 'em want to do right by you. You just don't use it. Why do you think I push you so damn hard?"

"Because you can't stand seeing someone idle?"

"Well, that, too," he admitted gruffly, "but it's mostly because you've got the gift. I wouldn't have been much of a father if I'd let you throw it away—like I did."

"Yeah, I know. You couldn't build a surgical practice because you got a woman with child and had to marry her."

"I didn't have to marry your mother; I wanted to." Daniel, Sr., wandered into the room, paused at the window, and tucked his thumbs into the pockets of his vest. "Your mother was the prettiest thing this side of Sweetwater, and I wanted her from the time I was old enough to set a razor to my chin. She used to let me practice on her when I got bit with the doctorin' bug; and after we got hitched, there wasn't a day that went by that she didn't have my instruments packed and my patients lined up. I couldn't have asked for a better nurse.

"After the war, all these damned medical association rules and regulations started coming into effect. Your mother pushed me to get the proper licenses so I could perform surgery legally. The more she pushed, the more inept I felt. It just tore us apart, and there didn't seem to be a damn thing either of us could do to make it right."

"Why didn't you just get the licenses?"

He didn't reply for a long while; just stared out the window at a pair of blue jays diving for worms. Finally, in an almost inaudible voice, he said, "Because I can't read."

"What?"

"You heard me," his dad barked over his shoulder, "I can't read."

Daniel fell back against the door frame, feeling as if the foundation he stood on had given away beneath his feet.

"Why the hell do you think all those bottles in there got pictures on 'em?" He jerked his thumb toward the apothecary.

Daniel couldn't reply. He'd always thought his dad put the symbols on the pharmaceutical containers as another prod to get him into medicine. He'd had no idea.

"I'll tell you why: because I don't know A from Z. I know numbers, and I know symbols. I even know how to spell my name, but I can't read the label on a damned tinned beef can."

"But you went to college," Daniel finally managed to say. "You got your physician's certificate—you were a field surgeon in the war!"

"How much book learning does it take to saw off boys' arms and legs?"

Daniel knew his father had done much, much more than that in the hospital camps. He might only have been in short pants at the time of the War Between the States, but he knew that a lot of men owed their lives to his father's skills with a scalpel.

"I apprenticed my way into doctoring, Daniel. In my day you didn't need any book-learning; you just hitched up with a doctor and did the job like he taught you. Half the time, a man didn't even need a license to practice medicine; he just hung a shingle and practiced. There were more damn quacks coming out of the woodwork than you could shake a stick at. And there wasn't a thing I could do about it, except treat my patients the best way I knew how and pray for the best."

"Why didn't you ever tell me?"

"And have my own son look down on me because I couldn't do something that came so easily to him?"

"I'd never have looked down on you, Dad. You are an excellent physician."

"I'm fair to middlin'. I do my job. But you, Daniel . . . " Daniel, Sr., closed the space between them and clapped a hand on Daniel's shoulder. "You are my greatest talent and my deepest pride. You've got the book smarts that I never had, and if you use them, they'll take you places I've only dreamed of. I couldn't let that go to waste."

Daniel stared into his dad's eyes, and the emotion that he saw in them filled him with a sense of acceptance he hadn't imagined possible. Years of discord and misunderstandings crumbled away, uncovering a trove of respect neither had expected to ever find.

Daniel cupped his dad's shoulder and, with a trembling smile, gave the old man a brief shake. If nothing else had gone right in the last few years, at least he and his father had finally made peace.

The jangle of cowbells and a sudden crash from the apothecary jolted both men. They turned as one and raced through the curtained partition.

Daniel's alarm turned to puzzlement at the sight of Robert Jarvis bracing himself against the frame of the front door. "Jarvis, what are you doing here? I figured you'd be halfway across Alabama by now." The town was still buzzing about the lamplighter's ascension in the new balloon. The *Herald* had even given it front-page coverage in the same issue that announced Addie Witt's engagement to Oren Potter.

Daniel had missed Jarvis's event, which was

probably for the best since he neither wanted nor needed any reminders of the day he and Linsey had touched the clouds. The wisest thing he could do was just forget he'd ever known her, forget he'd ever loved her.

"I ain't feelin' so good, Dan'l."

As Daniel approached his friend, he noticed the beads of sweat on his narrow brow, and smelled the humidity of his woolen clothes and coat. His instincts went on instant alert. Flushed, feverish, glassy eyes . . . "You been drinking Cooter's shine again?" he joked to hide his concern.

"Didn't ya hear? Cooter . . . gave up moonshinin'."

No sooner were the words out of his mouth than Jarvis went slack. Daniel raced to his friend's side, catching Jarvis under the arms just as his legs folded under him. "Jarvis, what's the matter with you?"

"You're the doc. You tell me."

And then he passed out.

Epidemic.

The word struck fear in the heart of any doctor, and Daniel was no different.

"Anybody who was at the wedding has been exposed," Daniel, Sr., gravely announced several days later.

"There were a hundred people there, Dad!"

"I know, son. We've already got six stricken down with the virus, and at the rate influenza travels, we'll have sixty more by Christmastime. You best get some sleep while you can. Soon enough, there won't be time."

Over the next week, close to twenty people—some whole families—were caught in the grip of the influenza virus, and the following week another fifteen were stricken down, keeping Daniel and his father in perpetual motion from one end of the county to the other. Some cases were milder, not exceeding the frontal-lobe headache, runny nose and sore throat, and general lame feeling associated with the virus. Others, though, had reached the more advanced stages of vomiting and respiratory cough. Those were the cases that concerned the doctors most, for they threatened to develop into catarrh pneumonia.

Finally, three days before Christmas, Daniel sank to his bed like a lead weight, grateful that the worst of the epidemic seemed to have passed. And miracle of miracles, they hadn't lost a single patient.

Only when Daniel felt a sting to his knuckles did he realize he'd been knocking on the wooden nightstand for luck.

With a deep scowl, he thrust his fist under his pillow. Would Linsey never leave him alone? No matter where he went, or who he was with, his thoughts turned to her. He hadn't seen her since that night beside Horseshoe Creek, when she'd given herself to him without reserve and made herself so much a part of him he feared he'd never be cured of her.

Even now, bone-deep weary and wanting only to catch a few winks, he couldn't get her out of his mind.

His last thought before falling into a sleep fit

for the dead was that she'd better have had
enough sense to keep clear of those infected
with the illness.

He wouldn't talk to her. He wouldn't look at
her. He wouldn't even walk on the same side
of the street as she did.

With a dejected slump of her shoulders, Linsey turned away from the darkened apothecary window and started for home. Even
shopping for Christmas gifts with Addie
hadn't lessened the heavy weight on her heart
since her parting with Daniel two weeks earlier.

She tried to find some comfort in the fact
that she and Addie had mended their broken
fences. They spent their evenings planning
Addie's wedding, yet nothing diminished this
aching loneliness she'd been feeling since the
night of Jenny and Noah's wedding, when her
world had gone from hell to heaven and back
again.

Reaching Briar House, she paused on the
veranda steps with a hand to her stomach and
closed her eyes, willing away the nausea
churning inside her.

Aunt Louisa had lied to her, she thought,
dragging herself into the house and up the
stairs. Love didn't make a girl's toes curl and
her breath catch and her fingers tingle.

It made her stomach roll and her muscles
ache and her throat sting.

She crawled under the thick quilts of her
bed and tried to remember a time when she'd
ever felt so miserable, but couldn't. There

wasn't a place on her that didn't feel bruised or swollen.

And as the days passed, the feeling grew worse, becoming so bad that she could barely drag herself out of bed each morning. She made excuses to Aunt Louisa and Addie, not wanting them to worry over a simple case of broken heart. But when general misery steadily developed into painful breathing and hot chills, Linsey began to worry herself.

She brought the quilt tighter around her shoulders as a chill overtook her body, and still she couldn't seem to get warm.

As much as she hated to face it, she knew what was happening. Her time had come: she was dying. As surely as the sun set each night, the omen was coming true.

It was nothing like she'd thought or hoped. Nothing fast or painless. This heavy, miserable sensation wasn't a simple case of heartache. Influenza claimed its victims slowly.

A knock came on the door, and a second later Addie appeared with a tray balanced on her hip. "You didn't come down to dinner, so I thought I'd bring you up something to eat."

Linsey held a cough deep in her lungs. They strained and burned, feeling as if they were being pressed through her spine with each breath she took. "I'm not hungry."

"Will you at least try? You've hardly eaten enough to sustain a bird." She set the tray on the bedside stand and sat down on the edge of Linsey's bed. "Are you feeling all right?" Without waiting for a reply, she pressed a cool, slim hand to Linsey's brow, only to jerk back. "For heaven's sake, Linsey, you feel on fire!"

"Funny, I feel as if I'm made of ice."

"I've got to get Daniel."

"No." She shook her head. "I don't want to see him, any more than he wants to see me."

"You are ill, and you need a doctor. If you won't see Daniel, I'll send for Doc Sr."

"It won't do any good, Addie." She turned her face against the pillow and stared out the window, feeling hollow, aching, and weary. So weary. "My time is almost up."

"Don't say that!"

"We've known this was coming."

"No." Addie drew back in horror. "You've made yourself believe this would happen."

"You sound like Daniel," Linsey said with a wan smile. "Addie, I only had two things left on my wish list. One was to make amends to Daniel. If I don't see him again, make sure he gets the letter I left for him in my vanity drawer. Perhaps when he reads it, it will help make up for all the pain I've caused him. The second thing left undone was to see you married to the man of your dreams. It doesn't look like I'll be able to keep my promise. But I want you to know that even if I'm not there in body, I'll be there in spirit, standing right beside you when you exchange vows with your Prince Charming."

"You stop talking this foolishness," Addie ordered, her eyes glistening with unshed tears. "You will live into the new year, and you will stand up at my wedding, do you hear me?" She dashed out the door.

Linsey blinked back the tears scalding her

eyes. Poor Addie. Didn't she know she was wasting her energy?

God knew, Linsey wished things were different. But a body couldn't fight fate. Her time had come to an end.

And not even Daniel could save her.

Chapter 21

*Sometimes the only luck left
is the luck we make ourselves.*

A violent shaking to his shoulder jolted Daniel awake. Disoriented, he glanced around the room until his gaze landed on a familiar blond woman standing beside his bed. He blinked. "Addie? What are you doing in my room?"

"I couldn't find your father."

Daniel snatched his shirt off the end of the bed and shoved his arms through the sleeves. "Granny Yearling took sick; he's over at her place. What's wrong?"

"It's Linsey."

He stilled, instant alarm snapping him to full alertness. "What about Linsey?"

"I think she's come down with the influenza."

Unmindful of Addie's presence, Daniel yanked a pair of trousers over his nudity, shoved his feet into his boots, and grabbed his medical bag.

They raced up Briar Hill. Daniel took the steps two at a time, burst through the front door, and tore up the stairs. His heart stampeding in his chest, he threw open each door down the hallway until he came to Linsey's room.

Even under a pile of blankets, she shook from chills. Three swift strides brought him to her side. "Linsey?" He brushed his hand tenderly against her brow, shocked at the heat emanating from her body. "For chrissake, she's burning up!"

"That's why I fetched you."

Daniel ripped his stethoscope from his bag and pressed the disk to Linsey's chest. "Her lungs are congested, her skin is dry—why in the hell wasn't I called earlier?"

"It just hit, Daniel, honest! She never gave any indication that she was ill."

"She's got the goddamn pneumonia!"

Addie's hand shot to her mouth. Tears welled up in her eyes.

Daniel fought to get his rampaging emotions under control. Bellowing at Addie wasn't going to do Linsey any good. She needed medical attention. He was a doctor. It was time he started acting like one.

After taking several deep breaths to clear his thoughts, he told Addie, "We need a fire going. I also need some clothesline to hang blankets up to warm, and a pot of water put on to boil."

Addie stood there, frozen.

"Now!"

That got her moving. As she dashed out the

door, Daniel brushed a wild red lock from Linsey's forehead. "Can you hear me?"

She stirred a bit, whether from his voice or his touch, he couldn't be sure. He was just thankful she responded.

"Daniel?"

"I'm here."

"I told Addie not to fetch you."

"Why would you tell her that?"

"Because there's nothing you can do. Because I didn't think you'd come."

"Wild horses couldn't have stopped me. And I'm going to do everything I can to make you better."

"It won't be enough."

"It will if you trust me."

All he got was tiny smile before she went out again, but it was enough.

Addie returned a short time later with all the items he needed. He had Addie make a pot of tea, to which he added several grains of powder to help break Linsey's fever and ease her discomfort. While Addie fed several spoonfuls between Linsey's chalky lips, Daniel warmed the blankets and piled them on top of her, and wrapped her feet in cloths soaked in hot water. Then he held her limp body over a kettle of a hot herbal mixture in the hopes that it would loosen the congestion in her lungs.

They continued the treatment through the night and all the next day. When Louisa Gordon came home that evening after caring for Persistence Yearling for two days, she was shocked to see her niece so ill. She pitched in without hesitation. By then, news of Linsey's illness had begun to spread around Horse-shoe. Several neighbors dropped by, but since Daniel wouldn't let them near her, they remained downstairs, supplying the family with food and comfort.

Even Oren had come by, and as was the way of pals, neither he nor Daniel spoke of their falling out. They just put it behind them as if it had never happened.

Day bled into night, then into day again, the hours becoming a blur of mechanical motion. Boil water, spoon-feed tea, administer medication, steam the lungs . . .

Daniel concentrated on the treatments he'd been taught, rather than on the fact that the woman he loved more than life itself was lying on death's doorstep. He refused to consider the odds of recovery. Linsey was young, she was strong, she was energetic. She'd pull through this.

But by the third day, when there was no change in her condition, Daniel began to doubt.

"Daniel," Addie said gently, "you can't keep this up. You must get some rest."

"I'm not leaving her." Not again.

"You won't do either Linsey or yourself any good if you don't lie down for a few minutes."

"I *won't* leave her." His gaze returned to Linsey's flushed face. What wasn't he doing? Why wasn't she getting better? He swallowed heavily and told Addie in a hoarse voice, "Fetch my father."

Daniel, Sr., arrived within the hour.

"It's bad, son, bad," Daniel's father

announced after a quick examination. "If she'd called one of us sooner, maybe, but now . . . I'll do what I can, of course. Boneset tonic, purging—"

"No. No purging. No bleeding, either. She's lost enough fluids."

"Fine. The acetanilid and salicylate of soda three times a day has been effective."

"She's beyond that. What about the atropine powders?"

"Might work for the catarrhal and nasal discharge. But I'd try the boneset tonic first. Has she been able to keep anything down?"

"Nothing."

"Keep feeding hot liquids into her to produce sweating. And try laying mustard plasters over her stomach to help curb the vomiting. Other than that, I don't know that there's much more we can do for her." He clicked his bag shut. At the door, he paused to glance over his shoulder and shake his head. "Helluva way to spend Christmas."

Daniel hadn't even realized that it was today. He looked at Linsey, who seemed so fragile. Her glorious hair had lost its luster and there were deep shadows beneath her eyes. As if she felt his study, her lashes fluttered, then her dull, glassy eyes focused on him.

"It's not good, is it?"

A lump of emotion shot into his throat. "I'm not done with you yet," he assured her.

Again that tiny, almost tolerant smile. "I have something for you. An envelope, in my top vanity drawer."

Reluctantly, Daniel released her hand. He fetched the envelope and brought it to her.

"Open it."

Resuming his seat on the hard chair, Daniel did as she bade. His eyes widened in astonishment. "What's this?"

"A gift for a gifted man. It's a fellowship, so you can continue your schooling and become a famous surgeon. I couldn't be your wife, so I wanted to give you something you've always wanted . . . to make amends. I hope that years from now, when you accept your degree from Johns Hopkins, you might remember me kindly."

Daniel laid his head on her belly, and for the first time in his life, he cried.

Christmas passed without much ado, as well as the days that followed. As Linsey faded in and out, Addie and Louisa took turns sitting with her, caring for her, surrounding her with the love that she'd given to them so freely all these years. All the while, Daniel watched in a numb state of disbelief.

Just when he didn't think she'd get any worse, she did.

Her respiration turned shallow and rapid, her face even more flushed, her spittle rusty. Her fever spiked. She tossed from side to side, kicked the blankets free, then curled up in a ball while chills wracked her thin body. Between him and Addie and Louisa, it was all they could do to keep her calm and warm.

During one of her quiet spells, as he sat at Linsey's bedside holding her hand in his own, his forehead against her wrist, he finally admitted to himself that nothing was working. He'd tried every remedy known to man, and not a single one of them appeared to be having any affect on her.

What if she was right?

What if fate had decreed that she would die? He thought of the night on the banks of Horseshoe Creek, the way she'd given herself to him without reserve and brought him pleasure he'd never felt before, and the day in the balloon, when she'd shown him a freedom he'd only dreamed of until that point. The idea of never seeing her cuddle a baby or curtsey to a horse or hear her cry out his name in passion sent anguish through his system.

"Damn you, Linsey, fight! Please! I know you can do this. You are strong and stubborn and you are so beautiful you take my breath away. Don't *leave* me. I can't do this . . . *living* thing without you. Who will laugh at me when I scowl, or smile at me when I've done well, or let me have it with both barrels when I'm ready to throw my hands up in frustration?"

There was no response.

He sprang from the chair, marched to her bureau top and scooped all her lucky trinkets into his arms. "Are these what you need?" He dumped them on the bed against her and started pushing them into her hands. "Take them, Linsey. Take them and make your wishes or spit over your shoulder or whatever it is that you do. Just . . . " His voice broke. "Don't leave me."

* * *

A warm breath against her neck reached deep into Linsey's glazed state, rousing her from the depths of a heat she couldn't escape.

It took all the strength she could summon to lift her hand to the head resting under her chin. She touched the silky hair, feeling weak as a newborn baby, yet compelled to comfort the man at her side. Somehow, she knew that he had been there all along. He hadn't left her

Her eyes went blurry at the thought of leaving him behind, of never being held by him again, never hearing him laugh. . . .

You'll fight for your sister, you'll fight for your friends, you'll even fight for me, but you won' fight for yourself. What are you so afraid of?

With the words echoing in her head, Linsey fell back against the pillows and stared into the cloudlike netting above her bed. What was she afraid of?

Failing.

It always seemed easier to blame things that went wrong on the signs, on fate's whim rather than accept that if she had only taken control, she might have been able to change destiny. She might have been able to stop her mother's death, her father's desertion, her own desperate need to be needed by those around her—even at the cost of their own independence.

Maybe Daniel had been right all along. Maybe things just happened because it was the way they were meant to happen. That sometimes, to gain something bigger, you had to take a risk.

What if, just once, she did doubt the signs

What if she actually let herself believe in another power—in Daniel's faith in her, in the love she felt for him, and the love he felt for her in return. What was the worst that could happen?

"Daniel?" His name slurred on her tongue. Strange, she felt so in command of her senses despite the fire burning in her body.

He bolted upright. "Jesus . . . Linsey?"

"What day?"

Again the words came out in a jumble.

"What?"

"What. Day?"

"Today? New Year's Eve."

Linsey closed her eyes. The last day of the year. It was now or never. Opening her eyes, she said in the same oddly garbled voice, "Take them away."

"Take what away?"

"The charms. Take them away. I am going to beat this."

"Good heavens, Daniel, she's delirious," Addie said, appearing behind him.

Linsey met Daniel's stare. He looked terrible—haggard and drawn and sporting a thick growth of black whiskers, as if he hadn't slept or shaved in days. Linsey willed him to understand her words, for she didn't think she had the strength to repeat them.

At last, a sparkle entered his eyes. He shook his head and told Addie, "No, she's lucid—though it might be the lull between attacks. The second attack is almost always more severe than the initial one."

"She won't survive it."

"I think she wants to try—on her own."

Linsey managed a crooked smile for him. He understood.

"You can do this, sweetheart," he told her, clasping her hand. "I'll be right here for you."

And she realized then, that if she weakened in her resolve, he'd become her strength. If she wavered in the belief in herself, he would be her faith. No matter what happened, that knowledge would live inside her.

Against her will, Linsey drifted in and out of awareness. She couldn't seem to fight this incredible weariness for long, and though it frustrated her, she refused to give up. Each time she felt herself being pulled under, she squeezed Daniel's hand and felt herself rise to the surface again, as if his strength fed hers.

Reaching midnight was all she could think of, all she could focus on as the day and night wore on. If she could just get past midnight she'd beat Fate at her own game. She'd hold Lady Luck in the palm of her hand. She would stand on the edge of that unknown place she'd always dreamed of, and look down, and feel the exhilaration of being someplace she'd never been before.

A sudden silence descended upon the room and she sensed that the time of reckoning had come. Daniel's hand squeezed hers tightly, Addie's arm curled around her shoulder, and Aunt Louisa's soft-skinned fingers held her other wrist.

She felt everyone hold their breath, and then she heard the clock. *One.*

Two.

Three.

Linsey clenched her eyes tight and braced herself. *I won't go without a fight. I won't leave Daniel, I won't leave Addie, I won't leave Aunt Louisa. . . .*

Twelve. The last strike echoed in the silence.

Then someone laughed—Daniel, she thought—and someone cried. Probably Addie. And someone sighed, no doubt Aunt Louisa.

Linsey simply smiled. She'd done it.

A gentle spring breeze ruffled the grasses alongside Horseshoe Creek, where the town had gathered to celebrate the double wedding of Adelaide Witt to Oren Potter, and Linsey Gordon to Dr. Daniel Sharpe, Jr.

There had been a time when Daniel had feared this day would never dawn. Linsey's recovery had been slow—sometimes agonizingly slow—but if he'd learned anything over his lifetime, it was that healing had its own timetable. The epidemic hadn't swept through Horseshoe without taking casualties—Granny Yearling and the Neely baby had both succumbed—and the town mourned their loss.

Though Daniel mourned along with them, he gave thanks that his Linsey had been spared. Neither quite knew where the credit should go for her recovery. Linsey's strong will, his own, or—Daniel's hand crept to his neck where a gold-lined amulet had lain against his heart since the night of December thirty-first—other elements, but he wasn't about to question it. All he knew as he stood beside this vision in blue, and listened to Reverend Simon say the words that would bind them together for the rest of their days, was that his life had never been more complete. He was due to start his first year at Johns Hopkins in the fall, and there were even rumors of a hospital being built there. Who knew? One day he might even work on staff at the hospital, and be a part of a surgical team of pioneers discovering new and innovative treatments.

Right now, life was good. And as he took Linsey's hand in his own, and slipped a thin gold band on her finger, he couldn't help but wonder how he'd ever gotten so damned lucky.

Dear Reader,

If you love westerns the way that I love westerns, then you won't want to miss Connie Mason's latest love story, *To Tempt a Rogue*. When Ryan Delaney—the third Delaney brother—leaves the family ranch on what he hopes will be a great adventure, he never expects to get mixed up with Kitty Johnson. Is Kitty really running from the law, or is this a case of mistaken identity? And as passion flares between them, Ryan must determine if he's thinking with his head...or his heart.

Lovers of contemporary romance won't want to miss Hailey North's delightful, delicious *Pillow Talk*! Meg Cooper has always believed in what she calls "possibles," but is it possible to become engaged to a stranger for only two weeks? Sexy, wealthy Jules Ponthier woos Meg with promises of this "innocent" proposition—but how long can she resist this irresistible man? If you haven't yet become a fan of Hailey North, I guarantee this will make you one.

Karen Kay has thrilled countless readers with her sensuous, unforgettable love stories with Native American heroes. Her latest, *Night Thunder's Bride*, highlights her heartfelt brand of storytelling as a young pioneer woman must become the wife of Night Thunder, a Blackfoot warrior.

Eileen Putman makes her Avon debut with the wonderful *King of Hearts*, a Regency rake who is plucked from a hangman's noose and unexpectedly rescued by Louisa Peabody, a golden-haired beauty who seems to be the only woman in England who can resist his many charms.

Until next month, enjoy!

Lucia Macro
Lucia Macro
Senior Editor

AEL 0699

Avon Romances—
the best in exceptional authors
and unforgettable novels!

Avon Romantic Treasures

Unforgettable, enthralling love stories,
sparkling with passion and adventure
from Romance's bestselling authors

❊❊❊❊❊❊❊❊❊❊❊❊❊❊❊❊❊❊❊❊❊❊❊❊❊❊❊❊❊❊❊❊

RAKE'S VOW **by Stephanie Laurens**
79457-8/$5.99 US/$7.99 Can

O WILD A KISS **by Nancy Richards-Akers**
78947-7/$5.99 US/$7.99 Can

PON A WICKED TIME **by Karen Ranney**
79583-3/$5.99 US/$7.99 Can

N BENDED KNEE **by Tanya Anne Crosby**
78573-0/$5.99 US/$7.99 Can

ECAUSE OF YOU **by Cathy Maxwell**
79710-0/$5.99 US/$7.99 Can

CANDAL'S BRIDE **by Stephanie Laurens**
80568-5/$5.99 US/$7.99 Can

OW TO MARRY **by Julia Quinn**
MARQUIS 80081-0/$5.99 US/$7.99 Can

HE WEDDING NIGHT **by Linda Needham**
79635-X/$5.99 US/$7.99 Can